Naomi Mitchison

# Naomi Mitchison

## A Writer in Time

Edited by James Purdon

EDINBURGH
University Press

Edinburgh University Press is one of the leading university presses
in the UK. We publish academic books and journals in our selected
subject areas across the humanities and social sciences, combining
cutting-edge scholarship with high editorial and production values to
produce academic works of lasting importance. For more information
visit our website: edinburghuniversitypress.com

Edinburgh University Press Ltd
The Tun – Holyrood Road
12(2f) Jackson's Entry
Edinburgh EH8 8PJ

Typeset in 10/12pt Goudy Old Style
by Cheshire Typesetting Ltd, Cuddington, Cheshire, and
printed and bound in Great Britain

A CIP record for this book is available from the British Library

ISBN 978 1 4744 9474 8 (hardback)
ISBN 978 1 4744 9476 2 (webready PDF)
ISBN 978 1 4744 9477 9 (epub)

# Contents

# Acknowledgements

*Naomi Mitchison: A Writer in Time* grew out of a research project supported by a Research Incentive Grant from the Carnegie Trust, and began to take shape in a symposium ('Naomi Mitchison: 20 Years On') funded and hosted by the School of English at the University of St Andrews in July 2019. I would like to record my gratitude to both organisations for their generosity. My sincere thanks also to the archivists and administrators of Columbia University Library in New York City; the Fondren Library at Rice University, Houston; and most especially the Harry Ransom Center at the University of Texas at Austin, where the story 'Europe' has been preserved in typescript. I am grateful to the Naomi Mitchison estate for their permission to publish this story, and to Georgia Glover at David Higham Associates for helping to secure the necessary permissions. Special thanks also to Jenni Calder, Kate Cowcher and Gill Plain for sharing their knowledge and expertise. This book had the great advantage of meeting with sympathetic and constructive readers at proposal stage; I am indebted to them, and also to Michelle Houston and Susannah Butler at Edinburgh University Press for their advice, patience and encouragement. This book – my own part in it, anyway – is for Kristen and Nye.

James Purdon
*University of St Andrews*

# Notes on Contributors

**Megan Faragher** is an Associate Professor at Wright State University. She is the author of *Public Opinion Polling in Mid-Century British Literature: The Psychographic Turn* (2021) and co-editor of the *Modernism/modernity* Print Plus 'Modernist Institutions' cluster. She has also published articles in *Textual Practice*, *Literature & History* and *The Space Between Journal*.

**Lesley A. Hall** FRHistS is a Wellcome Library Research Fellow and Honorary Associate Professor, Department of Science and Technology Studies, University College London. She has published extensively on gender and sexuality in the UK from the nineteenth century onwards. Her *Naomi Mitchison: A Profile of her Life and Work* appeared in 2007 from Aqueduct Press. She has been a judge for the Arthur C. Clarke and the Tiptree (now Otherwise) Awards.

**Nick Hubble** is Professor of Modern and Contemporary English at Brunel University London. They are the author of *Mass-Observation and Everyday Life: Culture, History, Theory* (2006) and *The Proletarian Answer to the Modernist Question* (2017). Nick is the co-editor of *Working-Class Writing: Theory and Practice* (2018) and six volumes of 'British Fiction: The Decades Series': *The 1970s* (2014), *The 1990s* (2015), *The 2000s* (2015), *The 1950s* (2018), *The 1930s* (2021) and *The 2010s* (forthcoming 2023).

**Catriona Livingstone** is the author of *Virginia Woolf, Science, Radio, and Identity* (2022). Her work has appeared in *Women: A Cultural Review*, *Woolf Studies Annual* and the *Journal of Literature and Science*. She co-organised the 2017 British Society for Literature and Science Winter Symposium and was awarded an Honourable Mention in the *Journal of Literature and Science*/BSLS Essay Prize in 2017.

**Leo Mellor** is the Roma Gill Fellow in English at Murray Edwards College, University of Cambridge. His first book was *Reading the Ruins: Bombsites, Modernism and British Culture* (2011) and he has written on aerial views in culture, Graham

Greene, and the lure of wilderness. His chapter comparing Dylan Thomas and Ceri Richards was part of the collection *Reading Dylan Thomas* (2019). He is currently finishing *The Long 1930s* and a short book about night trains and the European imagination.

**Adam Piette** is a Professor of Modern Literature at the University of Sheffield. He is the author of *Remembering and the Sound of Words: Mallarmé, Proust, Joyce, Beckett*; *Imagination at War: British Fiction and Poetry, 1939–1945*; and *The Literary Cold War, 1945 to Vietnam*. He co-edits the poetry journal *Blackbox Manifold* with Alex Houen.

**James Purdon** is Senior Lecturer in English at the University of St Andrews. He is the author of *Modernist Informatics: Literature, Information, and the State* (2016), co-editor (with Rex Ferguson and Melissa M. Littlefield) of *The Art of Identification: Forensics, Surveillance, Identity* (2021), and editor of *British Literature in Transition, 1900–1920: A New Age?* (2022).

**Henry Stead** is Senior Lecturer in Latin at the University of St Andrews. His research project 'Brave New Classics' explores the relationship between the Greek and Roman classics and the international left. He is author of *A Cockney Catullus* (2015), co-author of *A People's History of Classics* (2020) and co-editor of *Greek and Roman Classics in the British Struggle for Social Reform* (2015).

**Imogen Woodberry** completed her PhD at the Royal College of Art, London, with a thesis on the relationship between alternative forms of belief and art and literature between the wars in Britain.

# Introduction

*James Purdon*

> Sometimes I think of my life in terms of time: my own time and the very different times of other people.
>
> Naomi Mitchison, Memoirs of a Spacewoman (1962)

Naomi Mary Margaret Haldane – later Naomi Mitchison – was born on Monday, 1 November 1897, in an elegant Edinburgh townhouse overlooking the Water of Leith. Her parents belonged to the prosperous elite of Scottish society, and the milieu in which she grew up was in many ways that of the traditional, upper-class Victorian establishment. Her mother, Louisa Kathleen (née Trotter), could trace her ancestry back to Henry Dundas, First Lord of the Admiralty under Pitt the Younger, while her father, the physiologist John Scott Haldane, belonged to one of Scotland's most eminent families, the Haldanes of Gleneagles. There were nursemaids and servants, family worship on Sundays, and a public-service ethic of *noblesse oblige*. There were big, draughty houses in Edinburgh and Perthshire, as well as in Oxford, where J. S. Haldane was a fellow of New College, and where, aside from frequent Scottish holidays, Naomi would spend most of her childhood. Yet the Haldanes were also a family of progressive intellectuals: scientists, jurists, writers and free-thinkers with remarkably wide-ranging interests. Naomi's uncle, the barrister and statesman Richard Haldane, was an unseasonable admirer of Goethe and Schopenhauer, an important reformer of the British Army, and eventually Lord Chancellor in Ramsay Macdonald's first Labour government. Another uncle, William, was Crown Agent for Scotland (the most senior prosecutorial role in the Scottish justice system), while her aunt Elizabeth – a skilled administrator who helped to establish the Voluntary Aid Detachment – wrote studies of Descartes and George Eliot, and later became Scotland's first woman Justice of the Peace.[1]

Tradition and modernity; custom and curiosity; religious observance and scientific rationalism; success within the venerable institutions of British society coupled with an open, internationalist outlook: this combination of influences would feed Naomi Mitchison's imagination and shape a writing life that extended across most of the twentieth century. From her early childhood she acquired a strong sense of the reality of the past, and of writing as a way of bringing past, present and future together. Time and the variety of ways in which human beings experience it are enduring themes of Mitchison's fiction, from her earliest historical novels, through her interwar experiments with socialist narrative, to her later fantasy and science fiction tales and her stories of post-colonial Africa. Time, therefore, is also the central theme of this volume of critical essays, which ranges widely across Mitchison's writing, from her short stories of the 1930s to her mature fiction of the 1970s, bringing together new archival research with critical analysis of her major works.

The year of Mitchison's birth was the year of Queen Victoria's Diamond Jubilee, of Bram Stoker's *Dracula* and H. G. Wells's *The Invisible Man*. Motor vehicles were practically unheard of; moving pictures were a carnival novelty; radio was in its infancy. But the twentieth century, with all its achievements and horrors, lay just around the corner. By the end of her life, a little more than a century later, she had experienced two world wars; the beginning of women's suffrage; the demise of the British empire; the invention of the atomic bomb and the technological glamour of the space race; the rise – and fall – of the Soviet Union. In *All Change Here* (1975), her memoir of the years leading up to the First World War, Mitchison recalls reading a 'child's fable' in which 'a boy, wanting to be grown-up, unrolls the magic reel and *is* – irrecoverably'. The finality suggested by that one-way journey was not to her taste; fortunately, she had found an alternative. To be a writer, as she saw it, was above all to move freely in time: 'I want to go back and forth, as, in a way, I am doing now.' She was, as more than one critic has suggested, a kind of time-traveller.[2]

'All writers are shape changers', she wrote – 'or, if you like, so strung that they can play tunes in all modes.'[3] Whether or not this holds true as a general proposition, it was certainly true of Mitchison herself, who inhabited many different roles and identities in the course of her long life. The student scientist, barely eighteen years old, co-authoring a groundbreaking paper on Mendelian genetics with her beloved brother Jack (better known as the biologist J. B. S. Haldane). The breakout novelist, hailed in the modernist 1920s for her innovative reimagining of the genre of historical fiction. The pioneer of the modern fantasy genre, who was one of J. R. R. Tolkien's first trusted readers. The inquisitive traveller, reporting back from Vienna after the defeat of the 1934 socialist uprising, investigating the condition of Soviet society in the 1930s and again in the 1950s, and watching impatiently the slow dismantling of the British empire. She was a politician's wife, and politician herself, active in causes ranging from Scottish rural development and women's reproductive rights to decolonisation and nuclear disarmament. And, closer to home, she was both landowning laird and working farmer, sowing and reaping with the people of Carradale, her adopted home in the Kintyre peninsula on the west coast of Scotland.

Mitchison was a startlingly prolific writer who produced more than four dozen novels, for readers of all ages, across a wide range of genres, as well as plays, poetry, travel writing, journalism, political and philosophical essays, biographies and autobiographies – not to mention an extensive archive of diaries and notebooks, only some of which have so far appeared in print. While each of her many works has its admirers, it would be fair to say that her literary reputation rests primarily on a few major novels, of which the most significant are the epic *The Corn King and the Spring Queen* (1931), set in an ancient world tinged with elements of fantasy; the controversial social realist experiment *We Have Been Warned* (1935); the eighteenth-century family saga *The Bull Calves* (1947), which draws on the family history of the Haldanes; and the groundbreaking feminist science fiction stories *Memoirs of a Spacewoman* (1962) and *Solution Three* (1975). Yet this cross-section can only hint at the diversity to be found in Mitchison's wider oeuvre, which ranges from works of young adult fantasy such as the brilliantly unconventional *Travel Light* (1952) to political fiction dealing with decolonisation in sub-Saharan Africa (*When We Become Men*, 1965), and from a prescient Arthurian-themed satire of tabloid journalism (*To the Chapel Perilous*, 1955) to a painstakingly researched fictional account of life in prehistoric Orkney (*Early in Orcadia*, 1987).

True to her early training in evolutionary genetics, Mitchison put a high value on diversification. Yet, ironically, the variousness of her own writing may be one reason for its relative neglect in twentieth-century literary studies. Several key texts have been reissued by different publishers over the last four decades, while others have fallen out of print entirely. Not until the mid-2000s did a wider selection of Mitchison's writing begin to become available in a uniform edition under the general editorship of Isobel Murray.[4] Meanwhile, critical and scholarly commentary on that writing has been similarly scattered. Mitchison's multiple identities and interests – as a novelist (young adult, historical, science fiction, fantasy), dramatist, educator, memoirist, cultural ambassador, feminist, socialist – involved her in a number of areas which have come under intense re-evaluation in recent studies of literature in the modernist period and at mid-century. But that multiplicity has also meant that accounts of her work have tended to appear either in the form of isolated articles in specialist journals devoted to particular topics, or as single chapters, alongside commentary on other writers, in scholarly works concerned with broader themes.

Thus Isobel Murray, Angus Calder, Kirsten Stirling and Eleanor Bell have all written eloquently of the Scottish Mitchison, a writer deeply involved in reimagining national culture and politics.[5] Ruth Hoberman, Elizabeth Maslen and Diana Wallace have given us Mitchison the historical novelist, who turns the genre of historical fiction in unexpected directions, engaging with questions of feminism, imperialism and cultural memory.[6] There is the visionary Mitchison – emphasised by critics such as Donna Haraway, Gavin Miller, Natasha Periyan and Ashley Maher – whose feminist science fiction explores motherhood, eugenics, animal–human relations and the possibilities of utopian post-capitalism and post-humanism.[7] Meanwhile the Mitchison of the 1930s, deeply involved in socialist and anti-fascist political movements, has been brought into sharper focus by Nick Hubble, Nattie Golubov, Kristin Bluemel and Megan Faragher.[8] And there is the Mitchison of the Second World War, depicted by Gill Plain as a writer mining history for the means to sustain her feminist thought in a period shaped by masculine-coded militarism, and by Phyllis Lassner as an expert analyst of the connections between class conflict, patriarchy and the rise of fascism.[9] Others have explored – among other subjects

– Mitchison's travel writing, her anti-colonial activism, her moral philosophy, her intense interest in the supernatural, and her important role as a collector and champion of East African modern art.[10] While this research has illuminated the many strands of her work and its enduring appeal, what has so far been lacking is the opportunity to weave these strands together, and in doing so to consider how they intersect across the extensive body of work produced by this major twentieth-century writer.

Today, a century on from the publication of Mitchison's first novel, *The Conquered* (1923), the richness of that body of work is becoming more apparent than ever, owing to a gradual process of re-evaluation that can in part be attributed to changes in literary taste and wider cultural trends. General readers and literary scholars alike have learned to value and appreciate a wider variety of styles and genres; meanwhile, genres themselves have become more fluid, embracing forms of hybridity that once seemed disturbingly unconventional and dissonant. Critics of Mitchison's novel *We Have Been Warned*, for instance, have tended to deplore its juxtaposition of natural-ism and supernaturalism, in which socialist politics and realist descriptive style share the page with suggestions of witchcraft and second sight. To readers versed in more recent experiments in postmodernism and magical realism, however, such combina-tions no longer seem especially disturbing; nor are the novel's more autobiographi-cal elements likely to trouble readers familiar with works of twenty-first-century 'autofiction'. Similar changes in literary taste may help to explain why Mitchison's forays into fantasy and speculative fiction have found so many new admirers in the early twenty-first century: as the categorical divisions between literary and popular fiction have blurred, Mitchison's freewheeling approach to genre has come increas-ingly to seem ahead of its time. Of course, this also makes it all too easy to forget or diminish the freshness and innovativeness of her writing. To restore that awareness must be one priority of a volume such as this one.

But there are other reasons, besides changing tastes, for the revival of interest in Mitchison's life and her writing. One important factor has certainly been the loosen-ing of the grand narratives according to which the literary history of the century has, until quite recently, been organised, studied and taught. Over the last two decades or so, as the emphases of modernist scholarship have gradually shifted outwards from what was once a relatively narrow canon of major figures and texts, we have gained a much clearer view of the affinities as well as the differences between once-marginal figures such as Mitchison and their canonical contemporaries. Kristin Bluemel has pointed out that, like many other writers who first came to prominence in the 1920s and 1930s – and women writers in particular – Mitchison has not been 'well served by the vocabularies and genealogies of Modernism'.[11] Rather than a figure of canoni-cal modernism, then, Bluemel proposes Mitchison as an exemplary 'intermodernist': one of those many significant but neglected writers who (by virtue of genre, style, theme or period) inhabit and thereby define the margins of the modernist canon. To revisit the work of such writers is to complicate and expand the history of modern-ism itself, demonstrating that the desire to forge new literary forms in response to the conditions of twentieth-century modernity was not merely the obsession of a small avant-garde, but the common aim of many writers in the period.

In the case of Mitchison, whose social circle included Wyndham Lewis, Aldous Huxley and W. H. Auden as well the Woolfs and most of the Bloomsbury Group, it is especially clear that we are dealing with a writer carefully attuned to many of the key developments shaping early twentieth-century literary culture and responding to them in her own way. To take one early example, her novel *The Conquered* tells the story of Caesar's conquests from the perspective of the vanquished Gauls, proposing a cyclical vision of historical recurrence of the kind that is typically associated with the work of W. B. Yeats and James Joyce. The novel's verse epigraphs, drawn from Irish folk-song and poetry (including Yeats's own), establish important structural and thematic resonances between the historical narrative of Roman imperialism and the contemporary struggle for an independent Ireland.[12] Mitchison, in other words, had recognised for herself the literary potential in what T. S. Eliot, writing in praise of Joyce's *Ulysses* (1922), would later call the 'mythical method', whereby 'a continuous parallel' is established between ancient and modern times.[13] Similarly, Mitchison's accounts of the ancient fertility rituals central to *The Corn King and the Spring Queen* (1930) draw extensively on Sir James Frazer's anthropological study *The Golden Bough* (1890), which was also a key source for Eliot himself in *The Waste Land* (1922). In this respect, it is possible to see Mitchison as an early and highly self-conscious participant in the 'anthropological turn' which Jed Esty has proposed as a defining feature of modernism's development in Britain, with writers from the 1930s onwards shifting their attention from a disintegrating empire towards the particularity and value of a more narrowly defined national culture.[14] Yet Mitchison's intensifying sense of her own identity as a Scot, and her insistence on the importance and distinctiveness of a specifically Scottish national culture, also complicate any idea of this 'anthropological turn' as essentially a turn towards English nativism.

Mitchison's early fiction, then, shares more in common than might initially appear with the canonical works of high modernists like Eliot and Joyce, even if her status as a practitioner of the relatively unfashionable historical novel has tended to obscure those continuities. Indeed, 'continuity' – both conceptual and historical – is a key term here, since an awareness of Mitchison's three-quarter-century-long literary career can help us to see the wider patterns of twentieth-century literary culture not as a series of abrupt shifts or successive styles, but as a continuously developing process of individual and collective creative response to changing social conditions. Mitchison's mid-1930s shift to writing more overtly about contemporary politics can, for instance, be understood as part of a wider politicisation of literary life in the years before the Second World War. In that sense, reading an early work like *The Conquered* helps to clarify the connections between high modernism's mythical visions of history and the pressing political exigencies of the 1930s to which Mitchison was attempting to respond in *We Have Been Warned*.

Taken together, Mitchison's sustained productivity, her longevity and her continual experimentation with style and genre make her a key figure in historical narratives that emphasise how the economic conditions and political divisions of the 'long 1930s' continued to shape cultural life throughout the mid-century and beyond.[15] Perhaps the most striking example of this has been the re-evaluation of *We Have Been Warned*, once regarded almost universally as a muddled failure, yet now championed, by some critics at least, as a 'trailblazing' work of socialist-feminist fiction.[16] Rejected by three publishers on account of its frank depictions of extramarital sex and abortion, and dismissed by early reviewers as sentimental and politically naive, Mitchison's most divisive novel has been rediscovered not only as an example of left-wing feminist art suppressed by conservative and patriarchal censorship, but as a unique and compelling hybrid of Lukácsian realism with elements of the weird and the supernatural. The novel's protagonist, Dione Galton – a version of Mitchison herself, or one part of her – worries that, after a millennium or so has passed, 'men and women will be so different from us, so changed, to us now so terrible and shocking, that we dare not assess them or imagine the future'.[17] Given that the novel was written and set in the 1930s, a period when many British writers, including Mitchison, embraced revolutionary socialism, this expectation of total social and human transformation can be regarded as part of the period's zeitgeist. Yet the possibility of human solidarity across time is at the heart of Mitchison's vision of history and of literature, a vision to which her writing, in its invention of vanished pasts and possible futures, continually reiterates its commitment.

What makes this solidarity possible is Mitchison's understanding of human history as a continuous story grounded in productive (and reproductive) practices and activities: sowing and reaping; making and building; bearing and raising children. 'Stone and bone survive', she writes in the introduction to *Early in Orcadia*, one of her last and most ambitious works of imaginative history, and it is this physical substrate of experience – the shared material existence common to all human life – that grounds even her most speculative and fantastical fictions.[18] Time, for her, was neither an abstract trajectory of civilisational development nor a set of recurring mythic structures, nor yet a purely narrative construct developed in the present to make sense of the inaccessible past. It was a set of changing patterns: of evolving social arrangements, cultural traditions, languages, landscapes, technologies and genetic sequences, whose traces remained legible in the structure of present-day societies, in human minds and bodies, and in the shape of the natural world and the built environment.

No single literary study or collection of essays can hope to cover the full range of Mitchison's life and work, and there is a great deal that necessarily remains beyond the scope of this volume. Its nine chapters concentrate on her narrative fiction, ranging from the early historical novels and short stories of the interwar years to the speculative fictions she produced later in life. Together they comprise a convenient introduction to the major themes and contexts of Mitchison's work, as well as a point of departure for future scholarship. As their editor, I believe they also make a strong case for her status as one of the foremost Scottish writers of the twentieth century.

In the opening chapter, Leo Mellor draws on several volumes of Mitchison's short fiction in order to trace the influence of a 'documentary impulse' in her interwar stories, arguing that these fictional works are best understood not in relation to the longer historical epics that precede them, but to Mitchison's contemporaneous non-fictional writing: her diaries, letters, and, from the mid-1930s, her reports for the social research network Mass-Observation. For Mellor, Mitchison's stories, with their intense moments of emotional, physical or social transformation, demonstrate a historical imagination in which 'chasms of difference' can be crossed in 'moments of recognition', bringing 'the clouded past' into conversation with 'the yet-to-be-realised future'. Such moments help to situate Mitchison's progressive politics and her desire for the revolutionary transformation of society within the context of an archaeological deep time, in which sudden social change on a grand scale can be understood as a necessary and natural part of the development of civilisations.

One form of social change to which Mitchison was committed throughout her life was the transformation of gender relations, a goal which was for her inseparable from revolutionary class politics. As Nick Hubble explains in their chapter, Mitchison demanded far more than the superficial changes represented by the enfranchisement of women in 1928, the gradual extension of professional opportunities to women workers, or the new possibilities for sexual liberation through which some women had begun to assert their own bodily autonomy. Placing Mitchison's 1938 political essay *The Moral Basis of Politics* in conversation with two other feminist works of the same year – Virginia Woolf's *Three Guineas* and Ethel Mannin's *Women and the Revolution* – Hubble shows how Mitchison, like Woolf and Mannin, had arrived by the late 1930s at the conclusion that women's emancipation could be achieved only by overthrowing long-established attitudes to gender that were rooted deep in the British and European cultural consciousness. It was the potential for such a radical transformation, as well as its challenges, that Mitchison sought to evoke in the historical fantasy *The Corn King and the Spring Queen*, in which the sorceress Erif Der, despite wielding symbolic and magical power in the fictional kingdom of Marob, struggles to reshape its patriarchal structure.

For Mitchison, the dismantling of contemporary social mores concerning family life and monogamy was a crucial part of that struggle. A long-term advocate of non-monogamous relationships, Mitchison rejected what she called the 'repressions and formulae' of traditional sexual morality, living for many years in a contentedly open marriage with her husband, the Labour politician Dick Mitchison. This rejection of monogamy was for her partly a rejection of the patriarchal domination of women, and partly a joyful assertion of the bodily freedom and openness which she associated with the communal life of socialism. It went hand in hand with her practical political activism and her advocacy for women's reproductive rights. But it also had an idealist dimension. As Imogen Woodberry argues in her contribution, Mitchison's commitment to 'spiritualised sexuality', formulated under the influence of the consciousness-raising 'guru' Gerald Heard, developed along these lines from a technique of 'personal revolution' into a strategy of wider social transformation.

Mitchison's depiction of the transformative potential of sexual liberation reflects one of the broader themes of her writing, insofar as it suggests a way of reintegrating aspects of consciousness and experience that have been stifled and suppressed by the power structures of modern Western societies. In a similar way, her longstanding interest in scientific discovery – beginning with her youthful studies into genetic inheritance in guinea pigs and rats – was also shaped and conditioned by her strong attachment to the irrational, affective and qualitative aspects of human existence which a strictly rationalist and empirical understanding tended to exclude. As Catriona Livingstone's chapter shows, Mitchison was deeply knowledgeable about contemporary developments not only in biology, but in mathematics, chemistry and physics; her interwar writing draws on these scientific discourses even as it calls into question the tenability of the binary oppositions (masculine/feminine, real/ imaginary, rational/irrational) which create imaginary internal divisions within individuals and societies. Science also provided Mitchison with new ways of thinking about temporality, whether through the new cosmology of Einsteinian relativity or the distance-collapsing experience of connective simultaneity represented by radio broadcasting. It encouraged her, Livingstone argues, not only to imagine likely technological developments, but to think more ambitiously about 'disparate temporalities', the 'expansion of the self', and 'future forms of collective life'.

Picking up themes from both Woodberry's and Livingstone's chapters, Lesley A. Hall traces the development of Mitchison's thinking about 'the politics of reproduction', from her early dealings with the Eugenics Society in the 1920s, through the scandalous frankness of *We Have Been Warned* (which spooked several publishers with its references to contraception), to the high-concept science fiction of *Solution Three*. Set in a far future recovering from the devastation of racial conflict and nuclear war, *Solution Three* not only anticipates controversies surrounding cloning, genetic modification and the possibility of 'designer babies', but demonstrates the deep continuities between the racist and ableist programmes of early twentieth-century eugenic movements, and the ostensibly benign and salutary interventions in human reproduction made possible by post-war genetics and embryology. The product of a mind deeply invested in the capacities of science to unlock human potential, yet also sceptical of what Hall calls 'magic bullet' solutions to social problems, the novel is not only a key work in the history of feminist science fiction, but – in its depiction of a multiracial society in which homosexuality and polyamory have become social norms – a bold critique of heteronormativity, white privilege and bourgeois sexual ethics. The world of *Solution Three* is no utopia, as its inhabitants discover when it becomes clear that the standardisation of reproduction (through cloning) and education (through institutionalised conditioning) have created a brittle society, ill equipped to face unexpected challenges. Yet, as Hall argues, the novel demonstrates Mitchison's conviction that scientific innovation and social planning alone are not enough to create just societies: room must be left for dissent, for difference, for those who wish to live otherwise.

For a writer like Mitchison, raised in an intellectually curious but still socially conservative and class-conscious household, it was perhaps inevitable that the search for new ways of living would find expression not only in scientific inquiry, but in radical politics. Mitchison's own political education had been somewhat mixed. As a young girl she had absorbed and accepted the views of her mother, 'an active and constant propagandist for Tory imperialism', rather than the diffident Liberalism of her scientist father.[19] She became active in Labour Party politics in the early 1930s, when her husband unsuccessfully contested the seat of King's Norton at the 1931 general election; four years later, she herself stood as a candidate for the constituency of the Scottish Universities. And while she never followed the example of her brother, J. B. S. Haldane, in 'going over' fully to the Communist Party, her position on the Labour left quickly earned her a reputation as a 'fellow-traveller'. Indeed, that reputation was sufficiently enduring that Mitchison would appear as a 'silly sympathiser' on George Orwell's notorious deathbed list of individuals who could not be trusted with the work of Cold War propaganda. A sympathiser she may have been; yet as Henry Stead's chapter shows, she was by no means a silly one. While certainly a partisan commentator, Mitchison was also a perceptive and at times critical observer of Soviet society during her two visits there in 1932 and 1952. Drawing on archival records from both the National Library of Scotland and the Russian State Archive of Literature and Art, Stead tells the story of Mitchison's political development from a new angle, tracing not only her trajectory of disillusionment at the squandered potential of the revolution but also her relationships with the other left-wing British cultural figures with whom she visited the Soviet Union, including Doris Lessing and Alex Comfort.

Travel was an important part of Mitchison's life as well as of her literary practice. The 1932 junket to the Soviet Union, for instance, on which she travelled as part of a Fabian Society delegation, served as her model for Dione Galton's similar trip in *We Have Been Warned*. Her next novel, *The Blood of the Martyrs*, was also partly inspired by foreign travel, with dedicatees including the Austrian socialists she had met in Vienna in 1934 and the Arkansas sharecroppers whose living conditions had shocked her on her first visit to the United States the following year. One of Mitchison's less-studied and less well-known novels, published to little acclaim not long before the outbreak of the Second World War, *The Blood of the Martyrs* deals with the mythic formation of early Christianity and the persecution of Christians under Nero. In her contribution here, Megan Faragher reclaims the novel not only as a complex and timely examination of totalitarianism, political violence and collective agency, but as the beginning of a new 'material turn' in Mitchison's writing – a turn prompted partly by her admiration for the practical forms of solidarity she had witnessed among poor farmers in the southern United States, and partly by her recognition and rejection of the 'mystical undercurrents' of fascist rhetoric and propaganda as practised in Hitler's Germany. Mitchison's early Christians, Faragher suggests, appear in the novel less as mystics, theologians or symbols of holiness than as a community of ordinary individuals whose practice of solidarity, fellowship and underground resistance to political authority threatens the hierarchies of the Roman state. Throughout her life, Mitchison was attracted to such communities: to those marginalised and disempowered for reasons having to do with their religion, class, sexuality or race. Her own privileged background enabled her to speak relatively freely on issues of social justice, for instance in defence of Radclyffe Hall's classic of lesbian fiction *The Well of Loneliness* (for issuing which Mitchison's own publisher Jonathan Cape faced prosecution for obscenity in 1928), and as a vocal critic of the apartheid regime in post-war South Africa. But the fact of her privileged social position does not diminish her courage in taking up such issues of conscience when many others of similar status were content to remain silent. And, as the banning of her books (and her person) from South Africa shows, such solidarity was not entirely without personal cost.

Like much of Mitchison's historical fiction, *The Blood of the Martyrs* depends on a technique of temporal double exposure, in which the events of the distant past are overlaid on the present, or vice versa, in order to reveal the persistence of patterns in human feeling and conduct across time and across cultures. In *The Conquered*, the history of Gallic resistance to the Roman empire is allowed to rhyme with the modern Irish independence movement. *The Corn King and the Spring Queen*, published shortly after the success of the struggle for equal suffrage, uses a plausible depiction of ancient Sparta, along with Mitchison's invented Marob, to mount a wider critique of patriarchy that extends beyond the demand for equality at the ballot box. In *The Blood of the Martyrs*, the contemporary persecution of political and racial minorities circa 1939 – particularly Jews and communists – is refracted through the experiences of first-century Christians. This technique had two advantages for Mitchison. In the first place, it allowed her to present a simplified and compelling version of the ancient past in which characters' motivations and ways of understanding their place in the world are readily comprehensible to twentieth-century readers. But it also enabled her to use that depiction of the past in order to reflect on contemporary circumstances without the prejudices sedimented into contemporary political language. Readers unsympathetic to the radical left-wing political movements of the 1930s, she believed, might take a different view if their aims and their treatment at the hands of the ruling capitalist class could be shown to be comparable to that of early Christian martyrs in pagan Rome.

In her notes to *The Bull Calves*, Mitchison writes of this relationship between past and future as resembling the nets of the herring-trawlers that ply the seas around her home at Carradale: 'So, once again, the thing is a net, and the back-rope and sole-rope for ever apart and yet for ever bound to one another by the flow moving and giving and half seen and never letting us go.'[20] Strung between the 'back-rope' (the part of the net that floats on the sea's surface) and the 'sole-rope' (the weighted part that sinks into the depths) is the knotted mesh of language and history that binds together past, present and future. The image of the net is thus appropriately central to Adam Piette's reading of *The Bull Calves* as a novel binding together two mid-centuries: the wartime moment of its composition and the 'smooth mid-century' (as Mitchison calls it) of its setting, in the aftermath of the unsuccessful Jacobite rising of 1745–6. By borrowing the metaphor of the web or network – one of nineteenth-century fiction's most potent images of social connectedness – and by resituating it in the labour of Scottish fisher-folk, Mitchison imbues her own form of historical realism with a new political self-consciousness. It is this reimagining of the network as a model not only of social connectivity but of historical, linguistic, familial, erotic and political entanglement that characterises Mitchison's presentation of Scotland as 'an unfinished political ideal' in both the eighteenth-century past and her twentieth-century present.

After the Second World War, Mitchison made strenuous efforts, not only in her writing but in the world of local and regional politics, to achieve that ideal, working towards the goal of a modern, progressive, socialist Scotland. In 1945 she was elected to Argyll County Council as Labour representative for Kintyre East (a position she held twice, from 1945 to 1948 and again from 1953 to 1965), and in 1947 joined the

Advisory Panel on the Highlands and Islands, an investigative body reporting to the Secretary of State for Scotland on matters of economic and social development. She would serve on the Panel and its successor, the Highlands and Islands Development Consultative Council, for more than three decades. These bodies, however, still reported to Whitehall, and Mitchison frequently found herself frustrated by their slow progress and the bureaucratic caution that stood in the way of meaningful change. ('The Highland panel is rather hell', she wrote, 'as we are never allowed to do anything.')[21] By the early 1960s, she had begun to look elsewhere for opportunities to exercise her considerable skills as an administrator and activist.

She was to find them at last in Africa, where from the mid-1960s onwards she devoted large amounts of time and energy to the causes of decolonisation, Black African self-government and the anti-apartheid movement. An area of particular interest was Botswana (formerly the British protectorate of Bechuanaland), where she developed a close relationship with the Kgatla people and their hereditary leader, Kgosi Linchwe II. My own chapter here focuses on Mitchison's writing about Africa, and about Botswana in particular, in order to show how her relationships with Linchwe and the people of Botswana brought a new practical and personal dimension to her longstanding anti-imperialist political commitments. Among other things, writing about Africa compelled her to reflect on how the imposition of European attitudes to time – from the clock-watching efficiencies of industrial capitalism to the grand historical narrative of 'modernity' – had enabled and depended upon the suppression of African conceptions of temporality and history. In her efforts to understand and depict the disastrous consequences for Africa of colonial rule, Mitchison became an early proponent of the idea that real decolonisation would require not merely the substitution of Black African politicians and administrators in the place of white European ones, but the restoration of local cultural forms, traditions, social institutions and forms of knowledge.

Though she was proud of her Scottish roots – and became an early supporter, notwithstanding her Labour connections, of the Scottish National Party and its work towards the goal of an independent Scotland – Mitchison's outlook was never insular, always international. This internationalism found congenial expression in her lifelong work with the writers' and artists' organisation PEN (originally conceived as an alliance of 'Poets, Essayists, Novelists'; now simply PEN International), the Scottish branch of which now holds an annual lecture in her memory at the University of Glasgow. A proud member of PEN for nearly seventy years, Mitchison brought her usual energy and commitment to her work for the organisation, and frequently served as an unofficial ambassador while travelling. In 1947 she attended the second post-war PEN conference, in Zurich, and this volume concludes with a previously unknown and unpublished short story drawing on her experiences of that event. A modern folk tale of a kind, 'Europe' reflects – with a lightness of touch that belies its deep moral seriousness – on the individual and collective trauma inflicted by the Second World War and the Holocaust. In this brief but powerful story, Mitchison gazes unflinchingly into the 'black gap in the middle of Europe', recognising the immense challenge posed to the imagination, and to the human capacity for empathy, by the genocidal crimes of the Nazi regime.

For Mitchison, it was an article of faith that human solidarity was possible even across wide divisions of geography, race, gender, culture – and of historical time. To write, for her, was to open up the possibility of a special kind of community: a literary continuum in which the past might indeed be made recoverable in the present, even as the present is subsumed in the future that it shapes. It is this possibility that Dione Galton intuits at the beginning of *We Have Been Warned* when, engrossed in a book about an ancestor accused of witchcraft, she finds herself displaced from her own present, 'shifted [. . .] more in time than in space'. As she becomes aware that the old stone walls of the house in which she sits, and the unchanging rural Scottish landscape beyond, link her materially as well as spiritually to her seventeenth-century precursor, Dione is granted a vision of continuity: 'It was only the woman in the book and the woman who was reading it who were different.'[22] Through this experience of temporal solidarity, Dione comes to understand her own place in the pattern of history and to glimpse the utopian possibilities – as well as the dystopian risks – that still lie ahead.

Mitchison herself was no stranger to such moments of time-slippage. In *All Change Here* she recalls a period of her early life when she envisioned the relation of the present to the past as being 'something like two sheets of paper, each with a pinhole, moving against one another. If the pinholes accidentally coincided and one happened to be looking, one saw through.'[23] This vision of time – a vision influenced, perhaps, by discoveries in twentieth-century physics and cosmology with which the scientifically literate and intellectually omnivorous Mitchison would have been well acquainted – was a way of keeping faith with the vanished past by insisting on its reality, its persistence. Take, as a final example of such temporal solidarity, the following entry from Mitchison's wartime diary, written only a few years after *We Have Been Warned*, in which she records experiencing such a moment while researching her novel *The Bull Calves* in an Edinburgh library. The date is Thursday, 13 November 1941:

> I settled down with Macintosh of Borlum's *Enclosure and Fallowing* written from prison, from some place not half a mile from where I was sitting, written without malice or anger or anything but generous acceptance of events, the work of a good Fabian and oh such a damned nice man and so near one in time. By and bye I found myself sitting crying over my books in the Signet Library, because he was so nice and I could never tell him so, never give him back kindness, only two hundred years away in time, one could get at what he was and what he wanted.[24]

In the bleak middle of the Second World War, Mitchison is surprised into emotional communion with a long-dead Jacobite rebel who speaks to her across the centuries, close enough in character and outlook to take on the anachronistic guise of a 'good Fabian', yet so temporally distant as to provoke tears of grief at the unbridgeable gulf of the years. What makes this moment possible is, crucially, the communicative and preservative potential of the written word. Briefly, in the space of the library, history folds back on itself, granting writer and reader alike the gift of freedom to range freely across space and time. Just for a moment, as if by magic, the pinholes – the pages – align.

## NOTES

1. For full biographical information, see Jill Benton, *Naomi Mitchison: A Century of Experiment in Life and Letters* (London: Pandora, 1990) and Jenni Calder, *The Nine Lives of Naomi Mitchison* (London: Virago, 1997), revised as *The Burning Glass: The Life of Naomi Mitchison* (Dingwall: Sandstone Press, 2019).
2. Naomi Mitchison, *All Change Here*, collected in *As It Was: An Autobiography 1897–1918* (Glasgow: Richard Drew, 1988), p. 16. On Mitchison as time-traveller see, for instance, Ashley Maher, 'Memoirs of a Spacewoman: Naomi Mitchison's intergalactic education', *Textual Practice* 34:12 (2020), pp. 2145–65; Isobel Murray, introduction to Naomi Mitchison, *Memoirs of a Spacewoman* (Glasgow: Kennedy & Boyd, 2011), p. vii; and Carla Sassi, 'The Cosmic (Cosmo)Polis in Naomi Mitchison's Science Fiction Novels', in Caroline McCracken-Flesher (ed.), *Scotland as Science Fiction* (Lanham, MD: Bucknell University Press with Rowman & Littlefield, 2012), p. 50.
3. Naomi Mitchison, *African Heroes* (New York: Farrar, Straus and Giroux, 1969), p. v.
4. The Naomi Mitchison Library, published by Kennedy & Boyd, has so far reissued twenty-six volumes of Mitchison's writing.
5. See Isobel Murray, 'Novelists of the Renaissance', in Cairns Craig (ed.), *The History of Scottish Literature*, 4 vols (Aberdeen: Aberdeen University Press, 1987), vol. 4, pp. 103–17; Angus Calder, *Revolving Culture: Notes from the Scottish Republic* (London: I. B. Tauris, 1994), pp. 173–7; Kirsten Stirling, 'The Roots of the Present: Naomi Mitchison, Agnes Mure Mackenzie and the Construction of History', in Edward J. Cowan and Douglas Gifford (eds), *The Polar Twins* (Edinburgh: John Donald, 1999), pp. 254–69; Eleanor Bell, 'Experiment and Nation in the 1960s', in Glenda Norquay (ed.), *The Edinburgh Companion to Scottish Women's Writing* (Edinburgh: Edinburgh University Press, 2012), pp. 122–9.
6. See Ruth Hoberman, *Gendering Classicism: The Ancient World in Twentieth-Century Women's Historical Fiction* (Albany: State University of New York Press, 1997), pp. 119–35; Elizabeth Maslen, 'Naomi Mitchison's Historical Fiction', in Maroula Joannou (ed.), *Women Writers of the 1930s: Gender, Politics, and History* (Edinburgh: Edinburgh University Press, 1999), pp. 138–50; Diana Wallace, *The Woman's Historical Novel: British Women Writers 1900–2000* (Basingstoke: Palgrave Macmillan, 2005), pp. 43–52.
7. See Donna Haraway, 'Otherworldly Conversations, Terran Topics, Local Terms', in Stacy Alaimo and Susan Hekman (eds), *Material Feminisms* (Bloomington: Indiana University Press, 2008), pp. 157–87; Gavin Miller, 'Animals, Empathy, and Care in Naomi Mitchison's *Memoirs of a Spacewoman*', *Science Fiction Studies* 35:2 (July 2008) and *Science Fiction and Psychology* (Liverpool: Liverpool University Press, 2020); Natasha Periyan, 'Naomi Mitchison, Eugenics and the Community: The Class and Gender Politics of Intelligence', in Nick Hubble, Luke Seaber and Elinor Taylor (eds), *The 1930s: A Decade of Modern British Fiction* (London: Bloomsbury, 2021), pp. 91–122; Maher, 'Memoirs of a Spacewoman'.
8. See Nick Hubble, *The Proletarian Answer to the Modernist Question* (Edinburgh: Edinburgh University Press, 2017); Nattie Golubov, 'English Ethical Socialism: Women Writers, Political Ideas and the Public Sphere between the Wars', *Women's History Review* 14:1 (2005), pp. 33–60; Kristin Bluemel, 'Exemplary Intermodernists: Stevie Smith, Inez Holden, Betty Miller and Naomi Mitchison', in Maroula Joannou (ed.), *The History of British Women's Writing, 1920–1945* (Basingstoke: Palgrave Macmillan, 2015), pp. 40–56; Megan Faragher, 'Snoop-Women with Notebooks: Naomi Mitchison, Mass-Observation, and the Gender of Domestic Intelligence', *The Space Between* 12 (2017) and *Public Opinion Polling in*

*Mid-Century British Literature: The Psychographic Turn* (Oxford: Oxford University Press, 2021), pp. 132–73.

9. See Gill Plain, *Women's Fiction of the Second World War: Gender, Power and Resistance* (Edinburgh: Edinburgh University Press, 1996), pp. 139–65; Phyllis Lassner, *British Women Writers of World War II: Battlegrounds of Their Own* (Basingstoke: Palgrave Macmillan, 1998), pp. 58–103.

10. See Rebecca Kirsten Harwood, 'Reading Between the Lines: The Politics of Authenticity in Naomi Mitchison's *Vienna Diary*', in Clare Broome Saunders (ed.) *Women, Travel Writing, and Truth* (London: Routledge, 2014), pp. 124–38; Jacqueline Ryder, 'Speaking as Tribal (M)other: The African Writing of Naomi Mitchison', in Carla Sassi and Theo van Heijnsbergen (eds), *With and Without Empire: Scotland Across the (Post)colonial Borderline* (Newcastle-upon-Tyne: Cambridge Scholars Publishing, 2013), pp. 200–13; Suzanne Hobson, '"The Future of Our Movement": Bridging the Gap between Rationalism and Christian Ethics in Naomi Mitchison's 1930s Writing', in *Women: A Cultural Review* 31:4 (2020), pp. 401–15; Moira Burgess, *Mitchison's Ghosts: Supernatural Elements in the Scottish Fiction of Naomi Mitchison* (Edinburgh: Humming Earth, 2008). On Mitchison as a collector of African art, see the work of Kate Cowcher, especially the project 'Dar to Dunoon: Modern African Art from the Argyll Collection', available at http://www.dartodunoon.com.

11. Bluemel, 'Exemplary Intermodernists', p. 41.

12. Similar historical parallels are to be found in *The Blood of the Martyrs*, between Roman persecution of Christians and contemporary Nazi persecution of Jews.

13. T. S. Eliot, 'Ulysses, Order, and Myth' (1923), in Frank Kermode (ed.), *Selected Prose of T. S. Eliot* (New York: Harcourt Brace Jovanovich, 1975), pp. 175–8.

14. See Jed Esty, *A Shrinking Island: Modernism and National Culture in England* (Princeton, NJ: Princeton University Press, 2004).

15. See 'Introduction: The Long 1930s', in Benjamin Kohlmann and Matthew Taunton (eds), *A History of 1930s British Literature* (Cambridge: Cambridge University Press, 2019), pp. 1–14; Leo Mellor and Glyn Salton-Cox, 'The Long 1930s: Introduction', *Critical Quarterly* 57:3 (2015), pp. 1–9.

16. See, for instance, Hubble, *The Proletarian Answer to the Modernist Question*, p. 17; and Mara Dougall, '"What Does a Socialist Woman Do?" Birth Control and the Body Politic in Naomi Mitchison's *We Have Been Warned*', *The Cambridge Quarterly* 50:1 (March 2021), pp. 18–37.

17. Naomi Mitchison, *We Have Been Warned* (Kilkerran: Kennedy & Boyd, 2012), p. 66.

18. Naomi Mitchison, *Early in Orcadia* (Glasgow: Richard Drew, 1987), p. 7.

19. Naomi Mitchison, *Small Talk*, collected in *As It Was*, p. 87.

20. Naomi Mitchison, *The Bull Calves* (Glasgow: Richard Drew, 1985), p. 466.

21. Quoted in Calder, *The Burning Glass*, p. 266.

22. Mitchison, *We Have Been Warned*, p. 3.

23. Mitchison, *All Change Here*, collected in *As It Was*, p. 117.

24. *Among You Taking Notes: The Wartime Diary of Naomi Mitchison, 1939–1945*, ed. Dorothy Sheridan (Oxford: Oxford University Press, 1986), p. 169.

# 1. Naomi Mitchison's Interwar Short Stories

*Leo Mellor*

Introducing a recent edition of *The Fourth Pig* (1936), Marina Warner tried to eluci-
date why Naomi Mitchison had been so neglected by readers and critics:

> [S]ome of the writers with whom she could be compared – contemporaries such
> as Virginia Woolf (b. 1882) and Elizabeth Bowen (b. 1899), and others who
> were close friends, Wyndham Lewis (b. 1882) and Aldous Huxley (b. 1894) –
> were naturally modern. Whether by instinct, default, or choice, such writers
> belonged to the twentieth century and conveyed features of the time without
> needing to check their watches. But Naomi Mitchison is only partly modern.
> Or perhaps [. . .] she was oddly, but not entirely, modern. This quality, her fal-
> tering modernity, arises from many features of her life and work.[1]

This reading seems to function both as a biographical-literary-historical sketch and
as a way to ask an inescapable if implicit question: for if Mitchison is intriguingly
'partly modern', which of her texts might allow readers to understand this mode?
A predictable answer might reach for her most famous novels, but it is worth noting
the scale of the commitment they demand from a reader: *The Corn King and the
Spring Queen* (1931) – 720 pages; *We Have Been Warned* (1935) – 582 pages; *The Bull
Calves* (1947) – 532 pages. This is major fiction in both length and complexity; the
works cover vast amounts of time, both narrative time and reader's time. It is an art
of excess, intentional or not, and with that many other aspects of value can be elided.
But as well as writing novels Mitchison also wrote journalism, political tracts, poems
– and many short stories. And I believe it is in her short stories – with their intensity
and focus, as well as their craft and connection to the 'tale' and oral traditions – that
readers now can best understand Mitchison's aesthetic: her engagement with the
past; her testing of the form; and her conception of the political responsibilities of
any writer. This is a potent combination, and one in short (and shortness does have
many virtues) that best shows her version of being 'partly modern'.[2]

Mitchison is not alone in using a compact form for complex ends. For over the
course of the twentieth century the Anglophone short story became the form

which, more than any other, showed how literary experimentation negotiated with an inheritance from earlier eras. The short story allowed for the varying narrative possibilities of writers as diverse as Joyce, Mansfield, Hemingway and Stein, and of ideas ranging from 'artless narration' in writers such as Frank O'Connor to the *mise-en-page* elisions of speech and thought in Jean Rhys. Yet these writers were working with a form which had, from Poe and Kipling onwards, huge popular appeal, especially in the marketplace of magazines and in an age of mass literacy. The short story, then, as one of its most perceptive critics notes, was where experimentation met readerly demands and expectations; but it was also a form almost impossible to define by shape or word length (how to distinguish it from the sketch, the 'tale', the novella?) and thus highly resistant to totalising classification: 'no single theory can encompass the multifarious nature of a genre in which the only constant feature seems to be achievement of narrative purpose in a comparatively brief space'.[3] Indeed Mitchison's own stories themselves bear out such plural possibilities, refusing to conform to any easily discernible patterns or repeated templates, at times appearing as novels in miniature, or fragments from larger works, or meditations on a single idea or theme.

But Mitchison's complex use of shortness, and the critical problem of taxonomy raised by it, has to be set within a longer history. For many critics, including short story writers themselves, have tried to define what might be especially possible, lucid, or troubling in short stories, and how they have evolved. A notable and repeated point of interest is what the short story can do with time, and the human experience of time. The time of the short story is typically, perhaps inevitably, defined against that of the novel. As the Irish short story writer Frank O'Connor suggested: 'the short story represents a struggle with Time – the novelist's Time [. . .] it is an attempt to reach some point of vantage from which the past and future are equally visible'.[4] The dominance of the novel is not seen here as stifling; rather it functions as something short story writers overcome, and in such overcoming they allow readers a vista – rendered spatially and, crucially, described visually – where they can comprehend temporality. To do this within the tight confines of a short story means that, as Georg Lukács wrote, form *itself* has to work hard: '[t]he short story is the most purely artistic form; it expresses the ultimate meaning of all artistic creation as mood, as the very sense and content of the creative process, but it is rendered abstract for that very reason.'[5] Mitchison is not a writer to whose stories the term 'abstraction' has often been applied – her works are a long way from the poetical prose of Woolf's 'Blue & Green' (1921), those paired sketches where colours take on associative patterns and flow as connective fluid. But Lukács's intervention does capture what is happening structurally beneath the deceptively matter-of-fact tone of Mitchison's descriptions and her fragments of seemingly simple speech. For 'mood' in Mitchison's short stories is a way in which each story gestures to vast terrains: the unsaid, the unspoken and the unknown. These occur at both of the temporal compass points in O'Connor's topographical model: the clouded past of (mostly) unwritten events and sensations, and the yet-to-be-realised future, where, according to Mitchison's political beliefs, life for all will be transformed by socialism. And the visuality inherent in both O'Connor and Lukács also finds a corollary in

Mitchison's short stories, with their dependence on understanding history in terms of hidden depths, sightlines and visible encounters.

This chapter will draw on short stories by Mitchison across seven volumes – *When the Bough Breaks and Other Stories* (1924); *The Laburnum Branch* (1926); *Black Sparta: Greek Stories* (1928); *Barbarian Stories* (1929); *The Delicate Fire: Short Stories and Poems* (1933); *The Fourth Pig* (1936); and *Five Men and a Swan* (1957) – as well as some uncollected works.[6] But it will concentrate on four stories of the interwar period – 'The Wife of Aglaos', 'The Powers of Light', 'Beyond This Limit', and 'Five Men and a Swan' – all of which are included in *Beyond This Limit: Selected Shorter Fiction* (2008).[7] Its focus on the interwar stories is justified by the fact that they represent Mitchison's sustained inventiveness in matters of length, use of illustrations, and a plethora of different settings, but also because collectively they show how a voracious writer channelled and focused some historically specific ideas, especially those which elucidated why very short pieces, especially of detailed observation, might matter for culture and society. Mitchison's interwar short stories can thus be best understood, I believe, not as scaled-down versions of her novels but rather as counterparts to her other (non-fictional) short pieces – reports, letters and diaries. This comparative interpretative manoeuvre acknowledges the sheer variousness of Mitchison's oeuvre: her range of subject matter – from Greece in 500 BC to Scotland in AD 1940 – and her range of form, especially since two of the longer stories were published as individual, lavishly illustrated volumes.

Moreover, in thinking about how each of these stories functions as a 'report' of a different kind, a repeated issue of tone can be addressed. All of her stories are knowing, in different ways, about the art of storytelling, and about specifying what details or actions might matter in the limited number of words available. This artifice comes through the way in which Mitchison manipulates estrangement, the moments of similarity and recognition between the past and present which suddenly open up into chasms of difference – and, conversely, those moments of recognition where patterns from the past become visible and discernible to the reader. I thus want to make a reading which shows how Mitchison's impulse to record such moments of both recognition and estrangement – a process which vitally includes the imaginative reconstruction of the past as a way to be able to document what might have occurred – did not just shape works of reportage such as *Vienna Diary* (1934) or her later deep involvement with the Mass-Observation movement. For her interwar short story writing shows a version of what has been called the 'documentary impulse': a diffuse but prevalent British literary mode of the 1930s.[8] As an 'impulse' it is not a totalising attempt to simply list the visible features of whatever reality is being encountered, but rather one where the act of documenting is dialectically connected to previously existing literary forms, from an epic poem to an investigation of the state of the nation. But it was an impulse sparked by non-literary forces, as Storm Jameson remarked in her famous essay-manifesto 'New Documents' (1937). Jameson berates writers for individualist flaws, but then holds up a model:

> One technical difficulty remains to be solved. The solution may turn up any day, in the course of the experiments going on all the time. This is the frightful

difficulty of expressing, in such a way that they are seen at once to be intimately connected, the relations between things (men, acts) widely separated in space or in the social complex. It has been done in poetry [. . .]. We may stumble on the solution in the effort of trying to create the literary equivalent of the documentary film.[9]

Those literary works which might be said to answer Jameson's hopes were influenced both by such ideologies inherent in documentary film-making, and by political pressures for literature to comment upon the minutiae of the material world.[10] Mitchison's heterogeneous fictional works have not traditionally been seen as belonging in this sphere – but I hope this chapter shows how the very particularities of Mitchison's short stories – fragmented, urgent, and possibly, but not always, part of a greater whole – both accentuate and nuance how, as critics, we can now understand the broad-spectrum prevalence of this 'impulse'. Such a reading also matters for a wider literary history; for then – vitally – the multiple ways of documenting in other comparable writers, from Orwell to the pseudonymous 'Gunbuster' and from Storm Jameson to George Stonier, all start to look different if Mitchison's mode of short story writing is a comrade of kinds.

## REIMAGINING THE PAST

Mitchison's career as a writer began at the age of twenty-six with the success of her first novel, *The Conquered* (1923), which luridly traced a fraught relationship between siblings amid Caesar's conquest of Gaul. Over the following years, as well as her novels, she wrote many shorter texts which attempted to reimagine aspects of the classical past. In this respect she can be compared to other socialist interwar writers, such as Jack Lindsay and Rex Warner, who also saw the possibilities of extracting tutelary parallels from another era – seeing not just architectural templates, togas and philosophy but also, and of more relevance, dictatorships, empires and resistance. But Mitchison's approach was distinctive in that she used several, often overlapping, methods, representing the perspectives of those without power – especially slaves, children and women – in observing events which would later be come to be seen as foundational for European history.[11] Some of these stories of the ancient world are still fascinating and complex, and worthy of sustained attention from literary scholars of the period as well as general readers; but some, such as 'When the Bough Breaks' (1924), with its melodramatic piling up of high emotion and anachronistic detail, seem initially to invite cynical twenty-first-century responses:

> 'What's the matter?' asked Gersemi, and was answered in a torrent of sobs and 'Flavius – he's dead – they've killed him!'
>> Gersemi clutched at a curtain with her heart thumping. 'Are you sure?'
>> 'He's killed – my brother, my dear, dear Flavius!'
>> 'Who killed him?'
>> 'Your people – you Goth!'

Gersemi dropped the curtain and pressed her hands against her head: 'I'm not a Goth – but I'm going to have his baby!'[12]

One way to read this passage is as Victorian stage melodrama reimagined in a Roman context, with flourishes of hysteria doing the work of humanising the stock figures. Another, significantly more productive, way would be to follow what Jenni Calder notes about Mitchison's early short stories: '[h]er almost matter-of-fact tone and colloquial style, along with the distance in time and place, mask the genuinely experimental nature of what she was doing.'[13] Such a mode is not limited to the text of the stories themselves; Mitchison included a jauntily impressive bibliography tour to the complete volume of *When the Bough Breaks and Other Stories*, titling it a 'Note on Books and one's Funny Idea of Ancient History' (315). This could be a useful counterpoint to Eliot's notes to *The Waste Land*, if a compendium of broken classical references, laconic emendations, and veneration for J. G. Frazer is needed to show a rather more intriguing interwar history of classical reception.[14]

But Mitchison's work became significantly more sophisticated and tonally complex by the 1930s, as in 'The Wife of Aglaos' in *The Delicate Fire* (1933), a volume mixing stories and poems. This story is part of a five-story group which collectively recount how the former inhabitants of Mantinea survive after their city is destroyed by Antigonos of Macedonia in his wars against Kleomenes (229/228–222 BC). It follows a kidnapped upper-class Greek woman, Kleta, who survives as a slave, then as a runaway, and then triumphantly as shared mistress to a group of brigands. Her peripatetic physical journey is matched by an ideological one; she has repeated moments of realisation about power and status, but these are intercut with descriptions of the sheer laborious business of having to survive with children in the mountains. All this is addressed in second-person intimacy to the reader – 'You understand that, don't you' (103) – along with her free admission that she is using her knowledge and linguistic abilities to interpolate the thoughts of other characters: '[o]f course, the Helots didn't say that; they were hardly even thinking it; I got it out of them and put it into thoughts, for my practice with philosophic discussion enabled me to do so' (104). Kleta reflects upon the moments of change frequently, seeing her capture and enslavement, and her subsequent sexual liberation, as an educative process, and one which could not have come about peacefully. For what is displayed overtly here is praxis, with intellectual theories and ideas ('philosophic discussion') becoming embodied in the life Kleta comes to lead. This is visible when she compares how a theoretician or orator might understand her current situation with her own experience of the life she is actually living: '[h]e might easily have said that they were his brothers; that's good Stoic theory. But these outlaws of mine were a long way from theory and stoicism; they had the real thing' (114). This lauding of praxis and the 'real' in embodied experience is reinforced by another dimension of the text: its insistence on the sheer sensuality of living. This roots political experiences firmly in the body:

Damis felt he was free, but I felt something more than freedom. I suppose one would call it brotherhood. It was very odd: for here we were, still in danger

and with prospects of no more than a bare life among outlaws, and it was cold
when the wind blew and I knew it would be bitter cold at night; but still I had
an intense feeling of well-being all through my body, from my feet treading
strongly down into the sides of the mountains to my head in the air, I could
feel my muscles smoothly at work and my lungs breathing easily and my breasts
creeping with slow thick milk. (101)

Trying to find a language for the gendered sensuality of existing in the world, especially outdoors and with a knowledge of her own body, puts Mitchison into a context
of other visionary writers of the period who wrote in very different forms – notably
Nan Shepherd. A connection of a body with a landscape animates Shepherd's autobiographical meditation/prose-poem of the 1940s, *The Living Mountain* – for in her
words, 'the body is not made negligible – but paramount'.[15] This gives rise to litanies
which bear comparison with Mitchison's:

The hands have an infinity of pleasure in them. [. . .] The feel of things, tex-
tures, surfaces, rough things like cones and bark, smooth things like stalks
and feathers and pebbles rounded by water, the teasing of gossamers [. . .] the
scratchiness of lichen, the warmth of the sun, the sting of hail, the blunt blow
of tumbling water, the flow of wind – nothing that I can touch or that touches
me but has its own identity for the hand as much as for the eye.[16]

The similarities are worth noting, but so are the differences: Shepherd's corporeal
apprehension of the landscape does not centre itself, as Mitchison's often does, on
the female body defined through sexuality, reproduction, and especially childbirth.
Indeed the climax to 'The Wife of Aglaos' comes when Aglaos himself, having
escaped slavery, finds the bandit-cave in the hills. But Kleta now wishes to live with
– and love – other men, and she already has children with them. The story ends in a
discursive mode: it depicts first Kleta's rejection of Aglaos's plans to move and start
their life again on a well-irrigated farm complete with slaves – as Kleta says, 'you see
slave owning by now meant something quite different to me' (111) – before reaching the epiphany of Aglaos's acceptance of Kleta's agency as a woman (after he is
knocked out by her bandits): 'that was the end and the beginning between Aglaos
and me; there wasn't any going back after that' (121). The personal and political
resolutions are thus for Kleta fundamentally entwined.

  The frontiers of the classical world also provided the settings for Mitchison's most
sustained imaginative thinking about how existing cultures were supplanted by
Greece and Rome, cultures whose records might not survive in plays or histories but
rather in gnomic stories or signs on cave walls. The urge to document such traces
matter to those inside the stories, as well as to readers. In 'Babes in the Wood', collected in *Black Sparta* (1928), an Athenian family is settled on the newly conquered
and 'pacified' island of Melos. Melos had sided – albeit half-heartedly – with Sparta
in the Peloponnesian War and the Athenians had responded by besieging the island,
killing all the adult men, and selling the women and children into slavery. But the
Athenian colonial project here is, as even Thucydides' *History of the Peloponnesian*

*War* noted, literally built on unstable and hollow ground. The climax of the story comes when the twin children of its title accompany a wild boy, 'Skinny', into a cave – and there watch in fascinated horror the last few fugitive native inhabitants of Melos perform a religious ceremony: 'an altar in the middle of the cave with a red charcoal fire smouldering or just flaming on it [. . .] The people began to get more and more excited; they twitched their hands and stamped with their feet in time to the wailing.'[17] The boundary between the living and the dead is now indistinct, as one of the twins realises while running out of the stench-ridden cave:

> Suddenly Konnos caught hold of his sister and whispered: 'I know! I've thought what the smell is! It's the rest of the Melians, the ones who were killed, they're here and they've been worshipping too!' Then both of them looked from side to side of the cave entrance and saw the newer earth rammed and flattened under the rock, and felt under their feet where it had been dug up and then put back, and they ran whimpering out of the unclean place and past the Stone of the Snake.[18]

The cave as a sacred space was a continual preoccupation of Mitchison for her entire career, including in later works such 'Mithras, My Saviour' (1970). Mitchison's animation with narrative of the scant archaeological evidence available to her from digs in the 1920s can be better understood when she is seen as part of a wider pattern, with her works typifying what has been termed 'the archaeological imagination' in British culture of the long 1930s, a mode which came especially to the fore in those writers and artists who have been understood, *post hoc*, as neo-romantic.[19] The 1930s paintings of Alan Sorrell of scenes from Bronze Age and Roman Britain, all rendered as if from the air, would be one potent example; the poetry of David Jones in his 1930s pieces, some of which eventually became *The Anathemata* (1955), would be another; while Jacquetta Hawkes's *A Land* (1951) – an ecstatic and idiosyncratic survey of all of British history, interleaving the geological with the personal – shows how a non-fictional text can belong firmly in this category.[20]

The most virtuosic of Mitchison's attempts to dive into Deep Time and show how cultures articulate themselves is 'The Powers of Light'. This long story (sixty-two pages in the original lavish printing) was first published in 1932 as a complete book, with illustrations by Eric Kennington. It takes a nameless group of Neolithic people – again centring upon the symbolic potential of ceremonies in a cave – and meditates on the question of who gets to be an artist. Now the specific form matters acutely; for the modern short story has a long tradition of being a form that fuses together the intensity of a single, sustained aesthetic vision with implicit questions about the very practice of being an artist. The use of frame-narratives was a particular feature in impressionist works which experimented with decodings, withholdings, allusions and the ineffable, such as Conrad's 'Heart of Darkness' (1899) and many of his other short works; but such frames also intensify the terror of ghost stories of the period, as epitomised by the works of M. R. James. Moreover, the short story frequently both invites and embodies reflexive contemplation of the form and purpose of storytelling, as in Walter Benjamin's meditation upon the practice in his essay 'The Storyteller' (1936), which itself reads as a kind of story, or in Saki's rather more brutal and brusque expounding of what stories might do both to traumatise children and keep them quiet, in a brief 1914 tale of the same title.

Initially Mitchison does not make her attempts to describe hand-daubs on rock in flickering torchlight didactically and overtly transhistorical: she does not tell the reader she is thinking about the role of the artist in society. For the story begins simply by describing the quotidian life of a tribe – and the impossibility of indi-viduation: '[t]he rest of the men and women were They. It was They who decided things and settled things and killed anyone who broke the rules and said Why' (61). Against such collectivity the story follows individuals: the Surprised One who paints and Fire Head who makes fires. They fall in love – but only after the price of diverg-ing from the collective is shown brutally. When the Surprised One has an urge he cannot explain it, but '[i]t seemed to him that he must draw a woman' (72). He does so – a figure then depicted by Kennington in flailing lines which could perhaps best be described as sub-Omega-workshop decorous pornography – and this ensues:

> When They came back They saw he had drawn a woman. They pointed and Their lamps shook about, and They made all kinds of noises. They filled the long cave with the noises They made. They took hold of the Surprised One and some of Them held his hands against the wall of the long cave, against the black and red drawing of the woman, and They beat his hands with stones. They were beating the wickedness out of his hands. (73)

The story brutally fractures at this point between a language of art and craft, of pigment and detail, and a language of absolute collective certainty and violence, bluntly rendered with stone and blood, without shades or nuance. But the two named characters escape and tend to each other. They come out of the cave and onto a different mountainside, one replete with visual cues for pleasure, and where painting might not be punishable:

> Fire Head and the Surprised One sat among the very bright flowers and held one another's hands and rubbed their cheeks together. They had come to a very different place, to the powers of light. They were not frightened any more. They were both so very happy. (84)

'The Powers of Light' might be seen as anticipating another successful attempt to portray moments in a prehistoric past, and to create a narrative based around a point of change: William Golding's novel The Inheritors (1955). As in Mitchison's story, the central conflict Golding's novel describes, between some Neanderthals and a usurping group of Homo sapiens, 'the New People', also pivots on collectivity and individuality, and uses twentieth-century language to capture a world with barely any representational system at all. He also uses the figure of an artist (Tuami, a thug-gish woodcarver) as key. The presence of the artist figure in both works is structural as well as narrative. For Golding, like Mitchison, needs an artist both to show how such an alien world could be depicted, and to make the time-collapsing link to the twentieth century, with the continued imperative, despite the horrors of war, to create art.

## QUESTS AND LOST TICKETS

Questions of how to depict the figure of the artist, and what a society might do to an artist, are also central to 'Beyond This Limit' (1935). This was also initially published as a standalone work – and it was also lavishly illustrated, but this time by Mitchison's friend Wyndham Lewis. It is a work which resists conventional précis, but Marina Warner captures the rebarbative yet compelling weirdness well: 'an exuberant, crazy, phantasmagoric quest story [. . .] about an artist called Phoebe, who, armed with an alarmingly live crocodile handbag, cures herself of a broken heart and sets out for freedom'.[21] Jenni Calder describes it as 'an allegory, tinged with irony, of a woman artist breaking the bounds of convention',[22] and thus an autobiographical element is present, as Mitchison elucidated in her own account of the genesis of the book:

> In 1933 we had begun talking about doing a book together. *Beyond This Limit* (my title) was a total delight to do. I think it was my idea to start with but it developed jointly. I did the writing and he did the pictures but he came more and more into the story as we went along. There were two main characters: Phoebe, who is me, is usually drawn in a wide-skirted, unfashionable, not to say highbrow dress, which I used to wear at the time with a handkerchief knotted over my head – another highbrow fashion. The ticket collector, who is Hermes the guide of souls, becomes increasingly a self-portrait, especially the picture where he is clothed 'in authority' as a bishop.[23]

Mitchison's complex relationship to Lewis has been well excavated and this collaboration seems without precedent for either of them.[24] For while 'Beyond This Limit' is a hallucinatory story which starts in bourgeois realism – on a crowded bus in Paris – it ends in apocalyptic menace. It is filled with an apparitional and incarnational strangeness, especially with regard to the (re-)animation of carvings, statues and drawings; but at its centre is a fear – and a complex delight – about time itself as mutable. Yet Phoebe herself does not believe so at the start, resolutely thinking: 'the time for that was past. Odd that apparently one cannot interfere with past time, only remember it in very great detail, the exact texture of the skin between the eye and the temple, the exact shape of the leaf on the tree . . . Dangerous to start thinking about such things' (4). The 'dangerous' nature of allowing such thoughts to begin comes to fruition as the story shows exactly how one can 'interfere' with time; or rather how non-linear time – the interpenetration of multiple kinds of past into the present – can both terrify you and set you free of expectations, be they gendered or artistic. But the story wishes first to destabilise *place* – as Phoebe travels in a whirlwind from Paris:

the great curve of the world spinning under her, shouldered away the after-
noon; important to keep inside the pull of gravity. The smudge of London
dirtied green England, trailing off arterial legs, blotched with the red and the
brown of suburbs. The Thames valley was a deeper green, wound through by
the blue Thames, brooded over by cloudy Phoebe. (11)

This expansive view might link this story to other moments of delirious aeriality
in interwar literature, moments when from above there is both recognition and
estrangement; and writers such as Evelyn Waugh in *Vile Bodies*, or Virginia Woolf
in 'Flying Over London', use such vistas, and their concomitant sensations, for
aesthetic and political ends.[25] But for Mitchison the aerial is just the start of disori-
entation. For when Phoebe reaches her apparent haven of the British Museum its
contents come, spectacularly and terrifyingly, to life. Here again, as in Mitchison's
stories of the classical world, time has been collapsed – and the past and present are
interlocked. Now, however, this does not occur through the text imagining ancient
gossip, speech and social mores transposed into the vocabulary of the 1930s, but
rather by having a recognisable scene of the present, and a modern heroine, sur-
rounded by the literally animated objects of classical antiquity: not just statues of
heroes and gods, but 'a charcoal burner from Acharnae' (36) as well as minotaurs,
scarab-beetles and ants. All of these are recorded and depicted in Lewis's black-
and-white pen drawings, with the slashingly strong individual lines rendering every
creature both distorted and familiar, his approach mixing a Vorticist legacy and an
attempt to mimic the styles in which the creatures were first painted or carved. So
Lewis's rams look like children's toys from classical Greece, while his birds seem
taken from Egyptian friezes.

Yet the anxieties that assail Phoebe in this extraordinary zone do not only come
through her encounters with the menagerie, or even the unspecified and menacing
creature – the 'IT' – which is tailing her. Rather their source is quotidian:

a few minutes later, in a hideous mist of shame, Phoebe Bathurst was turned
out of the Reading Room, not only having made a noise and disturbed the
sacred peace of the rightful, the householder guaranteed, readers, but also NOT
HAVING HER READERS TICKET. Unforgettable humiliation for a high-
brow, for a respectable, museum-conditioned bourgeoise! Because of Phoebe,
hard things would justifiably be said of women, above all of women artists,
newspapers would publish cruelties, Phil would see them – or worse, May. (38)

The artist here is not as physically vulnerable as in 'The Powers of Light', but here
too society is ready to judge them violently and absolutely. But, again, escape is in
the air – or actually through the air: 'freedom now for swallow-Phoebe, steel-blue,
streamlined, ever falling with careless velocity forward on to air-currents which
cushioned her light body and stiffened wings into a guided bounce' (48). Even so,
escape does not come easily; first Phoebe is interviewed by the frightening ticket
collector at 'Hotel Terminus' – accompanied by more of Lewis's menacing drawings
– and then is offered a way out 'underground'. She feels 'very tired, very unwilling

to go for her interview in Hades. She would have liked a small sherry' (60). But go she must:

> The lift sank uniformly from beneath their following weight. Stairs and plaster decorations sailed upward; they did not stop. We must be at the basement now, thought Phoebe, and then, we must be below the basement. But the other two were not expecting it to stop yet awhile. No need for her to worry then. So the lift continued still with its smooth, its improbable, its clearly apprehended descent. (60)

The story ends without Phoebe being able to return from whatever limit she has exceeded, she is caught within the symbolism of the downward descent, but she has as a guide the (now kindly) ticket inspector, and a selection from the animated menagerie. If any of Mitchison's 1930s short stories pointed towards her later science fiction works, with open-ended imaginative potential emerging from a combination of the familiar and the phantasmagoric, it was perhaps this one.

## REALISM AND MAGIC SWANS

If incursions of the magical and the animation of the inorganic lead towards the darkness of the unknown in 'Beyond This Limit', then other stories by Mitchison, especially those written on the verge of the Second World War, offer visions that are at once more conclusive and more hopeful, albeit implausibly so. They give a glimpse of how her 'use of fantasy for Utopian possibilities', as Nick Hubble sees it, was not just limited to novels such as *We Have Been Warned* (1935), with its idiosyncratic mix of commissars and kelpies.[26] Partly this glimpse comes through Mitchison's retelling of fairy stories and myths, forms that allow a playfulness with wilful anachronisms and jarring images of the past crashing, violently but matter-of-factly, into the present. In 'Frogs and Panthers' (1936) the God Dionysus turns up in contemporary Scotland, insolently smoking cigarettes in a motorcar and seducing workmen away. But sometimes the playfulness stops abruptly, such as in 'Sketch for a Slave Market' (1933), where the reader assumes all the action is taking place in ancient Rome as terrified men, women and children are haggled over – until in the last paragraph where a 'Mrs Hepburn in a grey alpaca dress' says 'And this is Cape Town, and this is the year 1897. It seems as if nobody believes in justice.'[27]

If Mitchison's 'documentary impulse' had ranged widely across past eras in her earlier stories it now found material to record closer to home, but for similar – revolutionary and revelatory – ends. In her late 1930s pieces the focus is firmly on realistic depictions of labour, and this marks a notable shift after her move to Carradale, on the Kintyre peninsula in Argyll, in 1937. These works, especially the story 'Five Men and a Swan' and the long poem 'The Alban Goes Out', have to be seen in a specifically Scottish interwar context of literature which attempted in both form and content to approach issues of collectivity and the political. One example would be James Barke's novel *Major Operation* (1936), which intercuts a didactic message of growing class consciousness with Joycean linguistic play.[28] But Mitchison's form of hyper-local realism, which drew on her acquaintance with the fishing communities of Kintyre, perhaps more immediately recalls the documentary film-maker John Grierson's interest in North Sea herring fishermen in his pioneering and influential *Drifters* (1929). In both Mitchison's and Grierson's work, the fishing trawler serves as a model of tight-knit community while the fates of crew and catch alike illuminate the vagaries of the unfair market.

'Five Men and a Swan' was written in 1940 but not published until much later. It is worth examining to see how Mitchison renders a transformative moment – and does so by attempting to inhabit the consciousness of those to whom it occurs. In the story, the captain of *The Highland Mary* finds a swan-woman while walking drunkenly home at night; then he, and others in his crew, proceed to have a graphically described sex life with her: 'when the Swan came out of the water Black Rob caught hold of her, for he was never one for beds and houses when there was bracken on the braeside' (127). But Alec, the captain, wants something akin to bourgeois respectability with the swan-woman, and Mitchison thus counterpoints moments of mythopoetic shorthand – 'an angry skipper makes poor fishing, forby a white wing blinding his mind when he needs judgement quickest' (127) – with careful itemisation and descriptions of Alec's house as he prepares to welcome her:

> Alec got a cake and a bottle of sweet port wine, the kind that they were telling him the ladies would like, and he put a new red cloth with fringes on the table and a mug with some snowdrops, and he put his budgie cage into the window, with the two budgies that his aunties looked after for him during the week. (130–1)

Such oscillation between the Mass-Observation mode of sociological listing (all the objects here have class signification) and her attempts to transform fishing as an activity into something mythopoetic, Mitchison finds in her story versions of the modes she was trying out in her poetry at exactly the same time. For in 1939 Mitchison published 'The Alban Goes Out' as a privately printed pamphlet from the Raven Press; this had wood-engravings by Gertrude Hermes, including lacework-like black-and-white tracery of nets being drawn in, and the cover boasted a stylised gannet diving for fish. It drew upon her close relationship with the fishermen: indeed, she worked on a trawler in 1939 and later owned a part share in one.[29] It is a narrative poem which alternates between two distinct kinds of time, each meriting a different rhyme scheme, metre and energy; the first captures meditative context, the long, continuous temporality where relationships, tides and friendships matter:

> Sandy alone aboard, in the wheel-house, keeping
> The engine slow but a constant strain on the tow-rope
> Between boat and boat, and so on the net, lest, slack,
> The herring escape it. And he watches, across on the lighted Amy,
> His four sons hauling at the net; Colin and Dick and Bob and Alec:
> A share each for the house and a heart-lift for a father.[30]

The second mode, all end-rhymed, depicts the discrete yet interconnected actions of fishing itself:

Men and engines grunting and hauling,
The nets dripping, the folds falling;
The spring-ropes jerking to the winches' creaking
Wind in by fathoms from their sea-deep seeking,
Steady and long like a preacher speaking.[31]

Yet Mitchison also has, in her story rather than the poem, all the sociology and political context that these mythopoetic night scenes, with the constellations above and easy comradeship on board, might miss. An example comes when Alec tries to think what marrying the Swan might mean, reducing the problem to an economic one, rather than the fact that she periodically shape-shifts into a bird:

And a great shame came over Alec, thinking how they were only poor fisher-men, with no education beyond the age of fourteen and no chances at all, and some years there would be little herring in it, and if any pair did well then the rest would be angry at them and jealous, and if at any time there were plenty of herring, then the buyers would get together and force the prices down, or maybe they would be needing to dump their catch at Ayr, and there was no way out of it for the fishermen, and what kind of a man was he to think he could be marrying such a bonny one as the Swan? (133)

These polysyndetic sentences build up towards a despair that Alec cannot himself articulate – and indeed the story seems to be heading fatalistically towards the utter impossibility of love and happiness under capitalism, even with a magical swan as bride. But then the war begins and Alec is called up. The last page describes his terrors on a patrol boat, and the long sentences now act to slow down and track the near instantaneous action of sudden violence:

Then, on a clear day and out of the eye of the sun, a bomber came down on them. [. . .] Then a bomb came through one of the hatches and there was Alec trying to do a dozen things at once, and in the middle of it he saw his overalls were on fire, and he beat them out, and someone shouted to him to come up, and he saw his right hand was bleeding all over the iron rungs of the ladder though he could feel nothing at all in it yet, and first he was in a boat and then after the next explosion he was in the sea and swimming, but he did not think he would be able to keep it up for long, the way he was. (138)

The swan however finds him, and, precisely because he was kind to her and let her go (shades of 'The Wife of Aglaos'), she rescues him. This is *deux ex machina* in action, and yet the reworked Yeatsian symbolism is abruptly ended by a sailor trying to work out what was the 'white parachute' (140) he saw in the sky. This bird has now flown in every sense, and with it any possibility of explanation.

But what totalising explanations could there be for how, writing in 1940, Mitchison welded together socialist-realist detail, proto-magic-realist urges, careful enumeration of domestic signifiers, and sexual explicitness? Much better, rather, to try and understand this story – like the heterogeneous others Mitchison wrote in the interwar years – as being fuelled by an impulse to document multiplicity, and especially to observe specifics, to try to find a language for them, and then, from such glimpses, to extrapolate narratives. Such narratives though, being short and discrete units which collect and retell moments, do not have to function as part of the architecture of the novel and its generic inheritance; rather they can find affinities with other forms being created in the period – notably short documentary films and the 'day-reports' of the Mass-Observation movement. Mitchison's belief in Mass-Observation, as a way of democratically understanding a collective subconscious, has been well recognised, notably in *Among You Taking Notes* (1985), the compendium of her wartime diaries. But it is also fascinating to understand what attracted her to the very idea of Mass-Observation, especially the movement's affinity for bricolage which is at its most Surrealistic in the 'day-reports' of Humphrey Jennings, but would eventually be expressed in M-O's vast tapestry of individual diary records. For in understanding the unsettling power of Mitchison's complex short stories as encoding and reworking the idea of what it might mean to document, and even to document what cannot be known first-hand – by instead using archaeological traces or reworked mythic paradigms as sources – it is possible to see in those stories the ghost of a future yet to come: the imaginative possibilities for Mass-Observation *avant la lettre*.

## NOTES

1. Marina Warner, 'Introduction' to Naomi Mitchison, *The Fourth Pig* (London: Princeton University Press, 2014), pp. 1–21 (p. 10).
2. To locate Mitchison's short work within her oeuvre see Elizabeth Maslen, 'Naomi Mitchison's Historical Fiction', in *Women Writers of the 1930s: Gender, Politics and History* (Edinburgh: Edinburgh University Press, 1999), pp. 138–50; Janet Montefiore, *Men and Women Writers of the 1930s: The Dangerous Flood of History* (London: Routledge, 1996), pp. 163–8; 'Men, Women and Comrades', in Christopher Whyte (ed.), *Gendering the Nation: Studies in Modern Scottish Literature* (Edinburgh: Edinburgh University Press, 1995), pp. 69–84.
3. Valerie Shaw, *The Short Story: A Critical Introduction* (London: Longman, 1983), p. 21.
4. Frank O'Connor, *The Lonely Voice: A Study of the Short Story* (London: Melville House, 2004), p. 105.
5. Georg Lukács, *Theory of the Novel*, trans. Anna Bostock (Cambridge, MA: MIT Press, 1974), p. 51.
6. There is no definitive count of the short stories Mitchison wrote in her lifetime. They number at least a hundred and fifty, and while most were collected in her own sequences and in later anthologies such as J. F. Hendry's *Penguin Book of Scottish Short Stories* (Harmondsworth: Penguin, 1970), others remain fugitive.
7. Naomi Mitchison, *Beyond This Limit: Selected Shorter Fiction*, ed. Isobel Murray (Glasgow: Kennedy & Boyd, 2008), p. 48. All further references to this edition will be given in the text.

8. See Leo Mellor, 'The Documentary Impulse', in Matthew Taunton and Benjamin Kohlmann (eds), *The Cambridge History of 1930s British Literature* (Cambridge: Cambridge University Press, 2019), pp. 257–70.

9. Storm Jameson, 'New Documents', *Fact*, 4 (1937), p. 11.

10. For more analysis see Laura Marcus, '"The Creative Treatment of Actuality": John Grierson, Documentary Cinema and "Fact" in the 1930s', in Kristin Bluemel (ed.), *Intermodernism: Literary Culture in Mid-Twentieth-Century Britain* (Edinburgh: Edinburgh University Press, 2009), pp. 189–207.

11. For Mitchison's engagement with Greece and Rome see Ruth Hoberman, *Gendering Classicism: The Ancient World in Twentieth-Century Women's Historical Fiction* (Albany: State University of New York Press, 1997).

12. Naomi Mitchison, 'When the Bough Breaks', in *When the Bough Breaks and Other Stories* (London: Jonathan Cape, 1924), p. 223.

13. Jenni Calder, *The Nine Lives of Naomi Mitchison* (Virago: London, 1997), p. 71.

14. Mitchison, *When the Bough Breaks*, pp. 315–18.

15. Nan Shepherd, *The Living Mountain* (Edinburgh: Canongate, 2011), p. 106.

16. Ibid. p. 102–3.

17. Naomi Mitchison, 'Babes in the Wood', in *Black Sparta: Greek Stories* (London: Jonathan Cape, 1931), pp. 178–9.

18. Mitchison, *Black Sparta*, p. 183.

19. See Kitty Hauser, *Shadow Sites: Photography, Archaeology, and the British Landscape 1927–1955* (Oxford: Oxford University Press, 2007).

20. For an overview see David Mellor, *A Paradise Lost: The Neo-Romantic Imagination in Britain 1935–55* (London: Lund Humphries, 1987).

21. Warner, 'Introduction', pp. 11–12.

22. Calder, *The Nine Lives of Naomi Mitchison*, p. 134.

23. Naomi Mitchison, *You May Well Ask* (London: 1979), p. 148.

24. See Michael Hallam, 'In the "Enemy" Camp: Wyndham Lewis, Naomi Mitchison and Rebecca West', in Andrzej Gąsiorek, Alice Reeve-Tucker and Nathan Waddell (eds), *Wyndham Lewis and the Cultures of Modernity* (Farnham: Ashgate, 2011), pp. 57–76.

25. See Leo Mellor, 'Aeroplanes: Rethinking Aeriality in a Long 1930s', in Alex Goody and Ian Whittington (eds), *The Edinburgh Companion to Modernism and Technology* (Edinburgh: Edinburgh University Press, 2022), pp. 91–104.

26. See Nick Hubble, *The Proletarian Answer to the Modernist Question* (Edinburgh: Edinburgh University Press, 2017), p. 15.

27. Naomi Mitchison, *The Delicate Fire* (London: Jonathan Cape, 1933), pp. 338–41 (p. 341).

28. See Leo Mellor, 'Listening-in to the Long 1930s', *Critical Quarterly* 58:4 (December 2016), pp. 113–32.

29. Calder, *The Nine Lives of Naomi Mitchison*, p. 159.

30. Naomi Mitchison, 'The Alban Goes Out', in *The Cleansing of the Knife and Other Poems* (Edinburgh: Canongate, 1978), pp. 2–11 (p. 6).

31. Ibid.

# 2. 'She had her hand on the plow': Shame, Uncertainty and Transformation in *The Corn King and the Spring Queen*

*Nick Hubble*

And Jesus said unto him, No man, having put his hand to the plough, and looking back, is fit for the kingdom of God.

Luke 9:62

When you put your hand to the plow, you can't put it down until you get to the end of the row.

Alice Paul, 1920

Naomi Mitchison has been the subject of a mixed critical reception since the 1930s. Two of the major novels she wrote in that decade, *The Corn King and the Spring Queen* (1931) and *We Have Been Warned* (1935), elicited very different responses despite focusing on similar themes of social change and female agency. While the literary reception of British fiction in the 1930s is also now in a state of flux, until relatively recently the decade was mythologised as 'the Thirties', characterised by a seemingly unique conjunction of literature and communist-inflected popular-front politics.[1] From such a perspective, Mitchison has always appeared a curiously marginal figure. She is mentioned only cursorily in influential critical texts, such as Samuel Hynes's *The Auden Generation* (1972) and Valentine Cunningham's *British Writers of the Thirties* (1988), and even the more extensive discussion in Janet Montefiore's *Men and Women Writers of the 1930s* (1996), which corrects the masculine bias of earlier canonical constructions of the decade, takes pains to identify her as a liberal feminist in sharp contrast to 'Marxist contemporaries'.[2] In this chapter, I am concerned with situating Mitchison within a different context that allows us to judge her work for what it is rather than by the standards of what it is not. In particular, my aim is to show that *The Corn King and the Spring Queen* reflects Mitchison's desire to push on from the equal voting rights for women achieved through the Equal Franchise Act of 1928 in pursuit of a much more fundamental transformation of gender roles within society.

Early on in the novel, Mitchison's protagonist, the titular Spring Queen Erif Der, is described as having 'her hand on the plow'.[3] This phrase refers to the biblical verse of Luke 9:62, featured variously in gospel songs and the culture of the US Civil Rights movement. Significantly, the verse was also cited by the American suffrage activist Alice Paul in relation to her decision, after the passing of the 19th Amendment in 1920 (which gave women the vote), to keep campaigning for a further amendment to enshrine equal rights for women in the US Constitution: 'when you put your hand to the plow, you can't put it down until you get to the end of the row'.[4] Likewise, Mitchison's argument in *The Corn King and the Spring Queen* is that it is not enough for Erif to have a hand on the plow, or for women to have the vote in Britain: only by keeping control of the plow and using it to reconfigure the field, or society, can full freedom be achieved.

The novel was a well-received literary success, with Winifred Holtby going so far as to suggest that its author was 'of the calibre of which Nobel prize-winners are made'.[5] However, as Jill Benton notes, the fact that the reviews 'screened out' the Spring Queen, Erif Der, and concentrated on the masculine elements of the novel might have alerted Mitchison to the fact that she had transgressed 'acceptable limits of fantasised behaviour for women'.[6] Drawing on Benton's analysis, Kristin Bluemel argues that one of the clear limits to the apparent radicalism, 'whether of the right or left', of British literary culture of the 1930s is that there was 'little interest in narratives that insisted women were entitled to the same privileges of sexual and emotional and social experience as men'. Therefore, her depiction of female sexual agency and self-actualisation was either ignored, as in the case of *The Corn King and the Spring Queen*, or – when unavoidably foregrounded within a contemporary political setting, as in Mitchison's next novel, *We Have Been Warned*, with its portrayal of free love, rape and abortion – was 'universally despised'.[7]

However, times have changed. Mitchison may not yet have 'recovered her literary reputation in England', but as Anna McFarlane comments, *We Have Been Warned* became 'a compelling read in contemporary Scotland in the aftermath of the 2014 Independence referendum and the ongoing discussion about the nature of nationalism'.[8] More generally, Mitchison's sexual politics speak to the intersectional imperatives of the twenty-first century. Stephen Brooke shows that Mitchison, alongside others such as Dora Russell, set out in the 1930s 'a politics of sexual liberation and pleasure within a context of sexual reform and socialist politics'.[9] He suggests that her writing forms a link between the work of earlier utopian sex reformers, such as Edward Carpenter and Stella Browne, and women's liberation in the 1970s. Drawing on the work of Marshall Berman, Brooke goes on to argue that Mitchison was a '"subject" of modernity', 'attempting to live and promote "freedom, dignity, beauty, joy, solidarity"'.[10] In what follows, I first discuss Mitchison's position within the wider context of British women's writing in the 1930s and then analyse how writing *The Corn King and the Spring Queen* helped Mitchison develop the new kind of sexually and socially liberated modern subjectivity that she desired.

## BOTH WORLDS: WOMEN AND THE MORAL REVOLUTION IN THE 1930S

Reflecting on reviewing for *Time and Tide* – in her words, 'the first avowedly feminist literary journal with any class, in some ways ahead of its time' – Mitchison recalled:

> Lady Rhondda was always tremendously encouraging and gave gorgeous parties. I remember driving back from one of them, cautiously since there had been a fair consumption of alcohol, but feeling splendid, as though the whole world was opening up and everything would work out, not only for myself, but for women in general.[11]

Mitchison belonged to the generation of 'Professional Women Writers', discussed by Kristin Ewins, who, unfazed by the Victorian spectre of the 'Angel in the House', 'were able to inhabit the intellectual spheres of journalism and literary writing with new legitimacy'.[12] However, the new structure of feeling which made possible this 'formation of professional writers who substantially shaped intellectual culture across the decade' was not restricted to the parameters of equality.[13] When she drove back from Lady Rhondda's party, Mitchison was not simply imagining an egalitarian media but a more fundamentally transformed society. In her 1930 booklet 'Comments on Birth Control', she declared that:

> Intelligent and truly feminist women want two things: they want to live as women, to have masses of children by the men they love and leisure to be tender and aware of both lovers and children; and they want to do their own work, whatever it may be. [. . .] They insist – as I think they should – on having both worlds.[14]

Although Mitchison was clearly not speaking for all women in voicing this particular combination of desires, her insistence on having both worlds expressed a wider belief that a fundamental change in the dominant worldview was necessary in order for women to live freely. Similar ideas, for example, were implicit in Virginia Woolf's instruction that 'one must be woman-manly or man-womanly' in *A Room of One's Own* (1929) and explicit in Ethel Mannin's declaration that 'the only intelligent and satisfactory principle of life is that of determining both to have one's cake and eat it' in her bestselling autobiography, *Confessions and Impressions* (1930).[15] For these writers, the social shift in the 1930s that created an environment supportive of professional women writers was not an end in itself but part of an ongoing revolutionary change in women's place in society. Mitchison explained how she thought this change might be accomplished in *The Home and a Changing Civilisation* (1934): 'there must be no social ownership, no patriarchy [. . .] I cannot see how it is going to be done without some form of equalitarian society.'[16] The emergence of an environment that supported women's writing and publishing, as represented, for example, by the success of *Time and Tide*, created a readership and a potential market which made the publication of these kinds of ideas viable.

In 1938 all three of these authors published major political works: Woolf's *Three Guineas*, Mitchison's *The Moral Basis of Politics* and Mannin's *Women and the Revolution*. While all three books expressed awareness of the threat of fascism, they were primarily concerned with analysing the everyday structures of patriarchy of which fascism was seen as just one, albeit the most extreme, manifestation. In *Three Guineas*, Woolf described the public voice of men as women experience it over the radio and through the daily press: 'There are two worlds, one for women, the other for men.'[17] She urged that women should have full access to both worlds, not just in the name of equality but as a necessary prerequisite for a good, peaceful and just society:

> There are two good reasons why we must try to analyse both our [women's] fear and your [men's] anger; first, because such fear and anger prevent real freedom in the private house; second, because such fear and anger may prevent real freedom in the public world; they may have a positive share in causing war.[18]

For Mannin, the characteristic feature of modernity, and progressive society since the First World War, was the revolutionary change in the lives of women that had already taken place. What was happening in Nazi Germany was a backlash:

> All that progressive women have worked for for years has been lost. Women professors, doctors, civil servants, have been sacked. Women are no longer eligible for Government posts, and may not be appointed to municipal positions. That women should be displaced in medicine and teaching, two spheres in which women can do such valuable work, seems fantastic, but it is all in line with the Nazi policy of woman's subservience to male domination.[19]

In the least overtly feminist of the three books, Mitchison went back to first principles in order to make sense of the politics in the aftermath of the overwhelming victory of the National Government in the 1935 General Election, in which she had unsuccessfully contested the seat representing the Scottish Universities on behalf of the Labour Party. However, her approach to this investigation anticipated later ideas of 'the personal' being 'political' in its realisation that 'politics was not a special kind of game for skilled players but rather a whole aspect of life'.[20] *The Moral Basis of Politics* is, therefore, a wide-ranging attempt to understand life in order to understand politics. To this end, Mitchison bemoaned the lack of data on what ordinary 'people in an average Western European culture pattern, particularly men and women in England and Scotland' wanted, and in a footnote actually touted for money for the recently formed auto-anthropological project Mass-Observation, in which she was a participant.[21] She hypothesised that fun is more important to people than security and reflected that:

> Sex activity is for many people the only kind of free fun there is. Everything else costs money. In the middle and upper classes sex usually costs money too, but this gets less necessarily so, as one descends the social scale. Such data as I

have, at least, tend to substantiate this, but I am waiting for Mass Observation. I think it will be found that the need for fun is a very overwhelming one . . .[22]

The reason that Mitchison's and Mannin's books have remained largely neglected in the history of politically committed literature in the 1930s is because their arguments do not fit the communist-influenced popular-front ideology that until recently largely determined the reception and evaluation of 'Thirties' writing. Of course, *Three Guineas* does not fit this model either; but Woolf's position at the centre of elite social and literary networks, and her subsequent canonical status, means that it has always been widely read. All three books in their different ways envisaged a moral revolution which would fundamentally alter the values underpinning the organisation of society. Lady Rhondda, of *Time and Tide*, was referring to *Three Guineas* when she noted that 'it could not have been written two years earlier' – but the same could equally be said of the other two.[23] However, the paradigmatic shift that all three works represent in their respective authors' thinking was not simply the product of their immediate context but of longer creative processes that originated with the perception by women writers that the Equal Franchise Act of 1928 was not the end point either of women's emancipation or of social development, but rather the point of departure for building a new kind of society.

Mitchison was much more in favour of Soviet communism than either Woolf or Mannin. She is sometimes portrayed in political terms as a naive, fellow-travelling figure of the 1930s; as, for example, by George Orwell, who referred to her as a 'silly sympathiser' and as 'unreliable' in one version of his notorious list of crypto-communists and fellow travellers.[24] It is easy enough to read *The Moral Basis of Politics* as a somewhat tortuous version of the reasoning by which a member of the upper class such as Mitchison 'went over' to the side of the people in response to the political conditions of the times. However, this is to miss the point of a work that is preoccupied with the relationship between values and social change. Specifically, Mitchison was concerned with the question of how everyday culture needed to change in response to the possibility of post-scarcity economics so that people adapted their patterns of living to pleasure, play and plenty. Her consequent diagnosis that the success of the Soviet Union would depend on its success in entrenching economic equality over the next twenty years, as a precursor to a planned society in which that pleasure, play and plenty would be guaranteed for everyone, reveals her in retrospect to have been one of the few clear-sighted thinkers on the subject.[25]

Mitchison realised that 'for the first time in history' it was 'essential that somehow we make a change so as to ease the dislocation between our thought and social habits and the material conditions of our lives'.[26] The dominant 'Western culture pattern' had previously been based on competition but given that there was now enough food and materials for all, it was time to change the moral basis of politics: 'the present culture pattern is founded on economics of scarcity, and scarcity is now an abnormality except in times of war (when the culture standards of our immediate past always seem to become more valid)'.[27] Ultimately, one of the reasons that the Soviet Union eventually failed was precisely its inability, despite extensive efforts, to develop the fully functioning post-scarcity economics required to support its experiments with a new culture pattern of living that so excited Mitchison.[28] She would have liked the same freedom as the Soviet women workers she portrayed in *We Have Been Warned*: to have been able to have children while remaining single. She went on to argue in *The Moral Basis of Politics* – from the experience of her 1932 trip to the Soviet Union, which predated full-blown Stalinism – that 70 per cent of Soviet citizens were 'free to choose the kind of work they want to do, the kind of pattern they want to make with their lives'.[29] While the Soviet Union never delivered on this early promise, it provided an example of a system, in which women had economic independence and bourgeois morality was being discarded, that showed how society could be transformed to allow women to live freely.

Like Woolf's *Three Guineas* and Mannin's *Women and the Revolution*, *The Moral Basis of Politics* was the culmination of a train of thought developed by its author since the end of the 1920s. As noted above, the existence during the decade of a publishing culture encompassing professional women writers enabled this to happen, but the writers still had to find their way to these unprecedentedly radical positions. For example, Mitchison had a huge struggle to get her 1935 novel, *We Have Been Warned*, published. The combination of the contemporary context – as opposed to the classical settings of her other fiction at the time – with frank sexual content and open discussion of contraception meant that in the end she had reluctantly to accept cuts insisted upon by the publisher, Constable, and even these did not prevent the hostile reception discussed at the beginning of this chapter. However, as I have argued elsewhere, writing the novel about a thinly disguised version of herself, Dione Galton, had a self-developmental function which helped Mitchison in her ongoing transition from a subject position orientated to the liberal norms of bourgeois society, albeit with a progressive outlook, to one orientated to a transformed future; hence her description of it as a 'historical novel about my own times'.[30]

Mitchison's radical self-transformation was enabled in part by her treatment of shame as what Helen Merrell Lynd would later describe as 'a positive experience of revelation'.[31] For Lynd, shame is crucial to understanding the relationship between an individual's identity and the society they inhabit because it is not just a response to transgressing social or cultural norms, which would be a feeling of guilt, but also a realisation that other ways of life are possible and, therefore, also a judgement on one's own society. Shame can only be understood with reference to 'transcultural values, [. . .] [the] awareness of values beyond one's own society'.[32] It is a two-part process involving first 'feeling shame for things that one believes one should feel ashamed of and feeling shame that one is ashamed of feeling because one does not actually accept the standards on which it is based'.[33] Dione undergoes this sequence when she experiences shame at being kissed by working-class Donald in the street and immediately feels more shame as a socialist for being ashamed because of bourgeois standards of behaviour. Lynd argues that the two main responses to shame are either to retreat from the position of exposed selfhood back into a life lived according to societal conventions – in which case Dione would never go on to declare herself a 'Red' as she eventually does in the novel but instead remain a bourgeois liberal – or to face up to it and treat it as a revelation of oneself, society and the

wider possibilities which existing social conventions prohibit – which leads Dione
to embrace the idea of a future in which the British moral and social norms of the
1930s no longer hold sway.

Mitchison herself clearly underwent a similar process of self-recognition from the
late 1920s onwards. In the early 1930s she had a relationship with John Pilley – a
contributor to her *An Outline for Boys and Girls and Their Parents* (1932) – which
was based in part on the idea that 'comradeship meant sharing bodies as well as
ideals'.[34] According to Benton, 'With Pilley's help, she came to believe that as a
socialist gesture she should share her body sexually with others, non-possessive of
them, non-possessive of self' and she put this sexual altruism into practice on her trip
to the Soviet Union in 1932.[35] In this respect, *We Have Been Warned* was clearly a
reflection on her own transition beyond the social norms of her age. However, this
transition had long been prefigured in her historical fiction of the 1920s – from her
first novel *The Conquered* (1923) up to and including *The Corn King and the Spring
Queen* – which may be seen as providing a fictional space allowing her, or at least
her fictional avatars, to explore different ways of living beyond the norms of society
and cultural tradition.

In particular, a subplot in *The Corn King and the Spring Queen* anticipates not only
Mitchison's own sexual practice in the Soviet Union but progresses through almost
the same stages of self-recognition that Dione experiences in *We Have Been Warned*.
The titular Spring Queen, Erif Der, who is transparently an alter ego of Mitchison,
finds herself unexpectedly 'bitterly and deeply ashamed' because she refused to sleep
with her sister's retainer, Murr, and subsequently he has killed himself through fear
of her.[36] The point is not that one should always sleep with men who want it but
rather that Erif realises that her refusal stemmed from perceiving him as less than an
equal. This shame opens her understanding of the need for female sexual- and self-
actualisation to coincide with new patterns of living in relationship to the common
people; an understanding which was crucial to shaping the feminist literary structure
of feeling of the 1930s discussed above.

## THE CORN KING AND THE SPRING QUEEN: REWRITING THE WESTERN CULTURAL TRADITION

*The Corn King and the Spring Queen* was written over a period of six years between
1925 and 1931, during which Mitchison's life underwent a number of significant
changes. She gave birth to a fourth son and a second daughter, but her oldest son,
Geoff, died of meningitis. Her marriage went through various phases of being an
open marriage. Politically, Mitchison and her husband moved towards the left.
Benton reports that neither sympathised with the workers during the General Strike
but by 1930 they had joined the Labour Party, which would become central to their
lives for decades to come: 'Naomi's novel actually charts her metamorphosis into a
socialist Labourite'.[37] While the novel cannot simply be read autobiographically,
it is easy to see how Mitchison combined insights from her reading of the period
– which according to Benton included Marx's *Capital*, Freud's *Civilisation and Its*

*Discontents* and Frazer's *The Golden Bough* – with a personal sense of the accelerated social changes of her own time and inserted them into the fictionalised landscape of classical antiquity that she had developed in her novels of the 1920s. *The Corn King and the Spring Queen* may therefore be thought of as an example of what Max Saunders describes as 'autobiografiction' in which, through her alter ego Erif Der, Mitchison is able to imagine for herself a new pattern of living in relation to the common people centred on participation in sexual rituals connected with the harvest.[38] The novel's epilogue suggests that through such interactions, Erif inspires a revolutionary tradition that will pass down through the people and eventually become dominant over the hierarchical and patriarchal structures of classical Greek learning and culture venerated in Mitchison's present.

Unlike *We Have Been Warned*, *The Corn King and the Spring Queen* was at least republished by Virago in the 1980s, yet it seemed to function then more as a fantasy than a text representative of 1930s political concerns; a point that Montefiore reinforces even while trying to resituate it within that context: 'its energy lies in a feminism whose insights Marxists tend to ignore, but its socialism is much less convincing, mainly because it deals almost entirely with the lives and minds of royalty'.[39] For all that Montefiore's book broke ground by expanding the Thirties canon to include writers such as Mitchison, this interpretation of *The Corn King and the Spring Queen* is very much in keeping with the former dominant paradigm governing Thirties criticism of privileging of the communist popular-front line. However, when viewed from an intersectional twenty-first-century perspective, the politics of the novel appear in a more radical light.

Erif Der might be the 'Spring Queen', but this is a symbolic role rather than a royal position as conventionally understood, and much of the tension of the text lies in Erif and Tarrik, the Corn King, working out how to deal with the individuality they experience beyond these symbolic roles. At the beginning of the novel, written before the death of Mitchison's son, both main characters are still very young. Benton describes these opening pages as formulaic and faintly condescending, 'signalling another children's tale', but sees the rest of the novel as 'grippingly describ[ing] the brutality and the dignity of human experience'.[40] However, such a combination today suggests the genre of the contemporary young adult novel and it seems likely that the recent revival of interest in Mitchison's books is due to their appeal to the readership of this genre. The imperative of her young protagonists is not simply limited to overcoming challenges thrown up by the plot but also to avoid replicating the hypocrisies and failings of the adult generation. Being points of identification for a 1930s readership seeking to break free of residual nineteenth-century values of duty and decorum, Erif and Tarrik differ from the Spartan King, Kleomenes, despite his relative youth. The latter is both a recognisable tragic hero and also representative of a king who has to die for his people. Mitchison wrote about tragedies – referring to the examples of *Hamlet* and *Oedipus Rex* – in *The Moral Basis of Politics* and argued that they form a model for getting an audience to first realise their complicity with the unsatisfactory social relations of the contemporary world, before undergoing a process of catharsis and change of heart.[41] But while the fate of Kleomenes is a powerful element of *The Corn King and the Spring Queen*, it is the intervention of Erif after his death, protecting his body in the form of a snake, that ensures his story becomes a legend among the dispossessed.

Mitchison's use of royal protagonists may also be seen in the light of the anarchist tradition of fantasy writing from Hope Mirrlees and Mervyn Peake through to Michael Moorcock and Ursula Le Guin. As James Gifford has recently suggested in his discussion of these authors, this tradition often associates the power of the protagonists, symbolic or otherwise, with their exercise of conscious human agency. It is Mitchison's tendency to show subjectivity determining material conditions rather than the other way round (or in other words, her tendency to show how moral values shape the material configuration of society) which leads Montefiore to group Mitchison with liberal feminists such as Winifred Holtby and Storm Jameson rather than Marxists of the period. However, Mitchison's radical potential surely lies – to paraphrase Gifford's discussion of Le Guin – in both 'the liberation of the subject' and the 'radicalisation of society'.[42] In this respect, the novel is not fundamentally about the lives and minds of royalty but rather about the possibility of transforming the agency of kings and queens into the agency of commoners.

It is the exploration of how this social transformation might take place that requires *The Corn King and the Spring Queen* to be a sustained consideration of the relationships between art and practice, feminism and the class struggle, and the centre and the margins – as represented by the peripheral location of Mitchison's invented Black Sea kingdom, Marob, in relation to revolutionary Sparta and the decadent court of Ptolemy in Alexandria. Not only do these relationships map onto Mitchison's various contemporary concerns, ranging from the influence of Lenin to the nature of the relationship between England and Scotland, but they also give the novel an intersectional dimension. Tarrik, Erif and her brother Berris are always othered as barbarian Scythians because nobody 'civilised' has ever heard of Marob and so there is always a complex interplay of class, ethnic and gender identities within the novel.

The key 'culture patterning' of the various agrarian societies encountered in the novel – Marob, Sparta and Egypt – is around the annual harvest and related seasonal rituals, such as 'Plowing Eve' in Marob, which is only finally described in full detail more than two hundred pages into the novel.[43] The delay in detailing this key rite is significant. While the sexual symbolism of Erif as Spring Queen lying passive before the 'plow' of the Corn King is obviously one of female submission, we have already seen Erif being forced to submit to Tarrik at the beginning of the novel when he takes her to be his wife. She resents the power he holds by sexually attracting her and resolves to kill him through her magic: 'He shan't change me.'[44] However, the struggle for mastery between Erif and Tarrik is complicated by the desire of Erif's father, Harn Der, to become Chief of Marob in Tarrik's place. She is acting on her father's wishes when she originally magics Tarrik into wanting to marry her, but the plan has always been to kill him after a period of a few months. So, therefore, while Erif holds power through her magic – acknowledged, as we have seen, in Mitchison's biblical phrase 'she had her hand on the plow' – she is caught in the patriarchal trap of having to support either her father or her husband. While this situation in the novel is not a simple allegory, it is nonetheless indicative of the position of women after the Equal Franchise Act of 1928, which left them with symbolic power but still ensnared within the patriarchal structures of society. At this early point in the novel, it is really not clear how Erif will be able to keep her hand on the plow and continue on to the end of the row.

Proceedings are further complicated by the washing up from a shipwreck of the Stoic philosopher Sphaeros, whose teachings cause Tarrik to question the difference between appearance and reality. This ultimately helps Tarrik escape Erif's attempt to enchant him so that he is killed by bulls. However, it also leads him to question the entire nature of his role as Corn King and he thereby becomes ineffective in fulfilling his duties. Tarrik leaves Marob with Sphaeros and eventually goes to Sparta, where he joins Kleomenes' revolution. It is only after Erif follows him to Sparta and rescues him from imprisonment from Kleomenes' enemies in the Achaean League that the two are reconciled and return to Marob in time for the ceremonies of Plowing Eve, which Tarrik is able to perform successfully with a modern double consciousness, simultaneously aware of both the appearance of what he is enacting and its mythic role in ensuring the fertility of the fields.

Erif is still caught within the patriarchal dilemma of having to choose between father and husband but, through her shame following the suicide of Murr, she herself learns uncertainty and a painfully modern double consciousness of appearance and reality. Therefore, she is unable to perform another key ritual, the Corn Play, unselfconsciously. All too aware that the figure of the Corn Year, whom she is supposed to symbolically reap, is her father Harn Der, she slashes his throat for real in a deliberate, albeit impulsive, act of patricide. While the ritual is saved by Tarrik leaping in to take on the role of the Corn Year so that the rites can be completed, this has the amusing consequence that he starts thinking of himself as Harn Der and, thus, the repeating structure of patriarchy is laid bare by the text. Erif escapes this patriarchal order by henceforth always joining in with the common people in the harvest rituals and associated sexual celebrations of whichever of the novel's settings she happens to be in. By not running away from but working through the experience of shame she felt over Murr, Erif has come to what Lynd would describe as a transcultural awareness of values beyond those of her upbringing and society. In this way, Mitchison is able to explore through autobiografiction what it might be like to live freely as a woman by allowing her alter ego to enjoy moments of classless existence in antiquity.

The novel is not utopian in any easy or straightforward manner. At one point late in the novel, when the action has moved on to Egypt, the young son of Erif and Tarrik, Klint-Tisamenos, demands, 'Will you take me out, mother, if no one will? I want to see the lighthouse!'[45] This is clearly a reference to Woolf's To the Lighthouse (1927) in which, as Matthew Taunton observes, the lighthouse may be seen as 'emblematic of a kind of radiant future' but is nonetheless never actually reached.[46] However, in the novel's epilogue, set some years after the rest of the action, Klint-Tisamenos has himself become Corn King and it is clear from the way that he welcomes an injured slave from a merchant ship into Marob that the times are changing.

Mitchison wrote about the fictional Marob again in other works including Travel Light (1952), which, on one level, is a charming fairy tale and, on another, is an even more profound rewriting of the Western tradition than *The Corn King and the Spring Queen*. We learn from Tarkan Der, a descendent of the long-ago Corn Kings, that Marob is now a Christian country in which the new and old values – such as those of the Marob of Klint-Tisamenos – coalesce in the ideas of goodness, justice and the meek inheriting the earth. Nonetheless, by the end of the novel, the protagonist, Halla, leaves Tarkan because the prospect of keeping house for him does not appeal, however fundamentally decent he might be. Instead, Mitchison uses the story of Halla, who is abandoned on a mountainside by her royal parents at the beginning of *Travel Light*, to subvert the Oedipus myth when, through a process of time dilation, she returns to her homeland centuries after her birth and rescues, rather than kills, the father figure. In rejecting both the Oedipal tragedy and the 'happy ending' with Tarkan Der, Halla finds a way to be free. Her instruction to us to 'forget the story' is an invitation to follow her advice and move outside the Western cultural tradition.[47]

## CONCLUSION

As Mitchison observed in *The Moral Basis of Politics*, 'On the whole people would sooner be boiled in oil than change their minds.'[48] The urgent problem to be solved, both in the 1930s and today, is how to get people to overcome this resistance and accept change, such as that driven by the successive waves of women's emancipation. Mitchison suggested that we could learn from the way in which industrial strikes were regarded: before the First World War, 'strikes against intolerable conditions which could be righted without upsetting the capitalist system were approved of by Liberals and some Conservatives'.[49] However, the moment a strike was seen as a political attack on the capitalist system, in the manner that the 1926 General Strike was, then it was ruthlessly opposed. To overturn this common habit of thought which sees the strike or demonstration or political campaign, rather than the authorities' response to it, as the aggressive or hostile act, Mitchison suggested an alternative perspective:

> Now look at the same thing from another point of view. If we believe that our idea of good is correct, and if we have the correct ensuing system of the implied good life, then the existing system is realised as an active attack on the Good – all the time it is stopping and hindering attainment of good. Our object is to defend the Good from attack, and so the same strike which was seen as an attack on the system is now a defence of the Good.[50]

The 1938 books of moral critique by Woolf, Mannin and Mitchison were all written with the knowledge that the social and cultural changes necessary for women to live freely would only overcome resistance if they could be associated with an obvious, overarching 'Good' that outweighed established societal norms. They were able to see this because, unlike most of their peers writing before 1930, they understood the full extent of the radical transition required. Woolf, Mannin and Mitchison underwent processes of self-recognition through their writing which allowed them to adopt a transcultural perspective. Now that parallels with the 1930s have become a commonplace of contemporary political commentary, it is surely a good idea for us to study these books again.

Maybe it was unrealistic to expect the uninhibited representation of female sexuality and agency to be accepted in the 1930s. After all, Woolf warned in 'Professions for Women', a lecture she gave in January 1931, that the 'consciousness of what men will say of a woman who speaks the truth about her passions' or her 'experiences as a body' acted as a very strong prohibition against writing freely about female experience.[51] However, viewed within the alternative timeline which Woolf had set out in *A Room of One's Own* of women eventually being able to write completely freely and without inhibition – provided 'we live another century or so' – the renewed interest and appreciation of Mitchison taking place in the twenty-first century is hardly surprising.[52] Mitchison was not just ahead of her time but also clearly sympathetic to Woolf's qualification that by 'we live' she was 'talking of the common life which is the real life and not of the little separate lives which we live as individuals'.[53] Not only did Mitchison understand the need to become part of the common life, she was prepared to work out symbolically what that would entail in her vision of Marob, where, as the new Corn King, Klint-Tisamenos, comments in the epilogue to *The Corn King and the Spring Queen*, 'we have got the thing straight', meaning that kings are expected to live and die for their people rather than the other way round.[54] In her afterword to the 1982 Virago edition of the novel, she comments that this 'ending is wrong' because 'clearly a lot more happened [. . .] that should have been told' in both Sparta and Marob in order to get to this resolution.[55] However, I don't think this should be taken so much as a judgement made from hindsight but rather as a side effect of being halfway through that period of a hundred years specified by Woolf as necessary for arriving at a form of women's writing entirely free from patriarchal structures. In 1982, it was possible to imagine in more detail the incremental steps necessary to get from Erif's hard-won consciousness of the need to participate in the common way of life of the people, to the freer, more modern Marob, which had been mostly a utopian aspiration when the book was first published. Mitchison's comment that those 'interested in what happened to Marob later [. . .] will find small clues in several of my books, especially *Travel Light* and *Cleopatra's People*' acknowledges that she had remained engaged in the need to resolve the relationship between the Spring Queen and the common people over the intervening decades. Nobody familiar with her body of work over her lifetime would accuse Mitchison of ever looking back or taking her hand off 'the plow' in the struggle to transform gender relations and create a society in which women could live freely as social and sexual agents. As Benton argues, what links *The Corn King and the Spring Queen* and *Travel Light* – and *Memoirs of a Spacewoman* (1962) – is a concept of 'the female hero' who transcends binary limitations, such as the patriarchal dilemma over father and husband, and is 'gifted with empathy', capable of communicating 'with all forms of life in the universe'.[56]

NOTES

1.  For recent revisionist accounts of the literature of the 1930s see Leo Mellor and Glyn
    Salton-Cox (eds), 'The Long 1930s' [Special Issue], *Critical Quarterly*, 57:3 (2015); Benjamin
    Kohlmann and Matthew Taunton (eds), *A History of 1930s British Literature* (Cambridge:
    Cambridge University Press, 2019); Nick Hubble, Luke Seaber and Elinor Taylor (eds), *The
    1930s: A Decade of Modern British Fiction* (London: Bloomsbury Academic, 2021).
2.  Janet Montefiore, *Men and Women Writers of the 1930s: The Dangerous Flood of History*
    (London: Routledge, 1996), p. 164.
3.  Naomi Mitchison, *The Corn King and the Spring Queen* (London: Virago, 1983), p. 66.
4.  Quoted in Peter Dreier, *The 100 Greatest Americans of the 20th Century: A Social Justice Hall
    of Fame* (New York: Nation Books, 2012), p. 149.
5.  Quoted in Jenni Calder, *The Nine Lives of Naomi Mitchison* (London: Virago, 1997), p. 100.
6.  Jill Benton, *Naomi Mitchison: A Biography* (London: Pandora, 1992), p. 69.
7.  Kristin Bluemel, 'Exemplary Intermodernists: Stevie Smith, Inez Holden, Betty Miller, and
    Naomi Mitchison', in Maroula Joannou (ed.), *The History of British Women's Writing, 1920–
    1945* (Basingstoke: Palgrave Macmillan, 2012), p. 51.
8.  Benton, *Naomi Mitchison*, p. 106; Anna McFarlane, 'Naomi Mitchison's *We Have Been
    Warned* in Post-Referendum Scotland', *The Bottle Imp* 19 (June 2016), p. 2.
9.  Stephen Brooke, *Sexual Politics: Sexuality, Family Planning, and the British Left from the 1880s
    to the Present Day* (Oxford: Oxford University Press, 2011), p. 65.
10. Ibid. pp. 84–5.
11. Naomi Mitchison, *You May Well Ask: A Memoir 1920–1940* (London: Flamingo, 1986),
    pp. 168–9.
12. Kristin Ewins, 'Professional Women Writers', in Benjamin Kohlmann and Matthew
    Taunton (eds), *A History of 1930s British Literature* (Cambridge: Cambridge University Press,
    2019), p. 58.
13. Ibid. p. 59.
14. Mitchison, *Comments on Birth Control* (London: Faber and Faber, 1930), p. 25.
15. Virginia Woolf, *A Room of One's Own/Three Guineas* (Harmondsworth: Penguin, 2000),
    p. 94; Ethel Mannin, *Confessions and Impressions* (Harmondsworth, Penguin, 1937), p. 95.
16. Quoted in Brooke, *Sexual Politics*, p. 86.
17. Woolf, *A Room of One's Own/Three Guineas*, p. 269.
18. Ibid. p. 257.
19. Mannin, *Women and the Revolution* (New York: E. P. Dutton & Co., 1939), pp. 196–7.
20. Mitchison, *The Moral Basis of Politics* (Port Washington, NY: Kennikat Press, 1973), p. viii.
21. Ibid. p. 320. For Mitchison's involvement with Mass-Observation, see Nick Hubble,
    'Documenting Lives: Mass Observation, Women's Diaries, and Everyday Modernity', in
    Adam Smyth (ed.), *A History of English Autobiography* (Cambridge: Cambridge University
    Press, 2016), pp. 345–58.
22. Ibid. pp. 326–7.
23. Quoted in Angela V. John, *Turning the Tide: The Life of Lady Rhondda* (Cardigan: Parthian,
    2013), p. 320.
24. George Orwell, 'Names sent to Celia Kirwan, 2 May 1949', in Peter Davison (ed.), *The Lost
    Orwell* (London: Timewell Press, 2006), p. 146.
25. See Mitchison, *Moral Basis of Politics*, pp. 82–92.
26. Ibid. p. 308.
27. Ibid. pp. 14, 15.
28. On Soviet attempts to create a post-scarcity economy, see Francis Spufford, *Red Plenty*
    (London: Faber & Faber, 2010).
29. Mitchison, *Moral Basis of Politics*, p. 69.

30. Hubble, *The Proletarian Answer to the Modernist Question* (Edinburgh: Edinburgh University Press, 2017), pp. 10–21; Mitchison, *We Have Been Warned* (Kilkerran: Kennedy & Boyd, 2012), p. xxi.
31. Helen Merrell Lynd, *On Shame and the Search for Identity* (London: Routledge & Kegan Paul, 1958), pp. 19–20.
32. Ibid. pp. 35–6.
33. Ibid. p. 37.
34. Calder, *Nine Lives*, p. 109.
35. Benton, *Naomi Mitchison*, pp. 81–2.
36. Mitchison, *The Corn King*, p. 270.
37. Benton, *Naomi Mitchison*, p. 63.
38. Autobiografiction exceeds basic autobiographical fiction in part by allowing the author to put themselves into different times and places and thus reveal aspects of the self that have not been shown in real life. See Max Saunders, *Self-Impression: Life-Writing, Autobiografiction, and the Forms of Modern Literature* (Oxford: Oxford University Press, 2010).
39. Montefiore, *Men and Women Writers*, p. 168.
40. Benton, *Naomi Mitchison*, p. 64.
41. See Mitchison, *Moral Basis of Politics*, pp. 114, 288.
42. James Gifford, *A Modernist Fantasy: Modernism, Anarchism, and the Radical Fantastic* (Victoria, BC: ELS Editions, 2018), p. 73.
43. Mitchison, *The Corn King*, pp. 240–7.
44. Ibid. p. 74.
45. Ibid. p. 699.
46. Matthew Taunton, *Red Britain: The Russian Revolution in Mid-Century Culture* (Oxford: Oxford University Press, 2019), p. 54.
47. Mitchison, *Travel Light* (London: Virago, 1985), p. 140. See also Hubble, '"The Kind of Woman Who Talked to Basilisks": Travelling Light through Naomi Mitchison's Landscape of the Imaginary', *The Luminary* 7 (2016), https://www.lancaster.ac.uk/luminary/issue%207/Article%205.pdf [accessed 24 August 2022].
48. Mitchison, *Moral Basis of Politics*, p. 301.
49. Ibid. p. 194.
50. Ibid. p. 195.
51. Woolf, *A Room of One's Own/Three Guineas*, pp. 359–60.
52. Ibid. p. 102.
53. Ibid. p. 102.
54. Mitchison, *The Corn King*, p. 719.
55. Ibid. pp. 721–2.
56. Benton, *Naomi Mitchison*, p. 145.

# 3. Varieties of Sexual Experience: Naomi Mitchison, Mysticism and Gerald Heard

*Imogen Woodberry*

Raised as an agnostic by a mother convinced that religion was a matter for the servants, in adult life Naomi Mitchison maintained a generally antipathetic attitude towards the church.[1] Eschewing church attendance (to the disapproval of her Scottish neighbours), while she could write sympathetically of early Christianity, she was generally critical of its institutional formation.[2] Her sexual progressivism, in particular her advocacy of birth control, made her a controversial figure within Christian circles and her writings attracted repeated clerical denunciation. But although it's easy to assume a straightforwardly oppositional relationship between Mitchison's sexual progressivism and religion, in this chapter I'm going to argue that consideration of her oeuvre in the 1930s complicates the seeming antithesis between the two spheres. I'm going to investigate the way in which her advocacy of new social mores was, in fact, deeply permeated by spiritual notions, albeit ones that operated outside of the church.

Consideration of the networks in which Mitchison participated is instructive for understanding the intersection between metaphysics and progressivism during the interwar years. In the late 1920s Mitchison was part of a group of writers who became enamoured with the teaching of the guru-esque Gerald Heard. Mitchison's correspondence indicates something of the excitement Heard provoked in British intellectual circles; she wrote enthusiastically about his ideas to associates including E. M. Forster, Olaf Stapledon and W. H. Auden.[3] Her friend Aldous Huxley became similarly enthused with Heard's thought, joining forces with him to advance a form of spiritualised pacifism within the Peace Pledge Union. Heard exerted a hold that can be hard to understand from his writings alone. But his personal charisma appears to have been considerable, with contemporaries often describing his social charm and polymathic knowledge.

Fusing the theological and the anthropological, Heard's thought centred on a developmental notion of consciousness; he was convinced that humanity's present state of separation, or 'self-consciousness', represented a fall away from an earlier condition of connectivity. Primitive humanity, he opined, lacked a sense of separation, existing in a form of 'co-consciousness': a prelapsarian harmony that could be regained. Arguing that the impulse towards communality currently existed as a latent strand that could be fostered and cultivated, he believed that the present period of individuality would be transcended by a new age of 'super-consciousness' in which the boundaries of the self would fall away. This theory was expounded by Heard in a series of works published throughout the interwar years.[4] In the first section of this chapter, I will focus on Mitchison's pamphlet *Comments on Birth Control* (1930) to explore the way in which Heard fostered an eschatological note in Mitchison's ideas about sexual liberalisation. I will consider how her advocacy of new sexual freedoms fused the pragmatic with the apocalyptic, the practical grounds on which she advocated changed forms of intimacy situated alongside her belief that non-monogamy would emerge as the manifestation of a new age of connected being.

I will use the teleological dimension of Mitchison's ideas about sexual liberalisation to advance a reading of her novel *The Corn King and the Spring Queen* (1931) as an exercise in exploring alternative forms of living. The use of the historical novel in the 1930s to comment on the contemporary political moment has been widely noted by commentators. Building on Perry Anderson's observation that such fictions offered 'signposts to the future', and Diana Wallace's stress on the politically subversive potential of the genre, I will consider the way in which the influence of Heard can be discerned in the novel's portrayal of spiritualised sexuality.[5] The dual lens of Heardian temporality – the sense that the harmonious past offers the vision of an idealised future – provides a means of reading Mitchison's celebratory depiction of free love within the tribal group as a model of connectedness for the future.

This orientation to the novel's depiction of sexuality is reinforced, I will argue, by the centrality of renegotiated forms of personal intimacy to socialist futurity in her contemporaneous novel *We Have Been Warned* (1935). The final section of this chapter will undertake a recuperative reading of this widely criticised text. I'm not going to advance claims for its formal brilliance – instead I will make the case for its importance as an ideological document. While I think that there's a limit to the way in which Mitchison's oeuvre can be reclaimed in artistic or aesthetic terms, her writing is still highly significant for the nuanced quality of her social and political thought. A polymathic writer, she used her fiction as a crucial forum for the development of ideas she was also articulating in these separate spheres.

I will argue that there's a greater sophistication to the sexual ethics of *We Have Been Warned* than has been previously acknowledged. I suggest that Mitchison makes intriguing use of the element of autofiction to query her idealised notion of sexual liberation as the harbinger of a new age, by placing it in tension with the disappointments of her lived experience of polyamory. The heroine Dione (closely modelled on Mitchison) embarks on a course of free love as a way, she believes, of enacting her socialist principles – a commitment seemingly endorsed by the signs of impending revolution. But her attempt to construct a new lifestyle within the old order is met with disappointment, frustration and the loss of autonomy, rather than liberatory gain. The conflict between the novel's seeming optimism in the coming of a new age and Dione's difficulty in constructing a lifestyle geared to the revolutionary tomorrow offers, I will argue, a nuanced reappraisal of Mitchison's idealistic notions of the contribution that personal sexual freedom could make to the good of the social whole.

## 'THE REVOLUTION OF CONSCIOUSNESS'

Mitchison's excitement about Heard's writings was reflected in the pages of the feminist periodical *Time and Tide*, in which she wrote repeatedly endorsing his ideas in the early years of the 1930s. In 'Good News', Mitchison examined Heard's notion that the unconscious holds beneficent powers, arguing that accessing its latent impulse towards group love holds the power to transform society in both a personal and political sense. The 'charity of the group', she claims, will take the 'bitterness out of sex, bringing with it, inevitably, a communism based not on fear and hate but on love.'[6] Reviewing his *Ascent of Humanity* (1929), also for *Time and Tide*, Mitchison spoke of it as 'the book of perhaps the last revolution, the revolution of consciousness', a millenarian note that she also sounded in her review of his later work, *The Social Substance of Religion* (1931) ('It must be read intently, and – I believe – joyfully, for peace is in sight').[7] Her memoir went on to label him a prophet.[8] Mitchison became involved in Heard's practical schemes aimed at fostering new states of consciousness, helping to organise the Engineers Study Group. From Heard's description of the meetings, which Mitchison later recorded, they appear to have been spartan affairs. They were weekly gatherings of around twelve people, seated together in a darkened room, whose attempts to cultivate feelings of togetherness were aided, if at all, only by music.[9]

In what sense were these undemonstrative, small-scale meetings 'revolutionary'? In 1929 Mitchison had introduced Heard to W. H. Auden, who also became enthralled by his ideas. Auden's poem 'A Summer Night' ('Out on the lawn I lie in bed . . .'), from 1933, describes a moment of communion in a garden, in a feeling of togetherness and warmth with 'colleagues'. But the moment is troubled by the recognition of the political inequality that has enabled this happy sensation; the 'doubtful act' that 'allows/Our freedom in this English house', which is anyway 'rent' by the revolutionary flood.[10] Samuel Hynes reads the poem as an account of the death of the bourgeoisie, of how 'private feeling' is part of a 'drowning world'.[11] But in the final verse *agape*, or divine love, re-emerges as the power that assists the world's rebuilding after the revolution has spent its force. Auden's belief in the political acumen of Heard's thought is reinforced by consideration of his incomplete epic 'In the Year of My Youth', written in the same year as 'A Summer Night'. In this poem, intended to explain why communism would be hard to establish in Britain, Heard appears as a Virgilian 'perfect teacher' guiding the poet through modern life.[12]

Although Heard focused on the transformative power of *agape*, there was an implication in his thought that the erotic could also have a healing power. This suggestion is found in *The Social Substance of Religion*, in which Heard argued that sex had been used in early forms of religious practice to reaffirm the sense of community that had been lost once co-consciousness had broken down. He claimed that early religious ritual used orgies as 'life-associative' techniques to bridge the gap between individuals. Monthly the tribe would come together in an 'explosion of unity' from which the individual would leave 'purified, balanced, at rest'.[13]

There is a similar imbrication of sex and anthropology in Mitchison's pamphlet *Comments on Birth Control* (1930), based on the talk that she gave at the Third International World Congress on Sexual Reform, which took place in London in 1929. The pamphlet uses Heard's developmental view of the self to speculate on a future of non-monogamy. Although advocating polyamory as the ambition of '[i]ntelligent and truly feminist women', Mitchison recognises the problems with its establishment as a way of life in the present moment.[14] The solution that the pamphlet primarily looks to is the emergence of a new form of corporate identity. She compares the uncoordinated, separated self of the industrial present with an idealised, tribal form of connectivity. Taking Heard's soft primitivist lens, she applies it not to palaeolithic humanity, but rather the Trobriand islanders. Mitchison argues that the Trobriand women have a form of spiritual and physical connectivity so strong that they are able to control the time they become pregnant so as to suit the life of the tribe. Citing Heard, she claims that, by contrast, modern Western humanity is currently living in a state of separation; but she speculates that the future will see the emergence of a new psychic state, 'the super-conscious community', in which the importance of an intense heterosexual bond between couples will have been superseded.[15]

### 'MAKING PEACE IN THE HOUSE OF MAROB'

In this section I will argue that the ideas articulated by Mitchison in her pamphlet underpin her contemporaneous novel *The Corn King and the Spring Queen* (1930) in its depiction of a tribal society whose sense of communality is fostered by a form of mystical eroticism. I will then seek to contextualise this aspect of the novel by considering its relationship to writings on a more liberatory approach to sexual mores among her contemporaries.

Mitchison's novel centres on the relationship between the rulers of the fictional Marob society – the witch Erif Der and the king, Tarrik – whose romantic love for one another is almost entirely untroubled by their non-monogamous lifestyle. This involves varied forms of sexual conduct: Erif has repeated casual encounters with her Marob subjects, with men and with women. There is a distinctly untroubled approach to the active nature of Erif's desire – sex with a man she cannot see is presented as the healthy release of pent-up energy ('she had not realised how much she had wanted a man all these weeks of summer').[16]

But rather than a manifestation of vampish barbarian 'otherness', Erif is rendered in unthreateningly childlike guise, with her sexual desire presented as an aspect of tribal loyalty. When she reflects on whether to have sex with another member of the tribe she muses, in joyful refrain, on how the act would facilitate the community's prosperity: 'Surely she was making it easier for the rain and the warmth to come, for the corn to spring, for beasts and women to breed! Surely she was making peace in the household of Marob!' (238).

The duty of promiscuity is underlined most starkly in Mitchison's imaginings of the religious life of the tribe which centre upon the fertility rites of the 'Plowing Eve', a ritual performed by the Spring Queen and the Corn King to ensure the agricultural well-being of the community for the year ahead. The members of Marob society share in the psychic energy released by this ritual through sexual coupling with one another. The purpose of the event, which bears a close similarity to the description of tribal spirituality found in Heard, is community solidarity; the women 'stayed for the men to be able to work their own and only magic and help the Corn King to help the year' (216).

At the end of the 1920s Mitchison and her husband, Dick, decided to open their marriage; he formed a long-term relationship with the social reformer Margery Spring Rice, and she with the classicist H. T. Wade-Gery.[17] Both also had multiple other liaisons. In a letter to a disapproving aunt, Mitchison wrote earnestly of the way this lifestyle represented a serious attempt to forge a new form of social conduct: 'We have to try and make a world for ourselves, basing it as far as possible on love and awareness, mental and bodily, because it seems to us that all the repressions and formulae, all the cutting off of part of our experience [. . .] have not worked.'[18] The letter cites D. H. Lawrence as one of the contemporary formulators of her 'doctrine'. Interestingly there's a Lawrentian hue in her account of the sexual coupling of the King and Queen at Plowing Eve, in the lyrical description of how 'his body curved and shot down towards her' and 'the seizing in ultimate necessity on woman's flesh' (213, 214).

The novel, in its elision of sexual radicalism and lyric pastoralism, would seem to be aligned with Lawrence's vision of the rural as the locale for self-actualisation via sexual awakening. It could also be connected to E. M. Forster's figuring of the 'greenwood' as the utopic site for the abandon of suburban restraint. The impact of the literary rendering of erotic freedom on advocates of sex reform has been noted by Stephen Brooke, who draws attention to the way – particularly – Lawrentian stylistics infiltrated the writing of campaigners. In an article on Dora Russell, Brooke identifies elements of literary embellishment in works of otherwise sociological or political argumentation. Russell's feminist pamphlet *Hypatia* (1925) concludes with a flamboyant description of men and women as 'things of fire intertwining in understandings, torrents leaping to join in a cascade of mutual ecstasy', a note similarly struck in her *The Right to be Happy* (1927), where sex is characterised as 'the most vital [. . .] experience [. . .] which bears fruit in a union in which body and soul cry out: "For this, for this I was born!"'[19]

Russell's use of poetic language insists on the absolute importance of sex in order to argue – an implication that can also be gleaned from Lawrence and Forster – that to force individuals either to forgo the experience altogether, or to refrain from engaging with the person uniquely capable of arousing such sensations, would be cruelly repressive. But I don't think that Mitchison ever came to more than a surface application of Lawrence's thought. She turned to Lawrentian vocabulary as a convenient resource for describing sex in celebratory terms, but her idea of what was at stake in an erotic encounter was fundamentally at odds with his vision. I want now to probe this difference by reading Mitchison against the grain, proposing that a more apt comparison to her writing can be drawn, not with her advanced contemporaries, but the patrician insouciance of Mitford prose.

In his article 'Poor Hitler', Andrew O'Hagan discusses what he characterises as the 'posh aesthetic' of the Mitford sisters' letter writing.[20] He identifies the way their style was typified by a rejection of earnestness; an eschewal of 'effortfulness' in favour of the tonally girlish or childish enlivened by provocation – or what O'Hagan identifies as the 'ear for the unacceptable note'.[21] The unacceptable typically manifests itself in a kind of spiced-up Wildean inversion; in the Mitford universe 'a head cold is an utter tragedy and the invasion of Poland a bit of a bore'.[22] In Nancy Mitford's novel the *Pursuit of Love* (1945), when the main protagonist, Linda, is about to embark on a long train journey alone, her cousin Fanny comforts her with the idea that perhaps she will have a companion after all as 'Foreigners are greatly given, I believe, to rape.' Linda responds to this play on the 'unacceptable' with sang-froid: 'Yes, that would be nice, so long as they didn't find my stays' (a reference to money that she has smuggled in her underwear).[23] We also find this teasing inversion of values in her later *Love in a Cold Climate* (1949) when Fanny's uncle is horrified that she has accepted an invitation to a party at which he knows she will be unable to perform well socially. Comfort is at hand, though, in the thought that 'fun and games' might be in Fanny's reach as she's just about young enough to still attract the attentions of a paedophilic family friend.[24]

Although without Mitford's mischievously teasing play, in Mitchison there's still a strongly playful note and sense of *épater la bourgeoisie*. When Erif Der travels to Egypt:

> A rather charming girl [. . .] suddenly fell in love with her and felt no awkwardness about demanding her satisfaction there and then. Erif protested and finally ran out of the palace, her ears tingling with everyone else's laughter. She was annoyed with herself afterwards, thinking: why not? Why be unkind? (507)

This jollity pervades Mitchison's personal reflections on her sexually experimental past. In her autobiography she recalls beating her homosexual director friend, Rudi Messel ('Once he asked me to tie and beat him, which I did, making fierce faces and quite enjoying it') and her publisher's 'fatherly pawings'.[25]

Rather than identify these moments as awkward examples of dated turns of phrase, I want to argue that they're crucial to the implicit argument that lay behind Mitchison's advocacy of sexual freedom. As I've noted, if an argument can be extrapolated from the writings of figures such as Lawrence and Forster, it's that the denial of erotic autonomy is wrong because of the overwhelming quality of the passions at stake. But the implicit argument of much of Mitchison's writings is that sexual prohibitions are misguided for the very opposite reason. Sex doesn't arouse intense feeling; it's something that it makes no sense to curtail, for the very reason that the emotions at play are inconsequential. I think it was this sensibility that led her to speculate on human sexuality, not so much as significant in and of itself, but as a force that could be made meaningful when harnessed towards some other goal. In the next section I shall consider how Mitchison developed this idea in her

exploration of how the erotic life of the individual could be connected to a commitment in the socialist cause.

## WE HAVE BEEN WARNED AND THE 'TRANSGRESSIVE QUEST'

The relationship between Mitchison's progressive ideals and her privilege as an
upper-class woman was traced in early criticism of her work. One of the liveli-
est responses to her writing was a venomous critique of her novel *We Have Been
Warned* by Queenie Leavis. A partly autobiographical text, the work was based on
Mitchison's involvement with socialism, of which she became a supporter in 1932.[26]
Leavis's attack was directed at what she perceived to be the superficial and performative nature of Mitchison's political commitment; it was a socialism, she argued,
in which 'you may retain your leisure, servants and cocktail parties with an even
enhanced complacency provided you only learn the Russian alphabet and take a trip
to the USSR'.[27] Leavis's criticism focused particularly on the fashionable radicalism
of the novel's sexual politics, which, she argued, involved a lazy conflation of the
progressive mores of her social set with the question of how to improve the lot of the
working classes – utopia would be 'attending a Bloomsbury studio party'.[28]

Leavis's criticism is cited in Valentine Cunningham's account of the novel as
representative of the association between sexual and political liberation within the
Thirties left: an imbrication that he treats in a similarly derisory vein.[29] But in more
recent years there has been a change of approach. One recurrent strategy in attempts
to recuperate Mitchison's importance involves emphasising her significance as a
writer of female sexual autonomy. Noting with outrage that Mitchison's regular
publisher refused *We Have Been Warned*, her biographer Jill Benton argues that her
ideas were simply too progressive for the male-dominated world of the interwar left:
'In no quarter of Labourite socialism were men accepting Naomi's socialist-feminist
tenet that women had a right to possess their own bodies, and to share their bodies
with whoever and as many as they might choose or, for that matter, not share with
anyone.'[30]

A writer of female emancipation she may have been, but of unconstrained
agency, she was not. The novel explores the notion of altruistic sexuality, in which
the central female protagonist is liberated from the constraints of a monogamous
marriage to meet with a new obligation to promiscuity, understood by her as a means
of assisting the establishment of a socialist collective. The sex is bad, the values
uncomfortable, but rather than sound a Cunningham-esque sneer, I will argue that
there is an intentional awkwardness to the sexual ethic Mitchison inflicts on her
middle-class protagonist. Instead of a glib gesture towards the difficulty of recon-
ciling fashionable bohemian mores and revolutionary acts, I want to suggest that
it provides a serious reflection on the difficulty of constructing new ways of living
within the old order.

Again, I want to use Lawrence as a way of thinking about what was at stake in
Mitchison's project. Lawrence retained an importance within the Thirties' leftish

imagination, for the way that his writings stressed the need for rupture and revolution; as Stephen Spender reflected in 1935, 'his writing was a constant search for a new life and a new form of life in which civilisation might survive or be re-created'.[31] In Cecil Day-Lewis's 'Letter to a Young Revolutionary', he cites Lawrence to gesture towards the sense of metaphysical rebellion he deemed necessary to communist commitment – 'Be still in your own soul, as Lawrence would say: do you feel new life springing there?'[32] But the problem was the individualistic focus of this rebellion, something that Spender highlighted in his review of the posthumous collection of Lawrentiana, *Phoenix* (1936). While not rejecting the appeal of the Lawrentian revolt, he argued that it was necessary first to strive for structural change.[33]

Mitchison's novel was written at a transitional moment, when her own interest in personal revolution (represented by her association with Heard) started to wane and she, too, was placing greater emphasis on change in structural, political terms. In *The Destructive Element* Spender claims that the Marxist revolutionary attempts 'to accomplish the sacrifice of individualist traits, to achieve the fulfilment of a more united and wider humanity, by a historic act of the will which makes him reach forward and forcibly impose on the present the visualised, completed social system of the future'.[34] It is in its depiction of such an effort – in its exploration of the complexity of harnessing the personal present in the service of a teleological goal – that *We Have Been Warned* is most successful, and most interesting.

Valentine Cunningham has explored the performative dimension of the bourgeois literati's attempt to connect with the working classes, setting out the pervasiveness of motifs of disguise. The examples that he cites are literal in form: changes to accent, clothes, nomenclature or appearance – he cites Christopher Isherwood's attempt to eat lots of sweets to disguise his 'good bourgeois teeth'.[35] But I want to think about a subtler form of disguise that Mitchison develops in her novel: the trick of dissembling to the self through the pretence of desire. In the early 1930s, in correspondence with John Pilley, Naomi evolved an ethic of sexual altruism that led her to become intimate with a sexually inexperienced young communist on her trip to Russia. She wrote to Pilley expressing her mixed emotions about the experience:

> John, I am really rather frightened; you have landed me with being a priestess, when my individual self wants to be your lover and nothing else. I am very inexperienced and I am so afraid of doing something which will leave a bad memory for him (and, for that matter, for me).[36]

The encounter formed the basis for the central episode of *We Have Been Warned*: Dione's departure for Russia in the company of a young communist, whom she helps to escape Britain after he has murdered a newspaper proprietor. On the boat she sets about his confused seduction.

One of the (many) dismissive lines taken by Cunningham towards the socialism of figures such as Auden and Stephen Spender was that it involved a sentimentalisation of their desire for working-class men; their writing about the proletariat was 'vitiated by the bourgeois bugger's specialist regard'.[37] More recently, rejecting this statement, Glyn Salton-Cox instead sets about its 're-valorisation', tracing the lively and mutually constitutive relationship between queer desire and communism.[38] His account presents communism as a liberatory space for queer love in the early 1930s: an arcadia lost towards the end of the decade with the increasing association, among some on the left, of homosexuality with fascism.

Although I will build on this account of the imbrication between sexual radicalism and left-wing politics, I also want to temper its celebration of the way 'erotic love could emerge from a shared relation to a radical collectivity'.[39] Returning to earlier critiques of the decade, we can find articulations of a different relationship between desire and activism – one in which a sexuality fostered by politics is a rather more stuttering affair. Something of this strain (albeit idealised) was pointed to by Frank Kermode in his account of how the 'transgressive quest' of the bourgeois writer to find 'some kind of genuine meeting with the worker [. . .] the unknown, the wholly other' often settled upon romantic love as the agent of this leap. Kermode notes this strain in Edward Upward's *The Spiral Ascent* (1977), which describes the love affair between an upper-class young man who has recently converted to communism and a working-class and plain schoolteacher. He is so repulsed by her that he calls out, 'Oh Elsie, you're so ugly!'; yet, recognising that this sentiment is no more than a 'bourgeois hankering after romantic beauty', he marries her out of commitment to the party.[40] By virtue of her role as an agent of class solidarity she is ultimately rendered a desirable being in her own right.

Mitchison's novel, however, dramatises the failure of socialist commitment to redeem the object of desire. Campaigning with her husband Tom, who is standing as a socialist MP, Dione is pervaded by a sense of apartness from his constituents. The sentiment takes on a visceral charge in her Upwardesque reflection: 'they were ugly; they didn't know they were ugly; they moved badly [. . .] they would be horrible to be made love to by' (54). By means of her affair with the young communist Donald, Dione seeks to correct the bourgeois niceties of her sexuality.

Although she initiates the encounter, when the two become intimate the sense of Dione's control is more uncertain. In a psychoanalytically informed discussion of consent, Judith Butler points out that agreeing to sexual contact, rather than necessarily being an 'active and clear-headed' decision, can be more of an exploration, a way of trying out new experiences and roles.[41] An agreement to sex can sometimes 'articulate a fantasy of being one *who can* agree to such things, of being more open or capacious than one is [. . .] sometimes in saying "yes" we seek to overcome a sense of limit in ourselves that we simply wish were not there'.[42]

I want to argue that the encounter between Dione and Donald is an exploration of performative desire, of the difficulty faced by trying to enact a form of sexuality dictated by the wish to stake a claim for a political identity. When Dione and Donald begin to be sexually intimate with one another, Dione attempts to obfuscate the question of personal want. Forcing herself to kiss Donald passionately, she attempts to frame the question of her pleasure as unimportant: 'Did she like it or didn't she? Very probably she did. Anyway, who cares' (252). This line is continued in conversation with Donald where she tries to rationalise her own enjoyment away: 'Donald, I respect you [. . .] I think you have power and you'll use it well. That's what matters, isn't it, not one's silly personal desires?' (251). When they begin to be physically intimate Dione reflects: 'now they were pushed off, in the current, there was no need for her to do more than be very kind and very certain. If she could be.' She then corrects this note of hesitancy with the assertion 'A Socialist woman must be' (238).

After having read a draft of the novel, the critic David Garnett wrote a letter to Mitchison criticising her focus on Dione's intellectualising of her affairs rather than exploring her sense of passion.[43] Garnett's response represents an inattention to Mitchison's intent to present passionless passion, of desire that runs counter to the physical act. This is sex in which eroticism is absent, that only occurs by virtue of its intellectualisation. What's interesting and unnerving about the encounter is that Mitchison doesn't simply resort to vagueness – to a general implication that it's probably all justified in the socialist cause – but includes a distinctly troubled note. While Dione may attempt to obfuscate the question of her enjoyment, her approach is undercut by a narrative that frequently implies her actual distress. When Dione and Donald first embrace, the only physical sensation that she is aware of is the pain of being squashed against the metal of the boat. Similarly, when he begins to kiss her, although this is an encounter that she has initiated, it is Donald who is described in predatory guise: he is 'hungry', 'starved', and 'bones of his face hurt her' (240).

Dione's husband Tom seems to fare better at his own attempt at non-monogamy, starting an affair with one of the beautiful young Russian women with which the couple find the country teeming. But his emotional response to the end of this affair shows that he, like Dione, has also not developed a properly socialist form of sexuality. The Russian woman, Oksana, can treat Tom with total lack of possessiveness – untroubled that the affair will end when he returns to England. But Tom is overcome by acquisitive distress, desolate at the thought that he won't be able to see her again.

In a contemporaneous work tracing the history of the home, Mitchison argued that the idea of intimate relationships in the USSR had changed as a result of the way in which the society fostered a primary sense of devotion to the group – 'the factory, the learned Institute, the Collective' – rather than to the claims of the home.[44] The novel also reflects on the way material conditions shape emotional responses. When Dione reports on the death of a working-class acquaintance and Tom asks whether her husband is upset, Dione responds: 'I don't know. They're all so matter of fact. They make me feel as if I was another race, full of elaborate hot-house, high-brow feelings. Are we as bad as that?' Tom responds with a determined lecture on how strong emotional attachments are no more than an indulgence enabled by material wealth: 'The Two Worlds [. . .] Yes, a lot of our fine feelings are just a very unimportant by-product of too much money. That's why I can't stand all these novels and poems about them' (117).

The novel adheres to Tom's strictures in the barren simplicity of its rendering of the emotional exchanges on display in the USSR. Tired of Dione's hesitancy, Donald finally loses his virginity to a young Soviet woman, Marfa. Marfa displays none of Dione's irresolution; when Donald explains to her that he is still a virgin her response is to laugh before declaring, 'I teach you. Then – you teach Nina.' Her friend Nina approaches the situation with an equal degree of pragmatism:

'She translated to the other who laughed too. "Nina, she say, she comsomol, she like sleep first time with Scottish Party comrade. But – I show you first"' (274). Soviet sexuality represents one of the more problematic arenas of the novel; it was Mitchison's writing in these passages that attracted the particularly snide asides of Leavis and Cunningham. There is an inescapable ridiculousness to the scenario, but the difficulty arises from Mitchison's attempt to imagine a sexuality that stems from an emotional culture enabled by a political dispensation of which she had little first-hand awareness.

The novel is dominated by a proleptic tenor in which the quotidian is continually unsettled by hints that revolution is at hand; the everyday is repeatedly ruptured by the motifs of violence. The homely safety of Dione's Oxford dwelling – calmly populated by naughty children, tea with strawberries and cream and 'roses at their best' (196) – is punctured by the arrival of Donald with the announcement that he is wanted for murder. Donald is aware of the incongruity of his presence, exclaiming, after having been offered some of the family's food: 'I've killed a man and you give me strawberries and cream' (209). Dione also reflects on the destabilising effect of violence within a quotidian space; the sight of a man hurt by the police prompts her to exclaim on the oddity of 'being alone in the middle of London – yes, there was the Marble Arch! – with a wounded man' (454). These hints culminate in the final three chapters, which present alternative visions of the future, of both a socialist election and a fascist uprising.

Even more striking than Leavis's objection to the novel was Isobel Murray's intro- duction to its 2012 reissue, in which she labelled the work a 'disaster' for Mitchison's literary reputation.[45] Much of Murray's criticism centres on what she feels to be the uncomfortable alliance of the novel's socialist realism with elements of magic. These recur throughout the text: Dione's ancestor is a witch, Green Jean, who haunts her in the present day. Policemen in Oxford transform into an elephant; Dione's sister Phoebe is chased through her home in the south of England by two Highland ghosts, who also appear to Dione at a party 'cleverly disguised as moderns' (205, 133). But rather than structuring a comprehensive framework governed by magical laws, the supernatural merely fringes the drama. The characters might meet ghosts and see the odd magical portent, but these have minimal impact on the events of the narrative.

While Murray claims that this attempt to integrate realism and magic represented a failure on Mitchison's part, relegating the magic to mere 'whimsy', I want to argue that it's the very impotency of the magical realm within the text that gives it a crucial, structural role. The motifs of enchantment function as a playful variant of the metaphysical symbolism within Thirties writing: a capricious futurity mediated by witches, sprites and ghouls in contrast to the divine certainty of Auden's purging flood. The flood as the symbol for revolution was also used by Day-Lewis in his polit- ical parable from 1936, *Noah and the Waters*. Samuel Hynes comments on its lack of subtlety; the way it symbolises a pre-determined commitment: 'In the end, Noah accepts the Flood. But then, we knew all along that he would – how could he not?'[46]

The magical flourishes of Mitchison's novel set up a less certain conclusion. At the beginning of the narrative, when Dione speculates with glib enthusiasm on the swift and easy coming of revolution, Tom chides her for her magical thinking:

'Your difficulty,' he said, 'is that you talk about the revolution as if it were some nice, magic hey-presto. Press the button and a new England comes out of the hat, complete with nationalised industries, the classless society, bankers and bricklayers playing ring-a-ring-of-roses round the may-pole on May Day.' (144)

The actual reality, he claims, would be a tedious, messy and drawn-out affair. Yet the novel is itself guilty of replicating Dione's magical notion of change with the two images of political transformation it offers infused by motifs of enchantment. When Dione returns home from the USSR she muses on it with a sense of unreality: while a 'good country' it is a 'fairyland' that entices its travellers with 'fairy fruit' (312). At the end of the novel it is the figure of the ancestral witch, Green Jean, who offers Dione the image of Britain transformed by revolution: a vision of a future socialist Britain, conjured by looking through a magical white stone with a hole at its centre. However, the image quickly dissolves and Dione returns back to the capitalist present and the comfort of her Highland estate.

Mitchison had greater qualms about the socialist cause than the often giddily optimistic tenor of the novel would suggest. She had mixed feelings about the way of life she saw on display in Russia and her decision to become a socialist was made after some delay. Benton records her wavering commitment, quoting a further letter that Mitchison wrote to Pilley: 'I do believe that in time capitalism will give way to socialism of some kind, yet it may not be a kind that we would care for or recognise.'[47] Rather than taking a predictive lens, the mood of *We Have Been Warned* is optative; presenting the 'what might be' rather than the 'what will'. While Mitchison had happily yoked sexual liberation to the Heardian eschaton, the marriage of sexuality and socialism is complicated by the questioning of whether individual desire should be linked to the ambiguous good of such a futurity. Even if individual experiments in such sexual liberation might work towards the emancipation of the group, the novel acknowledges that the immediate result is likely to be the loss of autonomy rather than liberatory gain. It may be too far a step to argue that *We Have Been Warned* rates as an artistic success, on the whole. But I would suggest that it powerfully demonstrates the constructive dynamic relationship between Mitchison's literary and political writing. Ultimately, it was through the transformation of her personal experience into literary form that she achieved a nuanced and critical perspective on her own sexual idealism and, by extension, demonstrated the possibility of a productive relationship between personal activism and literary production.

## NOTES

1. Jill Benton, *Naomi Mitchison: A Century of Experiment in Life and Letters* (London: Pandora Press, 1990), p. 7.
2. Ibid. p. 118.
3. See E. M. Forster's letters to Naomi Mitchison, including: 15 June 1927, 8 January 1926, National Library of Scotland Acc. 6610; and Olaf Stapledon's to Mitchison, 20 January 1931, 12 December 1935, National Library of Scotland Acc. 7644.
4. This account is a brief summary of Heard's ideas expressed in: *The Ascent of Humanity*

(London: Cape, 1929); *The Emergence of Man* (London: Cape, 1931); and *Social Substance of Religion: An Essay of the Evolution of Religion* (London: G. Allen & Unwin, 1931).

5.  Perry Anderson, 'From Progress to Catastrophe', *London Review of Books* 33:15 (28 July 2011); Diana Wallace, *The Woman's Historical Novel: British Women Writers, 1900–2000* (Basingstoke: Palgrave Macmillan, 2005), pp. 2, 6.

6.  Naomi Mitchison, 'Good News', review of *Social Substance of Religion* in *Time and Tide* 12 (June 1931), p. 894.

7.  Naomi Mitchison, 'The Book and the Revolution', review of *Ascent of Humanity* in *Time and Tide* 11 (January 1930), p. 80.

8.  Naomi Mitchison, *You May Well Ask* (London: Victor Gollancz Ltd, 1979), p. 107.

9.  Ibid. p. 114.

10. W. H. Auden, *The English Auden: Poems, Essays, and Dramatic Writings, 1927–1939* (New York: Random House, 1977), pp. 136–8.

11. Samuel Hynes, *The Auden Generation: Literature and Politics in England in the 1930s* (London: Pimlico, 1976), p. 135.

12. See Lucy McDiarmid, 'W. H. Auden's "In the Year of My Youth . . ."' *The Review of English Studies* 29:115 (1978), p. 290.

13. Gerald Heard, *Social Substance*, pp. 114–16.

14. Naomi Mitchison, *Comments on Birth Control* (London: Faber & Faber, 1930), pp. 5, 22.

15. Mitchison, *Comments*, p. 31.

16. Naomi Mitchison, *The Corn King and the Spring Queen* (Edinburgh: Canongate, 1990), pp. 337–8. Further references to this edition are given in the text.

17. Benton, *Naomi Mitchison*, p. 49.

18. Ibid. pp. 50–1.

19. Dora Russell, *Hypatia; or, Woman and Knowledge* (London: Keegan Paul & Co., 1925), p. 33; and *The Right to be Happy* (London: G. Routledge & Sons, 1927), p. 128. Works cited by Stephen Brooke, 'The Body and Socialism: Dora Russell in the 1920s', *Past & Present* 189 (2005), p. 166.

20. Andrew O'Hagan, 'Poor Hitler', *London Review of Books* 29:22 (15 November 2007).

21. Ibid.

22. Ibid.

23. Nancy Mitford, *Love in a Cold Climate and Other Novels* (London: Penguin, 2000), p. 91.

24. Ibid. p. 162.

25. Mitchison, *You May Well Ask*, pp. 78–9.

26. Benton, *Naomi Mitchison*, pp. 79–80, 85.

27. Q. D. Leavis, 'Lady Novelists and the Lower Orders', in G. Singh (ed.), *Q.D. Leavis, Collected Essays*, 3 vols (Cambridge: Cambridge University Press, 1989), vol. 3, p. 318.

28. Ibid. p. 322.

29. Valentine Cunningham, *British Writers of the Thirties* (Oxford: Oxford University Press, 1988), p. 247.

30. Benton, *Naomi Mitchison*, p. 95.

31. Stephen Spender, *The Destructive Element: A Study of Modern Writers and Beliefs* (London: Jonathan Cape, 1935), p. 182.

32. Cecil Day-Lewis, 'Letter to a Young Revolutionary', in Michael Roberts (ed.), *New Country* (London: Hogarth Press, 1933), p. 42.

33. Stephen Spender, *The Thirties and After: Poetry, Politics and People* (New York: Random House, 1979), p. 27.

34. Spender, *The Destructive Element*, p. 165.

35. Cunningham, *British Writers*, p. 254.

36. Quoted in Jenni Calder, *The Nine Lives of Naomi Mitchison* (London: Virago, 1997), p. 117.

37. Cunningham, *British Writers*, p. 150.

38. Glyn Salton-Cox, *Queer Communism and the Ministry of Love: Sexual Revolution in British Writing of the 1930s* (Edinburgh: Edinburgh University Press, 2018), p. 17.
39. Ibid. p. 106.
40. Edward Upward, *In the Thirties*, in *The Spiral Ascent: A Trilogy* (London: Heinemann, 1977), p. 214.
41. Judith Butler, 'Sexual Consent: Some Thoughts on Psychoanalysis and Law', *Columbia Journal of Gender and Law* 21:2 (2011), p. 20.
42. Ibid. p. 23.
43. Benton, *Naomi Mitchison*, p. 94.
44. Mitchison, *The Home and a Changing Civilisation* (London: John Lane, 1934), p. 117.
45. Isobel Murray, 'Introduction', in *We Have Been Warned* (London: Kennedy & Boyd, 2012), p. v.
46. Hynes, *The Auden Generation*, p. 201.
47. Quoted in Benton, *Naomi Mitchison*, p. 85.

# 4. Scientific Temporalities in *We Have Been Warned* and 'Beyond This Limit'

*Catriona Livingstone*

'All my life,' Naomi Mitchison writes in an article of 1987, 'I have been on the edges of science.' She describes playing as a child with blobs of mercury in the laboratory of her father, the Oxford physiologist J. S. Haldane, and receiving presents of Danish dolls' house furniture from the physicist Niels Bohr. As young adults, she and her brother (the biologist J. B. S. Haldane) conducted genetics experiments on guinea pigs, and later jointly published 'a paper on color inheritance in rats'. In her article, Mitchison considers the question of why she did not pursue a scientific career:

> I suppose it was because I always thought of guinea pigs not as figures in a genetics problem but as people. So I began to write, and I seem to be still writing. But when I began on science fiction, I was no stranger in the other world.[1]

Mitchison's early refusal to consign her scientific researches to a purely rationalist realm – her incorporation of science into a whimsical world of play – leads her, in her fiction, to explore the emotional and imaginative significance of science. Though Mitchison's point here is that her scientific background enriched her postwar science fiction, science also has an explicit presence in her earlier novel *We Have Been Warned* (1935) and in her shorter work 'Beyond This Limit' (1935). In these texts, Mitchison incorporates interwar science – its debates, its technological productions and its popularisation – into the idiosyncratic imaginative lives of her women characters.

This chapter demonstrates that science (especially relativity, mathematics and radio science) is crucial to Mitchison's attempt, in *We Have Been Warned*, to envision a future which, though based on rationalist socialist principles, takes into account the emotional and imaginative experience of women. The incongruities of *We Have Been Warned*, particularly its mixture of social realism and whimsical fantasy, have prompted much negative criticism, both at the time of the novel's publication and since. Elizabeth Maslen, for instance, writes that Mitchison 'seems to have lost her sense of artistic decorum which limits what modes of expression can sit comfortably with each other'.[2] However, the incongruous presence of the fantastical within the novel's account of 1930s local politics is effective insofar as it highlights women's exclusion from the rationalist, scientific patterns of thinking that dominate their society. Mitchison herself describes retreating into the 'huge areas of fantasy' that existed 'outside' her father's physiological work.[3] In *We Have Been Warned*, science is associated with a masculine, rational domain (as personified by Phil Bickerden, the Oxford physicist). Fantasy, meanwhile, is a realm particular to women, which at once marks their exclusion from this masculine domain and provides a space in which to formulate new forms of society.

However, science has a more complex existence in the novel than this account might suggest. The scientific concepts of the period – relativistic motion, non-Euclidean geometry, radio valves – intermingle with witches, kelpies and elephants in Mitchison's symbolic fantasy worlds and dreamscapes. Indeed, the women characters employ scientific images to articulate their own exclusion from a patriarchal, rationalist society – and to conceptualise a future in which the barriers to women's access to science are removed. By occupying 'the edges of science', then, Mitchison (like the fictionalised versions of herself, Dione and Phoebe) is able to attach new metaphorical meanings to scientific concepts for her own feminist and socialist ends.

The conflict between binary principles – the masculine and the feminine, the rational and the irrational – features prominently in Mitchison's fiction. At the same time, as recent criticism highlights, Mitchison destabilises such binaries by grounding scientific knowledge in a bodily and emotional context – thus creating, in Gavin Miller's terms, 'an alternative feminine ethical rationality'.[4] Anna McFarlane argues that Mitchison's estranging depictions of medicine challenge the '"two cultures" view of the world', which places science in opposition to feeling.[5] Fran Bigman, meanwhile, demonstrates that Mitchison's writings about reproduction replace 'a male technocratic model of science' with a model 'more responsive to local situations and disempowered groups'.[6]

This chapter builds on such insights by demonstrating that Mitchison constructs a form of scientific imagination rooted in women's emotional life. Furthermore, in line with recent work in modernist studies that has identified numerous resonances between early twentieth-century science and literary depictions of time and space, it demonstrates that in her interwar writings Mitchison evokes the spatial and temporal distortions produced by relativity theory, radio, and non-Euclidean geometry to create links between heterogeneous temporalities. In 'Beyond This Limit' – Mitchison's collaboration with Wyndham Lewis, and the most obviously modernist of her writings – Phoebe's fantastical journey resonates with descriptions of relativistic motion in contemporary popular physics. In *We Have Been Warned*, the distortions of relativistic space-time cause the Campbell Women, figures from the days of clan conflict, to appear in modern Scotland, while the connectivity of radio creates a link to the potential future represented by the USSR. Ultimately, Mitchison's scientific imagination enables her to conceptualise a utopian future that emerges from past and present.

INTERWAR PHYSICS

Mitchison writes that in the early twentieth century, 'Physics especially was still intel-
ligible to the ordinary educated person.'[7] She herself studied physics alongside biology
and chemistry as a home student at St Anne's College, Oxford; though her autobiographical writings emphasise her struggles with the subject, they also express her
determination to be 'competent' at it.[8] Relativity attained especial prominence in the
public consciousness following Albert Einstein's much-publicised visit to England in
1921 – during which he stayed with Viscount Haldane, Mitchison's uncle – and there
was a huge demand for popular explications of its difficult concepts.[9] Mitchison herself
participated in the popularisation of the new physics; *An Outline for Boys and Girls
and Their Parents* (1932), the book on science and history that she edited, contains
a section by Richard Hughes which provides a fairly detailed account of relativity.[10]

*We Have Been Warned* comments explicitly upon the contemporary popularisation of physics. In particular, it critiques the writings of Arthur Eddington, a physics
populariser whose highly successful books combined an emphasis on physics' destabilising conceptions with memorable thought experiments. Eddington used his science
writing to promote an idealist, religious philosophy, a decision for which he was
much criticised. In *We Have Been Warned*, when the physicist Phil Bickerden advises
Tom Galton to read 'Darwin's book on Physics', Tom objects that he and his fellow
economists are 'still all romantic and Eddingtonian', to which Phil responds emphatically that 'There should be a censorship' of Eddington's books: 'We are, after all,
supposed to be educating people, not trying to give them religion!'[11] The book that
Phil recommends instead, which is almost certainly Charles Galton Darwin's *The
New Conceptions of Matter* (1932), is decidedly un-Eddingtonian, containing not a
single deviation into philosophy. Darwin explicitly states his intention to depart from
recent popular physics books which emphasise the difficult, counterintuitive nature
of physics; it seems likely that a reference to Eddington is intended here.[12] In praising
Darwin's book, Phil rejects Eddington's speculative popular physics as unscientific.

In *The Nature of the Physical World* (1928), Eddington argues that physics is an
artificial 'schedule of pointer readings'. The ultimate 'background' 'behind the
pointer readings' is, he suggests, 'something of spiritual nature of which a prominent
characteristic is *thought*'.[13] In *We Have Been Warned*, Dione similarly speculates
about the 'background' that exists behind human mental constructs, but explicitly
rejects Eddington's conclusions:

> What does one hope to find if one looks hard enough? Pattern. Purpose.
> Reason. A nice Eddingtonian reason that one will be able to understand the
> day after to-morrow if one is a good girl and thinks hard enough! Well – is it
> likely? Why should the universe happen to fit in with the ideas of the upper
> middle classes of north-west Europe and North America at this particular and
> non-significant moment of time?[14]

As kitt price writes, left-wing commentators were critical of the 'bourgeois individualism' implied by Eddington's suggestion that his readers' 'own thoughts had a

cosmic significance'.[15] Dione evidently shares this attitude, dismissing Eddington's argument as anthropocentrism. Her own solution is an empathetic socialism that utterly rejects the human construct of exchange.

Phil remarks of Darwin's book, 'It over-simplifies, of course. The thing's *not* simple.'[16] Lacking a grasp of the mathematics which formed the basis of relativity, readers outside scientific institutions were forced to rely on simplified, often analogical descriptions provided by popular explications. The idea that such a reader will achieve understanding if she 'is a good girl and thinks hard enough' is therefore illusory. The gendering of Dione's criticisms is significant. The passage not only expresses her disapprobation for Eddington's patronising tone and idealist conclusions; it also conveys her frustration with the exclusion of women from institutional science. Later she comments, 'Annoying that women are never taught to think mathematically.'[17] Mitchison's autobiographical writings starkly highlight the mechanisms by which exclusion occurs; she links her struggles with physics to her experience of being sexually harassed by a lecturer.[18] Given this experience, it is unsurprising that it is through reference to physics, rather than to biology, that Mitchison explores the exclusion of women from science in *We Have Been Warned*.

Mitchison consistently links the confinement of scientific knowledge to male-dominated institutions to an artificial and distorting separation between rationality and emotion. This separation is explored through the relationship between Phoebe and Phil, which has recently ended when the novel begins. Phil functions as an embodiment of science; within the idiosyncratic system of symbols that Phoebe shares with her sister Dione he is King Hoopoe, or the 'Scientific Intellect'.[19] When he and Phoebe separate, he becomes Kay in the Hans Christian Andersen fairy tale 'The Snow Queen' – the character who, after a fragment of ice is lodged in his heart, forgets his love for Gerda and becomes obsessed with mathematical problems.[20] Phoebe, meanwhile, becomes alienated from scientific knowledge. She remembers how 'Once she had trailed her hands over the side of the punt high up the river towards Islip, and Phil had discussed relativity and she had understood.'[21] The word 'Once' effectively conveys the vagaries of attempting to conceptualise the new physics, while also implying that Phoebe's understanding is dependent on Phil's instruction; now they have parted, it eludes her. In representing their separation, then, Mitchison depicts Phoebe's exclusion from a realm of pure masculine rationalism.

Later, during a fantasy in which Phil instructs Phoebe to make a radio apparatus in order to escape from the Campbell Women, she cries out to him:

I have no glass tubes, no mercury, no wire, no batteries; oh Phil, don't you understand, a woman never has the materials for doing anything important! But he didn't understand that, he couldn't hear, and then it was night, and in the morning he was gone.[22]

The fissure in understanding goes both ways; it is Phil's inability to empathise with Phoebe's experience, as well as her lack of technical expertise, that separates them. The assignment of rationality to the masculine realm and emotion to the feminine is limiting and exclusive. When the two realms are united, however, a form of understanding is achieved that is at once intellectual and emotional. Phoebe and Phil reunite during a garden party at which they discuss nuclear spin. The narration comments, 'For the moment at least, she understood; it had made a contact.'[23] Intellectual understanding brings about emotional fulfilment; the phrase 'it had made a contact' aligns the connections formed in Phoebe's brain with the re-establishment of their relationship. Following this conversation, science regains its proper proportions in Phoebe's mind; rather than feeling excluded from understanding, she reflects that 'I very much like hearing about physics. It's the kind of thing that seems to me worth while having a conversation about.'[24]

In general, the novel implies that science is a necessary ingredient in both individual and societal happiness. In Dione and Phoebe's fantasy world, happiness is experienced by 'those people who have used Intellect and Imagination for the good of life, of the Birds, for the citizens of Cloud Cuckoo Borough'.[25] The 'Scientific Intellect', then, is only negative insofar as it fails to combine itself with 'Imagination'. When Phil asks Phoebe what she thinks of his recent paper, she replies, 'It was rather dull – by itself.' Their conversation during the garden party, which successfully combines fact and feeling, is prompted by Phoebe's question, 'Well, how are the old electrons?' – a question that, while expressing genuine scientific interest, also contains the vague suggestion that electrons, like guinea pigs, are people.[26]

RELATIVISTIC TIME AND SPACE

In her treatment of relativity, Mitchison explores science's exclusiveness while also highlighting its imaginative potential (the capacity of physics, as she writes in An Outline for Boys and Girls and Their Parents, to lead us 'far beyond the realm of ordinary common-sense').[27] Einstein's special theory of relativity revealed that measurement is dependent upon one's frame of reference, so that two observers moving relative to one another at a velocity close to the speed of light will experience significant divergences in their measurements. In particular, lengths in each frame of reference will appear, from the point of view of the other, to shorten along the line of motion. Correspondingly, each observer will perceive time to pass more slowly for the other.

The opening of We Have Been Warned centralises temporal and spatial displacement. The narration comments that the book Dione is reading about her Scottish ancestor, the witch Green Jean, 'shifted her in time and space'. However, any expectations of science-fictional transportation raised by this statement are rather deflated by the next sentence: 'It shifted her more in time than in space.'[28] Relativity theory combines time and space into a four-dimensional entity, space-time. By separating them, Mitchison displaces relativity in favour of the Scottish historical tradition, grounded in a particular place. Later in the novel, however, there is a direct reference to relativistic motion. Green Jean's persecutors, the Campbell Women, reappear in the present day. Aided by kelpies, they pursue Dione as she drives in the dark in the Highlands: 'naturally they'd follow. And it wouldn't help you to go fast. A question of relativity. They would be geared to one's own speed.'[29] This scene closely resembles the analogy used by Richard Hughes in *An Outline for Boys and Girls and Their Parents* to illustrate the fixed value of the speed of light. Hughes asks the reader to imagine that they are driving along a road, pursued by a police car (which, in his analogy, stands in for a light-beam):

> Such police-cars, we know, go very fast indeed: moreover, they always go at the same pace. Well, we can go fast too: if we can go nearly as fast as the police-car, it won't overtake us so quickly, we suppose. So we go faster. And now the nightmare gets really bad; for we find that, however fast we go (relative to any ordinary car on the road), that magic police-car still overhauls us [. . .] at *exactly the same pace!*[30]

It is significant that the kelpies and Campbell Women occupy the role of the police car in Hughes's analogy; for Dione they consistently embody the various forces which demand social conformity. Despite often being equated with relativism, relativity identifies several absolutes in the physical world (most importantly, an absolute value for the speed of light). In *We Have Been Warned*, as in Hughes's description, these absolutes create a nightmarish reality in which the individual cannot escape the violent enforcement of social norms.

Relativistic motion recurs, with ambiguous significance, in Mitchison's short story 'Beyond This Limit'. Phoebe appears in this story, journeying to Paris to try to forget Phil. On the Paris metro, she inadvertently ventures beyond the point at which tickets become invalid, and subsequently visits various locations in estranged versions of Paris, Oxford and London in pursuit of an elusive Creature. In its exploration of the experience of moving beyond social limits, the story depicts distortions of time and space that recall popular expositions of relativity. When Phoebe pursues the Creature 'into the middle of Etoile', this metro station, in accordance with its name, takes on the physical qualities of the centre of a star. As the ticket inspector explains to Phoebe:

> 'Naturally, the pressure is more intense there. You can manage densities?'
> 'I think so,' said Phoebe, 'but are we all closing in?'
> 'Closing or expanding, according to whether you're going back or forward. What do you expect? My horse says you look like an expander: try. Of course, you'll probably get there first. If so, hold on.'
> 'How do I start?'
> 'Well, just remember what's going to happen and follow it up very closely.'[31]

Here, the physical conditions at the centre of a star – pressure and density – are combined with relativistic effects. An object moving close to the speed of light will appear, from the perspective of a stationary observer, to contract. Popular expositions illustrated this effect with descriptions of distorted human bodies; Eddington, for example, describes a six-foot-tall man who appears to have a height of three feet.[32] Moving relative to the star, Phoebe similarly alters in size, at first expanding and then contracting 'down to about three foot six'.[33]

Clearly, the text does not describe any definite series of motions; it almost reads as a parody of Eddington's estranging descriptions. Asking his readers to 'Imagine you are on a planet moving very fast indeed,' Eddington writes, 'The inhabitants copy Alice in Wonderland; they pull out and shut up like a telescope.'[34] This statement is a little misleading; objects in a moving frame will appear to contract, not expand (though the degree to which they contract can decrease). 'Beyond This Limit' extrapolates from Eddington's rather inaccurate description by referring to Phoebe as 'an expander'. As kitt price writes of Dorothy L. Sayers and William Empson, Mitchison pushes Eddington's 'expository analogies to their extremity to see what happens when they break'.[35] Phoebe thus transcends the limits even of the disorientating effects of special relativity. The result is her complete disintegration, as she begins to move relatively to her own body: 'bits of her are in different places [. . .] And going different ways, and some faster than others.'[36]

According to relativity theory, objects which travel close to the speed of light, or which occupy a gravitational field, exhibit time dilation. Phoebe both moves at a great speed and spends time at the centre of Etoile. As a result, she arrives at the future ('what's going to happen') more quickly than other people. She comes to Earth to find that her acquaintances, including Phil, have aged considerably. Her experience resembles that of Eddington's hypothetical space-traveller, who ages only one year while those he leaves behind age seventy years.[37] What is not consistent with relativity, however, is the suggestion that Phoebe can, by moving quickly, 'remember what's going to happen'. '[T]he points along the track of any material body', including a person, 'are in the absolute past or future of one another.'[38] By apparently experiencing the same events twice, Phoebe again flouts the restrictions of the relativistic universe.

In some respects, however, Phoebe cannot escape the universe's limitations. Conversing with various mythological figures at the British Museum, she comments that it is 'a second-chance universe'. 'Mechanically, yes,' responds Ariadne, 'in the shape. But not in the internal structure. There is only re-discovery and mutation.'[39] Einstein posited a universe that was 'finite but unbounded', such that, as popular expositions emphasised, travelling far enough 'brings us back towards the earth from the opposite direction'.[40] As Ariadne says, it is a 'second-chance universe' as far as the 'shape' is concerned. However, her assertion that the 'internal structure' does not allow second chances is also consistent with contemporary popular science, which emphasised that time only moved forwards.[41] This limitation is highly significant for Phoebe, as it means that she cannot regain either her lost respectability or her earlier relations with Phil. By exploring the interplay between destabilising motion and absolute limitations in relativity theory, Mitchison highlights the ambiguous nature of a life beyond social limits, which at once flouts social mores and is determined by those mores. Phoebe, despite experiencing estranged, relativistic motion, is unable to escape disapprobation and judgement.

However, the narrative does gesture towards an improved future – a future which Phoebe's motion through time enables her to glimpse. By the 1930s, the universe was known to be expanding, a phenomenon that Mitchison alludes to several times. For instance, when Orpheus appears in the present day, he feels dazed 'due perhaps to the tumult of wave-lengths through which he and his lute had passed during an expansion of three millenia [sic]'.[42] Phoebe is occasionally able to align her own alterations in size with the expansion of the universe and hence to travel backwards and forwards in time; when she attends the opera she 'ingeniously allowed herself to expand very slightly over-size and then contracted sufficiently to remember the first two acts'. She uses this control to glimpse the future:

> Expanding and softening again after her bullet-headed swallow flight, she perceived for a moment the future of liberty, the great sausage, of mankind no longer impacted and painfully colliding, but close and yet mobile as the swallow-pack, aware of proximity yet unhampered by touches.[43]

Here, the expansion of the universe is aligned with social progress. Elsewhere in the story, as we have seen, the laws of physics stand in for more terrestrial laws which constrict Phoebe's actions. In this scene, however, Mitchison implies that Phoebe's existence beyond social limits enables her to move in time and hence to glimpse an improved future: one in which 'proximity' to the community is no longer oppressive. As an outsider, then, Phoebe is able to attach new, radical meanings to scientific concepts – in particular, to envision the 'density' of the past giving way to a more expansive future in which liberty can be found within society, rather than apart from it.

## 'AN ABSTRACT AND TEASING MATHEMATICS'

Mathematics has a similarly ambiguous function in We Have Been Warned; its self-contained, abstract nature at once stands in for the limitations placed upon women and suggests a means of transcending those limitations. In Modernism, Fiction and Mathematics, Nina Engelhardt highlights the duality in historical attitudes towards mathematics, whereby it is associated with 'the extreme end of scientific rationality' while also exploring 'ideal constructs that escape the restrictions of the given world'.[44] In We Have Been Warned, mathematics both encapsulates an oppressive denial of emotion and produces a shift beyond the boundaries of the real.

Mathematics primarily features within the fantastical visions that Phoebe experiences while working on her illustrations for 'The Snow Queen'. In the original fairy tale, the Snow Queen entraps Kay by making him work on a puzzle represented in ice. Phoebe conceives of the Snow Queen as 'pure intellect [. . .] an abstract and teasing mathematics' and her puzzle as 'planes, mathematically linked, sliding over one another like – like the molecular sliding in graphite or something. I want the ice-block-puzzle crystalline, a crystal lattice, a moment of atomic cohesion.'[45] Crystals have a regular molecular structure, characterised by parallel lines and planes. Chemistry and geometry, then, collude in Kay's entrapment. Later, Phoebe

plans to include 'some mathematical formulae' in her picture of the ice puzzle –
'Those squiggles that mean square root or infinity or go back to where you started
from; only she'd be sure to get them wrong' – and repeatedly regrets that her separation from Phil means she cannot seek his help.[46] Once again, the narration links
Phoebe's lack of understanding of science to a fissure between the masculine and the
feminine. It thus replicates the gendered dichotomy of emotion and rationality that
is prominent in the original fairy tale, in which Gerda's love for Kay ultimately saves
him from his obsessive rationalism.

In the interwar period, the formalist approach to mathematics attained particular
prominence. According to this approach, maths was defined by 'a complete and consistent set of axioms', such that truth was determined by internal consistency rather
than by reference to the external world.[47] As Hughes put it in *An Outline for Boys
and Girls and Their Parents*, 'The mathematician [. . .] builds up a logical and imaginary system which *cannot* be "wrong", for he doesn't care at all whether it accurately
describes the things the physicist finds in the universe.'[48] Phoebe's image of a cohesive crystalline puzzle presents mathematics as just such a self-contained system:
one which prevents Kay (and Phil, with whom he is identified) from experiencing
emotion. The specific symbols Phoebe includes are significant. In the original fairy
tale, the solution to the puzzle is the word 'eternity'; by including the mathematical
symbol for infinity, $\infty$, Phoebe accords this solution a mathematical significance,
highlighting the pretensions of contemporary mathematics to completeness. The
symbol which means 'go back to where you started from' is rather more obscure; it
likely refers to a mathematical inverse, represented in many branches of maths by
the symbol $^{-1}$. Where a function $f(x)$ maps the values of a domain onto a range, the
inverse function $f^{-1}(x)$ maps the range back onto the domain. If this is indeed the
symbol to which Phoebe refers, her explanation of its meaning – 'go back to where
you started from' – emphasises the self-contained nature of such mappings. Phil's
emotional alienation from Phoebe is thus represented in terms of mathematics'
closed formal systems.

However, the fact that the puzzle is represented in a picture undermines the
notion of maths as a self-contained system which precludes the emotional and
imaginative aspects of experience. For Phoebe, the geometry of the puzzle – its
interlocking planes – is as much an artistic problem as a mathematical one. Later,
she identifies affinities between Phil's scientific work and her artistic craft, charac-
terising both as a struggle with 'Technique'.[49] Hughes posits similar affinities when
he describes geometry as 'a work of art built by logic on a basis of imagination – built
on the peculiarities of those *imaginary* beings, the point, the line, and the plane'.[50]
The resonances between maths and imagination are foregrounded in *We Have Been
Warned*, as the mathematical content of Phoebe's illustrations quickly becomes
absorbed into her fantasy world. The Campbell Women and kelpies emerge from
one picture and entrap her in a fairy-tale tower:

> Phil came riding by in armour; he had a clever plan to rescue Phoebe; he was
> going to dig a passage right under the root of minus one and come out into the
> middle of the Tower. He had made such a long equation that it would turn into

a ladder and she could creep down on it. But he dug and dug, and there was no way under the root.[51]

The 'root of minus one' is the imaginary number $i$; its presence in the fairy-tale world has already been hinted at by two symbols in the ice puzzle, $\sqrt{}$ and $^{-1}$. Phil's solution tests the limits of the ice puzzle's geometry in a way that accords with contemporary mathematical discourse. When representing complex numbers (numbers which can be expressed as the sum of a real number and an imaginary number), mathematicians used a coordinate system, with a horizontal real axis and a vertical imaginary axis. Phil's proposed tunnel, which goes down into the earth 'under the root of minus one', follows the direction of the imaginary axis. By utilising this vertical direction, moreover, Phil circumvents not only the tower but also the puzzle, which lies on the Earth's surface. Imaginary numbers contributed to the idea that maths, as Engelhardt writes, 'escape[s] the restrictions of the given world'; here, they open up new trajectories.[52]

Phil's proposed solution hints at another aspect of contemporary mathematics: non-Euclidean geometry. The discovery that several geometric systems were 'equally possible' undermined the conception of maths as 'the language of nature that arrives at certain truths about the world'.[53] One of Euclid's five axioms was the parallel postulate: the assertion that 'Given any straight line and a point not on it, there "exists one and only one straight line which passes" through that point and never intersects the first line.'[54] Within non-Euclidean geometries which assume a curved space, this axiom no longer holds. Phoebe's fantasy stages a conflict between Euclidean and non-Euclidean geometry. The ice puzzle is a system of parallel lines. Phil's tunnel, however, follows a curved line; it takes the curvature of the Earth into account, and so evades the puzzle. Non-Euclidean geometry came to particular prominence in early twentieth-century science when Einstein used it to theorise a curved space-time. Here, it enables Phil to imagine alternative ways of moving through space.

Engelhardt demonstrates that Thomas Pynchon's *Against the Day* uses both imaginary numbers and non-Euclidean geometry to explore 'parallels between maths and literary fiction regarding their potentials not to undo worlds but to build alternative ones'.[55] In Phoebe's fairy-tale fantasy, fiction, art and mathematics similarly collude to construct new realities. It is significant, however, that Phil's plan fails: there is 'no way under the root'. Imaginary numbers and non-Euclidean geometry undermine any stable relation between mathematics and reality; although they consequently have affinities with the imagination, they also, by the same token, reinforce the idea that maths is a self-contained system.[56] Ultimately, neither concept can provide an escape for Phoebe because they are part of the system that entraps and excludes her. Eventually she is rescued by Dione, who destroys the tower with a tractor (a symbol of progress towards a socialist future). They go to an assembly of birds, and Phil (in his persona as King Hoopoe, or the 'Scientific Intellect') offers to protect Phoebe, only for an elephant (a symbol of conformity to public opinion) to attack and kill the birds.[57] Finally, Phoebe escapes on her own drawing of Gerda's boat. Science is shown to be vulnerable to the destructive effects of public opinion; it is socialism and art that ultimately prevail.

RADIO CONNECTIONS

In her representation of radio, however, Mitchison integrates science into her vision of a socialist future. Following the inception of the British Broadcasting Company in 1922, the wireless became a ubiquitous aspect of British cultural life. For left-wing commentators, BBC radio encompassed conflicting political potentialities. On the one hand, it was a vehicle for debate and, in transcending national borders, a potential means to an internationalist future; on the other hand, its conservative management tended to censor divergent viewpoints, and many of the broadcasts had a strongly establishment tone. In her autobiographical writings, Mitchison refers to 'the over-respectability' of BBC radio and to its failure to represent a full range of opinion.[58] In We Have Been Warned, meanwhile, Tom reflects that the BBC has 'done us [the Sallington Labour Party] a good deal of harm'.[59] Later, Dione discusses the potential effects radio will have upon the village of Auchanarnish:

> 'I take it that's the only reason why people here still play fiddles and pipes and so on, and sing as well as they do – they aren't getting it nicely packed up and sent out to them by the Glasgow transmitting station.'
> 'Yes,' said Dione, 'the wireless would do in bonfires and dancing and working spells or whatever they're doing, in a very few years. And no doubt they'll soon have invented some way of getting the beastly stuff sent through the hills.'[60]

By transmitting a packaged version of Highland culture, this exchange implies, radio has the effect of destroying its genuine manifestations, with their potential to access the supernatural. Paddy Scannell and David Cardiff's history of the early BBC demonstrates that regional radio in the early 1930s was deprived of support by the central organisation, which demanded that it limit its productions to narrowly defined 'local' material; Mitchison's suggestion that radio imposes a top-down, impoverished version of Scottish culture aligns with this account.[61]

Despite her criticisms, however, Mitchison was an active participant in BBC radio. She delivered her first talk in 1943 and would continue to broadcast over the next fifty years. In the interwar period, she wrote many historical plays for the BBC's Schools programming, and another broadcast play, As It Was in the Beginning (co-written with Lewis Gielgud, brother of the head of the BBC Drama department Val Gielgud). Significantly, Mitchison participated in the BBC's dissemination of Scottish culture; one of her plays for children, 'My Ain Sel'', broadcast in 1930, draws upon Celtic folklore and makes extensive use of Scottish dialect. Mitchison's foreword to the published play states that it is 'meant to be acted [. . .] in a field or garden in Scotland or wherever there are Scots'.[62] In 1944, moreover, she delivered a talk on her own family history as part of a series entitled 'Some Scottish Links with the Continent'. Notwithstanding her concerns about its potential homogenisation of Scottish culture, then, Mitchison herself used radio to promote widespread engagement with Scottish history and myth.

In *We Have Been Warned*, when Phil's plan to tunnel under the tower to rescue Phoebe fails, his next solution involves the construction of a radio valve, or vacuum tube:

> He called to her what to do; she was to make a vacuum in a tube and put a current through it; she was to creep in at the cathode point and be whirled through with the electrons to the anode; he would be there to catch her at the end. But, she cried down to him, I have no glass tubes, no mercury, no wire, no batteries; oh Phil, don't you understand, a woman never has the materials for doing anything important![63]

Contemporary commentators celebrated the capacity of radio to collapse distance and produce intimacy. Phoebe imagines that, by merging with radio's electronic signals, she can overcome her entrapment and her separation from Phil. Unfortunately, the liberatory potential of radio is counteracted by women's exclusion from scientific and technical expertise.

It becomes clear, however, that this exclusion is far from inevitable. In her depiction of the USSR, Mitchison shows that radio, and science more generally, can be fully integrated into women's lives. The first hint of this integration occurs when the boat to the USSR has a woman wireless operator. Later, Dione and Tom encounter Oksana, a 'radio specialist' with whom Tom has a relationship. Oksana's job is aligned with her communism; she constructs the radio sets for a new town that she and Tom visit, conceptualising this task as her contribution to the collective future.[64] As we have seen, the association of science with an exclusive masculine realm means that scientific concepts frequently have an oppressive function in Dione and Phoebe's fantasies. In Oksana's case, however, radio forms part of her dream-world without these negative associations. She dreams that she is making corrections to a blueprint for a new radio apparatus: a dream which reflects her corrective, expansive effect on the other characters' political and emotional lives. She expands Tom's political consciousness beyond the moderate social democracy of the Labour Party, enables Tom and Dione to establish the open marriage that they both seek, and provides a personal connection to the USSR that persists even when they return to Britain. These political and emotional transformations are explicitly linked to the connectivity of radio; Oksana conceives of the way that she and Tom enrich one another's politics as 'like making something [. . .] a new five-valve set [. . .] a set that gives me something new – some station I have never heard'.[65] In establishing new connections, radio expands the self.

In Mitchison's presentation of the USSR, then, science does have a progressive, liberatory function. This appears to be because in her fictionalised USSR, unlike in Britain, science is not exclusive, but forms part of women's everyday existence. When Dione first visits Oksana's home, she is reading a book with 'a picture of a three-propellered aeroplane engine on the cover'; similarly, when Donald visits another family of communists:

> Maria showed him proudly her pile of books, an algebra book with the page doubled at the beginning of quadratic equations, one on elementary physics,

several copy-books half-full of what might have been essays, and three text-books of economics or Marxist history.[66]

Julia Chan writes that 'Soviet Russia in the 1920s and 1930s was widely considered to be the vanguard in transforming women's social position and daily life.'[67] For Mitchison, it encapsulates a future in which science (alongside other forms of knowledge) is integrated into women's experience.

Mitchison's presentation of science is inextricable from her progressive socialist and feminist politics. She imagines a future in which science no longer occupies the limited domain of masculine rationality, but forms part of collective life. As Stephen Brooke persuasively argues, the socialism that Mitchison advocates in her non-fictional writings looks beyond the practical 'economic planning' of contemporary Fabianism to the centring of emotion and collective transformation that characterised 'An earlier tradition of ethical and utopian socialism'.[68] We Have Been Warned is undoubtedly a socialist novel, but one which constantly tests the rational aspects of socialist economics against emotional imperatives. Towards the end of the novel, Dione is torn between a strong desire to keep her unborn baby and the conviction that 'Properly speaking, we [the bourgeoisie] oughtn't to perpetuate our kind.' She consults a biologist friend, who advises her to follow her own emotional impulse and keep the baby, saying 'Don't be reasonable [. . .] be intelligent!'[69] A real scientific intelligence, he implies, is one which accounts for emotional experience. The future envisioned in We Have Been Warned is conceived according to a rationalism that takes as its aim the enrichment of emotional and imaginative life.

Physics, mathematics and radio science all participate in what Nick Hubble calls the 'complex utopian temporality' of Mitchison's fiction. They do so by establishing connections between disparate temporalities: the Scottish past, the present, a projected socialist future.[70] In We Have Been Warned, relativity's temporal distortions cause the Campbell Women to appear and to re-enact their oppression of Green Jean in present-day Scotland, while in 'Beyond This Limit' Phoebe aligns herself with the expansion of the universe so as to glimpse a future form of community which has room for her idiosyncratic motions. Imaginary numbers and non-Euclidean geometry, meanwhile, contribute to the construction of an alternative, fairy-tale world and offer new means of moving through space which circumvent the closed, exclusive system of masculine rationality. Finally, radio, though producing a homogenised version of Scottish culture, also brings about an expansion of the self in the present day which provides the basis for future forms of collective life. Science, then, has an estranging function; it colludes with fantasy to shake characters free of the temporal and spatial limits of their surroundings, into possible futures.

## NOTES

1. Naomi Mitchison, 'Growing Up Saturated with Science,' The Scientist, December 1987.
2. Elizabeth Maslen, 'Naomi Mitchison's Historical Fiction', in Maroula Joannou (ed.), Women

*Writers of the 1930s: Gender, Politics and History* (Edinburgh: Edinburgh University Press, 1999), p. 143.

3. Naomi Mitchison, *Small Talk with All Change Here* (Isle of Colonsay: House of Lochar, 2000), p. 123.
4. Gavin Miller, 'Animals, Empathy, and Care in Naomi Mitchison's *Memoirs of a Spacewoman*', *Science Fiction Studies* 35:2 (2008), p. 251.
5. Anna McFarlane, '"Becoming Acquainted with all that Pain": Nursing as Activism in Naomi Mitchison's Science Fiction', *Literature and Medicine* 37:2 (2019), p. 279.
6. Fran Bigman, 'Pregnancy as Protest in Interwar British Women's Writing: An Antecedent Alternative to Aldous Huxley's *Brave New World*', *Medical Humanities* 42:4 (2016), pp. 265–6.
7. Mitchison, 'Growing Up'.
8. Mitchison, *Small Talk*, p. 11.
9. kitt price, *Loving Faster than Light: Romance and Readers in Einstein's Universe* (Chicago: University of Chicago Press, 2012), p. 10; Mitchison, *Small Talk*, p. 77.
10. Richard Hughes, 'Physics, Astronomy, and Mathematics or Beyond Common-Sense', in Naomi Mitchison (ed.), *An Outline for Boys and Girls and Their Parents* (London: Victor Gollancz, 1932), p. 339.
11. Naomi Mitchison, *We Have Been Warned* (Kilkerran: Kennedy & Boyd, 2012), pp. 148–9.
12. C. G. Darwin, *The New Conceptions of Matter* (London: G. Bell and Sons, 1931), p. 2.
13. Arthur Eddington, *The Nature of the Physical World* (Cambridge: Cambridge University Press, 2012), pp. 259, 331.
14. Mitchison, *We Have Been Warned*, pp. 438–9.
15. price, *Loving*, p. 6.
16. Mitchison, *We Have Been Warned*, p. 148.
17. Ibid. p. 80.
18. Mitchison, *Small Talk*, p. 111.
19. Mitchison, *We Have Been Warned*, p. 9.
20. Ibid. p. 163.
21. Ibid. p. 10.
22. Ibid. p. 167.
23. Ibid. p. 204.
24. Ibid. p. 371.
25. Ibid. p. 9.
26. Ibid. pp. 203–4.
27. Mitchison, *An Outline*, p. 8.
28. Mitchison, *We Have Been Warned*, p. 3.
29. Ibid. p. 368.
30. Hughes, 'Physics', p. 339.
31. Naomi Mitchison, 'Beyond This Limit', in *Beyond This Limit: Selected Shorter Fiction* (Kilkerran: Kennedy & Boyd, 2008), p. 11.
32. Eddington, *Nature*, p. 34.
33. Mitchison, 'Beyond This Limit', p. 12.
34. Eddington, *Nature*, p. 9.
35. price, *Loving*, p. 14.
36. Mitchison, 'Beyond This Limit', p. 44.
37. Eddington, *Nature*, p. 39.
38. Ibid. p. 125.
39. Mitchison, 'Beyond This Limit', p. 34.
40. Eddington, *Nature*, pp. 80, 167.
41. Ibid. pp. 48, 50.

42. Mitchison, 'Beyond This Limit', pp. 33–4.
43. Ibid. p. 49.
44. Nina Engelhardt, *Modernism, Fiction and Mathematics* (Edinburgh: Edinburgh University Press, 2018), pp. 1–2.
45. Mitchison, *We Have Been Warned*, p. 120.
46. Ibid. p. 161.
47. Engelhardt, *Modernism*, p. 10.
48. Hughes, 'Physics', p. 349.
49. Mitchison, *We Have Been Warned*, p. 204.
50. Hughes, 'Physics', p. 350.
51. Mitchison, *We Have Been Warned*, p. 167.
52. Engelhardt, *Modernism*, pp. 1–2.
53. Ibid. p. 7.
54. Matthew Szudzik and Eric W. Weisstein, 'Parallel Postulate', *MathWorld: A Wolfram Web Resource*, https://mathworld.wolfram.com/ParallelPostulate.html [accessed 16 March 2021].
55. Engelhardt, *Modernism*, p. 31.
56. Ibid. pp. 7, 35.
57. Mitchison, *We Have Been Warned*, p. 9.
58. Naomi Mitchison, *You May Well Ask: A Memoir 1920–1940* (London: Fontana, 1986), p. 91.
59. Mitchison, *We Have Been Warned*, p. 79.
60. Ibid. p. 138.
61. Paddy Scannell and David Cardiff, *A Social History of British Broadcasting: Volume 1 – 1922–1939, Serving the Nation* (Oxford: Blackwell, 1991), pp. 322–6.
62. Naomi Mitchison, *Nix-Nought-Nothing: Four Plays for Children* (London: Jonathan Cape, 1928), p. 9.
63. Mitchison, *We Have Been Warned*, p. 167.
64. Ibid. p. 291.
65. Ibid. p. 311.
66. Ibid. pp. 290, 272.
67. Julia Chan, 'The Brave New Worlds of Birth Control: Women's Travel in Soviet Russia and Naomi Mitchison's *We Have Been Warned*', *Journal of Modern Literature* 42:2 (2019), p. 39.
68. Stephen Brooke, *Sexual Politics: Sexuality, Family Planning, and the British Left from the 1880s to the Present Day* (Oxford: Oxford University Press, 2011), pp. 83–4.
69. Mitchison, *We Have Been Warned*, pp. 500, 497.
70. Nick Hubble, 'Naomi Mitchison: Fantasy and Intermodern Utopia', in Alice Reeve-Tucker and Nathan Waddell (eds), *Utopianism, Modernism, and Literature in the Twentieth Century* (Basingstoke: Palgrave Macmillan, 2013), p. 75.

# 5. Send in the Clones? Naomi Mitchison and the Politics of Reproduction and Motherhood

*Lesley A. Hall*

Themes around reproduction manifested early in Naomi Mitchison's life, even though she was brought up in the sheltered fashion appropriate to upper-middle-class Edwardian girlhood.[1] As far as specific sexual knowledge in adolescence went she could only evoke 'a real memory blank, a depth of embarrassment, into the bottom of which my fishing memory cannot reach'.[2] But health problems (perhaps) had led to her sharing her mother's bedroom from the age of ten, 'fairly certain that my presence was to ensure that my father should not be allowed in',[3] either to avoid family increase – though her mother spoke vaguely of 'Malthusian capsules' to Naomi in the prelude to her marriage, indicating some knowledge of contraception – or from distaste for marital sex.[4]

Her mother, an adherent of Edwardian feminist social purity eugenics, instructed Naomi that if anyone proposed marriage, to 'ask whether he had ever had anything to do with another woman'.[5] This was both an ideological commitment to attacking the sexual double standard, which saw sexual licence as permissible to men but to be condemned utterly in respectable women; and practical concern about the possibility of contracting venereal disease from men who engaged in sex outside marriage.[6] Mitchison's autobiographical comments upon the prioritisation of conventional social expectations – 'the standards and fine distinctions' around class and gendered behaviour supposed to be known 'in some subconscious way' – suggest that her mother did not take her feminist eugenics any further.[7] More radical agendas of the period advanced by the New Woman novelists and polemical writers such as Frances Swiney put the case that, freed from economic and social constraints, women might choose mates with an eye to their potential for fatherhood.[8] Shortly before Naomi's marriage to Dick Mitchison, her mother tried to convey the facts of life: 'I thought because I had kept guinea-pigs for many years and understood Mendelian genetics as far as it had then gone, that I already knew everything.'[9] In fact, their first couple of years of marriage were very unsatisfactory until, as for so many of her generation, illumination came from Marie Stopes's pioneering marriage manual, *Married Love*, in 1918.[10]

Early in the 1920s she became active in promoting birth control, which she later described as 'something . . . happening for women which was going to be almost as important an agent of social change as the National Health Service'. Mitchison, in line with the official ideology of the movement, seems to have understood birth control mainly as 'family spacing and helping in the emancipation of women', rather than a means either of population control or enabling 'permissiveness'.[11] She was a founding member of the committee of the North Kensington Women's Welfare Centre, established in 1924 to provide contraception to the working-class women of this deprived area by her friend (and Dick Mitchison's lover) Margery Spring Rice. A few years later she joined another of Spring Rice's initiatives, the Birth Control Research Committee, including volunteering for testing contraceptives: which 'could be embarrassing'.[12]

She had connections with the Eugenics Society – not unusual among birth control activists of the period – though the relationship was uneasy. Birth control activists in general wanted to give individuals agency over their own reproductive destiny: however, whatever their private beliefs and practices, for tactical reasons their public propaganda well into the post-World War II era focused on married women and happy planned families, emphasising maternal and child well-being. Eugenicists, on the other hand, tended to believe that there were entire groups within society which should, or should not, be reproducing.[13] According to the records of the Eugenics Society Mitchison was elected a Fellow in July 1925.[14] She appears to have become fairly rapidly disenchanted, since she wrote to Julian Huxley (in an undated letter, on internal evidence written sometime between 1925 and 1930), that she had 'chucked' the Society due to the 'dear old ladies who appeared at all the meetings longing to sterilise the unfit': but added that, if Huxley thought that birth control propaganda could be done in it, she would rejoin.[15] She was well-informed about modern genetics – not surprisingly, given her own scientific education and the work of her brother, the geneticist J. B. S. Haldane – and probably had a rather more sophisticated understanding of the complexities of inheritance than the Society's more rabidly enthusiastic members. She had a certain, though by no means unqualified, pride in her own heredity: writing to Cora Hodson, the Society secretary, in 1929, she mentioned 'several epileptics' in her mother's family and recalled that she had 'made up [her] mind early on not to marry anyone belonging to a Scottish family which was in any way related to [her] own'.[16] Similar eugenically inflected concerns over familial health issues were pervasive in the interwar period, and were reflected in the many personal queries received by the Eugenics Society and in letters to Marie Stopes.[17] By the early 1930s Mitchison's politics had moved further left, although she did not follow her brother into the Communist Party. She informed Carlos Paton Blacker, the General Secretary of the Society, that she felt she should resign since the 'general trend of opinion' in the Society was out of tune with

> my own position of one who wants to see the present state of society completely altered, and new sets of social and individual values substituted for the old ones. . . . I also feel very doubtful about such measures as the sterilisation of the unfit. They put such a terrible power into the hands of a government and bureaucracy which may yet prove tyrannous.[18]

During this period she did not embody her ideas in science fiction, in spite of the significant tradition in British literary circles of using scientific speculations as a basis for fiction: Aldous Huxley's *Brave New World* (1932) is probably the best known example of the era, but Mitchison's sister-in-law, Charlotte Haldane, had already published *A Man's World* in 1926.[19] Such fictions tended to depict dystopian future societies as a warning to the present. Other novels presented apocalyptic visions of the downfall of civilisation and the rise of barbarism, the grimmest of which is probably Katharine Burdekin's *Swastika Night* (1937), in which women have been reduced to the condition of breeding animals.[20]

Mitchison was, nevertheless, thinking against the grain of received ideas about birth control. In 1929 she presented 'Some Comments on the use of Contraceptives by Intelligent Persons' to the World League for Sexual Reform Congress held in London.[21] She expanded this into a pamphlet, *Comments on Birth Control*, for the Criterion Miscellany series.[22] In this she expressed 'some of the difficulties and criticisms' being raised by 'reasonably intelligent women', countering the tendency of those in favour of contraception to 'write and talk as though the control of conception solved all sexual problems and most social ones'.[23] This interrogated the issue from a different perspective from the one usually invoked by the birth control movement, which for prudent tactical reasons laid heavy emphasis on the sufferings of overburdened working-class women.

Mitchison had already been musing on these questions: in 1928 she wrote to Julian Huxley:

> I wonder when anything certain will be invented. The statistics are all right, but it won't make much difference to individual happiness until one can be sure one isn't going to be the 2% of failure oneself. I do also think the psychological aspects of it want studying by someone more sensible than the very old lady doctors and such who do it now.[24]

In *Comments on Birth Control* she articulated her suspicions of the missionary tendencies of Neo-Malthusians 'trying to force their doctrines on the world'. Those who already wanted birth control wanted knowledge of the best and safest methods; it should not be forced upon the unwilling when the unwillingness was not 'a product of bad education and artificial religious prejudice'.[25] She was sceptical of received wisdom within the birth control movement on the desirability of delaying parenthood for the first few years of marriage, or the virtues of carefully planning the family.

She also, daringly, considered the actual, rather than the ideal, effect on marital sex life of the 'previous and deliberate action' of contraception by the woman, in particular given that women were societally constructed as passive and consenting, rather than active, partners in sex.[26] Female barrier methods were advocated by the birth control movement and the ones most widely provided in their clinics, on ideological grounds (placing control in the hands of the woman) and also in the belief that these methods (occlusive cap plus spermicidal chemical) were the most reliable. Only in the mid-1930s did the introduction of the latex process vastly improve the reliability and user-experience of condoms. The problems that this posed given female sexual ignorance and attitudes towards sexuality within marriage have been well delineated by the oral history researches of Kate Fisher and Simon Szreter on gendered responsibility for contraceptive decision-making and practice within early twentieth-century marriage.[27] Mitchison spoke out about the issues that even well-informed women like herself experienced in practice with barrier methods that had to be inserted in advance of intercourse. Problems with the contraceptive cap became something of a literary trope in the decades between the end of the Second World War and the advent of the Pill.[28]

While she thought contraception 'altogether admirable on social grounds', Mitchison considered that the practicalities made for 'emotional difficulties which were not there before'.[29] Some women, she suggested, came to find the whole business 'so wildly boring' that they preferred to 'take the risk and be operated on from time to time'.[30] She found 'very few appreciable differences in methods which are at all reliable', though she held out some hope for 'the new German method'[31] – presumably the Gräfenberg ring, an early intrauterine device garnering interest in Britain at the time[32] – which she considered trying herself.[33] While conceding the male sheath was 'a possible makeshift', she did not personally find it a desirable alternative:[34] her originally explicit reference to the revolting feel of a rubber condom in the rape scene in her novel *We Have Been Warned* became, in concession to publisher's sensibilities, more euphemistically 'the foul, horrifying touch of the thing', with a later allusion to 'precautions'.[35] There was not, she pointed out, whatever the propagandists might preach, any 'perfectly safe, cheap, pleasant and fool-proof contraceptive'.[36] She advanced the radical possibility that couples might engage in non-penetrative forms of sexual activity – 'there are many kinds of mutual caresses and pleasures'[37] – and that in long-term relationships, periods of consensual abstinence might also have a place, 'cutting out the sex side of life, which may have become both over-emphasized and duller over a perhaps long period of years'.[38] The existing situation was 'at best . . . a compromise'.[39]

Mitchison argued that 'Intelligent and truly feminist women' wanted 'two things': 'they want to live as women, to have masses of children by the men they love and leisure to be tender and aware of both lovers and children; and they want to do their own work, whatever that may be'. They wanted to have 'both worlds, not specializing like bees or machines'.[40] (This was a period during which women were expected, if not compelled, to resign from paid employment upon marriage.) She was concerned that contraceptives, 'like many other excellent modern contrivances . . . may be agents for habit-forming and pattern making' – 'Life is destroyed that way'.[41] This anxiety about becoming stuck in habits and set patterns, like her puzzling over the question of whether the begetting of children should be intentional or spontaneous,[42] was a theme that would recur in her fiction of the 1960s and '70s.

The topics of contraception, family planning and abortion weave throughout Mitchison's 1935 social realist novel *We Have Been Warned*. On the first page Dione Galton is depicted as thinking 'She knew she mustn't have any more children'[43] – and her husband Tom passingly muses 'Ought I to have let Dione bear me four children?' alongside other sources of liberal guilt.[44] In a moment of marital cosiness, she remarks that 'All I mind about are these beastly contraceptives', as Tom acknowledges her desire for a large family.[45] (It is rather curious that in a novel in which discussions of issues of eugenics are notable for their absence, except for assumptions about superiority on grounds of breeding being significantly undercut, the central couple have the surname 'Galton'!)

Later, Dione walks through Sallington, the Midlands industrial city based on Birmingham, where Tom is standing as a Labour candidate for parliament. They pass through a quiet middle-class suburb – 'No good for us', with its 'dear little, dull little houses, little home-nests, families of two children only, the rest birth-controlled'.[46] This stultifying and sterile conventional pattern contrasts with the even less desirable dire and chaotic state of affairs Dione encounters in the slums – women dying young in childbirth, large families, couples ignorant of contraception practising long-term abstinence.[47] While there is a local birth control clinic, 'struggling to keep in existence by collections at drawing-room meetings and amateur theatricals', it is located a significant tram-journey's distance from the slums of Marshbrook Bridge.[48]

Several situations indicate how utopian in the existing state of society was Mitchison's ideal of women having meaningful work and motherhood and tenderness with love. One of Tom Galton's 'most hopeful pupils' in Oxford, a young woman studying at Ruskin College, reveals that she is engaged to an electrical engineer active in the Labour Movement, and going to 'chuck – all this'. Tom wonders whether, even if she remains politically active, 'this is [her] best way of helping to build a new world'. He daringly recommends the birth control clinic in London run by his apolitical but feminist sister Muriel.[49] She takes this advice: Muriel, a former suffragette, remarks 'Such a nice girl . . . going to spend all the rest of her life doing the work of a four- or five-roomed house . . . and forget all she's had such a struggle to learn. Yes, and it's a waste of our struggle . . . for women's education.'[50] Meanwhile, Agnes Green, the communist schoolmistress in Sallington, is dedicated to political activism and the work of educating the masses by way of the state school system, an occupation she would have to quit if she married;[51] she also mentions a former pupil who lost her job on becoming pregnant out of wedlock.[52] Dione's sister Phoebe struggles with her art, grieving for the loss of her lover and experiencing sexist condescension from male artists.

Things are somewhat different for the Russian women encountered in the 'Under the Red Flag' chapters. Marfa cheerfully admits that she divorced her husband Dmitri because he did not want her to work, and has no qualms about bearing another child, while having no intention of marrying again.[53] However, all is not idyllic in this depiction of the Soviet Union. In particular there is the harrowing scene in an abortion clinic,[54] based on the one Mitchison 'rather reluctantly saw' on her own visit to the USSR in 1932.[55] There are several other allusions to abortion at a period when it was illegal in England but nonetheless obtainable with money and the right connections: many years later, Mitchison stated: 'Of course we all knew one or two people who could do planned abortions. It was highly illegal and probably all the committee helped people who were in desperate trouble. We all did. The amount of prison sentences that I could have accumulated!' She added that she had no regrets.[56] There are passing mentions in the novel of the ineffective remedies sold in chemists' shops.[57] However, somewhat curiously, there are no scenes of 'backstreet' abortions, very prevalent at the time, except for a fleeting thought by the communist working man Donald MacLean –'old women who did things . . . it was dangerous, it was horrible'. These unsafe procedures were a major reason for the rise of an articulate movement for the legalisation of abortion, the open discussion of which by respectable middle-class women shocks Donald and provokes this thought.[58]

Eventually Dione finds herself pregnant as the result of contraceptive failure – Tom suggests that perhaps she 'subconsciously wanted it'. She responds: '"Of course it can be dealt with." She spoke rather impersonally: "It's expensive in this country – or else not safe – but I have the name of someone in Paris."' The cost, she suggests, would be about £20. ('Harley Street' abortions at this period were likely to cost around £100, and going abroad for the operation was not uncommon among those who could afford to travel.)[59] She adds – looking back to the unanaesthetised operation she saw in Moscow – 'They give anaesthetics properly on the Continent.'[60] However, they eventually decide to continue with the pregnancy: the final line of the novel – following Dione's dreadful vision of fascist counter-revolution – is 'The baby was coming alive and moving in her for the first time.'[61]

It is not entirely clear why, in her sixties, Mitchison turned towards science fiction as a medium to dramatise political and social issues. In her foreword to the twentieth anniversary edition of *Solution Three* (1975) she remarked:

> The interest of writing novels is to see what people will do in situations which one has invented for them. This seems to me to be supremely so in S.F. There are of course S.F. fans who are more interested in the details of the invented situations than in the people, and equally, there are S.F. writers who are better at handling the situation than the characters. I was brought up to biology rather than to physics: perhaps this shows through.[62]

It was possibly an outcome of her friendship with Olaf Stapledon, although her science fiction takes a very different line from his. She admired his cosmic history, *Star-Maker*: but reading it in manuscript circa 1933, suggested that she most enjoyed the parts that were 'about people who aren't impossibly remote', and exhorted Stapledon to avoid 'encourag[ing] the idea of the patriarchy' and not to make God 'so MALE all the time'.[63] Eschewing his concerns with transcendence and the posthuman, Mitchison's science fiction is very much about the limits and potential of being human.

She published *Memoirs of a Spacewoman* in 1962. Recent reproductive health developments included the introduction of the contraceptive Pill (though obviating the problems Mitchison had described with existing female methods, it brought its own issues)[64] and revelation of the teratogenic effects of Thalidomide on the developing foetus, revivifying the somewhat quiescent movement for abortion law reform.[65] Women were no longer required to leave their jobs on marriage, but combining careers and maternity remained a problem. The novel deploys interweaving strands concerning love, work and reproduction, in particular maternity. Mary, the narrator, apparently enjoys a situation enabling women 'to live as women, to have masses of children by the men they love and leisure to be tender and aware of both lovers and children; and . . . to do their own work'.[66] Her own work is as a space explorer specialising in establishing communication with very different beings.

The theme of reproduction and parenthood appears on Mary's first expedition, with the introduction of the possibility of her having a child with her colleague T'o M'Kasi. Mary states that she was already thinking that it would be a good idea to have a baby on her return to Terra (Earth), and that the preference among her colleagues 'to make several explorations before they allowed themselves the pleasure of a baby' seems to her a 'strict and even unbiological mode of behaviour':[67] a thought echoing Mitchison's earlier views on the received wisdom of delaying parenthood. However, she finds that her very ability to establish rapport with the starfish-like 'radial entities' they encounter, and to get into harmony with their very non-human mental patterns, renders her incapable of making definite binary choices: so she is unable to make the decision to have a child with T'o in spite of her attraction to him. She does not have her first baby for some years.

In the tense aftermath of disaster that befalls a later expedition, the androgyne alien Vly inadvertently activates one of Mary's ova, leading to the development of a haploid foetus (that is, one with half the usual number of chromosomes). Mary decides to bear the child, whom she names Viola.[68] This unexpected outcome of a traumatic disaster, who is unusually small and has various health problems – Mary remarks that she would have terminated the activation under more normal circumstances[69] – becomes Mary's most loved child. The narrative contrasts Viola with Mary's second child, whose father, 'a distinguished explorer for whom I still have the greatest respect', Mary chooses 'almost too sensibly and deliberately', producing a son tepidly described as 'intelligent and satisfactory'. In spite of continuing to have 'happy relations' with father and son, she does not choose to have a second child with him.[70] This resonates with Mitchison's remarks in *Comments on Birth Control* deploring what she feared was a new tyranny of the carefully planned and limited family with no room for spontaneity and surprise. By contrast, an unexpected meeting with T'o M'Kasi as he is about to depart on an expedition leaves Mary 'in no condition' to take part in the expedition she herself was planning on joining, as she becomes pregnant with her third child. She describes the outcome of this spontaneous occurrence – having to remain on Terra in order to 'stabilise' the child – as 'delicious', if rather incongruously an experience 'just like a twentieth-century Mum! . . . It must have been just like that in the old days.' She adds 'Only I could get away, that was the difference. How marvellous it was, in spite of the tiny prickles of regret, to be back in a ship among my instruments and tables, thinking intently and uninterruptedly.'[71]

The male characters in the novel are frequently assessed for their potential as fathers: during an expedition rather lacking in challenges upon which she can exert her own skills, Mary dallies with Quinag, a 'smoothy' from the Minerals Ministry, as 'a pleasing way of passing the odd half-hour when nothing more important is happening', but does not consider him suitable for fatherhood: 'one does, after all, demand more than good looks and expertise'.[72] When she later has a child with her fellow explorer and mentor Peder Pedersen she wonders 'why there had not been a rush to choose him as a father'.[73] This undercurrent recalls the early twentieth-century feminist eugenics of female choice, and also, perhaps, pokes oblique criticism at the kind of contemporary science fiction which tended to assume that women's prime value lay in their sexual attractiveness and capacity as breeders.

'A fairly complex moral problem' manifests itself when Mary joins an all-women group expedition to a habitable planet.[74] They encounter large caterpillar-like creatures displaying consciousness and intelligence, living in algae bogs and making pleasing elaborate patterns with the shiny coloured pellets that they evacuate. They turn out to be the larval form of butterfly-like creatures which communicate with psychic emotions. The butterflies attack the caterpillars with sensations of guilt and misery, to prevent their pattern-making and their enjoyable quasi-sexual wallowing in the bogs. The butterflies believe, though it is never clear whether this is correct, that pattern-making causes deformity in wing-development (the imperfect are ruthlessly destroyed as they hatch) and wallowing leads to egg-laying, which kills the butterfly in pain and trauma. There is no parental emotion: eggs hatch into an alien life-form capable of independent survival. It is impossible to convey to the caterpillars that they will become butterflies, and the butterflies feel no compassion towards the caterpillars, which are to be disciplined for an ultimate goal.

The expedition members are conducted into the presence of a very old, apparently immortal butterfly radiating blissful emotions of extreme happiness and peace: does this transcendence, as the butterflies indicate, justify the pain and misery visited upon the caterpillars? Some members of the expedition feel intense sympathy for the caterpillars and fiercely object to the cruelty they are subjected to: in particular, Françoise, one of the youngest members of the team, develops what are explicitly framed as quasi-maternal feelings for 'her damaged and miserable caterpillars. Her children. She had not yet had any babies of her own.'[75] This leads her to deliberately murder the undying butterfly, an act of interference that means she will never be permitted to engage in space exploration again.

This episode evokes troubling resonances around inflicting suffering in the present for the good of a possible future state and sacrificing the many for the sake of a few. While Mary comments 'Isn't it more like what has been done in human history in the name of religion?',[76] it also has strong resonances with eugenic ideology. The scenario makes further riffs on the pervasive themes of reproduction and parenthood: the sexual act, with fertilisation taking place (if it does) in the bog-wallowing caterpillars, is completely dissociated from the eventual agonising and mortal parturition of the butterfly. There is complete estrangement, amounting to antipathy, between the two forms. Meanwhile, Françoise's maternal emotions for the caterpillars lead her to a violent and career-destroying act.

This image of estrangement and antagonism between parent and offspring and the theme of dangerous maternal feeling takes another twist in the novel's very creepy episodes of body-horror involving the experiments with the alien grafts which Mary undertakes. In these, instead of alienation, boundaries are almost completely and perilously erased. The 'grafts' encountered by Mary's expedition are entities consisting of 'a tissue so alien that it is not recognised even as an enemy so that no anti-body is produced',[77] and thus can be grafted onto a mammalian host, with the rather surprising effect that the grafts develop, and pick up a certain degree of behaviour from the host animal. Mary volunteers as the first human host. Her initial experience, with a graft she names 'Ariel', is distressing and puzzling. She begins to lose her scientific objectivity, feels possessive towards the graft, 'maundering about it'.[78] When the graft separates, 'instead of being relieved . . . I felt I couldn't bear it.'[79] There remains a bond between the graft and Mary, and even a form of communication, until the graft inexplicably dies, leaving Mary grief-stricken.

Following the traumatic experiences on the butterfly planet, Mary returns to the centre where the graft experiments are continuing, to discover that more has been found out about the life cycle of the organism on its native world. The grafts evoke maternal feelings in the females of the other native species, the large lizard-like 'Diners', which appear to play some part in their reproductive cycle. What happens on this occasion, when Mary and the other participants in the experiment are given fresh grafts, is that their protective maternal instincts are, as it were, taken over and hypertrophied by the imperatives of the grafts: '[W]e had not reckoned . . . that the grafts would affect us in such a way that we would be highly suspicious of all tests, and . . . we would want to huddle over them secretly instead of speaking about them or even experimenting on them, openly.'[80] All the participants increasingly feel the urge to mate and be fertilised and to submerge themselves in water, following the grafts' reproductive imperative: Mary reports of herself, 'I was completely under the influence of the graft, except that far down, almost smothered, there was still a very small quietly struggling observer.'[81] Only external intervention saves her.

This idea of a woman and an offspring to which she is not genetically connected but with which she feels an intense and overpowering emotional bond is given another, more positive, twist in Mitchison's next science-fiction novel, *Solution Three*. She dedicated the novel to her friend Jim Watson, the co-discoverer of DNA, 'who first suggested this horrid idea'. However, the set-up has intriguing resemblances to the scenario imagined by Mitchison's brother, J. B. S. Haldane, in his 1924 lecture *Daedalus: or the future of science*: a world where sex and reproduction were completely separated. Haldane depicted this as involving the selection 'as ancestors for the next generation' of men and women 'so undoubtedly superior to the average that the advance in each generation . . . is very startling'. This was accomplished by the implantation of fertilised ova into 'ectogenetic mothers', by 'an operation which is somewhat unpleasant, though now no longer disfiguring or dangerous': their position was 'an honour, but by no means a pleasure'.[82] This foreshadows major themes in *Solution Three*, although reproductive science had moved on: Haldane also first suggested human cloning, in an essay of 1963.[83]

The background to the novel is a world that has suffered 'annihilation, as living and food-producing spaces, of large parts of the Earth's surface, including many major cities'.[84] A transnational, multiracial Council carefully administers depleted resources by applying a Code of harmonious living, mutual tolerance, and non-aggression based on the lives, example and teaching of two individuals simply known as He and She. Long dead by the time the action takes place, He and She are now being perpetuated as clones: the first generations of these clones are already young adults taking an active part in the Council's work. One may wonder if the dedication to Watson was somewhat backhanded. He was already notorious for sexist and racist views: not only are Council, and leading characters, in *Solution Three* of a range of ethnicities and predominantly women, but He was an African American man 'right in the middle of the race war' and She was an unmarried (with subtextual hints that she may have been lesbian) woman doctor from Shetland.

The Clones are implanted into 'Clone Mums'. The first of these 'had been high I.Q.s, very responsible, very much aware, people like Mutumba and splendid Lisa'; and initially 'there had been certain risks and dangers which had now been ironed out'.[85] Mutumba, now Convenor of the Council, recalls 'her own difficult clone birth' though also 'the enchantment of her blue-eyed white baby'.[86] In those days 'they had been still more severe' about separating the Clones from their Mums and Mutumba 'had no idea what had happened to her little flax haired Clone, whom she had cried for secretly and long'.[87] She only discovers the fate of A16, now Ellen, when her death is reported as the result of an outbreak of social unrest leading to aggression: 'the grey-curled head seemed to quiver a little. Then she sat up straighter than before'.[88] She subsequently develops a quasi-maternal relationship with Anni, the Clone who brings back this report. By the time the action of the novel takes place Clone Mums are 'quite ordinary young women, chosen on physical standards only; the genetic background made no difference', who receive a number of desirable privileges for the task: 'for the moment, every Clone Mum was a person of deep importance'.[89] They are allowed limited contact with their Clone in later life and a few even have the privilege of choosing their Clone's name.[90]

The Mums are kept soothed and happy throughout the process of pregnancy and parturition and the early nurturance of their infants. However, 'The Clones didn't belong to the Mums who had been their nests and love givers. . . . If anything it was the other way, the Mums belonging to the Clones, for little children must have love.'[91] The Clone Mum Lilac's recollections of feeling 'lulled . . . chosen, privileged . . . buoyed up . . . carefully looked after', have a certain similarity to Mary's feelings as host to the parasitic graft in *Memoirs of a Spacewoman*.[92] Maternal feelings are instrumentalised for the care of the precious Clones. It seems possible that Mitchison was responding to post-war ideologies of motherhood influenced by John Bowlby's theories of attachment, in which the interests of the mother became subsumed into care for the developing child.[93]

The population is socially conditioned to believe 'that attraction between the sexes was only a snare and an aggression'. Approved relationships are homosexual and non-reproductive.[94] However, some people adhere to older patterns: in particular, 'the Professorials', scientists and researchers, are less susceptible to the gentle persuasion away from heterosexuality and continue to have children in the usual way, although birth control is available. Miryam, one of the leading characters, is a plant geneticist with two children, married, as is still permitted, to Carlo, a cytologist, though the small space of their assigned living quarters means that they cannot cohabit. Her life rather more resembles that of a 'twentieth-century Mum' than did Mary's, involving issues over childcare – 'she was lucky there was still a day nursery at the lab, with a couple of old ladies in charge, too old to disapprove' – and the distractions these create for her work.[95] The Councillor Jussie is fairly sympathetic to Miryam, but nonetheless finds it somewhat unreasonable that she refuses to be 'normalised' or to have the children taken away to a nursery so that they will no longer 'bother' her.[96]

While women may have (same-sex) lovers and meaningful work, there are significant limitations upon the extent to which they can experience and enjoy motherhood. If they have reproductive heterosexual unions they are mildly stigmatised and subject to the difficulties Miryam experiences. If they miss the chance to bear a clone, and enjoy the experience of nurturing until the clone is taken away, that is that: Jussie muses that she 'had been too deeply involved, first as a mining engineer, and then in Council work during the years when she might have been a Mum, and perhaps, for that matter, it was not really her thing'.[97] Clone Mums normally only get a single opportunity: Jussie and the Council are somewhat bewildered by 'the usual' bother with the Clone Mums 'Wanting a second go'.[98] Those like the meek and compliant Gisela, however, 'extra good, all the time . . . might have another turn later'.[99]

Most of the Mums accept that, at a certain stage of development, their infants are taken away from them for the 'strengthening' process meant to replicate the adversities that made He and She into the extraordinary beings they were. But Lilac, instead of succumbing, has begun to think critically about the system, and the soft policing and hidden persuasion of social conditioning that characterises it. She says of He and She: 'supposing They'd only had kindness, well then, what would They have been? . . . At one period He showed what they call artistic leanings': and would rather her little F90 became a composer or a painter.[100] The infliction of what is perceived as a necessary cruelty for a higher purpose, although on beings considered superior rather than lower, foreclosing pleasurable and aesthetic activities, troublingly echoes the butterfly–caterpillar relationship in *Memoirs of a Spacewoman*. Susan Squier has suggested an influence from Mitchison's deep ambivalence over the accepted practice in her upper-class milieu of sending young sons away to school;[101] Mitchison herself observed that she and Dick were criticised for keeping their sons at home until the age of nine.[102]

Rebellious Lilac will not be chosen again to be a Clone Mum, and unlike her lover Gisela, will not be allowed to name or eventually meet F90 in future. But what does become possible for Lilac is to use her intelligence to research the so far understudied effect of 'non-chromosomal maternal influence from the cell material' and the fact there are differences between the Clones – 'not merely the difference between one uterus and another, but . . . also considerable interchange of fluids between the foetus and its hosts'.[103] It has already been observed that the Clones clearly distinguish themselves one from the other and recognise their own Clone Mums. Two of the Clones, Anni and Kid, even fall in love with one another in a 'deviant', i.e. heterosexual, fashion.

There is a very obvious ecological theme in *Solution Three* in which the urgent issue of failing crops caused by a lack of biodiversity – a topic Mitchison would revisit in *Not By Bread Alone* (1983) – is mirrored in the eugenicist assumptions of the Clone project. However, the theme of stultifying and eventually destructive 'habit-forming and pattern making' is also present in the imposition of the 'strengthening', the rigid norms around motherhood, and the treatment of the Mums as vessels to be cosseted for a period but of no individual significance: something that Lilac's projected research, it is suggested, will counter. Shortly after what she perceives as her unsatisfactory exchange with Miryam, Jussie says to Ric, the Council historian, 'We have to be careful not to become too completely patterned, haven't we?' This sets up 'chains of historical recollection' for Ric, reminding him that 'The areas which had been difficult for the wave [of social transformation] were just those which were too patterned and institutionalized.' He responds that 'Yes, flexibility is essential.'[104] It is to Ric that Bobbi, a Clone boy, remarks that 'it makes us Clones a bit too alike, a bit dull, all having the same genes' (the strengthening process must also produce similarities).[105]

Mutumba, shocked by Anni's revelation of the mutual attraction between her and the male Clone Kid, starts thinking of ways to handle this 'problem':

> This thing that had happened was something new, but she was trying to find out ways of containing it. . . . Instead of going with the wave. If it was a wave. . . . If deviancy was entirely wrong, were the Clones capable of it? Or was it something she had been looking out for, under her breath, the tiny, first sign of a change. For two centuries there had been the anxiety to stabilize . . . the world had needed it so desperately. But now there was a counter-danger of subsiding into unquestioning confidence and security in the thought of the Clones taking over.

Was 'a slightly other kind of excellence needed now? . . . A planned accident? In an unplanned plan?' Mutumba asks herself whether she is 'too deeply conditioned into the idea of meiosis as sin'.[106] While fiercely rejecting genetic engineering as against the Code, she and Jussie still find it hard to think beyond already proven excellence as the basis for permitting reproduction.[107] As with birth control in the interwar years, 'Solution Three' is an improvement on the situation it came into being to cope with, but not a stopping place in itself: it generates further questions and challenges.

Throughout these works, from the thirties to the seventies, Mitchison was posing questions and setting up thought experiments rather than claiming to have answers: except that flexibility is a virtue and the good life is one that allows openness to happy accidents and women combining motherhood, work and loving relationships. One can, with little difficulty, imagine her by no means enthusiastic reaction to contemporary exhortations to young women to put motherhood on hold and freeze their eggs (at considerable expense) until such time as they may feel secure enough to procreate.[108] As these novels demonstrate, she looked sceptically at even the most apparently benign of 'magic bullet' solutions and at the soft authoritarianism of social pressures to conformity.

## NOTES

1. Naomi Mitchison, *Small Talk: Memoirs of an Edwardian Childhood* (London: Bodley Head, 1973); *All Change Here: Girlhood and Marriage* (London: Bodley Head, 1975).
2. Mitchison, *All Change*, p. 86.
3. Ibid. p. 15.
4. Mitchison, *Small Talk*, p. 52; Naomi Mitchison, *You May Well Ask: A Memoir 1920–1940* (London: Victor Gollancz Ltd, 1979), p. 34.
5. Mitchison, *All Change*, p. 86.
6. Lesley A. Hall, 'Women, Feminism and Eugenics', in Robert A. Peel (ed.), *Essays in the History of Eugenics: Proceedings of a Conference Organised by the Galton Institute, London, 1997* (London: The Galton Institute, 1998), pp. 36–51.
7. Mitchison, *All Change*, p. 83.
8. Angelique Richardson, *Love and Eugenics in the Late Nineteenth Century: Rational Reproduction and the New Woman* (Oxford: Oxford University Press, 2003); George Robb, 'Race Motherhood: Moral Eugenics vs Progressive Eugenics, 1880–1920', in Claudia Nelson and Ann Sumner Holmes (eds), *Maternal Instincts: Visions of Motherhood and Sexuality in Britain, 1875–1925* (Basingstoke: Macmillan, 1997), pp. 58–74.
9. Mitchison, *Small Talk*, p. 52.
10. Mitchison, *You May Well Ask*, pp. 69–70.
11. Ibid. p. 34.
12. Lucy Pollard, *Margery Spring-Rice: Pioneer of Women's Health in the Early Twentieth Century* (Cambridge: Open Book Publishers, 2020), ch. 5 [e-book]; Mitchison, *You May Well Ask*, p. 34.
13. Lesley A. Hall, 'Movements to Separate Sex and Reproduction', in Nick Hopwood, Rebecca Flemming and Lauren Kassell, *Reproduction from Antiquity to the Present Day* (Cambridge: Cambridge University Press, 2018), pp. 427–41.
14. Secretary of the Eugenics Society to Mrs Mitcheson [*sic*], 17 July 1925, Eugenics Society archives in the Wellcome Library, London, SA/EUG/C/391, https://wellcomelibrary.org/item/b16899118 [accessed 1 February 2021].
15. Naomi Mitchison to Julian Huxley, n.d.: J. S. Huxley papers in the Woodson Research Center, Fondren Library, Rice University, Houston, Texas, MS. 050 Series III, file 47.2.
16. Mitchison to Cora Hodson 12 [no month] 1929, Eugenics Society archives in the Wellcome Library, London, SA/EUG/C/391, https://wellcomelibrary.org/item/b16899118 [accessed 1 December 2020].
17. Lesley A. Hall, 'Marie Stopes and Her Correspondents: Personalising Population Decline in an Era of Demographic Change', in Robert A. Peel (ed.), *Marie Stopes, Eugenics and the English Birth Control Movement: Proceedings of a Conference Organised by the Galton Institute, London, 1996* (London: The Galton Institute, 1997), pp. 27–48.
18. Mitchison to the General Secretary of the Eugenics Society (C. Blacker), 29 May 1933, SA/EUG/C/391, https://wellcomelibrary.org/item/b16899118 [accessed 1 December 2020].
19. Susan Squier, 'Sexual Biopolitics in *Man's World*: The Writings of Charlotte Haldane', in Angela Ingram and Daphne Patai (eds), *Rediscovering Forgotten Radicals: British Women Writers, 1889–1939* (Chapel Hill: University of North Carolina Press, 1993), pp. 137–55.
20. Katharine Burdekin, *Swastika Night*; with an introduction by Daphne Patai (London: Lawrence and Wishart, 1985).
21. Naomi Mitchison, 'Some Comments on the Use of Contraceptives by Intelligent Persons', in Norman Haire (ed.), *Sexual Reform Congress, London 8–15: IX: 1929. World League for Sexual Reform. Proceedings of the Third Congress* (London: Kegan Paul, Trench, Trubner & Co., 1930), pp. 182–8.

22. *A Series of Series: 20th-Century Publishers Book Series*, 'Criterion Miscellany', https://seriesof
series.owu.edu/criterion-miscellany/ [accessed 19 November 2020].

23. Naomi Mitchison, *Comments on Birth Control (Criterion Miscellany no 12)* (London: Faber
and Faber, 1930), p. 6.

24. Mitchison to Julian Huxley, 1928: J. S. Huxley papers, file 9.9.

25. Mitchison, *Comments*, pp. 7–8.

26. Ibid. pp. 17–18.

27. Kate Fisher, *Birth Control, Sex, and Marriage in Britain 1918–1960* (Oxford: Oxford
University Press, 2006); Simon Szreter and Kate Fisher, *Sex before the Sexual
Revolution: Intimate Life in England 1918–1963* (Cambridge: Cambridge University Press,
2010).

28. Donna J. Drucker, 'The Symbolic Use of Barrier Contraceptives in American and English
Literature', *The MIT Press Reader*, 4 May 2020, https://thereader.mitpress.mit.edu/barrier
-contraceptives-in-american-english-literature/ [accessed 16 February 2021].

29. Mitchison, *Comments*, p. 18.

30. Ibid. p. 19.

31. Ibid. p. 19.

32. Norman Haire, 'Sterilization, Abortion and Birth Control'; Ernst Gräfenberg, 'Die
Intrauterine Methode der Konzeptionsverhütung'; Hans Lehfeldt, 'Contraceptive Methods
Requiring Medical Assistance', *Sexual Reform Congress*, pp. 109–15, 116–25, 126–32; letters
from Ethel Mannin to Douglas and Malin Goldring, n.d. (c. 1930s), Goldring papers in
Special Collections, University of Victoria, British Columbia, CA UVICARCH SC048-
1994-109, file 1.78–9; Caroline Rusterholz, 'Testing the Gräfenberg Ring in Interwar
Britain: Norman Haire, Helena Wright and the Debate over Statistical Evidence, Side
Effects, and Intrauterine Contraception', *Journal of the History of Medicine and Allied
Sciences* 72:4 (2017), pp. 448–67.

33. Mitchison to Julian Huxley, 1931, J. S. Huxley papers, file 10.9.

34. Mitchison, *Comments*, p. 20.

35. Mitchison, *You May Well*, p. 178; Naomi Mitchison, *We Have Been Warned* (London:
Constable, 1935), pp. 414, 419.

36. Mitchison, *Comments*, p. 25.

37. Ibid. p. 13.

38. Ibid. p. 21.

39. Ibid. p. 22.

40. Ibid. p. 25.

41. Ibid. p. 19.

42. Ibid. pp. 13–14.

43. Mitchison, *We Have Been Warned*, p. 3.

44. Ibid. p. 28.

45. Ibid. p. 145.

46. Ibid. p. 52.

47. Ibid. pp. 113, 386, 505.

48. Ibid. p. 398.

49. Ibid. pp. 152–3.

50. Ibid. pp. 195–6.

51. Ibid. p. 424.

52. Ibid. p. 419.

53. Ibid. pp. 267, 275.

54. Ibid. pp. 258–60.

55. Mitchison, *You May Well*, p. 188.

56. Transcript of interview with Naomi Mitchison by Barbara Evans, 1982, for biography of

Dr Helena Wright: Papers of Philip Rainsford Evans and Barbara Evans in the Wellcome Library, PP/PRE/J.1/24.

57. Mitchison, *We Have Been Warned*, pp. 227, 490, 518–19.
58. Ibid. p. 227.
59. See references in texts cited at http://www.lesleyahall.net/abortion.htm [accessed 23 November 2020].
60. Mitchison, *We Have Been Warned*, pp. 487–93.
61. Ibid. p. 553.
62. Naomi Mitchison, *Solution Three*. Afterword by Susan M. Squier (New York: The Feminist Press at the City University of New York, 1995), p. 5.
63. Naomi Mitchison to Olaf Stapledon, n.d, probably summer 1933, quoted in Robert Crossley, *Olaf Stapledon: Speaking for the Future* (Liverpool: Liverpool University Press, 1994), p. 230.
64. Lara Marks, *Sexual Chemistry: A History of the Contraceptive Pill* (New Haven, CT: Yale University Press, 2001).
65. Lesley A. Hall, *Sex, Gender and Social Change in Britain since 1880* (Basingstoke: Palgrave Macmillan, 2012), pp. 150–1.
66. Mitchison, *Comments*, p. 5.
67. Naomi Mitchison, *Memoirs of a Spacewoman* (London: Victor Gollancz Ltd, 1962), pp. 22–3.
68. Ibid. pp. 62–3.
69. Ibid. p. 66.
70. Ibid. p. 68.
71. Ibid. p. 70.
72. Ibid. pp. 74–7.
73. Ibid. p. 85.
74. Ibid. p. 88.
75. Ibid. p. 121.
76. Ibid. p. 127.
77. Ibid. p. 42.
78. Ibid. p. 49.
79. Ibid. p. 51.
80. Ibid. p. 158.
81. Ibid. p. 167.
82. J. B. S. Haldane, *Daedalus, or, Science and the Future: A Paper Read to the Heretics, Cambridge, on February 4th, 1923*; transcribed: Cosma Rohilla Shalizi, 10 April 1993; https://www.marxists.org/archive/haldane/works/1920s/daedalus.htm [accessed 10 November 2020].
83. J. B. S. Haldane, 'Biological Possibilities for the Human Species of the Next Ten Thousand Years', in Gordon Wolstenholme (ed.), *Ciba Foundation Symposium on Man and His Future* (London: J. & A. Churchill, 1963), pp. 337–61.
84. Mitchison, *Solution Three*, p. 7.
85. Ibid. p. 28.
86. Ibid. p. 14.
87. Ibid. p. 36.
88. Ibid. p. 87.
89. Ibid. pp. 27–9.
90. Ibid. p. 36.
91. Ibid. p. 35.
92. Ibid. pp. 94–5.
93. Mathew Thomson, 'Bowlbyism and the Post-War Settlement', in *Lost Freedom:*

*The Landscape of the Child and the British Post-War Settlement* (Oxford: Oxford University Press, 2013), pp. 79–113.

94.  Mitchison, *Solution Three*, p. 16.
95.  Ibid. p. 41.
96.  Ibid. p. 45.
97.  Ibid. p. 28.
98.  Ibid. p. 12.
99.  Ibid. p. 59.
100. Ibid. p. 63.
101. Susan Squier, 'Afterword', *Solution Three*, p. 180 fn. 5.
102. Mitchison, *You May Well Ask*, p. 41.
103. Mitchison, *Solution Three*, pp. 98–9.
104. Ibid. p. 57.
105. Ibid. p. 109.
106. Ibid. pp. 122–3.
107. Ibid. pp. 154–5.
108. Rebecca Grant, 'How Egg Freezing Got Rebranded as the Ultimate Act of Self-Care', *The Guardian*, 30 September 2020, https://www.theguardian.com/us-news/2020/sep/30/egg-freezing-self-care-pregnancy-fertility [accessed 30 November 2020].

# 6. From Argyll with Love: Naomi Mitchison and the Soviet Union

*Henry Stead*

Naomi Mitchison's writing provides us with a remarkably clear albeit esoteric window into the uniquely turbulent political climate of mid-century Britain, and not least into the personal lives of the wealthy British left and their struggle with and for socialism. The socialist alternative to capitalism in the shape of the Soviet Union loomed large in the contemporary left imaginary, but it is Mitchison's direct confrontation with Soviet reality on which this chapter focuses. From the 1930s to the 1950s in particular, communism's internationalism and irreverence for tradition was attractive to a great many artists, musicians and writers on the left.[1] Mitchison travelled twice to the USSR in this period. In 1932, she went as a member of the Society for Socialist Information and Propaganda (SSIP), an arm of the Fabian Society, to observe and report back on social progress in action. Then in 1952 she travelled as a delegate of the Authors' World Peace Appeal (AWPA) with the aim of fostering peaceful exchange across the Iron Curtain. In the 1930s Mitchison's allegiance was squarely in line with those Labour MPs calling for a united front – an alliance of leftist and leftish political parties – against rising fascism across Europe, but she was fascinated by the socially liberating potential of Soviet-style communism, even if ultimately she would not be converted from her personal loyalty to Labourite social democracy and the gradualism propounded by the majority of people in her milieu.

Her upper-class vantage point afforded both the benefits and drawbacks of distance from the sites of capitalist exploitation of the working class. It affected her views in similar ways to the travelogue style of the Etonian George Orwell in *The Road to Wigan Pier* (1937).[2] But her journey, as we experience it both in her fiction and her autobiographical writing, is more complex. Like her fictional avatars, she opens herself up to several cross-class 'intersubjective relationships' which, as Nick Hubble has discussed, transform her, or her protagonist's identity.[3] The USSR was 'The Debatable Land that lies between here and fairyland' from where 'one came back changed'.[4] Mitchison's writing about her first trip to the USSR, including her diary entries and *We Have Been Warned* (1935), show a determined attempt to inhabit Soviet reality, to challenge and ultimately override her native bourgeois identity. She was, to adopt another of her protagonist's metaphors, ready to give her 'mind to the plow tractors to furrow as they will'.[5] Her novel, her first book set in the modern day and not the ancient past, reads as both authentic social commentary, written by and apparently for the middle- and upper-class British elite, and a species of 'proletarian pastoral', showing the otherness and rustic value of Soviet alterity.[6]

One fascinating aspect of Mitchison's critically maligned novel, in which her characters travel with a similar determination and alienation through British working-class life and the USSR, is that she resists striking an objective pose. Her protagonist Dione Galton, also an aristocratic Labourite experimenting with communism, is openly horrified by certain aspects of working-class experience, including – for example – the state of Idris Pritchard's shared bathroom.[7] Dione excuses the Welsh working-class ice-skating instructor for raping her in part because of the squalid state of his bathing facilities. Pritchard's 'pathetic little bathroom' with its 'nasty-looking' toothbrushes becomes the symbol of the general deprivation of his class under the oppression of hers, for which she is explicitly ready to atone.[8] This is one example of Mitchison's keen interest in the socio-sexual, the intersection between socialism and free love to which I shall return shortly.

Dione confronts poverty and its causes earnestly and with little romanticisation, even if her aristocratic gaze might draw attention to her distance from working-class reality. The working-class and Soviet characters in Mitchison's novels are always deeply suspicious of her fictional avatars, and she only infrequently makes a point of proving them wrong. As a feminist, she fought for the rights of women, especially reproductive rights; as a pacifist, she campaigned against the capitalist warmongers and polarising Cold War mentality; and as a socialist, she worked energetically towards what often comes across as a fairly nebulous notion of social fairness which would inevitably lift the working class from their oppression, and necessarily bring about a material loss for herself and her class. She and her husband – Gilbert Richard (Dick) Mitchison (1890–1970), a senior lawyer and member of the Socialist League – were reconciled to such a material loss, she admitted in 1951, because from the advent of socialism 'morally we stood to win'.[9]

## 1932

In the 1930s Mitchison was on the left of the Labour Party, and was friendly with several literary Communist Party members and fellow travellers, including D. S. 'Prince' Mirsky (1890–1939) and Victor Gollancz (1893–1967). As an aristocratic and intellectually voracious socialist born in 1897, the Naomi Mitchison who boarded a ship to the Soviet Union in 1932 was perhaps most familiar with two British institutions: the conservative hierarchy of the English 'public school', i.e. the expensive fee-paying secondary schools attended by elite males (including her brother and male children), and the classical education delivered by those schools, i.e. the study of ancient Greek and Roman language and literature, which had for generations furnished the minds and shaped the moral life and imperial mentality of its wards. It was in the 1930s that several British leftist writers severely challenged the efficacy of the classical education to do anything other than 'arrest [. . .] the development of the individual mind'.[10] But that is another story. Mitchison's mind was furnished quite as abundantly with the tales and knowledge of Hellas and old Rome as the majority of Etonians and Wykehamists, if not more so. Since she was instructed by a governess and excluded from formal education from her early teens, she read her classical texts widely, freely and for the most part in translation, driven by pleasure and interest rather than by a relatively narrow, dry curriculum designed to reach the linguistic entry requirements to Oxbridge via the antiquated 'grammar grind'.[11] It should then come as no surprise that when she experienced the Soviet Experiment first-hand, as part of a Fabian Society delegation, she saw it in terms that recalled her 'real-world' experience. This is borne out in the observations of her protagonist Dione Galton in *We Have Been Warned* (1935):

> Sometimes it seemed to her that the whole place [the USSR] was like one vast school, all becoming more and more imbued with that public-school spirit which all sensible women are up against: here was the house spirit, government by public opinion and if necessary public chastisement, the dear old O.T.C. very much to the fore, and Stalin something between head-boy and head-master![12]

Although her observation of the Soviet Union through the distinctly upper-class lens of the British 'public school' might at first strike one as comically parochial, the view it affords is on closer inspection insightful. On her visit to the Soviet Union, Dione grows increasingly distrusting of the homogeneity and uniqueness of Soviet 'Liberalism', i.e. the constant and explicit kowtowing to propaganda, and the apparent intolerance for dissent, figured as a lack of space 'for the rebel, the boy or girl who wouldn't fit nicely into any orthodox scheme'.[13] It is this uniformity of opinion and insular self-government that reminds her of the kind of posh school her brother and his friends attended. The parallel is especially rewarding also because those schools, as has been widely documented, were sites of colonial indoctrination, where pupils were prepared explicitly for positions of power in the administration of economic exploitation at home and abroad.[14]

The Clarendon Report (1864) presented the results of a Royal Commission on the Public Schools conducted in 1861. It painted a damning picture of the educational quality of the nine 'great' schools of England, but – despite some lip service to modernisation and a brief lamentation over contemporary standards – upheld the idea that the education of the British ruling elite was still best performed by prolonged exposure to the languages and literature of the Greeks and Romans.[15] Even though, as the Report states, these leading institutions were failing their students *intellectually*, they were nevertheless deemed successful in their promotion of certain values – i.e. those 'principles, character and manners' which were becoming of and useful to an adult of a certain class.[16] In Mitchison's day the intellectual training of pupils in the great public schools was no longer failing quite so dramatically, but the rigid authoritarianism of the prefect system and the high levels of classical tuition (even if they were now accompanied by history and the sciences) were still very much operative both in the schools and popular consciousness.[17] When we consider that the public-school ethic and its rituals were also distributed around the empire in this period as a mechanism of oppression, appropriation and the upholding of the *Pax Britannica*, what appears at first to be a distinctly twee observation in Mitchison's tea-party prose becomes keenly instructive.[18]

In the central section of *We Have Been Warned* (1935), entitled 'Under the Red Flag', in which both Dione and Tom Galton visit the USSR, Dione (in ways that closely correspond to Mitchison's diary from her Fabian Society trip) sees the fledgling communist state in terms borrowed from her own classical experience. This partially came in the form of formal education at the Dragon School, Oxford, where she learned Latin in a class full of boys. But it was supplemented by her own reading of the classical texts in English translation during her governess-led education in her later teens and, of course, in later life too. Her passionate and informal classical education frequently informed the experience of her historical novels' protagonists. In turn, the experience of those characters would bleed into her experience of the world around her, and so on. In other words, the membrane between Mitchison's own experience and that of her characters, therefore, was always highly permeable.

Dione apologises for her habit of seeing life through comparison with the ancient world to Oksana, a Muscovite radio specialist and student who guides and befriends her: 'Sorry, Oksana, going off on to ancient history! I was brought up on it.'[19] What she apologises for here is the following whimsical digression as she admires the sporty Soviets at play in a park:

> It's very – Hellenic. [. . .] Like old Greece. It's obviously like Plato's *Republic*. And these parks – they're like Sparta – it would be lovely if everyone was quite naked, not only their arms and legs! I expect the Spartiates were a good deal more like your people here and less like English public-school boys than we make out, and your State is all Spartiates and no helots.[20]

In ancient Sparta, society was divided between full citizens, in Mitchison's terminology 'Spartiates', and 'helots', who formed a slave class and were (most ancient sources concur) cruelly mistreated by their masters.[21] The apparent absence of helots characterises the USSR as a classless society, an observation made also by Dione's husband, Tom: 'These people are all right; they aren't being oppressed. I should like living here. They're a cheery lot, but they're serious-minded too. It's like Scotland without John Knox.'[22]

The contradiction implicit in the social flatness of this Hellenising description of the USSR and its simultaneous parallel with the hierarchical structure of the British public school shows Mitchison's conflicted and conflicting impressions of the Soviet Union. Such contradictions neatly capture the unresolved paradoxes of the time, and show her attempt to anchor the confusing messaging in her own experience. She was not alone among Western intellectuals in being perplexed by the Soviet Experiment.[23] In 1932 she ran open-eyed a curious gauntlet, with the utopianism of the Soviet propagandistic projection on one side, enhanced as it was by the hopeful rosy tint of its British socialist reception, and on the other the

disappointingly familiar signs of strict and ideologically motivated governing structures of an autocratic regime. It is no surprise that she should have come away with
a complex perspective.

In *We Have Been Warned* (1935) both Dione and Tom Galton agonise over their
relationship with communism. They are – like Naomi and Dick Mitchison, on
whom they were certainly based – members of the aristocracy and both stand politically on the left of the British Labour Party.[24] In the novel Dione and Tom visit the
Soviet Union, become physically and emotionally attracted to individual comrades
and are seduced by the strict doctrine that governs the Soviet way of life. The
couple are deeply impressed by the political, social and sexual mores of their Soviet
comrades. Their liberal sympathies, especially those of Tom, are stretched to the
brink of revolutionary feeling, but their Fabianism ultimately holds firm. It would be
easy to interpret this as a rejection of communism, but this does not quite capture
the extent to which Mitchison became an advocate for rapid political change and
her commitment to a socialist future. Hubble puts it well when he writes that she
became 'a "Red" in the sense of being committed to the revolutionary future rather
than the liberal norms of bourgeois society'.[25]

Both Tom and Dione Galton struggle with the idea that they just have too much
skin in the game to break their allegiance to the Labour Party. Their way of life
and their responsibility towards dependents, especially children, steer Mitchison's
characters (and, we might conclude, herself) away from revolution towards gradual
social reform. Added to this was her strong sense that the tactics of the Communist
Party simply would not work for contemporary Britain, a view which Western
communists were slow to admit owing to an 'underestimation of the resilience of
capitalism and its supporting structures and ideologies'.[26] In *We Have Been Warned*
Tom and Dione are enthusiastic members of the internationalist left of the Labour
Party. Tom worries that it is only his 'social and economic position that kept him
compromising, that kept him where he wasn't directly attacking his own world'.
Mitchison presents a letter from Tom to Dione, mirroring her own political soul-
searching of the time:

> I don't feel that I'm a Communist [. . .] except in so far as I'm a Socialist and
> also accept most of the Marxian interpretations of history and society – but not
> all. I don't at any rate feel like joining the C.P., who wouldn't presumably have
> me. They'll never do the trick in England.[27]

Tom Galton, like Mitchison herself, was a supporter of the Marxist leader of Labour's
left wing, Stafford Cripps (1889–1952), and other members of that broad, and more
militant faction of Fabian Labourites which included G. D. H. Cole (1889–1959)
and Charles Trevelyan (1870–1958).[28] This aligns him – and Mitchison's milieu –
with upper-class advocates of the Socialist League and the United Front (against
fascism), who were gradually forced out of the Labour Party as the decade drew on.
Tom reports back to Dione via letters from the Labour Party Annual Conference in
Leicester (1932). 'It was', Dione narrates, 'the best Party Conference he'd been at,
but, all the same, it was a bit uninspiring after the USSR!'[29]

If we were in any doubt about how closely fiction and reality were blended in Mitchison's novel, reflecting in her 1979 memoirs back on her time in Vienna during the Austrian Civil War (1934) – the first mass working-class uprising against fascism on the European continent – she recalls the 'constant feeling that I was deeply one of the Second, Social Democrat, International, a European in brother-hood with European socialists'.[30] In the same autobiography, *You May Well Ask* (1979), she remembers that when Stafford Cripps was thrown out of the Labour Party she felt that it 'seemed to bring Hitler nearer, though I'm not quite sure why'.[31] Her curiously nebulous concession here is characteristic of her published autobiographical writing on politics, absent from her far more direct and assured diary writing. A breezy detachment is conveyed which does not reflect her actions during the 1930s or her fully engaged writing of that period, of which *We Have Been Warned* is the prime example. In any case, her internationalism and Crippsian alle-giance puts the Mitchison of the 1930s squarely in the United Front faction on the left of the Labour Party.

As an aristocrat and a leftist intellectual Mitchison was caught between at least two worlds. In some circles she was regarded as a dangerous radical, by others hope-lessly conservative. On the ship to Leningrad in 1932, she reflected in her diary: 'It is very odd, after being usually rather extreme wherever one goes in ordinary England, to become a reactionary and compromiser here; I hate being that, but I must be, being an intellectual, keeping those other values.'[32] In the USSR she learned that socialists were considered dangerous to the movement. On the way, she wondered whether she would find there the answers to her questions: for example, was she an individualist or a communist? 'Shall I find the strict doctrine of Communism so attractive, so pulling, so like a super-Catholicism? Or shall I be a Protestant?'[33]

Mitchison's experience of the Soviet Union in the 1930s and the turmoil of British anti-fascism led her seriously to question, like Tom Galton, how her class position affected her political goal. This comes out most strongly in her fictional writing of the time, but it is also present in a softer form in her retrospective auto-biographical writing:

> But what did we well-off middle- or upper-class men and women in the Labour Party think the end product of our socialist thinking and planning was going to be? What were we after and what future did we imagine 'after the revolution' in the sense at least of a revolution being a turning upside-down of society? [. . .] But did we believe that a socialist society would mean a complete destruction of our kind of life, as clearly a revolution with any reality ought to have done? Not really. That kind of belief is very, very difficult to hold for more than a few minutes, especially if you have children: hostages.[34]

Mitchison's brother J. B. S. ('Jack') Haldane (1892–1964) did, however, cross the line to become a card-carrying Communist Party member in 1942. He had, in fact, been an active member of the movement from the 1930s onwards, speaking at rallies and conferences and contributing regular articles to the *Daily Worker*, on the editorial board of which he also served as chairman from 1940 to 1950.[35] Mitchison effortlessly reduced this political activity to a matter of 'assuaging [. . .] the guilt of being born into the upper classes [. . .] He certainly tried to cut luxuries out of his life.'[36] But Haldane was no fair-weather communist. During the Spanish Civil War he visited Spain three times, as an observer and adviser to the Spanish government on defence against gas attacks and air raids, or as Mitchison tells it, in the construction of 'home-made bombs'.[37]

Mitchison was less passionate about the economic side of revolution than she was about forms of liberation closer to her own experience: 'Political change', she argues, 'was never envisaged as a boring redistribution, not only of wealth but of other standards.'[38] Her socialism was driven by a strong sense of sympathy and fairness:

> Some were in it because they saw the breakdown of capitalism coming and wanted an alternative. But I, more romantically, saw it as a moral issue, justice as fairness. Above all I felt that in a fairer world people would become automatically nicer, all social intercourse would be happier and easier.[39]

This fuzzy utopianism of 'niceness' might be difficult to take seriously, but Mitchison was clearly fascinated by the progressive potential of socialism in the social and cultural realms. Her earnest socio-sexual explorations in the fictional realm manifest themselves in sex scenes which, however tame for modern standards, would serve to hold up the publication of *We Have Been Warned* for years, and which are now (and almost certainly also were then) difficult to read with a straight face:

> 'You got – rubber goods – comrade? [. . .] That no matter. Nichevo. Maybe I have another kid. Maybe not [. . .]' She took his hands in hers and laid them over the cotton stuff stretched across her hips. 'You take – them pants – off me, Scottish comrade,' she said.
> He was trembling a good deal now.[40]

Her attitude towards 'non-possessive, generous' sexual relationships may seem 'ahead of her time', which she considered 'always a bore', but this particular literary genre of socialist soft porn has never quite caught on.[41]

That these anomalous fictional encounters have their base in reality is no secret. For example, Jenni Calder recounts in her biography *The Burning Glass* (1997) – from an exchange of letters between Mitchison and the communist academic John Pilley in the 1930s – how the 'sharing of bodies' was a serious attempt to enact and embody the communal theories of their shared politics, and to overcome class division through physical intimacy.[42] Drawing on the same letters, Calder has also discussed Mitchison's own adoption of the role of 'priestess' aboard the Leningrad-bound boat in 1932. In this role she helped an unnamed comrade overcome their historically conditioned sexual repression.[43] Calder points out correctly that Mitchison's 'Russia Diary' does not contain this episode,[44] which she unearthed in Mitchison's letters to John Pilley, who had played 'priest' to her sexual acolyte. Calder also sees no direct portrayal of this relationship in *We Have Been Warned*.[45] But it appears to be exactly this episode which underlies much of the second chapter of 'Under the Red Flag', where on the boat to Leningrad Dione Galton leads the sexually repressed Donald MacLean –an out-of-work riveter and Communist Party member who has fled the UK after committing murder – into a tenderly described intimacy between comrades, riffing as she goes on the refrain 'What does a Socialist woman do?'[46] By this intimate act, which exposes the vulnerability of both 'lovers', she shows an extraordinary commitment to 'live the same way that I think'.[47] 'How could I', she asks Donald, 'leave you all oppressed and bound as you were'.[48] Dione feels it is her responsibility to free her 'tovarish' from his historical conditioning, and his socio-sexual oppression.

Another glimpse, explicitly in the Soviet context, is seen in the novelist Doris Lessing's account of the first formal meeting of the 1952 delegation in which she and Mitchison both participated. Mitchison apparently scolded the assembled Soviet representatives for having become amorously reactionary and hostile towards free love, after regaling them with tales of 'bathing nude in the Moskva River with her lover, and all kinds of good times'.[49] In We Have Been Warned there are several pages dedicated to Tom and Dione Galton swimming nude with the 'most lovely golden-brown' Oksana.[50] This kind of supporting evidence might reassure critics in their delicate game of reading reality into Mitchison's fiction, but we ought still to be wary of equating wholesale the lives of writer and protagonist, even when it is supported and explicitly encouraged. Memory itself can be misleading, and reflections that occur significantly later, following disillusionment, tend to tidy up what might in that latter period be conceived as ideological infringements and/or embarrassments.[51] Lessing's own account of the 1952 delegation is couched in uncertainty:

> I have to say that these memories of that trip are not shared – for instance, with Naomi, as I discovered when twenty-five years or so later I found we were not remembering the same things: it was not a question of remembering the same things differently but as if we had been on two different trips.[52]

Before moving on to Mitchison's second visit to the Soviet Union, it is worth noting that in 1979 she recalled returning to Britain 'not converted' and 'with a somewhat ambivalent feeling about the Communist Party'. She explains that 'They were them, I was I.'[53] Taken out of context, this feeling of ambivalence might be interpreted as 'being undecided [. . . or] unconvinced by the merit' of the Party.[54] But her ambivalent state is qualified with the following sentence: 'This comes out clearly in We Have Been Warned.'[55] If we read her political ambivalence through the smoked prism of her 1935 novel, a more psychoanalytical meaning of the word seems to pertain, i.e. 'the coexistence in one person of profoundly opposing emotions, beliefs, attitudes, or urges towards a person or thing'.[56] That emotional state surely does 'come out clearly' in the 1930s novel, as the public-school and ancient Sparta parallels discussed above begin to suggest. The effect on the fictional Galtons of their trip to the USSR in 1932 is profound and their adoption of the Marxist/Leninist worldview is thoroughgoing, even if it never quite shakes their commitment to the Parliamentary Labour Party. Mitchison's casual and softening use of 'somewhat' and the lack of precision of the term 'Communist Party' (does she mean the Commnist Party of

Great Britain, or the Comintern?) confuse what is being communicated here. Even the most convinced British communists felt deeply ambivalent towards both institutions at some point or other. Lessing retrospectively recounts how 'Going to the Soviet Union had stirred up emotions much deeper than the political. My thoughts and my emotions were at odds.'[57]

Mitchison may have returned to Britain 'unconverted', but she also returned with a suitcase full of typed notes. These notes include a summary of her experience of the Soviet way of life. She remarked at some length on the living and working conditions in the USSR, explaining that in spite of temporary shortages, including severe food shortages, and a clear need for continued improvements, such material improvements appeared to be in process. She stressed the benefits of complete job security and free access to higher education and leisure activities, irrespective of class or gender. She also reported positively on the integration of the lives of 'brain workers' and 'manual workers'; the intellectuals were not – as at home – 'cut off [. . .] from the social and political life of their country'.[58] She also reported, less positively, that:

> the whole country is being run on one rigid system of doctrine, as expounded by a German two generations ago . . . the doctrine admits no fundamental or philosophical criticism. It admits no real deviation. . . . It suppresses 'freedom of thought', 'open-mindedness' and various other qualities which are usually valued by intelligent people. It suppresses individualism, which has, up to now, produced much of the best of our ideas and actions. . . . It is a religious system, but it will not admit that it is.[59]

Mitchison then, identifying specifically as a 'non-Marxian', admits that her criticisms are those of an outsider: 'For those who believe in it [Soviet communism], it appears to be completely satisfying. . . . There is no such thing as boredom or individual fear, general love is made possible and happiness such as is very rare in other countries becomes almost a matter of course. . . . At present only a minority believe with this intensity, but with every year of propaganda and education, more and more come to believe, and to find it completely satisfying.'[60] Mitchison also seems anachronistically cognisant of the purges: 'The present rigid system is essentially based on the proletarian dictatorship. This has meant bloodshed and the elimination of a great many people who might have been doing good and useful work, simply from class bias.' The fact that widespread murder is reported in such a utilitarian manner is chilling. Presumably she was not aware of quite how much truth she was speaking.

She laments the inefficiency of Soviets and the extremely high levels of bureaucracy, pitching them as polar opposites to the hurrying Americans, for whom punctuality and efficiency 'has killed happiness'.[61] She notes that the USSR is not yet a dangerous trade rival, but when she questions whether or not it is 'a dangerous rival to our system', she replies 'Yes, thank goodness!' While a 'non-Marxian', she clearly remains hostile to the capitalist status quo in Britain, but the most important problem that she determines that the Soviets have solved is 'the sex question', 'simply by giving women complete economic freedom and equality'.[62] Mitchison remains cautious, however: 'It remains to be seen what will happen when a higher standard is possible, whether with the return of silk stockings there will be a return of sex appeal and complexities. But just now there is wonderfully little work for the psychiatrists in the USSR.'[63]

After a few notes on the use of anaesthetics, or lack thereof, for childbirth and abortions, and some more casual digressions, her typescript diary, which was never published, ends with the following flourish, alluding to Rupert Brooke's 'Beauty and Beauty' (1912):

> That place [USSR] has got me still, the quality of life there – The Earth is crying-sweet And scattering-bright the air, Eddying, dizzying, closing round, With soft and drunken laughter: Veiling all that may befall After – after. But it hasn't got me out of the Labour Movement. Not here. Not yet.[64]

## 1952

The Soviet Union to which Mitchison returned in 1952 was a very different place to the one she had left in 1932, or the one her younger self had hoped to find twenty years on. The Great Patriotic War (1940–5) had devastated the Soviet economy and killed around 26.6 million people, 13.7 per cent of their pre-war population.[65] As Doris Lessing hauntingly recounts in *Walking in the Shade* (1998), when the delegates visited Moscow's main dance hall and asked where the men were, their guide replied that 'the men were all killed in the war'.[66] There is significantly less published documentation about Mitchison's second trip to the USSR, given the absence of both a *We Have Been Warned*-style fictional account and a *You May Well Ask*-style autobiographical account.[67] Lessing's account then is all the more important and it provides a colourful recollection of events. Mitchison, however, cuts a decidedly unflattering figure in it.[68] As mentioned above, the two women remembered the trip quite differently. According to Lessing, Mitchison was constantly playing the antagonist, constantly criticising the Soviet Union and patronising its inhabitants. She was especially vocal on agricultural matters – 'That's a very nasty bit of erosion' – and aesthetic taste: 'everything was ugly or second-rate'.[69] Lessing recalls vividly Mitchison's 'Oxford drawl', which 'for some reason is emphasized in Russia'.[70] Lessing's Mitchison is an insensitive and opinionated snob. There is however significant archival material, including letters between the Foreign Commission of the Board of the Union of Soviet Writers (*Inostrannaya Komissiya Pravleniya Soyuza Sovetskikh Pisateley*, or *Inkomissiya*) and delegates, which brings some nuance to this characterisation, even if it does not entirely refute it. The correspondence records in a far friendlier light the group's activities both during and after the delegation. These have lain undisturbed in the Russian State Archive of Literature and Arts (RGALI) in Moscow for some years.[71]

Mitchison was among the first group of British writers to reach Moscow since the outbreak of the Second World War. The 1952 delegation was made up of six writers. In addition to Mitchison there was A. E. Coppard (1878–1957), a bow-tie-clad

English short story writer and convert to communism who was the nominal leader of the delegation; Douglas Young (1913–1973), a gigantic, kilt-wearing Scots poet and Dundee lecturer in Latin; Richard Mason (1919–1997), an English novelist and ex-military man; Arnold Kettle (1916–1986), a prominent Leeds-based Marxist literary critic who would later become the first Open University Professor of Literature; and of course Doris Lessing (1919–2013).

The Authors' World Peace Appeal, under whose auspices the trip took place, was co-founded in 1951 by Mitchison and the pacifist author Alex Comfort, neither of whom were communists. But it was quickly populated by known Soviet sympathisers and widely considered a front organisation and part of the Soviet cultural offensive. The Appeal's original aim was to warm up relations between the Soviet Union and the West through discussion and negotiation. It was conceived as a genuinely cross-party and international alliance promoting world peace. Even while Mitchison continued to advocate for the Appeal, the Labour Party blacklisted it in 1953.

The two Scots, Mitchison and Young, were certainly among the more sceptical delegates, but on their return both fought against a tide of virulent anti-communist sentiment to argue for the Soviet Union's peaceful intentions. It is safe to say that Mitchison fought considerably harder than Young, who after stirring up all sorts of trouble in the Soviet Union mainly, as Lessing notes, by 'playing the jackass in his kilt', was glad to get back to his books. In a letter to *Inkomissiya* interpreter Oksana Krugerskaya, Lessing reports: 'As for Douglas Young, he has retired back to the classic calm of his university, with the remark: "Well, all that socialist uplift was very enjoyable, but now to the realities of life."'[72]

On returning to Britain, members of the delegation were simultaneously hugely divided in their politics and their impression of the Soviet Union, and – counterintuitively perhaps – united in their support of the Soviet Union against the virulent anti-Soviet sentiment of the British press. This is perhaps best illustrated by Lessing's description of the AWPA meeting in London, in a letter to Krugerskaya:

> If I say that Mr Coppard lost his temper and was extremely rude to Mr Young, and that this helped matters enormously, I daresay you'll find it strange. But as the chairman said – it was our friend Mr Alex Comfort – this disagreement goes to show that although our delegation differed so strongly among themselves on politics, their agreement on the main issue – that the Soviet Union wants peace – is all the more impressive.
>
> The trouble was that poor Mr Coppard was so tired and exhausted with emotion. He had been exasperated all the time in your country by the bad manners of Mr Young, Mr Mason and our Naomi, and could no longer control himself. Naomi and he are no longer on speaking terms, but that's all right, now we are safely back again.[73]

Lessing was conscious of the fact that it would be hard for Mikhail Apletin and Krugerskaya, both *Inkomissiya* officials who were in closest contact with British writers at the time, to understand the fall-out of the delegation. Apletin and Krugerskaya were not shy in relaying their impressions of Mitchison in particular, confirming that some of Lessing's unfavourable reflections on her behaviour were accurate. But Lessing defended them in letters following the delegation, explaining that 'people like Naomi and Douglas and Richard, who appear outright reactionary in your country, are worth their weight in gold here. The simple effect on them of the stupid things people say and believe about your country, turns them into passionate partisans of it.'[74]

Mitchison was in fact the most successful member of the delegation from a Soviet point of view because as an established writer and public figure she had the opportunity to address many meetings, and she even managed to get into print a fairly positive view of the USSR and the Soviets' commitment to world peace. She wrote and saw through to print an article about the trip, not completely censored, in the *Sunday Pictorial* (predecessor to the *Sunday Mirror*). This was not easy. Lessing herself failed:

> When I got back, I rang my agents, and said I had just returned home from the Soviet Union, and could write articles. Reply: 'What were your impressions, favourable or not?' Me: ('guilefully') Oh, favourable, on the whole. Final answer: 'Well, if you want to write critical articles, or course there's a large market, and plenty of money, but I'm afraid not for pro-Soviet articles.' And the same occurred with the BBC.[75]

It is clear enough that Apletin and Krugerskaya had indeed been offended by Mitchison's behaviour on the trip, and neither were they especially impressed with her article:

> During your stay here N. [Naomi] asked us a great many questions about freedom of the press in our country. This was done in a manner that would suggest that no such problem existed in Britain, since freedom of the press was taken for granted there.
> Her first clash with reality, however, showed her how mistaken she had been. That distortion of her article in the *Sunday Pictorial* must have been a lesson to her.[76]

Lessing's defence of Mitchison continued. The *Pictorial* article draft she had seen was 'for the most part, extremely sympathetic, and the things she would criticise in private – as she did inside the delegation, she doesn't mention at all publicly'.[77] This was something of an unspoken code of Soviet sympathisers in the early 1950s. In order to deny the anti-Soviet press, people felt obliged to keep their reservations to themselves and speak of them only in private. This attitude is described retrospectively by Lessing in 1956 and 1957 when she, along with yet another generation of Western comrades, felt betrayed by Soviet foreign policy following the brutal suppression of the uprising in Hungary. How, Lessing queried, could the USSR play victim when it had the Hydrogen bomb?[78]

In the meantime, Mitchison struck up a friendly correspondence with Krugerskaya. She shared an interview she had given in the *Campbeltown Courier* about the Soviet

Union in which she tells of how delegates were struck by 'the high standard of reading matter', the 'peaceful development schemes', 'full employment', crèche provision enabling women to work more easily, and, last but not least, the 'peaceful intention of all the Russian people their feelings of personal friendliness and their convictions that it is possible for two countries with different political systems to exist side by side in the same world'.[79]

It was also through Mitchison's organisational skills, her friends in high places and, ultimately, her tears, that the Soviet return delegation happened at all:

> I took one of them [Soviet embassy officials] by the shoulders and shook him. I burst into tears, always I find effective with males. Heads were turned in our direction. There were quick consultations. Then the man said yes, it could be arranged. I took him by the ears and kissed him.[80]

But *Inkomissiya* remained distinctly frosty towards Mitchison, at least in their letters to 'Comrade Doris'.[81] The criticism levelled at Mitchison suggests that she returned to her estate and busied herself with housework:

> I think you are being unfair to Naomi. Let me hasten to say I hold no brief for Naomi, and I disagree with her violently about politics. But given her political convictions, and the sort of pressure that had been put on her, I think she's done not too badly. After all, what do we expect? Naomi has been on the Left Wing of the Labour Party here for her whole life. Do we expect her suddenly to become a communist? I think not. [. . .] Naomi came to the Soviet Union full of prejudice, and convinced that the Soviet Union was one of the war-mongers. She came away profoundly convinced that the Soviet Union desires peace.[82]

Lessing was frustrated by the way that Mitchison was targeted while those other delegates whom she sees as the real offenders are ignored:

> The person you should be angry with is our young friend Richard [Mason], but I suppose it is not his fault for being an idiot. Naomi has got several articles in the Press. She was successful where the rest of us failed, because her husband is in Parliament and she is too respectable to be suspected as a Communist – which is precisely *why* she is so valuable, Mr. Apletin. It is a pity the delegation didn't consist entirely of Naomis, from that point of view, because she has been able to tell far more people that your country is peacefully inclined, than any of the rest of us.

Presumably none the wiser, Mitchison remained busy trying to compile and pitch to publishers a collection of essays on the Soviet Union written by the AWPA delegates. Despite valiant efforts and putting aside personal grievances, she failed to find a publisher bold enough to print a balanced and mixed view of the Soviet Union at that moment in the Cold War. The mainstream press was reluctant to print anything remotely positive about the USSR, and the left-wing press presumably reluctant to print anything that could fan the anti-communist flames. From 1952 to 1956, which is when my trail goes cold, Mitchison did more than most for Anglo-Soviet and Soviet-Scottish relations. She supported visa applications, and provided personal invitations to several delegations of Soviet writers to the UK. These delegates included Alexei Surkov (1899–1983), who was the editor of the Commission's journal, *International Literature*, and then the magazine *Ogonëk*, which in 1957 had a circulation of 850,000; the poet, translator (famously of Robert Burns) and children's writer Samuil Marshak (1887–1964); Boris Polevoy (1908–1981), Soviet writer and war hero, most famous for his popular novel *A Story of a Real Man* (1946); and the Soviet professor of English literature who wrote a biography of Burns, Anna Arkadyevna Elistratova (1910–1974).[83]

The visit that made the biggest splash in the Scottish newspapers was that arranged by Emrys Hughes, MP for South Ayrshire. In January 1955 Marshak, Polevoy and Elistratova arrived in Scotland and attended several events associated with the Burns Festival.[84] The way had been paved by Mitchison's bridge-building as part of the AWPA, and the fact that Burns was a bestselling author in the 1950s USSR was enough to thaw the Cold War for a spell. According to the *Glasgow Evening Times*, nine editions of Burns had been printed in the Soviet Union and 460,000 copies had been sold by February 1955. Burns's spirit, Professor Elistratova told the *Glasgow Bulletin*, was 'very much akin to ours – his spirit of freedom, his belief in the dignity of the common man, his feelings of a need for friendship between nations'.[85] Mitchison wrote to Marshak after he had returned home, saying:

> I believe your visit did a tremendous amount of good. Many of the people who are applauding you probably realised for the first time that it was possible to break through any barriers. But I wish you could come in the summer and stay peaceably with me among the fisher folk and perhaps do some writing, as you used to in Scotland.[86]

Marshak replied:

> With greatest pleasure I dwell upon my short stay in Scotland. I was deeply moved by real love and devotion of common people to Burns' poetry and his memory.[87]

Almost a month before Khrushchev's 'Secret Speech' of 25 February 1956, in which the Soviet leader denounced his predecessor for his crimes and the cultivation of a cult of the individual, Mitchison wrote to Alexei Surkov expressing shock over 'how much is being blamed on Stalin now'. She continues:

> I don't like these sudden changes of opinion; that isn't how history works. No doubt he was difficult, especially in his old age, and doubtless some of his underlings were real hell. But I feel he is something like our own Cromwell – not an entirely laudable figure, but a great man in his time. He too took the blame for everything immediately after his death.[88]

The description of Stalin as a 'difficult' man, is a lesson to anyone trying to read historical events through Naomi Mitchison's idiosyncratic and domesticating worldview.

In the 'Cold War' typescript (1980) Mitchison reflects on a political gaffe she made in March 1953 which damaged the credibility of the AWPA:

> But I did put my foot into it heavily. . . . Stalin died: what should we do? I consulted the only other committee member I could get hold of . . . and we took it on ourselves to send a telegram of condolence to the Union of Soviet Writers. This resulted in two of the executive resigning and perhaps they were right. My feeling had been that it was rather like Great Aunt Emma from whom one has expectations but whose demise has been eagerly awaited: one wears black for the funeral.[89]

On the death of Stalin, Mitchison also wrote a letter to Krugerskaya:

> My thoughts have been very much with you and all our friends over in the Soviet Union, during these last days. I know how very sad you must be feeling; it was all so sudden, and you must all be feeling dazed and shaken as though you had lost a real father. Do convey our very real sympathy to all our friends. I have not been in touch with the rest of the party but I am sure we shall all be feeling the same and wanting to reach out a hand to you all.[90]

As we have seen, Mitchison's relationship with the USSR spanned over twenty years, from 1932 to at least 1956. Her first taste of Soviet communism was as a 'non-Marxian' socialist revolutionary, on the left of the Labour Party. Her pseudo-Gramscian sense about the difficulty of ushering in socialist system change in the developed democracy of Britain now reads as politically insightful.[91] Her determination to lend her cultural and political powers to the socialist cause and her passion for what she witnessed as the dizzyingly exciting potential of communism (especially on the personal and spiritual level of citizens) can be clouded by hindsight, ours and her own. It was a different Mitchison and a different Soviet Union who reunited in 1952. Her belief in social democracy was more convinced and she could no longer fall in love with a Soviet Russia war-torn and ideologically calcified by decades of Stalinism. Her cause had been to negotiate peace at the height of the Cold War, and in 1980 she reflected that she was not sure they had achieved much for their time and their pains: 'The situation repeats itself, the arguments are the same. The lies are the same. The politicians are almost the same. Is anybody going to listen to the writers? I am afraid this is most improbable.'[92]

## NOTES

1.  For an excellent discussion of the influence of the Russian Revolution on British culture see Matthew Taunton, *Red Britain: The Russian Revolution in Mid-Century Culture* (Oxford: Oxford University Press, 2019).

2. On Orwell's life experience and writing see e.g. Raymond Williams, *Orwell* (London: Collins, 1971) and Raymond Williams (ed.), *George Orwell: A Collection of Critical Essays* (Englewood Cliffs, NJ: Prentice Hall, 1974).

3. Nick Hubble, *The Proletarian Answer to the Modernist Question* (Edinburgh: Edinburgh University Press, 2017), p. 15.

4. Naomi Mitchison, *We Have Been Warned* (Glasgow: Kennedy & Boyd, 2012), p. 312.

5. Ibid. p. 312.

6. See Hubble, *Proletarian Answer*, pp. 10–21 on Mitchison's 'proletarian pastoral', drawing on William Empson, *Some Versions of Pastoral* (London: Chatto and Windus, 1935).

7. Mitchison, *We Have Been Warned*, pp. 414–16.

8. Ibid. pp. 412–16.

9. Naomi Mitchison, 'Socialist Britain', *Pakistan Horizon* 4:1 (1951), pp. 12–20 (p. 12). On the Socialist League see Ben Pimlott, *Labour and the Left in the 1930s* (New York: Cambridge University Press, 1977).

10. Randall Swingler, 'Apropos of Translation', *Greece and Rome* 7:19 (October 1937), p. 7. Other examples include Cecil Day-Lewis, 'An Expensive Education', *Left Review* 3 (February 1937), pp. 43–5. See also Edith Hall and Henry Stead, *A People's History of Classics: Class and Greco-Roman Antiquity in Britain and Ireland, 1689 to 1939* (London: Routledge, 2020), pp. 485–8.

11. Mitchison studied Latin at the Dragon School, Oxford, and claimed to communicate in 'dog Latin' with Professor Marti in *You May Well Ask* (London: Gollancz, 1979), p. 189 – where she also proudly deciphers the Latin on a Neronian coin. On the grammar grind see Christopher Stray, *Classics Transformed: Schools, Universities, and Society in England, 1830–1960* (Oxford: Clarendon Press, 1998).

12. Mitchison, *We Have Been Warned*, p. 295.

13. Ibid. p. 295.

14. See e.g. P. J. Rich, *Elixir of Empire: The English Public Schools, Ritualism, Freemasonry and Imperialism* (London: Regency, 1989); Robert Heussler, *Yesterday's Rulers: The Making of the British Colonial Service* (Syracuse, NY: Syracuse University Press, 1963).

15. The explicit linking of Classics with social class was nothing new; it forms part of a tradition of elite education reaching back to the early eighteenth century. See Hall and Stead, *A People's History*, pp. 29–33.

16. Clarendon Commission, *Report of the Commissioners on the Revenues and Management of Certain Colleges and Schools and the Studies Pursued and Instruction Given Therein*, 4 vols (London: Houses of Parliament, 1864), vol. 1, p. 31.

17. Heussler, *Yesterday's Rulers*, p. 110.

18. See J. A. Mangan, 'Eton in India: The Imperial Diffusion of a Victorian Educational Ethic', *History of Education* 7:2 (1978), pp. 105–18; J. A. Mangan, *The Games Ethic and Imperialism: Aspects of the Diffusion of an Ideal* (London: Viking, 1986); Rupert Wilkinson, *The Prefects: British Leadership and the Public School Tradition* (Oxford: Oxford University Press, 1964); John Raymond de Symons Honey, *Tom Brown's Universe: The Development of the English Public School in the Nineteenth Century* (London: Millington, 1977); Gauri Viswanathan, *Masks of Conquest: Literary Study and British Rule in India* (New York: Columbia University Press, 1989); and Edward Said, *Culture and Imperialism* (New York: Vintage, 1994), pp. 111–12.

19. Mitchison, *We Have Been Warned*, p. 302.

20. Ibid. p. 302.

21. On Sparta see Paul Cartledge, *The Spartans: An Epic History* (London: Pan, 2013).

22. Mitchison, *We Have Been Warned*, p. 298.

23. For several accounts see Michael David-Fox, *Showcasing the Great Experiment: Cultural Diplomacy and Western Visitors to the Soviet Union, 1921–1941* (Oxford: Oxford University

Press, 2012) and Doris Lessing, *Walking in the Shade* (London: Flamingo, 1998), pp. 58–79.

24. On the closeness of fact and fiction in *We Have Been Warned* see Jenni Calder, *The Burning Glass: The Life of Naomi Mitchison* (Dingwall: Sandstone Press, 2019), pp. 162–5; see also Hubble, *Proletarian Answer*, p. 18.

25. Hubble, *Proletarian Answer*, pp. 18–19.

26. Ben Harker, *The Chronology of Revolution: Communism, Culture, and Civil Society in Twentieth-Century Britain* (Toronto: University of Toronto Press, 2021), p. 5 and passim. Mitchison's sense comes across in both her diary 'Not here. Not yet', National Library of Scotland Acc. 10888/7, p. 119, and, as we can see in the following quotation, in her fictional writing.

27. Mitchison, *We Have Been Warned*, p. 382.

28. Peter Clarke and Richard Toye, 'Cripps, Sir (Richard) Stafford (1889–1952), politician and lawyer', *Oxford Dictionary of National Biography*, https://doi.org/10.1093/ref:odnb/32630 [accessed 28 March 2021]; Marc Stears, 'Cole, George Douglas Howard (1889–1959), university teacher and political theorist', *Oxford Dictionary of National Biography*, https://doi.org/10.1093/ref:odnb/32486 [accessed 28 March 2021]; A. J. A. Morris, 'Trevelyan, Sir Charles Philips, third baronet (1870–1958), politician', *Oxford Dictionary of National Biography*, https://doi.org/10.1093/ref:odnb/36553 [accessed 28 March 2021].

29. Mitchison, *We Have Been Warned*, p. 381.

30. Mitchison, *You May Well Ask*, pp. 193–4.

31. Ibid. pp. 204–5.

32. Naomi Mitchison, 'A Visit to Russia', typescript journal, National Library of Scotland Acc. 10899, p. 10.

33. Ibid. p. 4.

34. Mitchison, *You May Well Ask*, pp. 191–2.

35. V. M. Quirke, 'Haldane, John Burdon Sanderson (1892–1964), geneticist', *Oxford Dictionary of National Biography*, https://doi.org/10.1093/ref:odnb/33641 [accessed 27 March 2021].

36. Mitchison, *You May Well Ask*, p. 191.

37. Quirke, 'Haldane'; Mitchison, *You May Well Ask*, p. 203.

38. Ibid. p. 192.

39. Ibid. p. 192.

40. Mitchison, *We Have Been Warned*, p. 275.

41. Dorothy Sheridan (ed.), *Among You Taking Notes: The Wartime Diary of Naomi Mitchison* (Oxford: Oxford University Press, 1985), p. 181.

42. Calder, *The Burning Glass*, pp. 147–9. See also Phyllis Lassner, *British Women Writers of World War II: Battlegrounds of Their Own* (Basingstoke: Macmillan, 1998), p. 71.

43. Calder, *The Burning Glass*, p. 157.

44. 'A Visit to Russia', typescript journal, National Library of Scotland, Acc. 10899.

45. Calder, *The Burning Glass*, p. 157.

46. Mitchison, *We Have Been Warned*, pp. 237–43.

47. Ibid. p. 241.

48. Ibid. p. 241.

49. Lessing, *Walking in the Shade*, p. 63.

50. Mitchison, *We Have Been Warneed*, pp. 305–7.

51. For a discussion of Lessing's anti-communist account of her communist years see Stead, '"Comrade Doris": Lessing's Correspondence with the Foreign Commission of the Board of Soviet Writers in the 1950s', *Critical Quarterly* 63:1 (April 2021), pp. 35–47.

52. Lessing, *Walking in the Shade*, pp. 60–1.

53. Mitchison, *You May Well Ask*, p. 191.

54. *Oxford English Dictionary*, 'ambivalence, n.', 1.b.

55. Mitchison, *You May Well Ask*, p. 191.
56. *Oxford English Dictionary*, 'ambivalence, *n.*', 1.a.
57. Lessing, *Walking in the Shade*, pp. 80–1.
58. Mitchison, 'Not here. Not yet', p. 116.
59. Ibid. p. 116–17.
60. Ibid. p. 117.
61. Ibid. p. 117.
62. Ibid. p. 118.
63. Ibid. p. 118.
64. Ibid. p. 119.
65. Michael Haynes, 'Counting Soviet Deaths in the Great Patriotic War: A Note', *Europe-Asia Studies* 55:2 (2003), pp. 303–9 (p. 303); Vadim Erlikman, *Poteri narodonaseleniia v XX veke: spravochnik Потери народонаселения в XX веке: справочник* [in Russian] (Moscow: Russkaia panorama, 2004), p. 54. For comparison, UK and crown colonies lost around half a million, less than 1 per cent of pre-war population. See Michael Clodfelter, *Warfare and Armed Conflicts: A Statistical Reference to Casualty and Other Figures, 1500–2000*, 2nd edn (Jefferson, NC: McFarland, 2002), p. 582.
66. Lessing, *Walking in the Shade*, p. 74.
67. The 'Cold War' typescript at National Library of Scotland, Acc. 10888/5, is only thirteen pages long. Although it quotes from a draft of Mitchison's foreword to a planned volume of essays written by the AWPA delegates, the typescript appears to have been written in 1980, given its reference to the recent death of Olivia Manning (1909–1980).
68. Lessing, *Walking in the Shade*, pp. 58–79.
69. Ibid. pp. 69–70.
70. Ibid. p. 68.
71. Many thanks are due to Goryaeva Tatyana Mikhailovna, Director of RGALI, The Russian State Archive of Literature and Arts, for granting access to the archival materials discussed, and to the Leverhulme Trust for funding my research project, 'Brave New Classics', http://bravenewclassics.info (2016–19).
72. Doris Lessing to Oksana Krugerskaya, 6 August 1952, RGALI 631.26.706. For more information on Krugerskaya see Stead, 'Comrade Doris', pp. 38–9.
73. Ibid.
74. Doris Lessing to Oksana Krugerskaya, 3 August 1952, RGALI 631.26.706.
75. Ibid.
76. Mikhail Apletin to Doris Lessing, 18 October 1952, RGALI 631.26.708.
77. Doris Lessing to Oksana Krugerskaya, 6 August 1952, RGALI 631.26.706.
78. Doris Lessing to Boris Polevoy (21.01.1957); RGALI, 631.26.830. For discussion see Stead, 'Comrade Doris', pp. 42–5.
79. Extract [no visible date] from *Campbeltown Courier* enclosed as cutting in Naomi Mitchison to Oksana Krugerskaya, 2 August 1952, RGALI 631.26.708.
80. Mitchison, 'Cold War', p. 9.
81. For an account of Lessing's correspondence with *Inkomissiya* see Stead, 'Comrade Doris'.
82. Doris Lessing to Mikhail Apletin, 20 April 1953, RGALI 631.26.708.
83. Anna Vaninskaya, 'Introduction: Scotland and Russia since 1900', *Studies in Scottish Literature* 44:1 (2019), pp. 3–10 (pp. 8–9). On Russian Burns see Robert Vlach, 'Robert Burns through Russian Eyes', *Studies in Scottish Literature*: 2:3 (1964), pp. 152–62.
84. Images of the press cuttings about the trip are presented at http://www.scotland-russia.llc.ed.ac.uk/robert-burns as part of the *Scotland–Russia: Cultural Encounters (1900–)* project.
85. These press cuttings are found in RGALI 631.26.708. They were originally published in the *Glasgow Bulletin*, 18 January 1955 and the *Glasgow Evening Times*, 18 January 1955.
86. Naomi Mitchison to Samuil Marshak, 7 February 1955, RGALI 631.26.708.

87. Samuil Marshak to Naomi Mitchison, 28 February 1955, RGALI 631.26.708.
88. Naomi Mitchison to Alexei Surkov, 29 January 1956, RGALI 631.26.708.
89. Mitchison, 'Cold War', p. 12.
90. Naomi Mitchison to Oksana Krugerskaya, 8 March 1953, RGALI 631.26.706.
91. The *Prison Notebooks*, in which Antonio Gramsci developed his ideas for alternative revolutionary strategies in Western countries, were written between 1929 and 1935, but not translated into English, or widely available before the early 1970s. See Ben Harker, *The Chronology of Revolution*, pp. 7–8.
92. Mitchison, 'Cold War', p. 13.

# 7. Fire or Blood? Aestheticising Resistance in Naomi Mitchison's *The Blood of the Martyrs*

*Megan Faragher*

This chapter will argue that Naomi Mitchison's late 1930s fiction represents a transition in her writing from an aesthetic approach informed by magic and mysticism to one increasingly informed by materialism. Of course, in adopting a more materialist approach to aesthetics, Mitchison would be far from the first interwar writer to be recognised for doing so. The re-emergence of a gritty materialism is evident in interwar novels like Walter Greenwood's *Love on the Dole*, George Orwell's *Down and Out in Paris and London* (both 1933), or John Sommerfield's *May Day* (1936). But, unlike these other writers, Mitchison was never one to dwell on the contemporary moment; her interwar fiction was almost exclusively historical in nature – not set in the streets of the present, but in the thoroughfares of the past. This made her brand of materialism more oblique, as she aimed to wrest the same political effects from stories about ancient Greece and Rome as one might normally draw from stories of the contemporary working class. Overwhelmingly, interwar writers were moved by an urgent presentism and compelled to sweep the cobwebs of modernism away in pursuit of aesthetic approaches more suitable to the times. Like her contemporaries, who shifted focus away from the sacrosanct realm of psychological interiority to the raw material of everyday life, Mitchison also turned away from psychologising in her fiction in the later years of the 1930s; more specifically, she turned away from the more mystical elements of psychology she had often utilised in her fiction up until that point. While myth, folklore and magic emerge in her earlier novels, Mitchison's late 1930s work, beginning with *The Blood of the Martyrs* (1939), reimagines historical fiction as situational, representing history as a series of punctuated political moments. Mitchison was prompted to revisit the politics of resistance in her writing by a series of life-altering journeys in the mid-1930s, during which she met destitute sharecroppers in the American South and Austrians traumatised by the civil war of 1934. These material witnesses to interwar political tensions made her own accounts of political events more material in turn. Mitchison's reprised approach to historical fiction – her shift from a spiritual understanding of politics to a more activist one – is an effort to realise a practical utopianism in light of political unrest and offer insights into how historical fiction, if rendered through a political sense, can provide guidance to the institutional nature of totalitarian regimes in the late 1930s.

One symbolic touchpoint stands in for the transformation I am tracing in Mitchison's work: her allusions to the Spartan king Kleomenes III. Kleomenes III is best known for inciting a failed populist uprising against Ptolemy IV, after which he committed suicide; his story intrigues Mitchison, who revisits it in several works, including *The Corn King and the Spring Queen*, published in 1930, and *The Blood of the Martyrs*, published nine years later. And while the repetition of this reference across both *The Corn King and the Spring Queen* and *The Blood of the Martyrs* might suggest a stalwart consistency in Mitchison's fiction, the radically different contexts of the reference in these novels mark a transformation of her historical fiction in the late 1930s. From her first historical novel, *The Conquered* (1923), to *The Corn King and the Spring Queen*, Mitchison tended to favour historical characters whose status was defended or elevated by the harnessing of mystical, supernatural authority. In *The Corn King*, this is most dramatically evinced by the death of Kleomenes, who dies by suicide at the climax of the novel having failed to stage a populist coup against an increasingly authoritarian power. But his posthumous iconic status is not secured by his rhetorical or political legacy; rather, his role as a symbol of proto-socialism is safeguarded by the actions of Erif Der, a witch from the fictional city Marob, who is in Sparta having been exiled from her own community. Erif Der is moved by Kleomenes's egalitarian politics and, to protect his corpse from Roman desecration, she morphs into a snake and slithers in protective vigil for the dead King. Erif Der's actions make the citizens 'more likely to worship' the dead king; as the tutor Sphaeros argues, '[t]hey will do that for Kleomenes when he is dead for the sake of a serpent, who would not lift a finger to help him when he was alive for the sake of his ideas.'[1] It is thus not the revolutionary insurrection of Kleomenes that moves the people to action, but the mystical powers of Erif Der, who lends Kleomenes a power greater than he acquired in the political sphere; it is only through the pure magic of creation that socialist values disseminate.

While mystical intervention remained a mainstay of Mitchison's oeuvre throughout the 1920s and 1930s, as epitomised in *The Corn King*, Kleomenes's re-emergence in the pages of *The Blood of the Martyrs* not only eschews the magic and mysticism of the prior novel, but actively rejects it. The allusion to Kleomenes in *The Blood of the Martyrs* arises not in the context of fifth-century BC Greece, but in that of first-century AD Rome, featuring Nero and his apocryphal fiddling at the burning city. Argas, one of a band of Christian slaves featured in the novel, contextualises Jesus's importance for his master Beric. For Argas, Jesus is not important due to spiritual power, but because he is one of a long list of populist philosophers who challenged authority to secure economic justice: 'Spartacus and Eunus and Kleomenes of Sparta and Nabis and Jesus Christ,' Argas lists, '[t]hey were all of them for the oppressed ones, the common people.'[2] Kleomenes thus emerges in *The Blood of the Martyrs* as an ideological precursor to Jesus who 'freed the slaves in Sparta and divided the land; but the rich got him in the end, and he was killed and flayed and staked in Egypt'.[3] The magical story of the snake, recounted in *The Corn King*, is absent here as an explanation of Kleomenes' cult status amongst anti-authoritarian rebels. But also absent, perhaps more surprisingly, is any reference to the miraculous Jesus; what replaces him is a Jesus most notable for his protean socialist vision. Even the news of Jesus's resurrection is met with a shrug by followers who simply reflect that '[h]e was of such a kind that this sort of thing might happen.'[4] While Mitchison was liberal in her reference to mystic or spiritual power in her early historical novels, *The Blood of the Martyrs* repeatedly, overtly and conspicuously rejects such tropes. In her contemporaneous polemic *The Moral Basis of Politics* (1938), Mitchison identifies Kleomenes' rebellion as one of many 'crude dilemmas of an intolerable situation'.[5] Such 'crude dilemmas' were ones Mitchison grappled with anew after seeing the horrendous conditions of Arkansas sharecroppers.

Mitchison's early work in the 1930s harnessed the supernatural power of individuals, particularly women, to symbolise the potential of collective action. However, after extensive travels in the decade and recognition of fascism's more mystical undercurrents, Mitchison, too, makes the 'material turn'. In tracing the transition in her historical fiction – from plots fuelled by magic and mysticism to those fuelled by collective action – this chapter contends that Mitchison's approach to the historical novel was transformed by the bravery and solidarity she witnessed in her travels of the 1930s: particularly in the United States of America, where she was confronted by both scenes of abject oppression and instances of moving solidarity. But additionally, Mitchison's rejection of the supernatural was informed by an increased scepticism towards the aestheticisation of politics she witnessed in the emergent Third Reich. These two factors pushed her towards a new model of historical fiction that she believed more capable of working towards a utopian political praxis born of community, love and friendship.

## MITCHISON'S INTERWAR TRAVELS

Mitchison's travels in the 1930s influenced her for the rest of her life. She spent the summer of 1932 in the Soviet Union on a trip with the Fabians, where she listed her areas of expertise as '[a]rchaeology and abortion'.[6] Then, in February 1934, she went alone to Vienna amidst a civil war, documenting the atrocities of the violent Nazi occupation and the repression of the left; her records from that time were published by Victor Gollancz as *Vienna Diary* (1934). A year later, in February 1935, she and her friend Zita Baker made their trip to the American South, going against advice to not give strangers 'lifts' and leading a march with the Southern Tenant Farmers' Union in Arkansas.[7] In response to this hectic time in Mitchison's life, Olaf Stapledon asked her in a letter, 'Don't you go the pace too much in everything you do?'[8] She certainly did. Upon return from these journeys and the passing of her father John Scott Haldane, Mitchison settled at Carradale in Argyll just in time to house war-displaced refugees. But her time in America had inordinate value for her and even at age ninety-three she remained a member of the Southern Tenant Farmers' Union (STFU), an organisation with which she had first made contact over half a century earlier, and which sought to protect the wage-earning potential of sharecroppers and restore dignity to their work.

While Mitchison admits her debt to historians like Martin Charlesworth and Guy Chilver in her dedication to *The Blood of the Martyrs*, her memoir recognises another influence: 'the shadow was beginning to fall, Hitler over Europe'.[9] The preface of *The Blood of the Martyrs* makes clear the relevance of early Christian persecution to the contemporary moment. Thanking historians, who provided the backbone of her work and who helped 'guide and tidy' her work, she credits both the 'Austrian socialists in the counter-revolution of 1934' and the 'sharecroppers in Arkansas in 1935'. In both instances she writes that these groups, in their resistance to oppression, stood 'against tyranny and superstition and the worship of the State, witnesses of the humanity and reason and kindliness, whose blood is crying to us now and whose martyrdom will help to build the Kingdom which we all want in our hearts, and whose temporary manifestations in friendship and comradeship and collaboration give purpose and delight to our lives and deaths'.[10] The touching nature of this preface notwithstanding, the citation of 'superstition' as one of the forces 'against' which both activists and her novel are ranged suggests the pivotal transition in an aesthetic approach that had previously cited magic and superstition as key allegories for political resistance. But it was not only the Arkansas sharecroppers and the displaced Viennese who inspired a retrospective examination of early Christians; the inspiration worked both ways. In *The Moral Basis of Politics* Mitchison outlines the turn towards authoritarian hero-worship, arguing that people were 'breaking the second commandment as effectively as though we had set up the statue of Caesar-as-state-God and sprinkled incense before it'.[11] Under the conditions of emergent totalitarianism, she argues that 'we may now sympathize with the early Christian martyrs who refused to do this, although up till recent years their actions seemed rather ludicrous to those of us who were no longer believers'.[12] If the dispossessed in Austria and Arkansas refocused Mitchison's understanding of political intervention towards humanity, reason and kindliness, they also helped her re-evaluate how she had understood early Christian resistance to the Romans outside of a purely spiritual lens. This transition radically diverges from her previous work, which had consistently privileged superstition and spiritualism as symbols for political resistance.

One need only look briefly to her other works of the 1930s, including *The Corn King*, the story 'The Powers of Light' (1933) and *We Have Been Warned* (1935), to identify how important superstition and fantasy had been to her writing only a few years prior to this preface in *The Blood of the Martyrs*. Besides using her witchery to memorialise the dead King Kleomenes, Erif Der of *The Corn King* deploys it early in the novel to stage a coup against her soon-to-be-husband and reinstate her biological family to the monarchy of the fictional Marob. Her magical powers, though met with fear by those who wish to unseat her, nevertheless give her the power to determine her own fate within Marob. Erif Der's magic is passed down from her mother and grants Erif a circumscribed realm of female autonomy, symbolised when she commits patricide during a communal ritual. As Mitchison writes when Erif Der refuses to use her magic to harm her husband: 'she would be free again, to start another life of her own, not his nor her father's'.[13] In much of the novel, Erif Der battles to find her way back to Marob, banished for the curse that patricide has placed on the community. Exiled to Sparta, she backs the populist king Kleomenes and is freed from her curse after her metamorphosis into a snake.

'The Powers of Light' and *We Have Been Warned* revive similar themes in radically different contexts, the former staged in a primitive past and the latter set in the contemporary moment. 'The Powers of Light' presents a concentrated example of Mitchison's mystical vision of community formation, featuring two magicians, the female 'Fire Head' and the male 'Surprised One', who are castigated and abused by a community that simultaneously relies on them and fears them. Fire Head, able to produce sparks from her hair, is shunned when her powers aren't useful. The same is true for the Surprised One who, though he can materialise animals by drawing them, continues to be spurned: 'They would not let him be one of Them. They threw things at him and called him bad.'[14] 'The Powers of Light' mirrors from *The Corn King* the abject position of the mystics who harness the potential to control their communities. This short story emphasises that the position of such empowered beings is akin to that of the artist herself, who attempts to harness her power for the benefit of humanity but is cast aside and isolated by dint of her talents. The same dynamic will hold for Mitchison's only novel set in the interwar period, *We Have Been Warned*, where the powerful ghost Green Jean acts as a soothsayer for the leftist political wife Dione Galton. While Jean knows the truth about interwar politics, including the reality of a rising proto-fascist tide in England, Dione recognises that superstition would be met with horror by the men in her life. In the end, Jean's predictions are more accurate than those of cynical, rational men. Much the same reversal of fortunes takes place in 'The Powers of Light', when Fire Head and Surprised One abandon hostile tribes, only to find a new community that accepts their eccentricities and embraces their differences.

So when Mitchison writes that *The Blood of the Martyrs* is a testimony 'against tyranny and superstition and the worship of the State', it suggests an about-face from her longstanding interest in such superstition. And while it is undeniable that *The Blood of the Martyrs* is informed by the brave acts of resistance Mitchison witnessed amongst the sharecroppers and Austrians, it still may remain surprising to see Mitchison, so bound to superstitious allegories in her earlier writing, turning so actively against them. Arguably, the seeds for this rejection were inspired not only by her travels but also by fascism itself, which had taken on the very mystical undertones that had so marked her earliest fiction. Interwar discussions with Olaf Stapledon circled around this question of mysticism, with Stapleton insisting that the 'belief in magic [. . .] was part of a general sickness of the modern mind, a sickness that was producing fascism'.[15] As Stapledon cites, fascism's mystical undercurrents were becoming increasingly evident as the 1930s progressed. This connection between superstition and fascism would have been apparent to Mitchison, who identified in fascist ideology the mythologisation of the Aryan race, and probably noted the importation of the occultist symbolism of the Thule Society in the iconic swastika: a symbol wielded against both the Black sharecroppers of Arkansas and the Jews of Vienna.

Other of Mitchison's 1930s writings suggest the problematic homology between authoritarianism and the aestheticisation of politics achieved by means of occultist tropes. Mitchison wonders whether, in the interwar, it was really possible to 'do anything from above' or to produce a more just society by weaponising symbols of transcendence.[16] And while Mitchison had once been moved by Gerald Heard's spiritualist theory of human development, which argued that human evolution might lead to a species of peaceable telepaths (see Chapter 3 in this volume), she began to theorise that community-mindedness might be better realised in a practical sense. She and Stapledon began to turn away from theories of Heardian utopian telepathy; by 1942, Stapledon was arguing for the development of 'personality-in-community', the creation of a perfect social science that allowed for both individual agency and group cohesion. Mitchison would theorise something similar, identifying it with the German term *Sittlichkeit*: a secular negotiation of community that eschewed spiritualist conceits.[17] She likewise recognised that authoritarian beliefs were metaphysical in nature, stating that some political theories 'are obviously fantastic; they bring in some extra factor which is by definition beyond proof, and must either be believed in devoutly or else considered as nonsense, but cannot be rationally argued about'.[18] As Mitchison began to privilege the ethical obligations of the individual towards the community she witnessed in her travels, her fiction would likewise evince a similar turn, focusing on the practical construction of cohesive social groups that eschewed any sublimation of the individual will to authoritarian or transcendent agents.

## THE INDIVIDUAL IN HISTORY IN *THE BLOOD OF THE MARTYRS*

It was not just in her political works that Mitchison turned towards a more practical historical framework. The abject conditions of the Christians in *The Blood of the Martyrs*, faced with beatings, whippings and brutal deaths, are clearly inspired by the conditions she found in the depressed American South. When Mitchison visited Marked Tree, Arkansas in February 1935, she was horrified by the farmers' living conditions. In response, she wrote a spate of articles in which she tried to fulfil her duty to bear witness: 'the world should know what was happening to them'.[19] In the STFU archive lies a draft document from Mitchison, probably of a speech she gave after touring the farmers' homes. Her urgency in this early document was mirrored in the public writings and addresses that followed, but the tenor of the address was more personal and evocative: 'I have traveled over most of Europe and part of Africa but I have never seen such terrible sights as I saw yesterday among the sharecroppers of Arkansas.'[20] She wrote later in *The New Statesman* that one 'cannot travel' in America 'without being struck ill all the time by evidence of poverty, inefficiency – never have I seen such an untidy countryside, even in Poland or the Balkans'.[21] In another article she states that the sharecroppers 'are being starved to death, and not so slowly, either'.[22] But while Mitchison's pleas to the public sought to draw awareness to the farmers' plight, her private address to them proposed a more revolutionary solution: 'The sharecroppers have got to be treated as decent people [. . .] It will be better if this is done constitutionally and peaceably. But, if such means fail othermeans [*sic*] must be used. Justice carries the scales of peace, but it also carries a sword.'[23]

Presbyterian pastor and American socialist presidential candidate Norman Thomas inspired Harry Leland Mitchell and Clay East to form the STFU in 1934. The goal of the organisation was to highlight the structural inequities built into the New Deal's Agricultural Adjustment Administration, which privileged the power of landowners over sharecroppers, exacerbating economic inequities between the two.[24] The STFU was thus radical on two fronts. Its overt socialism was a threat to extant economic hierarchies. But additionally, the focus on class equity necessarily crossed racial lines. The STFU's cross-racial composition was a factor that Mitchison emphatically underscored. In the *New Statesman*, she argued that the STFU 'was dangerous, not only as any Union is dangerous to employers who have always had the best of the bargain so far, but also because in it, for the first time, there is absolutely no distinction between white and colored men and women'.[25] In a separate article she stated: 'For the first time in the United States, perhaps in the whole world, Negroes and white people are standing together in complete mutual trust and loyalty and friendship [. . .] The "poor whites" and the grandchildren of the slaves were banding together – they could no longer be played off against one another.'[26] This solidarity across demographics is recalled in *The Blood of the Martyrs*, which brings together Black slaves, white slaves, prostitutes, shopkeepers and even the disempowered Beric. The ability of political collectivity to unite such a wide and diverse cross-section of people was a point that Mitchison identified in Arkansas, highlighted for readers across the globe, and explored in fiction.

Like her other historical novels, *The Blood of the Martyrs* is dense with characters who represent intersecting networks of agency; the diversity of characters, crossing lines of gender, sex and race, mirrors the diversity amongst the unionised farmers that had so inspired Mitchison. As *The Blood of the Martyrs* reveals a cast of increasingly diverse characters, it traces the larger networks that encompass them, picturing the individual's part in a larger social network of resistance. Characters like Mannases, Josias, Eunice, Argas, Lalange and Sophrosyne are all slowly revealed as readers progress, all representative of the subaltern class of oppressed Christians who struggle to hide their faith from prying Roman eyes. But despite the abundance of characters, the novel revolves around Beric, the son of a former Briton king. Beric, disinherited by Roman imperial victory, finds himself between two worlds. Still treated to the privileges of his status as a courtesy, but denied the former authority of his father, Beric is both a part of Roman society and outside of it; he is even able to carry on an ill-fated affair with King Crispus's daughter Flavia, who is destined to marry Candidus. A liminal figure in Roman society, though not so much reduced as to be enslaved, Beric is confronted with his abjection by the marriage of Flavia, who rejects him as an 'impudent foreigner'.[27] Beric breaks down, only to be consoled by the prostitute Lalange, who ushers in his slow, careful conversion to Christianity. Increasingly entangled in a network of underground Christian rebels, the complexity of which Mitchison reveals throughout the novel, Beric inevitably finds himself torn between the desire to maintain his liminal social standing in the Roman state and his increasingly genuine affection for the down-and-out Christian slaves who have given him community and solace.

Beric's ambiguous position between two communities – Roman and Christian – suggests the possibility of institutional interventions that Beric might make using his cultural capital on behalf of the Christians. Like Mitchison, who uses her privilege to amplify the voices of the sharecroppers as war casts its shadow over Europe, Beric finds himself emboldened by connections to the Roman state while also being cowed by its power. But Mitchison is always keen to remind readers that Beric's liminal institutional power might compromise his activism. Beric has slaves, whom he supposedly retains in order to mask his complicity with Christian resistance. He even buys his eventual lover Argas in an effort to protect him from worse treatment by another master. Despite his complicity in parts of the oppressive Roman system, Beric is still selflessly accepted among the Christians, finally proving his dedication to the faith in the text's most tactile moment, when he takes part in a foot-washing ceremony. Such feelings of welcome are reflected by Mitchison's writings to STFU leadership, which thank them 'for having made me a Member of the union – that made me feel very proud'.[28]

In *The Blood of the Martyrs* small symbolic kindnesses stand in for the acts of magic and ritual that are featured in early novels like *The Corn King*. The prostitute Lalange explains Christian rituals of foot-washing in *The Blood of the Martyrs* in such terms: 'It's one of the funny things we do, to remind us that we're all one another's servants.'[29] As Lalange suggests, Christian rituals in Mitchison's novel are never designed to provide a magical method to overturn authority or stage revolution. Rather, rituals – which maintain pride of place in the Mitchison oeuvre – become symbols of collective identity and action. Mitchison pauses on the intimacy of the scene of foot-washing as freewoman Euphemia comments on Beric's 'trimmed toe-nails' and the slave Niger comments on the 'funny' look of his 'black hands on [Beric's] white legs'.[30] One after another, the Christians wash Beric's feet. That is, until Dapyx, the most abject of the slaves, with a boil on his neck, approaches. It is here that Mitchison reminds us of the limits of Beric's membership in this community, as Dapyx expresses hesitation about washing Beric's feet; Beric even attempts to think 'of something to say which would stop Dapyx being afraid of him [. . .] [b]ut he couldn't'. Dapyx washes Beric's feet, though Beric notes that '[Dapyx's] hands were shaking,' afraid of physical contact with someone more privileged than he.[31]

The stakes of this scene heighten when the positions are reversed and it is Beric's turn to wash the feet of the slaves. This reversal provides Mitchison a venue for emphasising the power of solidarity as greater than that of magic. Beric recognises that, in this symbolic act, he will be relinquishing his privilege: 'Beric knelt and undid [Manasses'] sandals. It was the hell of a queer mixed feeling. He'd never be the same again, never be able to be a master. A kind of panic caught him and he stopped, holding on to the edges of the basin, his head down.'[32] But Beric overcomes his anxiety and begins to relish in the delight of giving up his position of power. He kisses Lalange's feet as he washes them, and Mitchison details the line of feet as they move through Beric's hands, some 'old and white', some with 'interesting scars', 'a corn', and the feet of Niger, which 'had a different shape and smell from the others'.[33] When the turn comes for the anxious Dapyx, sores on his feet, to be washed, Beric is compelled to reveal the levelling of their status: 'Now listen, Dapyx, and try to be sensible. You still think nothing has altered between us except some magic. But everything's altered. I wouldn't be washing your feet for any magic! I do it because of our being in the Kingdom together, and you're stopping me getting into the Kingdom by hating me and fearing me still. I've washed your feet to show you that this is nonsense.'[34] The Kingdom here, far from symbolising a type of transcendent intervention that upends the social status of Beric or the Christians, represents the consecration of political community: it is this power of the 'Kingdom together', that justifies Beric's actions, not 'magic'.

But solidarity, like foot-washing, is a messy business, and this scene of intimacy in *The Blood of the Martyrs* cannot be left without a return to an important moment in Mitchison's travels to Arkansas. When she recalls her trip with Zita Baker, she notes the ramifications of cross-racial physical contact for Black people in the United States:

> I was asked to speak at open-air meetings; the custom was to begin every speech with a Bible quote, of which there are plenty applicable. I had no trouble with this, but my poor chairman at one meeting had bad trouble, for he put his hand on my shoulder introducing me: I was a white woman, he a black man. Someone duly shot into his house, but luckily he was warned and under the bed.[35]

The intimacy – and danger – of touch, which for Mitchison's early Christians is an act both of resistance and of solidarity, had been foreshadowed years earlier in this haunting vignette of American prejudice. At the end of *The Blood of the Martyrs*, Beric attempts to save the vulnerable Christians by trying to assassinate a high Roman operative. Yet in trying to save them, Beric escalates their oppression, leading to the deaths of most active Christians at the Circus Maximus. The violent reprisals against the Black activists in Arkansas live on in this novel, which stages the danger of political allegiance and solidarity in the face of injustice.

## TYRANTS DOING WHAT THEY HAVE ALWAYS DONE: MITCHISON'S REALIST HISTORY AS INSTITUTIONAL CRITIQUE

Mitchison sees friendship and community, above all, as ways of countering the challenges to individual freedom; the construction of cohesive social counter-movements, like the Christians, allows for the identification and critique of authoritarianism. *The Blood of the Martyrs* provides a model for meeting the historical moment, recognising the importance of institutional knowledge in the production of revolutionary counter-programming. As tutor Nausiphanes says in the novel, '[o]ne begins asking questions about the Universe [. . .] and ends by asking questions about particular institutions. And the answers may be rather startling.'[36] This reference, embracing institutional critique and social agency (as opposed to metaphysical questions about 'the Universe'), crystallises Mitchison's shifting focus, capturing the transition of her historical novels from ones that evoke the universal power of magic to those that embrace the value of communal political resistance, informed by an intimate knowledge of institutionalised authoritarianism. Mitchison's depictions of persecution (as institutional dysfunction) and her depiction of Christians (as a collective agency seeking to correct this dysfunction) revisit and revise her earlier political landscapes. While Erif Der's metamorphosis in *The Corn King* enables the restoration of her role in Marob, the family of Christians in *The Blood of the Martyrs* will inevitably be sacrificed. And yet, the public sacrifice of Christians at the Circus Maximus presents these deaths as means to an end: a civic demonstration of solidarity that inspires others to privilege community over authority. Even the guarantee of Christ's return and its promise of salvation is jettisoned by key Christian leaders in favour of the continued personal fight for justice. Christian ritual and doctrine, far from ushering in miraculous spiritual transformation, are always circumscribed as practices of intimacy and friendship, not as calls for divine intervention. After the Romans successfully quash the Christian resistance, Christian leader Eunice emphasises the stakes of this strategy by recognising the enormity of institutional power. She cautions Christians not to interpret authoritarianism as an eschatological omen. While Hadassa imagines the cruelty of Nero as precursor to the return of a Christ who will restore justice by fiat, Eunice is quick to remind her: 'This isn't the Coming, Hadassa. It's only a tyrant doing what they have always done.'[37] This explanation of injustice, framing it as a natural outgrowth of institutional authoritarianism, is witnessed directly in Mitchison's new political interventionism and reinforced by her journalistic interventions at the time, which raised public awareness of the institutional networks in which injustice proliferated.

Mitchison presents the Christians in *The Blood of the Martyrs* as a counter-institution: peace-loving, anti-authoritarian and, most importantly, democratic. Furthermore, she emphasises the importance of belonging for the consecration of counter-institutional organisation, demonstrated by foot-washing ceremonies and baptisms. She also recognises that any counter-institution must consider its tactical positioning; as various Christian leaders are arrested or killed, practical matters of leadership and meeting spaces become paramount. We even see the importance of counter-institutional structure emerge in Mitchison's chapter titles. While she names early chapters after individual characters ('Beric', 'Argas', 'Euphemia'), these titles evolve first into the names of rituals ('The Sign of the Cross', 'The Second Sacrament') and then, finally, into titles about tactics and counter-strategies, including 'Ends and Means', 'Difficulties of a United Front' and, perhaps the most enticing final chapter title in literature, 'Business Meeting'. In this final chapter, Mitchison describes the origins of a new generation of Christians, converted by the slaughter at the Circus Maximus. In other words, the counter-tacticians succeed, even if they never live to see the fruits of their labour.

In her interactions with the STFU leaders, Mitchison came to appreciate both the mundanity of bureaucratic resistance and its efficiency. It is perhaps for this reason that Mitchison encourages the readers of *The Moral Basis of Politics* to join the group

Mass-Observation in Britain, which might unearth the dangerous 'superstitions' that align with authoritarian movements.[38] In *The Moral Basis of Politics* Mitchison draws parallels between standard national mythologies and those fuelled by religion and superstition, locating in both the selfsame structures that 'bind us into a cake of custom'.[39] But the fragility of such institutional mythologies is evident. Mitchison argues that authoritarian mythologies are more liable to falter, as 'Nazi mythology will also fail as soon as economic pressure which it is under and which has created it has relaxed'.[40] In the face of these false mythologies, like Britain's Empire Day, which are vulnerable to their own hypocrisy, Mitchison cites the historical move-ment of Christianity, which turned from fragile mythologies to the ur-mythology: democracy. She counts 'democracy' as one of a number of 'transcendent' ideas, adding that 'an obvious parallel is the Christian idea of love [. . .] there is always an element of stretching out from the best one can produce towards something better still. So with democracy.'[41] While many of Mitchison's mythologies fall by the wayside, she remains steadfast to civic mythologies with transcendent aims, like democracy, which does not wilt under the light of sceptical examination. *The Moral Basis of Politics* suggests that this new pragmatic approach to politics might impact her trajectory as a writer: 'I am constantly attempting to turn power into something else: as with the power held by Erif, Tarrik and Philylla in *The Corn King and the Spring Queen*.'[42] But in *The Blood of the Martyrs*, she does not turn power *into some-thing else* (transforming her 'magic' to some other superstition), but reconceptualises power as real, tangible and consequential. Power was something to be taken literally and seriously. Mitchison thus forces readers to understand power as political, and resistance to that power as involving personal sacrifice.

To trace the costs and benefits of collective sacrifice, *The Blood of the Martyrs* repeatedly returns to the nuances of political theory. As Beric becomes more embed-ded with the Christians, he is less interested in the gospel than he is in 'the theory of the State and its rights over individuals'.[43] In the surreptitious meeting with his childhood tutor Nausiphanes, Beric looks for sources to help him understand the state, which has increased its violence against the Christians; Nausiphanes' privi-leging of institutional critique over universal critique, as I have noted, serves as a solution to the question of political resistance. Mitchison drives this point home when the Apostle Paul makes a cameo appearance in the novel. Paul argues that the main point of Christianity is that someone had 'died to show [Paul] his love' and that 'the sacrifice of the victim who gives himself out of his great love' is not just related to Christianity: 'It is Christianity.'[44] Paul's interlocutor Gallio translates Paul's teachings into institutional terms: 'If you believe in human beings, in the importance of the individual person, whoever he may be, then sooner or later that is an attack on the State which is bound to claim a super-authority and a super-value.'[45] This exchange between Paul and Gallio crystallises Mitchison's aims in the late 1930s in producing a historical novel about the early Christians under Roman rule. Christians in *The Blood of the Martyrs* are important because they represent a challenge to totalitarian rule, as the State threatens to subsume the freedom of the individual within an increasingly powerful institutional apparatus. The subversive, rhizomatic network of Christians threatens the state due to its flexible institutional structure, not because of reliance on transcendence. Jenni Calder writes that *The Blood of the Martyrs* plays with 'transcending the limits of the self'.[46] This is certainly true to the extent that Mitchison sees collectivity as a rejoinder to the selfish egotism that undergirds totalitarianism.

## CONCLUSION: COMMUNITY IN THE FUTURE TENSE

The problem that emerges in *The Blood of the Martyrs* is the same that emerged for Mitchison when she witnessed the resistance of the workers in Arkansas: if we are not to rely on supernatural intervention, from whence should effective resistance come? This is a problem that puzzles her throughout *The Moral Basis of Politics*, as she attempts to ascertain to what extent violence can work as an act of political resistance. While Mitchison's address to the STFU members, where she raised the spectre of justice's sword, might seem extreme, by the time she worked through the dilemma in *The Moral Basis of Politics* she had not completely put aside the use of violence as a force of resistance in self-defence or in extremis. But Mitchison recognises in *The Blood of the Martyrs* what is truly prescient in the story of Kleomenes III, as in that of the Christian resistance: it is the failed incitation of revolution that gives these stories power, not the spectral aura of any one personality. Acts of revolution are seldom successful and even violence seldom makes justice more secure. In *The Blood of the Martyrs* Beric attempts to assassinate one of the most heinous of the Romans, Tigellinus. He feigns that the assassination is in response to Tigellinus's treatment of his former lover, but he states to the Christians that it is truly for the community's sake. Mitchison is ambiguous about the extent to which Beric is fuelled by either motivation. The muddying of his motivations suggests, in Mitchison's thinking, a kind of marked ambiguity also demonstrated in *The Moral Basis of Politics* – an ambiguity she likewise expresses regarding the Soviet experiment. But Beric's efforts at assassination backfire, hurtling back to damage the most vulnerable. To some extent, this mirrors Mitchison's situation as well, as her position as a woman of relative privilege in her travels makes her worry about the ways her actions improve (or worsen) the fate of her allies. Just as her speech to the STFU was linked to an assassination attempt on her friend, Beric's efforts at solidarity miss the mark, only succeeding in riling up the political class against the underprivileged.

To see Mitchison's later historical fiction as proffering a new, more engaged vision of political community can help us in understanding her later works of science fiction, which continue to navigate the new ways that communities might coalesce despite differences across race, class or even species. Mitchison, as Nick Hubble writes, was consistently 'shedding [. . .] individualism in favor of [. . .] collective intersubjectivity'. I would agree that the corpus of Mitchison's work does precisely this; not only are her early mystical histories engaging in this turn but so, too, are the parts of her oeuvre which receive the most scholarly attention – her later works of science fiction. Both, as Hubble suggests, are doing the work of utopianism by producing a 'resolution of the utopian dialectic of identity and difference'.[47] But I would still suggest that some of Mitchison's grittier histories of the late 1930s and

1940s, which extend to her epic Scottish family genealogy *The Bull Calves* (1947), are unveiling new limitations of some of her earlier historical work, ones that push her towards science fiction to realise the potential of community in its fullest, cosmic, sense. Mitchison's disillusionment with institutionalised justice inspired new approaches in her writing, ones that emerged in the tenuous interspecies relationships in novels like *Memoirs of a Spacewoman* (1962). With an awareness of how the complexity and richness of Mitchison's histories began to emphasise the risky intractability of social belonging under authoritarianism, one might read her later science fiction as a way of experimenting with the body's capacity for love and community formation. As she turned from the internecine struggles of Rome in the interwar to the problems of interstellar community in the post-war period, her representation of new chasms of difference through the expansion of the human sciences would emerge as a more timely response to the political struggles of modern life.

## NOTES

1. Naomi Mitchison, *The Corn King and the Spring Queen* (London: Canongate, 1990), p. 625.
2. Naomi Mitchison, *The Blood of the Martyrs* (Whittlesey House: New York, 1939), p. 132.
3. Ibid. p. 133.
4. Ibid. p. 27.
5. Naomi Mitchison, *The Moral Basis of Politics* (London: Kennikat Press, 1971), p. 303.
6. Naomi Mitchison, *You May Well Ask: A Memoir 1920–1940* (London: Flamingo, 1979), p. 187.
7. Jenni Calder, *The Nine Lives of Naomi Mitchison* (London: Virago, 1997), pp. 136–7; Mitchison, *You May Well Ask*, p. 199.
8. Mitchison, *You May Well Ask*, p. 140.
9. Mitchison, *The Blood of the Martyrs*, p. viii; *You May Well Ask*, p. 171.
10. Mitchison, *The Blood of the Martyrs*, p. viii.
11. Mitchison, *Moral Basis*, p. 57.
12. Ibid. p. 57.
13. Mitchison, *The Corn King*, p. 54.
14. Naomi Mitchison, 'The Powers of Light', in *Beyond This Limit: Selected Shorter Fiction of Naomi Mitchison* (Glasgow: Kennedy & Boyd, 2008), p. 70.
15. Jill Benton, *Naomi Mitchison: A Century of Experiment in Life and Letters* (London: Pandora, 1990), p. 89.
16. Calder, *Nine Lives*, p. 155.
17. Olaf Stapledon, 'A Sketch-Map of Human Nature', *Philosophy* 17:67 (July 1942), p. 221. Benton, *Naomi Mitchison*, p. 89.
18. Mitchison, *Moral Basis*, p. 31.
19. Naomi Mitchison, 'Arkansas through British Eyes', *The Living Age* (May 1935) [Reproduced from *The Daily Herald*], p. 279.
20. Naomi Mitchison, Untitled document (1935), Southern Tenant Farmers' Union Archive.
21. Naomi Mitchison, 'White House and Marked Tree', *The New Statesman and Nation* (27 April 1935), p. 585.
22. Mitchison, 'Arkansas through British Eyes', p. 278.
23. Naomi Mitchison, Untitled document (1935), Southern Tenant Farmers' Union Archive.
24. Jerold S. Auerbach, 'Southern Tenant Farmers: Socialist Critics of the New Deal', *The Arkansas Historical Quarterly* 27:2 (1968), pp. 113–31.

25. Mitchison, 'White House and Marked Tree', p. 586.
26. Mitchison, 'Arkansas through British Eyes', p. 280.
27. Mitchison, *The Blood of the Martyrs*, p. 10.
28. Naomi Mitchison to Harry Leland Mitchell, 30 May 1935, Southern Tenant Farmers' Union Archive.
29. Mitchison, *The Blood of the Martyrs*, p. 142.
30. Ibid. p. 143.
31. Ibid. p. 144.
32. Ibid. p. 145.
33. Ibid. p. 145.
34. Ibid. p. 147.
35. Mitchison, *You May Well Ask*, p. 200.
36. Mitchison, *The Blood of the Martyrs*, pp. 195–6.
37. Ibid. p. 267.
38. Mitchison, *Moral Basis*, p. 320.
39. Ibid. p. 143.
40. Ibid. pp. 143–4.
41. Ibid. pp. 274–5.
42. Ibid. p. 338.
43. Mitchison, *The Blood of the Martyrs*, p. 195.
44. Ibid. p. 250.
45. Ibid. p. 250.
46. Calder, *Nine Lives*, p. 135.
47. Nick Hubble, 'Naomi Mitchison: Fantasy and Intermodern Utopia', in Alice Reeve-Tucker and Nathan Waddell (eds), *Utopianism, Modernism, and Literature in the Twentieth Century* (New York: Palgrave, 2013), p. 90.

# 8. 'The summoning urgent thing': *The Bull Calves* and the Drive to Experiment at Mid-Century

*Adam Piette*

The Highlander Black William, in Naomi Mitchison's wartime historical novel based on her Haldane family, *The Bull Calves* (1947), is listening to pipe music, and begins to feel in his body the call of history, sex and nation:

> But Black William was listening to the pipe music, the summoning urgent thing, the wee sharp waves of the tune beating on his stomach, the buzz of the drone shoving at his feet to come. Aye, to Kirstie.[1]

What is driving him to Kirstie is sexual attraction (so between the stomach and the feet), but is also a summoning thing, urgent as a drive or knot of drives, calling him to join in the dance with the Lowlander 'she-Haldane' as if by some nationalist, destinarian form of Darwinian sexual selection. It is nationalist since the conjoining of William Macintosh and Kirstie Haldane would marry the two poles of the new Scotland of the post-1745 Union, fulfilling the destiny of necessary integration after the disastrous civil strife of the Jacobite risings. The 'wee sharp waves' and the 'buzz of the drone' might be said to bring to union the drive to sociality and common future as enlightened nation (the overt music of the tune of the chanter), and the drive to fusion of the male and female moving from biological affect to kinship affection (the groundbass of the drone) – it is the tune which moves the sex drive (stomach), and the drone the social body (dancing feet), knotting together the political and erotic.

For Mitchison, that nationalist music of the Scottish body integrates, through kinship relations, families acting as survival zones for the communitarian potential and rootedness associated with the clan system that Culloden had destroyed.[2] This chapter examines the Haldane family network in the eighteenth century representing a Scotland entering a transitional, experimental phase triggered by the Knox Revolution, the Union, the Jacobite uprisings and the destruction of the clan system in 1745 as communicated to Mitchison through the female, not patriarchal, line. This network is consciously attended to in relationship to the post-1945 experiments in family, nation and class under feminist and communitarian reconfigurations that Mitchison supported and advocated. Using some of the material Mitchison produced for her Mass-Observation wartime diary, I'll explore the proposed unions of opposites as dialectical process, the contradictions and struggle in the encounter of male and female, Lowland and Highland, British-imperial and Scottish-communal, capitalist and communist. This dialectical union of opposites will be compared to a more complex model of encounter enacted by the novel, a knotting together of drives, as in the drone and chanter musics of sexual, kinship and national relations staged in the relationship between Kirstie and Black William: a knotting together in encounter that is non-linear, transhistorical, fusional, allowing for gaps and perplexities in ways that might challenge facile dialectic and the Union itself. These psychosexual knots, and the perplexities, secrets, repressions and shared accommodations they involve, suggest alternative ways into Haldane evolutionary genetics as social and family determinism. The 'bull calves' of the novel are both the male members of the Haldane family clan and representative of patrilineal dialectic in the novel according to the logic of evolutionary genetics. Mitchison stages this patriarchal dialectic as well as challenging it with the knots that bind rogue and Highland elements in the kinship system and favour the secret agency of the female side to the Haldane family. That knotting-in of female experience is accompanied by a similar reinscription of Scottish history and culture in terms of comparably covert progressive and communitarian projects and credences, aligning the political and erotic drives of the book.

In the extensive notes Mitchison published at the back of *The Bull Calves*, she dwells on the various social and nationalist projects secreted away in the historical novel as a documentary project. The obvious question – why write about the Haldanes soon after 1745 to explore the Scotland of 1945? – she only gets round to addressing in the notes to the second part:

> Some at least of my book people were working towards the same green pastures as lie in view for the bull calves of my own and the next generation. Between them and us was a time when, as far as we can judge, there was less sympathy with what we are after in the mid twentieth century. Two hundred years ago, in the mid eighteenth century, Scotland was in a transitional period. There was much questioning, much research and experimentation in science – especially agriculture and medicine – philosophy and literature. I think this makes it more possible to get the feel of eighteenth-century Scotland in words and phrases which come easily now to us in another transitional and experimental period, than it would be to get the feel of the nineteenth century when there was a hardening up into certainties and the uncharitable morality of technical and commercial success wrenched out of poverty, with the corresponding success-image of the dour Scot, almost always an east coast Lowlander. (464–5)

This prepares the ground for the complexity of the project, its many sides and valences: 1745 chimes with 1945 because the younger generations in both centuries were entering an 'experimental period' comparable in terms of politics and national history. The eighteenth-century generation tracked in the novel emerged from the wars of religion, from the brutal realities of colonialism at home and abroad, and faced the consequences of a new disciplinary form of enforced Union post-Culloden while trying to absorb the impact of the scientific discoveries of the Enlightenment; at the same time it was exploring the liberating potentiality of freedoms and democratic-nationalist idealism soon to be unleashed by the French Revolution. The younger Scottish generation in 1945 were also suffering a brutal war laying waste to progressive communities in Europe. Its members sought to rediscover Soviet-inspired communist and radical democratic sociality in popular nationalism enabling freedom from the Union, while absorbing the extraordinary new technologies and social practices of the mid-century as well as the transformations enabled by feminism and depth psychology.

The two mid-centuries match in that Scotland is presented at each of these junctures as an unfinished political ideal, with Mitchison speculating that the kinship bonds of her Lowland ancestors (the family seat at Gleneagles figuring as at the border between high and low)[3] were established to absorb and preserve Highland culture through intermarriage. The failed dialectic of Highland and Lowland is still operative as stalled potential in the two historical moments. But the match also suggests a way of forging a left-liberal consensus through a more subversive and radical knotting together of drives and social and sexual practices that might eventually lead to the desired revolution. The Haldanes prided themselves on their benevolent and pragmatic land stewardship in the eighteenth century, always aiming for just relations between the peasant farming community and their still semi-feudal but also Enlightenment-driven custodianship of the territory and agricultural practices. This stewardship is aligned, in *The Bull Calves*, with the form of proto-socialist communitarian power to bind together the people of low estate that had characterised the disappearing ideal of the clan system. This matches the comparable emergence of a Scottish generation in the twentieth century, hardened in the crucible of the total war effort, seeking to forge a new nation state that is both socialist and progressive: preserving the 1930s communism and communitarianism that the war and emergent security state had stopped in its tracks despite war socialism and the emergent welfare state and knotting it into a feminist, communitarian and nationalist vision of a polity made up of the two major Scottish cities bound together with the rural Highlands and Lowlands. The periods being compared – 1745 being forty years before the French Revolution, and 1945 being twenty-eight years after the Russian – merge as pre- and post-revolutionary texts, as Mitchison states in her notes. There is, she suggests, a line of continuity linking the effects of these two revolutionary periods:

> Bliss was it in that dawn to be alive. How well we know that feeling, some of us! But although less than a generation afterwards it appeared to be a false dawn to those who, to their horror, had seen Napoleon rise out of the ashes of liberty, yet we know that this was not so. The French Revolution had ended a particular kind of privilege in France, and, still more important, the idea and image of it in other countries. It had ended the idea of people as chattels, and had made possible the idea of nationalism as a human and, paradoxically, an international good. (415)

Stalin as Napoleon, communism as the liberation of the new chattels of capitalism, the internationalism of the Soviet vision of socialism in one country: Mitchison does not need to make the explicit parallels, but they are there implicitly and reveal her sense of the socialist principles of her own generation as necessarily radical and engaged with the potential for communal collective action inspired by the Russian Revolution of 1917. What is striking is how she knots together the class revolutions of 1789 and 1917 as nationalist: equally remarkable is her perception that the nationalism sponsored by the two revolutions has the power to foment progressive change internationally despite retrospective critiques of Napoleon and Stalin as imperial and totalitarian leaders. Class and nationalist revolutions are knotted together as paradoxically internationalist because of the exemplary demonstration of justice and liberation from oppressive domination that is one of the defining characteristics of a class revolution. Mitchison takes the Scottish socialism that is the fruit of both the French and Russian Revolutions as inspirational of radical democracy in all nations and constructs another knotting together of the two histories, imagining a conceptual marriage between nationalist and erotic bonds, a political union that is integrative, radical and complex insofar as it connects to a daring inclusive and dangerous coming together of lovers, the struggles and relational complications of the erotic bond. That bond enables, crucially, female influence and feminist counter-patriarchal measures to enter into the equation. These twin acts of knotted union, political and erotic, are, in the dual Scottish contexts of the eighteenth and (by allegorical translation) the twentieth centuries, designed to subvert the Act of Union as an instance of stalled and colonial dialectic through feminist interventions and reinventions. The act of political and erotic counter-hegemonic union is figured both in Kirstie's marriage to Black William and, by analogy, in Mitchison's project running her estate at Carradale on Kintyre: in both cases women are in charge of the transformations. Her political idealism about the estate as a potential Scottish Soviet occurs alongside her erotic affairs with the fishermen and ghillies of the estate and village and are recorded in the diary she wrote for Mass-Observation from 1939 to 1945. While she shuttled between Glasgow, Edinburgh and London during the war, it was Carradale as political and erotic project that formed the centre of her wartime experimental imagination, and it is Carradale as example of the knotting together of erotic and political projects which informs the other difficult knot, the knot binding together the strands of national and revolutionary praxis. It is Carradale which is allowed to shape her retrospective gaze, as historical novelist, on eighteenth-century Gleneagles. Both big houses are zones within which a radicalism is fostered that dares to imagine an end to privilege and chattel economics in the eighteenth century, and an end to the bonds of twentieth-century capitalism and of bourgeois and elite control over the means of production.

The communitarian act of union as defined by the erotico-political alliance between Kirstie and Black William in the novel is not straightforward, however. As we have argued above, the subversive union of opposites in this case does not follow the tidy logic of dialectical synthesis nor the linear clarities of facile allegory. The radical new form of union being imagined is totalising and fusional still, but it cuts no corners, allows for true and difficult, even impossible, contradictions. Its drive to union of the oppositional-erotic and nationalist-political is clearly still defined as a drive towards integration – in her notes to *The Bull Calves* Mitchison notes the influence of Jung's *The Integration of the Personality*, translated into English in 1940, which she read, she says, halfway through the book. Resisting its masculinist assumptions ('the man is the individual; women are a lump' [512]), Mitchison used the study to dramatise the psychological struggles of Kirstie and William: but in ways that ground true integration in a complex act of knotting together that is analytically messy and at best only notionally dialectical. Both characters have dark secrets in the novel, Kirstie's being her involvement in a witch's coven to escape the cruel misogyny of her Calvinist minister husband; William's the story of his captivity in America, where he was drawn into cannibalism and torture within a Native American tribe. These sensational plotlines are a Gothic subtext acting as the novel's generic unconscious, and stand in for the Jungian unconscious that is its chosen model of depth psychology. Kirstie, in the witch episode, 'had almost drowned in the dark waters of her own unconscious'; she imagines she is being pursued by the Devil, defined as her own animus. Submission, Mitchison tells us, is necessary at this stage of the integrative process, but in the text-world she submits instead to William, who arrives in the 'Nick' of time (513).[4] The animus is therefore projected onto William, and he becomes her soul. William also 'goes down into the dark waters', writes Mitchison, in his relationship with Ohnawiyo and then with Kirstie: 'He puts his dream on to Kirstie,' but has to meet her Indian counterpart in order to rid himself of pagan and royalist desires (514).

If we unpack the implications of the two unconscious back-stories, it becomes clear that what is being staged are two comparable acts of mental liberation. Kirstie has to destroy the Calvinist male at the heart of Christian ideology that has determined and dominated her before moving towards Black William as her equal partner: companionable marriage through sacrifice of the patriarchal sacrament. Similarly, William has to destroy the servile mentality of the colonial subject (the novel has interesting research into the Jacobites transported to America as indentured servants) by going through the trauma of the extreme horrors of the colony, before coming home to a post-imperial and post-patriarchal partnership – though traces of both imperialism and patriarchy remain in the fate meted out to Ohnawiyo.

The integration is not without its costs: both Kirstie and Black William go through protracted, soul-searching, pragmatic interrogations of what to reveal to and conceal from each other, and a complex play of special pleading and unconscious, deluded patterns of thinking and feeling, as they struggle with the difficult truths of their pasts and their circumstances within the familial, national, patriarchal and colonial histories in which their lives are embedded. These moments of resistance and obliquity are significant, we come to realise, because the doubts and pitfalls are where the novel really happens. Mitchison adapts George Eliot's trope of the web as image of the social relations being mapped by the kinship relations of her novel's plot; she turns to the image of the fishing net (taken as organising metaphor due to the importance of the fishing industry to Carradale) to describe the procedures of her version of the realist novel as a genre designed to represent social relations across classes and gender divides. Talking about the family trees of her own family and of her novel (reproduced as prefatory material in the novel), she writes in her notes of 'a close net-work of relationships', and the nets are made up of knots. 'When I was pretty far on with this book, another knot came in the net,' she writes, when recounting how a Free French young man during the war at Carradale had brought her into contact with a distant relative (412). What Mitchison terms 'family continuity' is a social network, a system of social relations where the knots bind people together into kin and nation in ways transcending class and gender. The knots are also, however, moments of psychological crisis, integrative traumas and secrets that also bind together the nation, through a shared secrecy about what it is necessary to forget or collectively to repress. And given the transtemporal connections between the eighteenth- and twentieth-century revolutionary moments that imbue the historical novel with its comparative force, one could argue that the knots are temporal networking agents too, binding together chronotopes through shared historical interconnections and necessary accommodations in the strategic understanding of an agreed common history.

Traditionally, the realist novel adjudicates comparisons between its act of representation of social relations and the manner in which social formations are structured and interrelate. That is, the relations that differentiate and attune individuals and communities are matched by the novel's modes of organisation of class and gender relations according to the plot and subtexts of the novel's stratifying strategies. What attracts and repels the characters in the realist novel, forcing them into conflict or binding and networking them together, matches the cultural formations in culture that govern conformities, clashes, fusions, encounters: such as war, kinship relations, courtship and marriage conventions, social prejudice and hierarchy, class differences and powers. For Mitchison, there is a relationship between the knots of feeling and the knots that bind people together, such that the patterns in a novel are knots of history affective and political that go beyond the local conventions governing what attracts and repels within communities, and therefore step beyond the fixed class politics of the realist novel as a nineteeenth-century genre. The knots of history allow for the individuals involved in the local encounters consciously and unconsciously to stand in for the political objects that are historical catalysts and binding agents, functioning a little like memory objects in Lukács's idea of the epic:

> Only in the novel and in certain epic forms resembling the novel does memory occur as a creative force affecting the object and transforming it. The genuinely epic quality of such memory is the affirmative experience of the life process. The duality of interiority and the outside world can be abolished for the subject if he (the subject) glimpses the organic unity of his whole life through the process by which his living present has grown from the stream of his past life dammed up within his memory. The surmounting of duality – that is to say the successful mastering and integration of the object – makes this experience into an element of authentically epic form.[5]

We might revise Lukács somewhat and define the epic memory object as an object that acquires a shared history through integration into epic narrative as a story combining psychological and national significances within the realist novel as a genre. That epic knowledge must be intradiegetic, held in common by the subjects within the story being integrated into history and memory.[6] This is not necessarily an easy or even positive force, since integration could be forced upon an object for evil purposes, as a manner of sabotage or disintegration. The net and knots that make the ropes into a net are not blameless objects either: Mitchison speaks, for instance, of the colonists rounding up Native Americans before removal as catching them in a net (277), and William gazes upon Kirstie thinking of 'the poor bull calves that were mashed in this nasty dark net of difficulties and obstinacies' (353). The net and its knots are fictional objects and political objects neither good or bad, but rather structuring processes in the 'surmounting of duality – that is to say the successful mastering and integration of the object'.[7]

An example might be those two moments in the novel when Kirstie and William do not quite tell the full story of how they faced their anima and animus, Jungian terms for the collectively defined other gender within the unconscious. It is the incomplete telling of the story (rather than the actual facing down) which allows for the marrying of Lowland and Highland poles in the experiment Mitchison is performing textually. Kirstie does confess to Black William her coven story, in Part 2, 'Ye Highlands and Ye Lowlands', and tells the truth about her mystical trance as a witch expecting the Devil to come and force her to submit. But she only does so because she still believes William is the Devil when she tells the story, and when she hears his accent, she tells him, 'and suddenly I thought, aye, it is true after all what is said and there is a connection between the highlands and hell!' (169). The two of them go over their dialogue of the night of the appearances (Kirstie is assailed by 'appearances', ghostly beings that accompany the devil in the world, at the psychic border). She cries *You have found me now and what are you asking of me?* (169) but she is talking to the Devil, not to William. William replies, *'I am asking you to be my wife in the name of God.'* The cross purposes only get resolved once the conversation is remembered at Gleneagles after Culloden; and Mitchison makes some comic play with the discrepancies between the dialogue they had then and the dialogue as recalled, noting the misprisions, evasiveness, misapprehensions. For example, when William tells Kirstie about why he took no advantage of her there in her short shift, defenceless and exposed:

> Maybe, lassie, you were like poor Scotland herself, and one more betrayal would have spoilt you clean. But before I had it well sorted out in my body or mind, you cried out: *'If you are not he, who are you?'* And I said: *'I am the one you found on the coal-road up from Gleneagles.'* (170)

We read this both with her sense of her own words as challenge to the pseudo-devil and stranger, and with his sense of his own words as those of a Highlander voicing his recognition of her tolerance and charity. The encounter is metaphysical insofar as we have the clash of mistaken identities, she believing him the very Devil, the leader of the appearances, to which she must submit in order to rid her mind and body of the influence of her Calvinist bully of a patriarchal husband: but what she seems to be submitting herself to is the master as parody of the Calvinist patriarch, a shape-shifting version of the counterpart enemy in Scottish Gothic, as with Gil-Martin in Hogg's *Private Memoirs and Confessions of a Justified Sinner*. Black William, conversely, is proposing to a memory, the woman who helped him escape and gave him money and disguise enough to sail to America as colonist and rebel outlaw. This *dialogue de sourds* reveals itself as pure drive at the time being narrated (she driven towards evil by Calvinist patriarchy, he still on the run as criminal and Highland devil, driven by desire for her that is close to a rape instinct); but it becomes political and social, and therefore Scottish, progressive and nationalist, once the dialogue is itself re-narrated with the secret drives and thoughts confessed, in a similar space and comparable time.[8] In other words, it is only by being reflected upon after the event that the psychological drives can be understood as political by the protagonists themselves: in a sense, the political meanings are constructed as well as construed by the retrospect.

Mitchison stages the double dialogue – Kirstie and Black William in dialogue remembering the dialogue they had – not only to unpack the cross purposes, but to dramatise the double temporality described by Lukács as characteristic of the realist novel and epic: 'Only in the novel and in certain epic forms resembling the novel does memory occur as a creative force affecting the object and transforming it.' The double temporality of the recalling of the dialogue matches the double temporality of the historical novel as genre inasmuch as the second iteration reveals the politics of the first as history understood, rather than history as raw event in time subject to conflicting motivation and secret forces. The event itself, or rather the dialogue spoken back then, becomes an epic memory object in Lukács's sense, and is integrated into a shared history and memory through the new iteration of that object in ways that enable it to become epic, not subjectively realist – this is the sense of William's comparison of Kirstie to Scotland – and, importantly, that enable a marriage of true minds to occur as the marriage vows performed back become real and substantial once properly understood as epic memory objects.[9]

At the same time, the marriage is also based on the shaping of memory objects (defined as stories told about the past that transform as well as shape them) according to a pragmatics of discretion. Black William tells Patrick of his cannibal feasts and sexual liaison with Ohnawiyo as a captive in America, but cannot tell Kirstie, though she intuits much of the story. Similarly, when she receives a visit from the sinister Phemie, Kirstie recalls her experiences during her first marriage, when she had visions of 'appearances' or devilish spirits and was tempted to a witch's traditional submissiveness to the forces of evil. Phemie's intervention triggers a recurrence of Kirstie's visions of a ghost bairn floating in the air: but she does not relate this to William. They agree at the end of the novel not to tell their secrets, but also to understand that this is a known and allowed secrecy on both sides – the drive to tell all is tempting, and becomes a motif in the story as 'a longing to drown in the deep waters' (405), a Lawrentian submersion as submission to unconscious death-wish, or submission to the mastery of others. The bringing to shared consciousness of the double secrecy ('I know fine you have secrets, William') is a sharing of a *lack* of knowledge to enable escape from the cycles of deception and betrayal that structure colonised and patriarchal Scotland.[10] It also at a stroke rewrites the epic memory object as less about mastery and integration than about shared *lack* of mastery and a consciousness of unintegrated material in political consciousness.

Mitchison learned a lot from her Mass-Observation war diary about confessions of this kind. She thought about her diary for the organisation as a form of confession:

> Earlier Rosemary had been writing to a friend who is very unhappy. I suggested Mass-Obs. Of course one realises that Mass-Obs is a kind of God-Figure – one confesses, one is taken an interest in, encouraged. Will Mass-Obs supersede psychiatry? I always recommend it myself.[11]

But it is a curious act of psychiatric confession to write a diary that is of service to the wartime bureaucracy and sociological values associated with Tom Harrisson's project. The diary at once confesses privacies and often scandalous material, such as the affairs and militant politics, yet at the same time passes over in silence the material suppressed both by the confessor and by Mass-Observation itself. As the editor of the published selection from the diary, Dorothy Sheridan, revealed, the diary was not written as autobiography but as a social and documentary project: 'she asserted to Angus [Calder] that her main motivation in taking part in Mass-Observation was not to put *herself* on paper but arose from her scientific and anthropological interest in the value of social documentary'. Indeed, there is telling evidence of self-censorship: Mitchison removed the carbon copy from the typewriter when typing sensitive material such as the black-market activities of locals, as the surviving top copy shows – and that secrecy matches the tact shown by Sheridan and Mitchison when in the 1980s they agreed, according to what Sheridan calls their 'knot of intersubjectivity', to withhold sensitive material with regard to those depicted in it who were still alive.[12] That self-censorship chimed with the censorship of wartime Britain: Mitchison knew the diary would be read and controlled as it moved through the postal service. She's told at one point 'that the censor's dept got parts of my letters and diary, which were copied (with dashes in places – but I don't think I ever said worse than bloody!)'.[13] The compliant agreed secrecy analysed in the Kirstie–William pact is analogous to the practice of self-censorship and the acceptance of censorship of the diary by the state.

At the same time, the diary is an ethnographic record, designed to reveal the links between erotic affections and desires and the political hopes and fears of Scotland as it weathered the storm of the war, generating a knot of intersubjectivity that binds the erotic and the political, in depth, connecting the drives of the collective unconscious to the complex weave of events according to a diaristic version of the novel's epic memory system. And just as Kirstie and William agree to abide by a mutual pact that tolerates secrecy, guilt and evasion, so the diary is designed to be read as a textual performance of epic form that shares its own obliquities as accepted censorship on both sides. The acceptance is deliberately belated, only coming into being politically as historical document once the diary is revisited, by Dorothy Sheridan and the Mass-Observation Archive at the University of Sussex. It is only as historical document that the diary can do the job it was designed to perform, which is to communicate the collective and national/international project of Scotland as a socialist ideal through the close-knit, knotty story of Carradale and Mitchison's erotico-political wartime.

The diary as a narrative of knots does afford one an intimate portrait of the work Mitchison was doing during the war: the political talks, the support for the SNP breakaway movement, John MacCormick's home rule party, the Scottish Convention.[14] As Antonia Kearton explains, 'the Scottish Convention (later Scottish Covenant Association) was a cross-party body that aimed to create a consensus for Home Rule. It did not contest elections, but organised several "Scottish National Assemblies", produced proposals for a parliament, and then produced a massive petition in favour of Home Rule, which was to gain around two million signatures before being submitted to Westminster'.[15] The Convention provided Mitchison with a material realisation of the revolutionary nationalism she had espoused insofar as it married SNP independence values with progressive politics. The diary also expounds her hopes and fears for a post-war communist Supreme Soviet of Scotland according to Soviet nationalism as internationalism, her sense of communism as enabling people to get 'out of the enclosing walls of the home, to get them to see things, not individually, but socially, to get them not to compete, but to co-operate'.[16] That Scottish Soviet ideal is conceived intersectionally, however, as necessarily a feminist project, and intersectionality might be another form the knotting complexity takes – preferred by Mitchison to standard dialectical materialism: the diary tracks the many ways she resisted the everyday patriarchal assumptions running the working-class movement. She aimed to proselytise for 'non-possessive generous human relations' as opposed to the patriarchy founded by and for the 'generations of owners, of possessors'.[17] The knotting together also takes as part of its scope the Highland–Lowland divide: the diary documents her every move across this divide, from the Lowland class of monopoly capitalists towards the 'Highland' working class. On a visit to Edinburgh in June 1942, she tells the diary, she has an epiphany:

> Queer going through this lovely town, which I am hoping won't be bombed, full of one's own class, a capital, and suddenly feeling this bubbling secret excitement because one is on the other side, when one sees the brass plate with Forestry Commission, one is part of it, either for or against, but in league with the roe-deer, the fairies, the foresters, against the keepers, the lunchers, the respectable. I have never felt this kind of thing, this sudden wave of sympathy with someone far off, except when I have been in love . . .[18]

This epiphany worked towards a secondary elaboration whereby she dreamed of a fusion of Edinburgh and Glasgow as sign of a Lowland–Highland alliance: 'Can we,' she asks in her notes to *The Bull Calves*, 'somehow, get the best of Glasgow and the best of Edinburgh and fuse them? [. . .] Can the Highlands break loose from the past and get into contact again with the rest of Europe and make their own statement, in life and in art, of its civilisation?' (436). The fusion of Glasgow and Edinburgh would enable a liberation of the Scots from capital: 'the pressure of competition, on the top of continuous betrayal by landowners and leaders whom they trusted, has made the Highlander fully as suspicious and hard and individualist as any other member of capitalist society' (436–7). Edinburgh, she argues, still connects with Europe and European civilisation, though vitiated by the dead hand of conservatism and Presbyterian censorship of the arts; whereas the Highlands were cut off 'and had to develop mainly on their own, scarcely feeling the impact of the Renaissance, still less the French Revolution' (435) with Glasgow's Marxist Clydeside also vitiated by poverty (434–5). Kirstie's marriage to Black William is analogous to an Edinburgh–Glasgow match, if we take north Glasgow (as Mitchison did) to stand for a progressive politics that connects to the Highlands. The match marries the best old qualities, Glasgow's Marxism free of the poverty and ignorance of colonial and capitalist subjection, Edinburgh's internationalism and art free of the Presbyterian censorship and complicity in capitalism and imperialism. But it would only work, Mitchison advises, if both sides of the progressive generation (the 'roe-deer, the fairies, the foresters, against the keepers, the lunchers, the respectable') were to agree to be understood as forgetting the other's dark historical secrets in a difficult and diplomatic act of mutual tolerance. The union of the two poles, a Highland internationale, is founded on a knotted construction of a socialist Scotland as imagined during the war years in the Convention, and as staged in the fusion of Haldane kindness and pragmatism (303). That construct is knotted because also tempered by feminist release from Calvinist patriarchy and animated by forgotten clan solidarities and rooted cooperative social memory. The machine of dialectic is transformed by the multivalent union of plural, shifting, transtemporal oppositions into a tactile and embodied, erotic and political epic memory system based on shared historicised dialogue.

Mitchison gave a talk in February 1941 at Ellary, a Christian Socialist house on Loch Caolisport:

> I talked about People's ways of working determining their social structure and ways of thought, but didn't say that was Marxist history. About monopoly capitalism with special reference to the Clyde monopolists and MacBraynes, about democracy, about Scottish and Russian history, about a Five Year Plan for peace and Planning for Scotland. I talked for about three quarters of an hour, and when I stopped they all began talking at once. It was very lively, fairly practical and very hopeful for the future.[19]

Mitchison is speaking the double speech of two cities, conjoining Marxist experience with the Highlands (the Ellary house on the loch) and a Soviet internationalism with a national project. Her speech is the fusion of poles dreamed of in the Kirsty–Black William marriage, alive to the shared social values, pragmatic about the need for discretion ('but didn't say that was Marxist history') – and full of the energy and drive to experiment at this moment of transition. The summoning urgent thing is a marriage of the two drives, the chanter tune of art and international cooperation, and the drone of socialism in one country. It is also a summoning of free embodied energies that bring men and women together, in a dance to the combined sharp waves of the tune and the buzz of the drone, attentive to the knots of desire in the stomach and the knots of memory in the handkerchief of shared history and story together, in tune with the intimate other, and wary of the authority of the self alone:

> [Black William] wiped his forehead with the cool silk handkerchief from his coat pocket, and rose. 'I am for the dancing too,' he said, 'or herself will be wild at me. And I am thinking I will go before my feet become their own masters.' (145)

## NOTES

1. Naomi Mitchison, *The Bull Calves* (Glasgow: Richard Drew, 1985), p. 145. Further references to this edition are given in the text.
2. See Mitchison on the effect of Culloden on clan solidarity, in her 'Open Letter to an African Chief', *Journal of Modern African Studies* 2:1 (March 1964), pp. 65–72: 'when the last of the clan chiefs who considered the clan as a body of people for whose welfare they were responsible were killed, some at Culloden, and were succeeded by men who had no such feelings, who instead considered themselves absolute owners of the clan lands, with no need to pay any attention to their vote-less, powerless clanspeople' (p. 66). The 1745 theme also, of course, ties her historical novel very firmly to Walter Scott's *Waverley*. For a useful account of Lukács on *Waverley* as a post-'45 historical novel, see Ian Duncan, 'History and the Novel after Lukács', *Novel* 50:3 (2017), pp. 388–96.
3. 'Gleneagles is only a short ride, even on bad roads, from the Highland line' (*The Bull Calves*, p. 413).
4. For a useful account of the witchcraft plot of the novel and their sources in the 1662 Crook of Devon trials and the Paisley trials of 1697, see the fourth chapter of Moira Burgess's University of Glasgow PhD thesis '"Between the Words of a Song": Supernatural and Mythical Elements in the Scottish Fiction of Naomi Mitchison' (2006), http:// theses.gla.ac.uk/5413/1/2006BurgessPhD.pdf [accessed 20 March 2021].
5. György Lukács, *The Theory of the Novel*, trans. Anna Bostock (London: Merlin Press, [1916] 1971), p. 127.
6. This chimes with Lukács's broader understanding of the impact of the French Revolution on citizens: it made manifest the force of history in ordinary lives of the masses, and led to the popularity of the historical novel as a genre as defined and practised by Scott. This is succinctly summarised by Lukács in *The Historical Novel*, trans. H. and S. Mitchell (Boston: Beacon Press, [1937] 1963): 'It was the French Revolution, the revolutionary wars and the rise and fall of Napoleon, which for the first time made history a mass experience, and moreover on a European scale' (p. 23).
7. Lukács, *Theory of the Novel*, p. 127.
8. Gill Plain makes a strong case that the accommodation and agreed repression of secrets staged in Kirstie's story dramatises the predicament of women under patriarchy at mid-century, the pressure either to conceal or conform. See her *Women's Fiction of the Second World War: Gender, Power, Resistance* (Edinburgh: Edinburgh University Press, 1996).
9. Kirsten Stirling discusses the nation-as-woman imagery in the novel in 'The Female Figure in the Scottish Renaissance', *Scottish Cultural Review of Language and Literature* 11 (2008), pp. 35–63. This relates to Lukács's reading of Scott's historical novels in terms of the ways characters are aware of their historicity after revolutionary crises that split the population in two: 'Scott, by disclosing the actual conditions of life, the actual growing crisis in people's lives, depicts all the problems of popular life which lead up to the historical crisis he has

represented. And when he has made us sympathizers and understanding participants of this crisis, when we understand exactly for what reasons the crisis has arisen, for what reasons the nation has split into two camps, and when we have seen the attitude of the various sections of the population towards this crisis, only then does the great historical hero enter upon the scene of the novel. He may therefore, indeed he must, be complete in a psychological sense when he appears before us, for he appears in order to fulfil his historic mission in the crisis' (Lukács, *The Historical Novel*, p. 38).

10. Douglas Gifford argues that white lies are also a strategy of companionability accompanying the divisions in the novel, in his article 'Forgiving the Past: Naomi Mitchison's *The Bull Calves*', in Joachim Schwend and Horst W. Drescher (eds), *Studies in Scottish Fiction: Twentieth Century* (Frankfurt: Peter Lang, 1990), pp. 219–24. The staging of mutually beneficial opacities in the couple may have a lot to do with Nick Hubble's sense of the novel as 'represent[ing] a final abandonment of the attempt to reconcile female experience with the patriarchal order and the role of the tragic king, which so strains – albeit often in exhilaratingly exciting ways – Mitchison's earlier fiction'. See '"The Kind of Woman Who Talked to Basilisks": Travelling Light through Naomi Mitchison's Landscape of the Imaginary', *The Luminary* 7 (Summer 2016), pp. 64–74 (p. 69).

11. Naomi Mitchison, diary entry for Sunday, 22 June, 1941, in Dorothy Sheridan (ed.), *Among You Taking Notes: The Wartime Diary of Naomi Mitchison, 1939–1945* (London: Phoenix Press, 1985), p. 154. Cf. Nick Hubble's essay on her MO diary and the utopian and communitarian effects it enabled, 'Documenting Lives: Mass Observation, Women's Diaries, and Everyday Modernity', in Adam Smyth (ed.), *A History of English Autobiography* (Cambridge: Cambridge University Press, 2016), pp. 345–58.

12. Dorothy Sheridan, 'Woven Tapestries: Dialogues and Dilemmas in Editing a Diary', *The European Journal of Life Writing* 10 (2021), pp. 45–67.

13. Naomi Mitchison, diary entry for 16 February 1941, in Sheridan (ed.), *Among You Taking Notes*, p. 121. As Dorothy Sheridan puts it, though it 'is difficult to ascertain the extent of internal censorship' of the diary, 'it was almost certainly examined from time to time when it was sent through the post' (*Among You Taking Notes*, p. 22).

14. *Among You Taking Notes*, p. 227.

15. Antonia Kearton, 'Imagining the "Mongrel Nation": Political Uses of History in the Recent Scottish Nationalist Movement', *National Identities* 7:1 (2006), pp. 23–50 (p. 37).

16. Ibid. pp. 169, 79, 120.

17. Ibid. p. 181.

18. Ibid. p. 200.

19. *Among You Taking Notes*, p. 123.

# 9. Mitchison, Decolonisation and African Modernity

*James Purdon*

The social and psychological consequences of empire and colonisation are a consistent theme of Naomi Mitchison's fiction. In her first novel, *The Conquered* (1923), Gallic resistance to Roman occupation in the first century BC serves as an effective if none-too-subtle allegory for the condition of twentieth-century Ireland under British rule. In *The Blood of the Martyrs* (1939), the Roman empire under Nero is an economic vampire, 'suck[ing] the blood' of its provinces in Greece and northern Europe.[1] And in *The Bull Calves* (1947), the refugee Jacobite Black William becomes intimately acquainted with Britain's own colonial exploitation – in his words, 'our cheatery' – of the Indigenous inhabitants of North America.[2] Born into the upper echelons of the British ruling class, Mitchison felt very keenly the implications of that *our*. For the first half of her life, the British empire was indisputably a major world power. At home, young Naomi absorbed and internalised the strong opinions of her mother, 'an active and constant propagandist', as she would later put it, 'for Tory imperialism'. (Her father, though more liberal, tended to avoid the subject of politics.) Yet as an adult, Mitchison herself would become a committed and outspoken *anti*-imperialist who, even as she recognised the effects of her mother's influence, was capable many decades later of feeling 'ashamed and embarrassed' at the pro-empire sentiments recorded in her childhood diaries.[3]

Towards the end of the 1950s, Mitchison began to take an active and energetic interest in present-day anti-colonial politics, with a particular interest in sub-Saharan Africa. No longer content to filter contemporary events through historical analogies, she became a vocal critic of apartheid, and a consistent advocate for Black African self-government throughout the region. In 1960, while hosting a British Council delegation at her home in Carradale, she struck up a friendship with a young delegate from the British protectorate of Bechuanaland, Linchwe, who a few years later would take up his hereditary role as *kgosi*, or chief, of the Bakgatla people. Linchwe would become a regular guest in Argyll, and Mitchison in turn accepted his invitation to visit Mochudi, the home settlement of the Bakgatla, in Bechuanaland (soon to gain independence from British rule as the Republic of Botswana). In 1963, she visited again, this time to attend and assist at Linchwe's installation as chief.

For the rest of her life, Mitchison would maintain a close relationship with Linchwe and his people, drawing on her knowledge of Botswana in novels, memoirs, poems, plays and stories spanning several decades. She became an adviser and confidante to Linchwe, and came to be known among the Bakgatla by the Setswana honorific *Mmarona*, 'mother'.[4]

That this title was freely bestowed on Mitchison by the Bakgatla themselves goes some way towards complicating what might otherwise seem a textbook case of white paternalism – or, in this case, maternalism. Formed as they were within a social, political and economic order born of European colonialism, her relationships with Black African friends could not be, as she often wished, thoroughly 'non-racial'.[5] As a white woman, and as one of the British elite, she possessed status, power and economic resources far in excess of those available to Black Botswanans. And her denunciation of European colonial violence, though grounded in the anti-imperialist political tradition of revolutionary socialism, was not part of a multi-generational legacy of dispossession as it was for the Black Africans she met and befriended in Botswana and South Africa. Yet her relationship with the Bakgatla, founded as it was on mutual respect, affection, reciprocal hospitality and acts of practical solidarity, endured for more than thirty years, during which Mitchison worked energetically both with and on behalf of Linchwe and his people in Botswana and in Britain.

Besides committing herself – politically, creatively and financially – to anticolonial, anti-imperial and anti-racist positions, she engaged in practical demonstrations of solidarity at considerable risk to her person and to her reputation. Her vocal support for the anti-apartheid movement resulted in a ban on her books, and their author, in the Republic of South Africa. She accepted that censure with pride. She visited Botswana regularly from the 1960s until the 1990s, helping to set up schools and scholarships, lobbying for infrastructural projects, and hosting Botswanan visitors back home in Scotland. She became a keen collector of East African and South African painting, both in her own right and on behalf of Argyll Council, on whose behalf she assembled an important and historically significant public collection intended for the use of local schools.[6] And she was an early and sincere advocate for African writing – by Chinua Achebe, Wole Soyinka, Camara Laye, Stanlake Samkange, Ngugi wa Thiong'o, and others – which she understood not as a homogeneous literary export for consumption by Western audiences, but as a varied and vibrant complex of regional traditions, each helping to sustain and renew the cultural life of modern Africa.[7]

The question of what that fraught term – 'modern' – might mean in an African context was one that Mitchison repeatedly confronted in her writing about mid-century Botswana. Was the rhetoric of modernisation, she wondered, no more than a covert way of advocating for the further Europeanisation of African society: a cultural and economic hangover of colonial rule? Or was it possible to conceive of an African form of modernity, a way of being modern that did not derive from or seek to mimic the developmental patterns of Europe? Central to these questions was her sense of the intersecting and sometimes clashing temporalities that shaped African life. As I shall argue in this chapter, Mitchison's fiction and non-fiction alike registered her growing recognition of decolonisation as not only a *geopolitical* process, but a *chronopolitical* one: a struggle between different conceptions and scales of temporal experience. At the heart of her writing of this period is a tension, not simply between advanced Europe and laggard Africa, but between competing conceptions of modernity, in which the citizens of newly self-governing African nations have the opportunity and the responsibility to determine the direction of their own societies. What Mitchison saw in Africa, and recorded in her writing about the continent and its people, was the gradual and often difficult progress of decolonisation, a process that required not just the redistribution of political power, but the dismantling of Eurocentric conceptions of modernity which had hitherto served to suppress the distinctiveness of African ways of life and the possibility of a distinctively African future.

'Modern' is a crucial term in Mitchison's writing about Africa, where it is subjected to repeated and careful examination. The characters in her African-set fiction repeatedly confront the question of what it means to be 'modern' – and, more specifically, what the orientation of society towards the achievement of 'modernity' might entail in an African context. As Aníbal Quijano and others have noted, the idea of 'modernity' is itself an invention of European historiography, associated with the rise of scientific and technical rationality and the expansion of mercantile and finance capital.[8] The colonisation of the Americas, India, South Asia, Africa and Australasia generated economic wealth, fuelling European scientific, economic, military and intellectual development from the fifteenth century onwards. Essential to this process was the suppression of pre-existing local forms of knowledge, kinship structures, cultural traditions, cosmologies and legal codes that might disrupt or challenge the colonisers' ability to extract economic or strategic value from colonised territories and their inhabitants. In ideological terms, the colony came to represent the 'primitive' or 'backward' other against which the development of European civilisation was measured; in material terms, it provided the seemingly inexhaustible reservoir of labour power and natural resources that enabled such transformations.

The teleological idea of modernity had supported these endeavours by enabling colonial powers to conceive of themselves not merely as more militarily powerful or more technologically proficient than the societies they had colonised, but as more advanced in every sense: situated further along the one-way street of historical development. *Modernity* came to be understood as a continually receding destination, one at which the concept's European originators were always destined to arrive first.[9] In consequence, the term took on implicitly spatial as well as temporal implications, producing what Peter Osborne has called 'the idea of the *non-contemporaneousness* of geographically diverse but *chronologically simultaneous* times'.[10] (To invert L. P. Hartley's celebrated line: it is not that the past is a foreign country, but rather that certain foreign countries are imagined as being in the past.) As the concept of modernity emerged out of the matrix of colonial exploitation, the colonised were thus relegated in the European imagination to a historically prior condition, a temporal as well as a geographical elsewhere. Only through processes of active and ruthless remodelling on European terms could they hope – always belatedly – to arrive at the goal of modernity.

Mitchison herself was clearly not immune to this kind of thinking, with its ten-dency to imagine twentieth-century Africa through the lens of European history. In her memoir *Return to the Fairy Hill* (1966), written relatively early in her relation-ship with the Bakgatla, she describes Botswana's transition to independence as 'a transition by 30,000 men, women, and children from one bit of history, if you like one technological epoch, into another'.[11] Similarly, in writing *When We Become Men* (1965) – the first of her African novels – she had sought, by means of 'research and imaginative sympathy', to immerse herself in the life of 1960s Botswana much as she had attempted to do in her 'reconstructions' of Gaul and Sparta. Her hope that Linchwe and other Botswanans would recognise in that novel an accurate depic-tion of their own society stemmed, as she explained, not only from a desire to write realistically about present-day Botswana, but from her conviction that success in doing so would confirm the validity of her approach to historical fiction: '[I]f *When We Become Men* was genuinely about the Batswana so that they genuinely recog-nised themselves, then it would show that I was justified in my working methods. It would mean that ancient history was perhaps something like I had imagined it.'[12] Yet in her efforts to write sympathetically about life in 1960s Botswana and South Africa – and in her efforts to demonstrate solidarity with her Black African friends as they began to build a new, independent society – Mitchison quickly began to understand the perniciousness of such comparisons. She became sensitised to the many ways that Europe's colonial domination of Africa had itself held back and distorted the development of African societies by seeking to remake African life in the image of Europe. For Mitchison, the challenge was to show how Africa could be modern in its own way, rather than by uncritically adopting European ways of life. As she saw first-hand the psychological and social consequences of colonialism, she became convinced that the independent nations of a post-colonial Africa would have to draw on traditional forms of knowledge and governance, and on indigenous cultural traditions, rather than relying solely on ideas of modernity imported from elsewhere.

Consider this pivotal scene in *Sunrise Tomorrow* (1973), in which Seloi, a nurse in the fictional town of Craigs, goes with her brother Rutang to see an exhibition of photographs depicting scenes from African rural life. Standing among the 'pictures of Zulu and Venda maidens wearing their traditional costumes', Seloi starts to feel uncomfortable in her European-style clothes: 'she began to hate her new mail-order dress with the pink roses and her pink and white hat'. After a violent quarrel with Rutang, she runs out of the exhibition hall back to the garden of the hospital where she works:

> She pulled off her shoes and stockings and stretched her toes out and began to wonder about everything and above all about being modern and whether she was being modern the right way. And was the way the hospital was being modern as right as she thought? Antibiotics, yes; asepsis, yes. But wasn't some of it just showing off? And what about all the hundreds of little villages and scattered houses and cattle posts that none of this ever reached? Was it modern to leave these out?[13]

Seloi's discomfort in this moment arises not just from her clothes, but from her recognition that she has embraced a version of modernity, represented by European-style fashion and European-style medicine, that suppresses and devalues the traditions and the history of her own community. Yet she also recognises that the images of Africa presented in the photographs of traditionally attired Zulu and Venda 'maidens' – like that anachronistic word itself – implicitly relegate African culture to a pre-modern condition. These images play into a romanticised and homogenised image of Africa which fails to accord with Seloi's own experience as a young girl who is, after all, neither Zulu nor Venda, but Kgatla. Confronted with two images of African culture – on the one hand, her own sartorial imitation of European-style modernity; on the other, a series of stereotypical images which do not represent either her own cultural heritage or her ambitions – Seloi ends up rejecting both. Unlike Rutang, who is training to be a mechanic, and for whom to be civilised is simply 'to have skills', Seloi cannot fully accept that being modern means adopting European ways of life. Instead, she wants to understand how Africans might shape their own forms of modernity: 'Because being African was as important as being modern. No, no, they were not two opposite things, they had to be brought together somehow.'[14]

Resistance to Eurocentric conceptions of temporality has been a central motif of post-colonial thought, from Frantz Fanon's insistence on the future rather than the past as the proper temporal horizon for any true movement towards the liberation of Black consciousness, to the Cameroonian philosopher Achille Mbembe's argument that African time is structured according to patterns and imperatives which are radically incompatible with European modernity's vision of linear historical progress.[15] 'African social formations', Mbembe insists, 'are not necessarily converging toward a single point, trend, or cycle. They harbor the possibility of a variety of trajectories neither convergent nor divergent but interlocked, paradoxical.' As an alternative to the perpetual forward motion of modernity, Mbembe posits a distinctive 'time of African existence' which he describes as the '*time of entanglement*'. This attitude towards temporal experience he conceives as 'neither a linear time nor a simple sequence [. . .] but an *interlocking* of presents, pasts, and futures that retain their depths of other presents, pasts and futures, each age bearing, altering, and maintaining the previous ones'.[16]

As a writer of historical fiction in which the past and future very often do interlock in just this way – through thematic resonances, but also at times by means of supernatural hauntings and prophetic visions – Mitchison was well primed to understand this aspect of African time. Nonetheless, she still struggled when in Africa to throw off her own ingrained attitudes to timekeeping. She recalled being 'a bit cross' when, having been kept waiting by a local teacher who claimed, by way of excuse, to be 'keeping African time', Mitchison 'turned on her as she is someone who should know better, and told her she'd better keep Israeli time – for that was where she had trained'.[17] Such unpunctuality annoyed her, partly because she felt it played into racist clichés of African unreliability, but also because, as she gradually came to recognise, she had been conditioned by her own upbringing to regard punctuality as a sign of respect, and to equate it with other kinds of probity. ('The English virtues', thinks Mitchison's alter ego Kate Snow, in the West Highland-set novel *Lobsters on the Agenda* (1952): 'honesty, truthfulness, punctuality'.[18] Rural Scotland, no less than rural Botswana, had tested her patience.) If she never quite managed to overcome that attitude, she nonetheless understood that perceptions of time in Botswana, and local habits of timekeeping, were conditioned by different historical, economic, climatic and technological factors:

> Perhaps things like accurate arrangements, phone calls, telegrams, doing things at one time rather than another, are matters which should not be expected. We Europeans have lived a long time with them, and probably being clock-bound is a very exhausting thing for us, though we are used to it.[19]

As the case of Kate Snow suggests, however, 'Europeans' here is too broad. For cultures of timekeeping, as Mitchison knew, were not uniform in 'Europe' any more than in Africa. Just as Kate, in *Lobsters on the Agenda,* finds the pace of the Highlands to be frustratingly unpredictable by comparison with city life, in Mitchison's first African novel, *When We Become Men* (1965), the Black African freedom fighter Isaac has to abandon his 'clock-bound' urban life in order to elude the South African authorities and go to ground in rural Bechuanaland. Among the possessions confiscated by his police captors at the beginning of the novel is his watch. After escaping by jumping from a moving train, Isaac and his co-conspirator Josh find refuge in Ditlabeng, the tribal capital of the Bamatsieng (Mitchison's thinly fictionalised version of the Bakgatla), in rural Bechuanaland, where they find that time is reckoned differently: 'What time was it? He did not miss his watch in the day time. One knew when it was light, one woke to the sound of inspanning, of goats' bleating, of cocks' crowing and the pleasant chirrups of little birds that went to sleep again in the heat of the day.'[20] The patterns of rural labour, animal husbandry and the rhythms of the natural world replace the clock face as temporal markers. Isaac adapts to these new rhythms, just as Mitchison did when, without electricity or reliable lamps, she found it impossible to read or write after sunset in Mochudi.

The friction between 'clock-bound' European time and the temporal codes of Africa is merely the most quotidian manifestation of the temporal disjuncture that arises from the imposition of European temporality in colonial settings. To demand that the colonised should regulate their activities according to the coloniser's clock and the coloniser's conventions of punctuality, is to repeat in miniature the larger demand that the colony must fall into step, must keep up, must chase after an ever-receding European form of modernity. The question of African temporality, however, has to do not just with the rationalised time of the clock, but also with the generational time of tradition and inheritance. When Isaac and Josh seek refuge in Ditlabeng, the old chief offers them sanctuary, persuaded to do so by an amiable (white) District Commissioner, against the wishes of the chief's nephew, the hot-headed Motswasele, who would rather turn Isaac and Josh in to the police in expectation of a reward. In the course of a heated discussion, which Isaac overhears, the District Commissioner argues for the men's right to political asylum on the basis of international law and a humanitarian moral imperative, citing the case of Jewish refugees from Nazi Germany. Motswasele, meanwhile, takes a strongly nationalist and anti-colonial position. 'We have to think of the whole country,' he insists, accusing the chief, his uncle, of allowing himself to be manipulated by the District Commissioner: 'He gets round you talking about honour. That's not modern' (19–22).

The chief himself prefers 'to think of the tribe', which for him stands as a bulwark of tradition against the disruptive transformations of national and global politics (19). In his experience, modernity names the force that has taken from him a large part of the authority wielded by his forebears; against it, he asserts the prerogatives of tribal identity and tribal justice, pointing to the assegai – the African spear – that hangs above the door to his office:

> That used to be for justice. Or against the disobedient. It has been taken from me. Perhaps that is right. It is not, what do you say, Motswasele, modern. Modern is napalm, is bombs dropping on people you do not see. But I say in the name of the tribe, that it shall protect these men. (23)

The assegai is a key symbol in the narrative, as it was in the tribal life that Mitchison gradually came to know. Crucially, Mitchison presents this sign of tribal authority not as the worn-out relic of a primitive order that has been superseded, but as the living symbol of a power that exists in the same temporal frame as napalm and bombs. In Mbembe's terms, the assegai evokes the time of entanglement in which past, present and future are all equally real, and equally to be valued. Even if some of its force has been usurped by an imposed European system of justice, it is not a meaningless artefact of a bygone era, but a symbol of the living power of the community, vested in the chief.

By the end of the novel, these contradictory positions – nation or tribe, tradition or modernity – will have been resolved in the figure of Letlotse, the chief's son, who having returned from school in Britain survives an assassination attempt by Motswasele and dedicates himself to the leadership of the Bamatsieng. Abroad, Letlotse has been trying to work out his own understanding of modernity, as he socialises with other anti-colonial students from other parts of Britain's former empire: 'They had talked in terms of exploitation, of the death of Imperialism and so on; perhaps these words were not very accurate; what mattered was the warm feeling between him and the Indian. And the thought that he must be modern, as modern as the Indian Congress party; more modern in fact' (75). For Letlotse, being 'modern' himself becomes a necessary step in the modernisation of his homeland. At this point in the novel, however, his vision of modernity has been shaped above all by his experiences in Britain. He has 'been to see one of the English new towns – oh, it was modern! Factories like little palaces, he could see a row of them at home all along the railway line, pink and blue and green' (75). Later still he will travel, as Mitchison did, to the USSR, and flirt with the idea of encouraging the construction of Soviet-funded factories in Bechuanaland.

In Europe, Letlotse dreams of starting a political party that would be 'against the chiefs', and would adopt a gradualist approach to self-determination, delaying

Independence 'until we are strong enough' (74). It is only after he returns to Bechuanaland that he comes to see traditional, tribal forms of kinship and community as a necessary component of a modern, independent African society. At the novel's climax, Motswasele plots to secure his hold on the Chiefdom by abducting and raping Letlotse's sister Seneo, and by having Letlotse and Isaac – now Letlotse's close ally – poisoned during Letlotse's initiation ceremony. Both men survive, thanks to Western antibiotics, while Motswasele is killed by Seneo and her family, leaving Letlotse to take his hereditary place. Now Chief himself, Letlotse has learned from the example of Motswasele: he no longer wants to create African modernity in the image of Europe, or of Soviet Russia.

Throughout *When We Become Men*, Mitchison undermines and complicates the idea of linear, historical progress according to which Africa represents merely an earlier stage on the path to European-style 'civilisation'. Accused of trying to 'go back to the past' by participating in Letlotse's initiation, Isaac comes to realise that 'It's not any wickedness this, we don't go into the past I think, or only a little, just to drink at old wells, to find our fathers and come back strengthened' (178). When near the end of the novel, he accepts Letlotse as his chief and takes a tribal name, Isaac explains how he has come to the realisation that it is white colonial ideology, and not African tribal culture, which is responsible for the idea of Africa as primitive and backward:

> '[. . .] Remember there was a time when I thought that all this about tribes and chiefs was nonsense, was wrong, was taking us back into the bad past, as surely as Verwoerd and Vorster would put us there. I thought a tribe was utterly against progress. Against freedom and democracy. As they try to make them in the Republic. In the Bantustans. I thought it was another kind of slavery.' [. . .] 'What I think now is harder to say,' said Isaac. 'Because I do not believe it has been said before. But it could be that our tribes are the kind of coming together, the kind of society, which we all want in our hearts.' (225)

After Letlotse has recovered from his poisoning at the hand of Motswasele's allies, the word 'modern' drops out of his thinking altogether, to be replaced with a different idea: 'Perhaps, thought Letlotse, perhaps it will not be so bad being chief. Perhaps there are ideas floating about among the Batswana and they may be caught and made into something. Perhaps I can get into the future after all.' (239) To *get into the future*, on his own terms, on African terms, thus becomes in Letlotse's thinking an alternative to the rigged game of catch-up implied by the imposition of European ideas of what it means to be 'modern'.

In *When We Become Men*, the initiation ceremony is depicted as a crucial element in the structure of African time. In *Return to the Fairy Hill* (1966), written shortly afterwards, Mitchison anticipates Mbembe's ideas about temporal entanglement in observing how 'African initiations tie people in to the past through songs and stories and above all the hidden meaning of words and phrases; they tie people into the future by giving them a sense of their responsibilities.'[21] Initiation is also, for Isaac and Letlotse in *When We Become Men*, a key moment in the formation of tribal identity and solidarity. For although both men are saved by the 'European medicine' that their friends steal from the local clinic, Isaac remains gravely ill until he is accepted and strengthened, psychologically and spiritually, by Letlotse, who embraces him while acknowledging his own responsibility to Isaac and to the rest of his people as the new Chief of the Bamatsieng. The elders of the tribe watch with approval:

> They spoke to one another softly behind the thin curtain of smoke from the fire; they spoke on and off through the night and into the dawn. 'This is not something he learned while he was away.' 'Not English education.' 'No, it was put into him; it has been brought out by the need.' 'From whom does it come?' 'I have heard it said that his mother's grandfather had also this power. He could have worked through Letlotse when Letlotse was himself open.' 'Open and also strengthened. But it is now known to the old ones that he is chief and we are his people.' (198–9)

For Mitchison, the time of temporal entanglement – the time in which 'the old ones' continue to exert ancestral power within the present moment – is not merely the absence of colonial clock-time, but a mode of temporal consciousness that insists on the equal significance of past, present and future alike. Nor does it represent a straightforward rejection of modernity; rather it represents a refusal to accept a vision of modernity for Africa that would prioritise a future defined in relation to European patterns of development. In Mitchison's African novels, the characters who triumph are those like Letlotse and Isaac in *When We Become Men*, and Seloi in *Sunrise Tomorrow*, who learn to live in both kinds of time, without becoming fully Europeanised, fully clock-bound. In doing so, they learn also to value and to recuperate distinctively African forms of knowledge and relation to the world, forms hitherto suppressed and denigrated, even within African communities, as a direct consequence of colonial rule.

Seloi, for instance, has been taught during her medical training to reject traditional healing practices as mere superstitions that belong to the past. One day a patient arrives for whose pains the hospital doctors can find no cause. When the man discharges himself, Seloi worries that he will die, but a friend reassures her that the man will go to an 'African doctor': a *dingaka*, or traditional healer. 'There are some things', she insists, 'that European medicine is not good for.'[22] In the course of the novel, Seloi gradually comes to understand that European medicine and African medicine both have a place in modern Africa. Her insight is affirmed when, near the end of the novel, an aeroplane carrying two white mining engineers crash-lands in Seloi's village while she is home visiting her family. One of the engineers suffers a broken arm; the other, concussed, starts shooting at the villagers who are trying to carry the survivors out of the wreckage. Eventually Seloi, wearing her nurse's uniform, manages to calm the men, treats the concussion, and helps to move the man with the broken arm to the house of the village *kgosi*, the chief. But Seloi does not know how to set a broken arm. Fortunately, her father has already gone to fetch the *dingaka*, Andrew:

Suddenly she began to cry. 'It is all right,' said Mr Tebogo. 'He will know what to do, but he will do it his way and if you did not believe you could make it go wrong. First, he will throw the bones on that beautiful rug which *Kgosi* laid out for him and then he will do all that is needed with his hands. There are two parallel ways of knowledge, with the bones – the ditaolo – and with hands. It is with hands that he will set the arm. You will see. [. . .] One can build with mud or stone or brick or concrete and some say with glass. In the end it is a house.'[23]

Andrew the *dingaka* does indeed set the bone, and when the mining engineer regains consciousness he sends for Seloi in order to ask who performed the operation. Embarrassed by his probing and insensitive questions, she equivocates when asked whether 'a native doctor' or 'a genuine doctor' was responsible. 'She was both ashamed and angry, but must hide both. Ashamed because she did not want to seem not modern, angry because he was looking down on what was African.'[24] As he recovers, the white engineer demands European medicine, including a course of anti-malarial tablets which Seloi, who knows very well that malaria is not a problem in her part of Botswana, considers unnecessary. In the face of his ingratitude, Seloi finds herself once more questioning what she has been taught:

> Was this right? And yet, thought Seloi, not so long ago I would have said it was the only way to become modern – to want the newest thing from the most modern country and to turn one's back on everything else – including Andrew [the *dingaka*] and his knowledge.[25]

Seloi's gradual awakening to the value of African knowledge helps her to understand not only the limits of European knowledge, but the needs and the capabilities of her Botswanan community.

*Sunrise Tomorrow* is a hopeful novel, in that it shows a younger generation grasping the responsibility to shape the future of Botswana in ways that reflect African modes of thought and African priorities. Seloi herself notes that 'some of the things in Botswana, some of the things which were admired, were only second-hand white things', like the nurse's cap she has to wear when working in the hospital, which keeps slipping because it has been designed to clip to white women's long hair.[26] 'Someone should think of an African cap,' teases her friend Aleseng; 'I know what you are going to say, Seloi, it would not be modern, it would not be like a European hospital. But this is an African hospital.' In this moment the small detail of a nurse's cap becomes a synecdoche for the many ways in which the unthinking imposition of European standards serves not to help Africans, but merely to constrain their agency by ignoring cultural and ethnic differences.

The treatment of people's names, in Mitchison's African fiction, points to another small but significant way in which such difference is suppressed. In the short story 'Out of School', collected in *Images of Africa* (1980), the children Kandisha and Chisalu attend school as 'Mary' and 'Jason': 'Both of them had two names, a home name and a school name, for two kinds of life which were sometimes very different and sometimes strangely twisted into one another.'[27] For Mitchison's Black characters, the adoption of a new African name, or the re-adoption of a suppressed one, thus frequently marks a moment of commitment or recommitment to their own community, and a self-conscious distancing from colonial manners and ways of living. In *Sunrise Tomorrow*, the delinquent who goes by the name of 'Tiger-Tiger' eventually decides to go straight, leaving behind both his nickname and his European name – Thomas – in favour of his ancestral name Motlakadibe. And in *When We Become Men*, Isaac is renamed 'Koboatau' by Letlotse as part of his cure: 'He knew also what he had become with the new name, someone small who had been put into the skin of the great lion, so that now he was safe against his enemies' (201).

In *Sunrise Tomorrow*, Seloi's 'church name' is 'Rebecca'. 'I am nurse Rebecca in the hospital,' she explains to her friend Mokgosi and her brother Rutang when she returns home on a visit. But Mokgosi is not impressed:

'That is a cold name, I think.'
   'It is my European name. It is more modern.'
   'It is not modern,' said Rutang unkindly. 'It is in the Bible, and that is very old – and dusty. You want a space-age name, then you must look at the films. Norma, Ulla, Goldie, Sandra, Shirley, Barbarella – oh, man, she was the one!'[28]

To Seloi, 'Rebecca' seems a more modern name simply by virtue of its association with white European missionary culture. To be modern here is merely to reject and devalue African naming practices. Rutang's preferred 'space-age' suggestions, meanwhile, speak of a different idea of what it might mean to be modern. But they also lay bare the absurdity of an ideology that expects colonial subjects to demonstrate their modernity by adopting a name steeped in many centuries of European religious and cultural tradition. It is as if, in order to become modern, Africans like Seloi must adopt social and religious practices that belong not to the present condition of European societies, but to the European past.

Like the assegai in *When We Become Men*, and like the techniques of African medical knowledge which Seloi learns to value in *Sunrise Tomorrow*, names in Mitchison's African fiction represent the power of a past that cannot simply be discarded, but which continues working in the present and into the future, carrying knowledge and power across generations. Names bind together communities; they inscribe individuals into their own stories, and into the stories of those who name them and accept their names. As Mitchison understood, the imposition on African societies of European forms of modernity was not accomplished solely by means of the regulation of everyday time and the suppression of local temporalities. It also required the denigration and dismantling of longstanding traditions across the whole of African life. Conventions of naming represent only one small part of that reorganisation. Pre-existing forms of government, legal codes, economic structures, trade networks, systems of social care and traditional medicine: all had to be replaced or remodelled along European lines, often with the active participation of African community leaders who saw European capital and power as a means of strengthening their own political positions, as Motswasele does in *When We Become*

*Men.* Yet to recognise and insist on the validity – and the modernity – of African names was, for Mitchison, one small way of recognising the value of cultural traditions and modes of kinship that were in danger of being suppressed in the headlong rush towards modernity.

'If you discard everything in order to be free to grasp the new,' Mitchison wrote in *Return to the Fairy Hill*, 'you are in for psychological and social trouble.'[29] Through her experiences in Botswana, she came to understand the profound repercussions – psychological as well as social – that had followed successive attempts by European empires to compel African societies towards their own vision of the new. She saw how her African friends were caught in an ideological double bind: urged to adopt European values and social forms as evidence of their readiness to enter the 'modern' world, yet constrained by a Eurocentric interpretation of social history in which their own cultures continued to serve as the very image of the primitive, the backward, that which must be left behind. In her African fiction she tried to expose and disrupt the conception of modernity as an essentially European condition, and to create a discursive space in which traditional forms of knowledge and governance could be legitimated, valued and celebrated as essential components of independent African societies.

Mitchison's efforts in this direction serve to remind us that twenty-first-century debates about decolonisation are part of a much longer history of political, practical, intellectual and imaginative struggle, and that such struggles have depended upon the forging of solidarities across lines of race, gender, nationality and economic class. A lifelong socialist, Mitchison placed a high value on the virtue of solidarity. Yet as a wealthy, white, upper-class woman who nonetheless believed in revolutionary socialism, she was also acutely conscious that genuine solidarity was more than merely an ethical orientation or rhetorical position. Political solidarity, and perhaps especially anti-colonial solidarity, is never simply a point of view; it involves, as Priyamvada Gopal has put it, an ongoing process of 'hard work, reciprocal un-learning and learning, and collective organizational efforts'.[30] In her relations with Africa, in her support for Botswanan independence, and in her writing about the Bakgatla, Mitchison challenged herself to do that work by confronting the difficulties of interracial and anti-colonial solidarity. Doing so tested the limits of her political commitment as well as the capacities of her imagination. It required her to re-evaluate her own status and her position in the imposed racial and social hierarchies that had sustained British imperial power. In the end, as Jacqueline Ryder notes, it 'brought into focus her own whiteness'.[31]

This is by no means to suggest that Mitchison was uniformly successful in her occasionally quixotic attempts to – as she put it – 'build bridges of understanding' between European and African modes of thought.[32] In trying to express the depth of her feelings of interracial solidarity, for instance, her writing sometimes veers uncomfortably between the roles of martyr and mother, as she speaks at one moment of her wish to fight (and perhaps die) in the struggle for African liberation, and at the next of her feelings of maternal care for Linchwe and the Bakgatla. Such moments, recorded most openly in *Return to the Fairy Hill*, clearly reflect Mitchison's powerful emotional attachment to Linchwe and to his people's struggle for self-determination, but they are nonetheless steeped in the iconography of colonial romance, as she herself acknowledged. Yet Mitchison's honesty in recording her failures, as well as successes, in showing solidarity, may be valuable precisely *because* those failures demonstrate the power of the ingrained psychological and cultural resistances that she worked to overcome in her writing and in her anti-colonial and anti-racist activism.

Solidarity, as she recognised, was not without its risks, among which must be counted the risks of misunderstanding and of being misunderstood, the risk of overstepping the bounds of hospitality, and the risk of giving offence. At its best, however, Mitchison's writing about Africa demonstrates not only a consistent ideological and practical commitment to anti-racism, anti-imperialism and decolonisation, but also a rare degree of humility and a willingness to listen to and learn from her African hosts. If she wanted to know whether the people of Bechuanaland 'recognised themselves' in *When We Become Men* partly in order to reassure herself of her own imaginative capacities, that point of professional pride should not be allowed to obscure the fact that, in writing about the lives of Black Africans, she took great care to solicit permission and approval from those whose cultures and communities she was trying to represent. It would not have occurred to many white writers of the period to do so.

## NOTES

1. Naomi Mitchison, *The Blood of the Martyrs* (Edinburgh: Canongate, 1988), p. 56.
2. Naomi Mitchison, *The Bull Calves* (Glasgow: Richard Drew, 1985), p. 276.
3. Naomi Mitchison, *As It Was: Small Talk and All Change Here* (Glasgow: Richard Drew, 1988), pp. 85–7.
4. For Mitchison's most extensive account of her early friendship with Linchwe and the Bakgatla, see *Return to the Fairy Hill* (London: William Heinemann, 1966).
5. Ibid. p. 1.
6. See recent scholarship by Kate Cowcher, and in particular the research project 'Dar to Dunoon: Modern African Art from the Argyll Collection': http://dartodunoon.com/ [accessed 22 January 2022].
7. See 'Further Reading', in Naomi Mitchison, *The Africans: A History* (London: Anthony Blond, 1970), pp. 221–3.
8. Aníbal Quijano, 'Coloniality and Modernity/Rationality', *Cultural Studies* 21:2–3 (2007), pp. 168–78.
9. For a detailed discussion of this geopolitical tendency, see John L. Agnew, *Geopolitics: Re-visioning World Politics*, 2nd edn (London: Routledge, 2003), pp. 35–49.
10. Peter Osborne, *The Politics of Time: Modernity and the Avant-Garde* (London: Verso, 1995), p. 16.
11. Mitchison, *Return to the Fairy Hill*, p. 86.
12. Ibid. p. 76.
13. Naomi Mitchison, *Sunrise Tomorrow: A Story of Botswana* (Glasgow: William Collins, 1973), p. 104.
14. Ibid. pp. 104–5.
15. See Frantz Fanon, *Black Skin, White Masks*, trans. Charles Lam Markmann (London: Pluto, 2008), pp. 174–81.

16. Achille Mbembe, *On the Postcolony* (Berkeley and Los Angeles: University of California Press, 2001), p. 16.
17. Mitchison, *Return to the Fairy Hill*, p. 137.
18. Naomi Mitchison, *Lobsters on the Agenda* (Isle of Colonsay: House of Lochar, 1997), p. 14.
19. Mitchison, *Return to the Fairy Hill*, p. 44.
20. Naomi Mitchison, *When We Become Men* (Glasgow: Kennedy & Boyd, 2009), p. 42. Further references to this edition are given in brackets.
21. Mitchison, *Return to the Fairy Hill*, p. 249, n. 3.
22. Mitchison, *Sunrise Tomorrow*, p. 95.
23. Ibid. pp. 148–9.
24. Ibid. p. 152.
25. Ibid. p. 153.
26. Ibid. p. 105, p. 72.
27. Naomi Mitchison, *Images of Africa* (Edinburgh: Canongate, 1980), p. 95.
28. Mitchison, *Sunrise Tomorrow*, p. 53.
29. Mitchison, *Return to the Fairy Hill*, p. 86.
30. Priyamvada Gopal, *Insurgent Empire: Anticolonial Resistance and British Dissent* (London: Verso, 2019), p. 22.
31. Jacqueline Ryder, 'Speaking as Tribal (M)other: The African Writing of Naomi Mitchison', in Carla Sassi and Theo van Heijnsbergen, *Within and Without Empire: Scotland across the (Post)colonial Borderline* (Newcastle upon Tyne: Cambridge Scholars Press, 2001), p. 203.
32. Mitchison, *Images of Africa*, p. iii.

# Naomi Mitchison's 'Europe'

*James Purdon*

In 1947 Naomi Mitchison travelled to Zurich to attend the second post-war congress of the international writers' organisation PEN. Founded in London in 1921, with the three letters of its acronym originally standing for 'Poets, Essayists, Novelists', PEN had quickly established a worldwide network of writers who shared its principles of internationalism, cooperation, peace and the free exchange of ideas. Mitchison had joined the London branch in 1931 – her name appears in the list of new members in the PEN newsletter for October of that year, alongside a note announcing the publication of *The Corn King and the Spring Queen* – and in 1938, having moved to Argyll, became a prominent member of Scottish PEN.

During the 1930s, in response to the persecution of writers and artists by European fascist governments, PEN had slowly transformed itself from an international but generally apolitical writers' club into a campaigning movement dedicated to freedom of thought and expression. A turning point came at the 1933 congress in Dubrovnik when, in the course of a heated debate to decide the organisation's official response to Nazi book-burnings, the four members of the German delegation walked out. Within a year, PEN had suspended the membership of its German branch and agreed to recognise a new group of German writers in exile. PEN also gave its backing to the Deutsche Freiheitsbibliothek (or, as it came to be known, the 'Library of the Burned Books') founded by the exiled Jewish communist Alfred Kantorowicz. In PEN's March 1934 newsletter, Mitchison is listed (alongside her brother and her sister-in-law) among the library's first supporters.[1]

The first international meeting of PEN after the war took place in Copenhagen, in the summer of 1946. Mitchison did not attend that event. But she enthusiastically signed up for the 1947 congress, in Zurich, where among the issues to be debated by delegates was the thorny question of whether PEN's branch in Germany should be re-established. (In the end it was, though the motion was opposed by the Yiddish and Hebrew centres, with eight other delegations abstaining.)[2] In her travel memoir *Mucking Around* (1981), Mitchison writes of the mixture of excitement and nervousness she and others felt at the prospect of meeting German delegates –

including, perhaps, 'actual Nazis' – and of her determination, as far as possible, to make 'a real effort towards brotherhood'.[3]

Under the circumstances, this was no easy undertaking. The war itself was barely two years in the past. The Nuremberg trials had concluded the previous October with the execution of senior Nazis, but the process of 'denazifying' German society was just beginning. There was, in addition, a heated and ongoing public discussion concerning the question of collective guilt. On one side of this debate, the novelist Thomas Mann, now living in exile in Los Angeles, had insisted that all Germans, and all German culture, must bear the taint of complicity in the crimes of the Nazi regime. (Mann attended the Zurich PEN congress, where he nonetheless spoke in favour of German re-admission.) Other German writers insisted, in response, that they themselves were victims of the Nazis, forced into compliance by a totalitarian state: a condition described by the novelist Frank Thieß as one of 'inner emigration'.[4] Mitchison seems, on balance, to have inclined towards the latter view: 'Even if they had acquiesced in the regime', she writes in *Mucking Around*, 'they cannot have approved.'[5]

The short story 'Europe' – written in or around 1947, and published here for the first time – is perhaps Mitchison's most direct attempt to grapple seriously in fiction with these questions of guilt and complicity, which for her were about more than just the behaviour or beliefs of German nationals. The story is set at an international writers' conference, clearly modelled on the one she attended in Switzerland. ('This must date from the Zurich PEN conference!' she later wrote on the cover page of the manuscript. 'Nobody ever published it.') At its dramatic centre is a failure of sympathy – a failure to recognise and care for the suffering of another human being – which, at its most mundane, results in a social *faux pas*; but which, taken to an extreme, leads on to the abyss of war and genocide. In the story, a tasteless joke made unthinkingly by one of the conference delegates causes a concentration camp survivor to relive his wartime trauma, and fills the narrator, who has shared in the joke, with a deep sense of shame and embarrassment. But Mitchison goes further than this, not only recognising the delegates' levity as tactless and inappropriate, but insisting, in the story's final words, that through their actions they have earned their portion of a more serious culpability: 'because of what had been said, there had been something added to the guilt of Europe'. There is, the story suggests, a link between such small-scale failures of sympathy – the inability or unwillingness to reckon with individual suffering – and the undermining of moral responsibility, on a far larger scale, which might enable a society to tolerate the systematic extermination of millions of human beings.

The narrator of the story is a well-meaning but rather glib British delegate: one sensitive enough to make the usual noises about feeling 'desperately sorry' for the suffering of those in the war-torn middle of Europe, yet so self-absorbed as to resent having to perform once again the obligatory rituals of sympathy. It is a carefully modulated voice, suave and mildly ironic, a voice that immediately assumes and encourages a shared point of view: 'After all, we are all tired and strained and needing – oh, vitamins and all that, a holiday anyway.' We are invited to identify with the owner of this voice, and the possibility of such identification is maintained by Mitchison's decision to leave the narrator's gender carefully unspecified. Yet how far should we be willing to go along with this voice, whose owner immediately complains about having to listen to so many stories of wartime trauma? One might think of Mitchison's first paragraphs as rehearsing in miniature both the wider theme and the technique of the story itself, which asks the reader to think about the possibility of real sympathy and the ethical stakes of complicity. She does this by adopting the voice and the point of view of a narrator whose own capacity for sympathy is, we quickly learn, somewhat limited, and by encouraging us to share in that perspective. As the narrator discovers how tempting it can be to forget about the suffering of others and drift into an easy complicity, so too the reader begins to see how questions of collective guilt and responsibility are not solely the inheritance of post-war German society.

The main action of the story takes place at the official dinner held on the last evening of the conference, as the delegates are enjoying 'a last blind' at the expense of their generous hosts. Speeches are being given and ignored; conversation is flowing. So too are large quantities of wine, to the approval of Mitchison's epicurean narrator. (This much, at least, seems to have been taken from life: reporting on the Zurich conference in the PEN newsletter, the Welsh novelist Wyn Griffith would also make a particular point of mentioning 'the enlightened generosity of the Swiss Wine Trade'.)[6] At the various tables, delegates are putting their differences aside and enjoying the evening. There are glimpses of the various delegations – quarrelsome French and Belgians, elegant Swedes – but the narrator, like everyone else, is particularly taken with Willi, a young delegate who has survived imprisonment in a Nazi concentration camp. The turning point of the story comes when, after dinner, the narrator draws another delegate's attention to an attractive South American woman sitting at the bar in a dress cut with gaps to expose the skin on her back. Ogling the bare flesh, and imagining himself to be talking confidentially, the other delegate indulges in a macabre joke: he fantasises, in an offhand way, about how nice the woman's skin would look, 'after she's been skinned and made into a lampshade'. Only when the words are out does the narrator realise that Willi has been listening all along.

Stories of lampshades and other objects allegedly made from the flayed skin of prisoners had begun to circulate widely after the liberation of Nazi concentration camps at the end of the Second World War. In 1945, prosecutors at the Nuremberg trials had presented, among other evidence of Nazi atrocities, a piece of tattooed, flayed skin said to have been prepared for Ilse Koch, the wife of Buchenwald commandant Karl-Otto Koch.[7] Testimony from camp survivors suggested that the Kochs had also possessed lampshades fashioned out of the same material, and while no firm evidence was ever found to corroborate the existence of these objects, the lampshade made of human skin had become, by the time of Mitchison's writing, a familiar image of the brutality of the camps in general, and of Buchenwald in particular.[8] Whether or not the lampshades themselves actually existed, their potency as an enduring symbol of Nazi brutality recognises the appalling and uncanny juxtaposition of the everyday domestic object with the acts of indescribable sadism implied in its manufacture. The Nazi lampshade, in other words, embodies the horrifying contradictions of the Holocaust itself: a brutal campaign of human extermination conducted by apparently ordinary human beings in a highly organised modern society. It confronts us with an extreme combination of the mundane and the monstrous that seems hardly to belong to the world of twentieth-century modernity, but rather to the fearful cultural unconscious that traditionally finds expression in the form of myth or folk tale.

Despite its contemporary setting, 'Europe', too, has something of the atmosphere of folk tale about it. There is the generalising vagueness of the setting established in its opening line ('These conferences in Europe are all the same in a way . . .'). There is the sense of childlike indulgence in the depiction of the conference dinner where the narrator gorges, like Hansel or Gretel, on the lavish spread, feeling at once 'guilty' at this demonstration of gluttony and disappointed not to be able to enjoy still more of the 'delicious cakes' on offer. And there is the way that this apparent abundance and satisfaction – achieved either through wartime neutrality or occasionally, the story hints, through black-market profiteering – is at last revealed as having been bought at a terrible cost. After the war, such traditional folk tales, or *Märchen*, were the subject of contention in Germany, where, having been appropriated by the Nazis for the dissemination of Aryan ideology, they were first banned by the occupying Allies before gradually being reclaimed by post-war German writers as a means of representing experiences that defied realistic depiction.[9] Mitchison was already steeped in such stories, having reworked several of them in her collection of modern-day fables, *The Fourth Pig* (1936). And it may be that 'Europe' owes something to this storytelling tradition, for it is, in its way, a kind of fairy tale. A tale in which the magic spell that has conjured a scene of luxury and bonhomie is suddenly broken by an ill-considered word, leaving narrator and reader alike to confront the bleak reality beneath the superficial glamour. A tale that, in the end, poses a question: has the monster really been defeated, once and for all?

## NOTES

1. [Anon.], 'Provisional Committee for the Foundation of the "German Library of the Burned Books"', *PEN News* 62 (March 1934), p. 4.
2. See R. A. Wilford, 'The Pen Club, 1930–50', *Journal of Contemporary History* 14 (1979), pp. 99–116.
3. Naomi Mitchison, 'Middle Europe', in *Other People's Worlds: Impressions of Ghana and Nigeria* and *Mucking Around: Five Continents over Fifty Years* (Edinburgh: Kennedy & Boyd, 2021), pp. 141–4 (p. 141).
4. Frank Thieß, Walter von Molo and Thomas Mann, *Ein Streitgespräch über die äußere und die innere Emigration* (Dortmund: Druckschriften Vertriebsdienst, 1945), p. 3.
5. Mitchison, 'Middle Europe', p. 141.
6. Wyn Griffith, 'Zurich, 1947', *PEN News* 150 (July 1947), pp. 21–2.
7. See Lawrence Douglas, 'The Shrunken Head of Buchenwald: Icons of Atrocity at Nuremberg', *Representations* 63 (Summer 1998), pp. 39–64.
8. David A. Hackett, *The Buchenwald Report* (Boulder, CO: Westview Press, 1995), p. 64. See also Joachim Neander, 'The Impact of "Jewish Soap" and "Lampshades" on Holocaust Remembrance', in Christina Guenther and Beth A. Griech-Polelle (eds), *Trajectories of*

*Memory: Intergenerational Representations of the Holocaust in History and the Arts* (Newcastle-upon-Tyne: Cambridge Scholars, 2008), pp. 51–78.

9. See Peter Arnds, 'On the Awful German Fairy Tale: Breaking Taboos in Representations of Nazi Euthanasia and the Holocaust in Günter Grass's *Die Blechtrommel*, Edgar Hilsenrath's *Der Nazi & der Friseur*, and Anselm Kiefer's Visual Art', *German Quarterly* 75:4 (Autumn 2002), pp. 422–39.

# Europe

# Europe

*Naomi Mitchison, ?1947*[1]

These conferences in Europe are all the same in a way, everyone is so desperately glad to have got out from behind their own particular iron curtain, to hear another language, see other kinds of houses and shops. To be without responsibilities as one can only be if one is a foreigner. We all start window-shopping, because of course the conferences are always held in places that were either neutral or that have recovered enough to stand an influx of foreigners. Everything always seems wonderful at first. The shops one sees are meant to look prosperous. It only begins to look different when one goes into peoples' homes and talks about ordinary things. When one can compare their rationing system, whatever it may be, with one's own. Meanwhile, of course, we eat at restaurants or at official parties, where the food and drink make up for having to pretend to listen to the speeches.

This conference was very much like the rest; the valuable part happened behind the scenes. There were far too many delegates; one didn't meet the ones one wanted to meet and as for the others, there were some one dodged like poison and others one was desperately sorry for and – well, sometimes one dodged them too. After all, we are all tired and strained and needing – oh, vitamins and all that, a holiday anyway. And to hear from them about the suffering, the chivvying across frontiers, humiliations and anxieties, partings, betrayals – well, you know what it is: one cannot stand hearing about it again, sympathising in creaking German, trying to avoid getting committed to anything which might mean action!

The boy was nice all the same, we couldn't help liking him. He and his aunt seemed to be the only ones of the family who had survived, and they had been separated for the years he had been in the Camp. But he had found her again and

1 'Europe' is reproduced by kind permission of the Naomi Mitchison Estate. The typescript is held in the Harry Ransom Center at the University of Texas at Austin, MS-2862, Container 8.5 [misdated to 1946], 9pp. The cover sheet reads: 'EUROPE / BY / NAOMI MITCHISON / CARRADALE HOUSE / CARRADALE / ARGYLL.' Above this is Mitchison's autograph inscription in blue ballpoint pen: 'This must date from the Zurich PEN / conference! Nobody ever published it.' Obvious typographical errors have been emended in square brackets.

both of them were quite gay and didn't seem to be asking anyone for anything. Which meant that we were all that much more prepared to give. And Willi was good at the conference sessions, he didn't go into hysterics like some of them. We said to one another that he had made a wonderful recovery, you wouldn't have thought he had been in a Camp. Anyhow not in that one.

Well then, it was the last evening and, of course, the conference was doing itself proud, some of the delegates felt, I expect, that they deserved a last blind. After all, something had come of it. I cannot say I felt that way myself to start with, in fact, I felt a bit ashamed at having taken things too lightly and at having slept or drawn little houses during the sessions. But then, what is one to do while the speeches are being translated into three languages? I felt guilty, anyhow, at having been so much more interested in food than anyone ought to be. And at the same time, it had been a little disappointing to find one just could not eat as many delicious cakes as one had thought one easily could. And on top of it all I was beginning to worry again about all the things there would be to do at home when I got back.

I had not very much liked my neighbours at the table. The French and Belgians had quarrelled again; they were almost as bad as north and south Ireland that way; and of course the Swedes thought they were better than any of the rest of us; they were better dressed anyway! Their wives and the women delegates all had stunning dresses, though not quite so glamorous as some of the South Americans.

Poor Great Britain looked terribly dowdy and pre-war and altogether like a small power. Some of the men were in black and managed to make the whole thing, with the bright lights and bowls of roses and flags of all nations, look like something out of a film. Not a very good film perhaps. But they were doing us well on the drinks and after a bit it began to seem like a better film and I began to think perhaps we had not done so badly and my French began to pick up, and the delegates with large woolly beards at the table behind, who had been quarrelling, suddenly made it up and kissed one another; they were Poles or Finns or something, anyhow from the other side. The other side, I mean, of that sort of black gap in the middle of Europe that had been so unpleasantly present during some of the discussions. Willi was at the same table as the woolly beards. He caught my eye and grinned. I was suddenly so very glad he was enjoying himself; I lifted my glass and he his. The others at my table saw who I was drinking with and lifted their glasses too. They said nice things about Willi; he was a boy of talent.

He would go far. He was not like 'ces autres'. Even the Swedes unbent.

Willi hadn't got a dinner jacket of course; he looked very nice all the same. There was something clean and pleasant about him; he had nice hands. I had been watching him take notes earlier on at one of the sessions. There was a scar across his thumb. I wondered if it had been made somehow in the Camp in some horrible way and if he had forgotten it. Because it looked as if he had. Could one? But if people cannot forget, then what is the use of all these conferences?

By the time we got to speeches and dessert things were more cheerful. People were beginning to talk about another conference, perhaps in Switzerland – or would Rome be all right by next year? – meaning would there be enough black market stuff for us to eat and drink. Not that we didn't perhaps deserve it more than some who get it, at least some of us – the youngest of the French delegates was beginning to look les[s] like a bag of bones and nerves since the beginning of the week – but it doesn't do to think too much along these lines, to make comparisons round the gap in the middle of Europe.

We were all given little keepsakes – edible I was glad to find! The winding up speeches were going on, but fortunately nobody bothered to translate them into any of the other languages. There were press photographs of the important, while the rest of us went on drinking; it seemed a pity not to finish the bottles; lovely green bottles, lovely white wine, lovely red wine, lovely sense that life was, after all, worth living, was, after all, going on again; that the quarrels didn't matter, had dissolved like bubbles in faintly sparkling wine, would always do so with a little care by everyone, a little friendliness, a few more conferences. And it seemed to be generally agreed that our own delegates had behaved with great good sense. Whenever a speech ended we cheered; after all, if we had happened to listen it might have happened to be good.

At last the talk was all over. Everyone had congratulated everyone else and we stood up and began to move around. There was a bar with low chairs under palms and soft lights, and a general drift set in towards it, circling round and back like flies round an uncovered joint. The delegations which had been scattered at the small tables now formed up again, feeling unequal to the strain of talking in anyone else's language or taking on anyone else's point of view.

Only the fluchtlinge refugees, seemed not to have a proper language of their own. Their native language was also the language of the place they fled from, the place of death and darkness.

The guards of the Camps had spoken that language. But there was no other which they knew so well, no other in which they were at home. Some of them spoke good English or French, wonderfully good, considering – Willi, for instance, understood every word one said, could swing his idioms about. Yes, and he was still looking gay. If the conference had not done anything else it had helped him!

I was sitting under a palm with another excellent little glass, beside one of our delegates – you would know his name if I told you. A first-class man in his own line and good hearted. One of the South American wives, that is, if she was a wife, was sitting on a stool at the bar with her back to us, and she had a deep violet dress on with some highly diagrammatic gaps in it. I expect it was the very latest in provo[c]ative fashion; I hadn't seen any clothes like that for years. Anyway the main gap set off a piece of prime back, an area of rippling and glossy cream that wriggled under the lights. I made some slightly catty remark about it to my neighbour, who began to be highly technical and make an estimate in square inches, then he put his head on one side and said he thought it would look better with some decoration: 'A flower, or what-not' I said, and Willi, who was talking to the young French delegate just at the edge of the next group, and saw what we were looking at, laughed and made a motion with his hands like someone untying something – the violet dress had one of those neck fastenings that look as if they would not stand up to a tug.

'Yes' said my neighbour, 'a little what-not. Yes, of course, it would look so damned well afterwards.'

'After what?' I said, hoping to be slightly shocked, I suppose.

'Yes' he said 'after she's been skinned and made into a lampshade. That's what she's kept for, you know.'

It doesn't sound funny now, but it seemed to be then, cause it was all spoken mock seriously, and he leaned towards [me] waggling his great eyebrows and we seemed to be making a littl[e] confident pool of laughter and ease among the lights and drink[s] and palm leaves. And he, I am sure, had the idea in the back of his mind to reassure me that fine clothes and success and all that didn't really matter, were only to be laughed at by the intelligent. But it didn't stop there.

You know the way talk switches and suddenly a thing said with an ironic inten- tion becomes real. And it only shows where we have got to now after all these centuries. For the next thing he said was, 'You've no idea how solid human skin is, very like pig skin in fact. Of course it has to be properly dressed and smoothed off –' I suppose I made a face, because he went on rather louder, 'Come, come, we must be objective! I saw a very fine piece of human skin, very fine indeed, a collector's piece with everything –'

And then I saw that Willi had been listening. His mouth was a little bit open and a little bit twisted at the corner. He had a glass in his hand and it had tilted and it was dripping on to the floor. I gave my neighbour a kick and whispered 'Shut up'[.] For a moment he went on; he thought I was just being squeamish. Trying to question his standards of unreality in a world that must be faced for the thing it is. Because he had really seen this piece of human skin and it was necessary for him to speak of it, to externalise it, to make it into something which could be referred to as a fact and then forgotten. For otherwise it would edge itself in and become a night mare.

But then he saw what I had seen. Willi had half turned his head away now; sud- denly he lifted the glass and drank off what was in it and set it down very carefully on the bar and walked away. We both knew which Camp he had been at. Not that this business of making lampshades out of human skin was confined to one Camp, nor indeed is it a particularly bad thing. It doesn't matter really what happens to the dead. No doubt Willi had seen a number of things which were worse. Oh, so much worse, that the rest of us don't want to think they happened. But they have.

My fellow delegate and I looked after Willi walking away and both of us were flooded with this terrible European feeling of guilt and of nightmare, of something we must not think about because it is beyond our putting right. The lights and leaves and dresses moved sickeningly and we knew that, because of what had been said, there had been something added to the guilt of Europe.

# Bibliography

ARCHIVAL SOURCES

**Canada**

Douglas Goldring Fonds, Special Collections, University of Victoria, British Columbia

**Russia**

RGALI: Russian State Archive of Literature and Arts, Moscow

**UK**

Archives of the Eugenics Society, Wellcome Library, London
Naomi Mitchison Papers, National Library of Scotland, Edinburgh
Papers of Philip Rainsford Evans and Barbara Evans, Wellcome Library, London

**USA**

Naomi Mitchison Collection, Harry Ransom Center, University of Texas, Austin
Papers of J. S. Huxley, Woodson Research Center, Fondren Library, Rice University, Houston


PUBLISHED SOURCES

[Anon.], 'Provisional Committee for the Foundation of the "German Library of the Burned Books"', *PEN News* 62 (March 1934), p. 4
Agnew, John L., *Geopolitics: Re-visioning World Politics*, 2nd edn (London: Routledge, 2003)
Anderson, Perry, 'From Progress to Catastrophe', *London Review of Books* 33:15 (28 July 2011)
Arnds, Peter, 'On the Awful German Fairy Tale: Breaking Taboos in Representations of Nazi Euthanasia and the Holocaust in Günter Grass's *Die Blechtrommel*, Edgar Hilsenrath's *Der Nazi & der Friseur*, and Anselm Kiefer's Visual Art', *German Quarterly* 75:4 (Autumn 2002), pp. 422–39
Auden, W. H., *The English Auden: Poems, Essays, and Dramatic Writings, 1927–1939* (New York: Random House, 1977)

Auerbach, Jerold S., 'Southern Tenant Farmers: Socialist Critics of the New Deal', *The Arkansas Historical Quarterly* 27:2 (1968), pp. 113–31

Bell, Eleanor, 'Experiment and Nation in the 1960s', in Glenda Norquay (ed.), *The Edinburgh Companion to Scottish Women's Writing* (Edinburgh: Edinburgh University Press, 2012), pp. 122–9

Benton, Jill, *Naomi Mitchison: A Century of Experiment in Life and Letters* (London: Pandora, 1990)

Bigman, Fran, 'Pregnancy as Protest in Interwar British Women's Writing: An Antecedent Alternative to Aldous Huxley's *Brave New World*', *Medical Humanities* 42:4 (2016), pp. 265–70

Bluemel, Kristin, 'Exemplary Intermodernists: Stevie Smith, Inez Holden, Betty Miller and Naomi Mitchison', in Maroula Joannou (ed.), *The History of British Women's Writing, 1920–1945* (Basingstoke: Palgrave Macmillan, 2015), pp. 40–56

Brooke, Stephen, 'The Body and Socialism: Dora Russell in the 1920s', *Past & Present* 189 (2005), pp. 147–77

——, *Sexual Politics: Sexuality, Family Planning, and the British Left from the 1880s to the Present Day* (Oxford: Oxford University Press, 2011)

Burdekin, Katharine, *Swastika Night*; with an introduction by Daphne Patai (London: Lawrence and Wishart, 1985)

Burgess, Moira, '"Between the Words of a Song": Supernatural and Mythical Elements in the Scottish Fiction of Naomi Mitchison' [PhD thesis, University of Glasgow] (2006), http://theses.gla.ac.uk/5413/1/2006BurgessPhD.pdf

——, *Mitchison's Ghosts: Supernatural Elements in the Scottish Fiction of Naomi Mitchison* (Edinburgh: Humming Earth, 2008)

Butler, Judith, 'Sexual Consent: Some Thoughts on Psychoanalysis and Law', *Columbia Journal of Gender and Law* 21:2 (2011), pp. 405–29

Calder, Angus, *Revolving Culture: Notes from the Scottish Republic* (London: I. B. Tauris, 1994)

Calder, Jenni, 'Men, Women and Comrades', in Christopher Whyte (ed.), *Gendering the Nation: Studies in Modern Scottish Literature* (Edinburgh: Edinburgh University Press, 1995), pp. 69–84

——, *The Nine Lives of Naomi Mitchison* (London: Virago, 1997), revised as *The Burning Glass: The Life of Naomi Mitchison* (Dingwall: Sandstone Press, 2019)

Cartledge, Paul, *The Spartans: An Epic History* (London: Pan, 2013)

Chan, Julia, 'The Brave New Worlds of Birth Control: Women's Travel in Soviet Russia and Naomi Mitchison's *We Have Been Warned*', *Journal of Modern Literature* 42:2 (Winter 2019), pp. 38–56

Clarendon Commission, *Report of the Commissioners on the Revenues and Management of Certain Colleges and Schools and the Studies Pursued and Instruction Given Therein*, 4 vols (London: Houses of Parliament, 1864)

Clarke, Peter, and Richard Toye, 'Cripps, Sir (Richard) Stafford (1889–1952), politician and lawyer', *Oxford Dictionary of National Biography*, https://doi.org/10.1093/ref:odnb/32630

Clodfelter, Michael, *Warfare and Armed Conflicts: A Statistical Reference to Casualty and Other Figures, 1500–2000*, 2nd edn (Jefferson, NC: McFarland, 2002)

Crossley, Robert, *Olaf Stapledon: Speaking for the Future* (Liverpool: Liverpool University Press, 1994)

Cunningham, Valentine, *British Writers of the Thirties* (Oxford: Oxford University Press, 1988)

Darwin, C. G., *The New Conceptions of Matter* (London: G. Bell and Sons, 1931)

David-Fox, Michael, *Showcasing the Great Experiment: Cultural Diplomacy and Western Visitors to the Soviet Union, 1921–1941* (Oxford: Oxford University Press, 2012)

Day-Lewis, Cecil, 'Letter to a Young Revolutionary', in Michael Roberts (ed.), *New Country* (London: Hogarth Press, 1933), pp. 25–42

——, 'An Expensive Education', *Left Review* 3 (February 1937), pp. 43–5

Dougall, Mara, '"What Does a Socialist Woman Do?" Birth Control and the Body Politic in

Naomi Mitchison's *We Have Been Warned*', *The Cambridge Quarterly* 50:1 (March 2021), pp. 18–37

Douglas, Lawrence, 'The Shrunken Head of Buchenwald: Icons of Atrocity at Nuremberg', *Representations* 63 (Summer 1998), pp. 39–64

Dreier, Peter, *The 100 Greatest Americans of the 20th Century: A Social Justice Hall of Fame* (New York, NY: Nation Books, 2012)

Drucker, Donna J., 'The Symbolic Use of Barrier Contraceptives in American and English Literature', *The MIT Press Reader*, 4 May 2020, https://thereader.mitpress.mit.edu/barrier-contraceptives-in-american-english-literature/

Duncan, Ian, 'History and the Novel after Lukács', *Novel* 50:3 (2017), pp. 388–96

Eddington, Arthur, *The Nature of the Physical World* (Cambridge: Cambridge University Press, 2012)

Eliot, T. S., 'Ulysses, Order, and Myth', in Frank Kermode (ed.), *Selected Prose of T. S. Eliot* (New York: Harcourt Brace Jovanovich, 1975), pp. 175–8

Empson, William, *Some Versions of Pastoral* (London: Chatto and Windus, 1935)

Engelhardt, Nina, *Modernism, Fiction and Mathematics* (Edinburgh: Edinburgh University Press, 2018)

Erlikman, Vadim, *Poteri narodonaseleniia v XX veke: spravochnik Потери народонаселения в XX веке: справочник* [in Russian] (Moscow: Russkaia panorama, 2004)

Esty, Jed, *A Shrinking Island: Modernism and National Culture in England* (Princeton, NJ: Princeton University Press, 2004)

Ewins, Kristin, 'Professional Women Writers', in Benjamin Kohlmann and Matthew Taunton (eds), *A History of 1930s British Literature* (Cambridge: Cambridge University Press, 2019), pp. 58–71

Fanon, Frantz, *Black Skin, White Masks*, trans. Charles Lam Markmann (London: Pluto, 2008)

Faragher, Megan, 'Snoop-Women with Notebooks: Naomi Mitchison, Mass-Observation, and the Gender of Domestic Intelligence', *The Space Between* 12 (2017), https://scalar.usc.edu/works/the-space-between-literature-and-culture-1914-1945/vol13_2017_faragher

——, *Public Opinion Polling in Mid-Century British Literature: The Psychographic Turn* (Oxford: Oxford University Press, 2021)

Fisher, Kate, *Birth Control, Sex, and Marriage in Britain 1918–1960* (Oxford: Oxford University Press, 2006)

Gifford, Douglas, 'Forgiving the Past: Naomi Mitchison's *The Bull Calves*', in Joachim Schwend and Horst W. Drescher (eds), *Studies in Scottish Fiction: Twentieth Century* (Frankfurt: Peter Lang, 1990), pp. 219–41

Gifford, James, *A Modernist Fantasy: Modernism, Anarchism, and the Radical Fantastic* (Victoria, BC: ELS Editions, 2018)

Golubov, Nattie, 'English Ethical Socialism: Women Writers, Political Ideas and the Public Sphere between the Wars', *Women's History Review* 14:1 (2005), pp. 33–60

Gopal, Priyamvada, *Insurgent Empire: Anticolonial Resistance and British Dissent* (London: Verso, 2019)

Grant, Rebecca, 'How Egg Freezing Got Rebranded as the Ultimate Act of Self-Care', *The Guardian* (30 September 2020), https://www.theguardian.com/us-news/2020/sep/30/egg-freezing-self-care-pregnancy-fertility

Griffith, Wyn, 'Zurich, 1947', *PEN News* 150 (July 1947), pp. 21–2

Hackett, David A., *The Buchenwald Report* (Boulder, CO: Westview Press, 1995)

Haire, Norman (ed.), *Sexual Reform Congress, London 8–15: IX: 1929. World League for Sexual Reform. Proceedings of the Third Congress* (London: Kegan Paul, Trench, Trubner & Co., 1930), pp. 182–8

Haldane, J. B. S., *Daedalus, or, Science and the Future: A Paper Read to the Heretics, Cambridge, on February 4th, 1923*, https://www.marxists.org/archive/haldane/works/1920s/daedalus.htm

——, 'Biological Possibilities for the Human Species of the Next Ten Thousand Years', in Gordon Wolstenholme (ed.), *Ciba Foundation Symposium on Man and his Future* (London: J. & A. Churchill, 1963), pp. 337–61

Hall, Edith, and Henry Stead, *A People's History of Classics: Class and Greco-Roman Antiquity in Britain and Ireland, 1689 to 1939* (London: Routledge, 2020)

Hall, Lesley A., 'Marie Stopes and Her Correspondents: Personalising Population Decline in an Era of Demographic Change', in Robert A. Peel (ed.), *Marie Stopes, Eugenics and the English Birth Control Movement: Proceedings of a Conference Organised by the Galton Institute, London, 1996* (London: The Galton Institute, 1997), pp. 27–48

——, 'Women, Feminism and Eugenics', in Robert A. Peel (ed.), *Essays in the History of Eugenics: Proceedings of a Conference Organised by the Galton Institute, London, 1997* (London: The Galton Institute, 1998), pp. 36–51

——, *Sex, Gender and Social Change in Britain since 1880* (Basingstoke: Palgrave Macmillan, 2012)

——, 'Movements to Separate Sex and Reproduction', in Nick Hopwood, Rebecca Flemming and Lauren Kassell, *Reproduction from Antiquity to the Present Day* (Cambridge: Cambridge University Press, 2018), pp. 427–41

Hallam, Michael, 'In the "Enemy" Camp: Wyndham Lewis, Naomi Mitchison and Rebecca West', in Andrzej Gąsiorek, Alice Reeve-Tucker and Nathan Waddell (eds), *Wyndham Lewis and the Cultures of Modernity* (Farnham: Ashgate, 2011), pp. 57–76

Haraway, Donna, 'Otherworldly Conversations, Terran Topics, Local Terms', in Stacy Alaimo and Susan Hekman (eds), *Material Feminisms* (Bloomington: Indiana University Press, 2008), pp. 157–87

Harker, Ben, *The Chronology of Revolution: Communism, Culture, and Civil Society in Twentieth-Century Britain* (Toronto: University of Toronto Press, 2021)

Harwood, Rebecca Kirsten, 'Reading Between the Lines: The Politics of Authenticity in Naomi Mitchison's *Vienna Diary*', in Clare Broome Saunders (ed.), *Women, Travel Writing, and Truth* (London: Routledge, 2014), pp. 124–38

Hauser, Kitty, *Shadow Sites: Photography, Archaeology, and the British Landscape 1927–1955* (Oxford: Oxford University Press, 2007)

Haynes, Michael, 'Counting Soviet Deaths in the Great Patriotic War: A Note', *Europe–Asia Studies* 55:2 (2003), pp. 303–9

Heard, Gerald, *The Ascent of Humanity* (London: Cape, 1929)

——, *The Emergence of Man* (London: Cape, 1931)

——, *Social Substance of Religion: An Essay of the Evolution of Religion* (London: G. Allen & Unwin, 1931)

Hendry, J. F. (ed.), *The Penguin Book of Scottish Short Stories* (Harmondsworth: Penguin, 1970)

Heussler, Robert, *Yesterday's Rulers: The Making of the British Colonial Service* (Syracuse, NY: Syracuse University Press, 1963)

Hoberman, Ruth, *Gendering Classicism: The Ancient World in Twentieth-Century Women's Historical Fiction* (Albany: State University of New York Press, 1997), pp. 119–35

Hobson, Suzanne, '"The Future of Our Movement": Bridging the Gap between Rationalism and Christian Ethics in Naomi Mitchison's 1930s Writing', in *Women: A Cultural Review* 31:4 (2020), pp. 401–15

Honey, John Raymond de Symons, *Tom Brown's Universe: The Development of the English Public School in the Nineteenth Century* (London: Millington, 1977)

Hubble, Nick, 'Naomi Mitchison: Fantasy and Intermodern Utopia', in Alice Reeve-Tucker and Nathan Waddell (eds), *Utopianism, Modernism, and Literature in the Twentieth Century* (Basingstoke: Palgrave Macmillan, 2013), pp. 74–92

——, 'Documenting Lives: Mass Observation, Women's Diaries, and Everyday Modernity', in Adam Smyth (ed.), *A History of English Autobiography* (Cambridge: Cambridge University Press, 2016), pp. 345–58

——, '"The Kind of Woman Who Talked to Basilisks": Travelling Light through Naomi Mitchison's Landscape of the Imaginary', *The Luminary* 7 (2016), https://www.lancaster.ac.uk/luminary/issue%207/Article%205.pdf

——, *The Proletarian Answer to the Modernist Question* (Edinburgh: Edinburgh University Press, 2017)

Hubble, Nick, Luke Seaber and Elinor Taylor (eds), *The 1930s: A Decade of Modern British Fiction* (London: Bloomsbury Academic, 2021)

Hughes, Richard, 'Physics, Astronomy, and Mathematics or Beyond Common-Sense', in Naomi Mitchison (ed.), *An Outline for Boys and Girls and Their Parents* (London: Victor Gollancz, 1932), pp. 303–57

Hynes, Samuel, *The Auden Generation: Literature and Politics in England in the 1930s* (London: Pimlico, 1976)

Jameson, Storm, 'New Documents', *Fact* 4 (1937), pp. 9–18

John, Angela V., *Turning the Tide: The Life of Lady Rhondda* (Cardigan: Parthian, 2013)

Kearton, Antonia, 'Imagining the "Mongrel Nation": Political Uses of History in the Recent Scottish Nationalist Movement', *National Identities* 7:1 (2006), pp. 23–50

Kohlmann, Benjamin, and Matthew Taunton (eds), *A History of 1930s British Literature* (Cambridge: Cambridge University Press, 2019), pp. 1–14

Lassner, Phyllis, *British Women Writers of World War II: Battlegrounds of Their Own* (Basingstoke: Palgrave Macmillan, 1998), pp. 58–103

Leavis, Q. D., 'Lady Novelists and the Lower Orders', in G. Singh (ed.), *Q. D. Leavis, Collected Essays*, 3 vols (Cambridge: Cambridge University Press, 1989), vol. 3, pp. 318–36

Lessing, Doris, *Walking in the Shade* (London: Flamingo, 1998)

Lukács, Georg [György], *The Historical Novel*, trans. H. and S. Mitchell (Boston: Beacon Press, 1963)

——, *Theory of the Novel*, trans. Anna Bostock (Cambridge, MA: MIT Press, 1974)

Lynd, Helen Merrell, *On Shame and the Search for Identity* (London: Routledge & Kegan Paul, 1958)

Maher, Ashley, 'Memoirs of a Spacewoman: Naomi Mitchison's Intergalactic Education', *Textual Practice* 34:12 (2020), pp. 2145–65

Mangan, J. A., 'Eton in India: The Imperial Diffusion of a Victorian Educational Ethic', *History of Education* 7:2 (1978), pp. 105–18

——, *The Games Ethic and Imperialism: Aspects of the Diffusion of an Ideal* (London: Viking, 1986)

Mannin, Ethel, *Confessions and Impressions* (Harmondsworth, Penguin, 1937)

——, *Women and the Revolution* (New York: E. P. Dutton & Co., 1939)

Marcus, Laura, '"The Creative Treatment of Actuality": John Grierson, Documentary Cinema and "Fact" in the 1930s', in Kristin Bluemel (ed.), *Intermodernism: Literary Culture in Mid-Twentieth-Century Britain* (Edinburgh: Edinburgh University Press, 2009), pp. 189–207

Marks, Lara, *Sexual Chemistry: A History of the Contraceptive Pill* (New Haven, CT: Yale University Press, 2001)

Maslen, Elizabeth, 'Naomi Mitchison's Historical Fiction', in Maroula Joannou, *Women Writers of the 1930s: Gender, Politics, and History* (Edinburgh: Edinburgh University Press, 1999), pp. 138–50

Mbembe, Achille, *On the Postcolony* (Berkeley and Los Angeles: University of California Press, 2001)

McDiarmid, Lucy, 'W. H. Auden's "In the Year of My Youth . . ."' *The Review of English Studies* 29:115 (1978), pp. 267–312

McFarlane, Anna, 'Naomi Mitchison's *We Have Been Warned* in Post-Referendum Scotland', *The Bottle Imp* 19 (June 2016), https://www.thebottleimp.org.uk/2016/06/naomi-mitchisons-we-have-been-warned-in-post-referendum-scotland/

——, '"Becoming Acquainted with all that Pain": Nursing as Activism in Naomi Mitchison's Science Fiction', *Literature and Medicine* 37:2 (2019), pp. 278–97

Mellor, David, *A Paradise Lost: The Neo-Romantic Imagination in Britain 1935–55* (London: Lund Humphries, 1987)

Mellor, Leo, 'Listening-in to the Long 1930s', *Critical Quarterly* 58:4 (December 2016), pp. 113–32

——, 'The Documentary Impulse', in Matthew Taunton and Benjamin Kohlmann (eds), *The Cambridge History of 1930s British Literature* (Cambridge: Cambridge University Press, 2019), pp. 257–70

——, 'Aeroplanes: Rethinking Aeriality in a Long 1930s', in Alex Goody and Ian Whittington (eds), *The Edinburgh Companion to Modernism and Technology* (Edinburgh: Edinburgh University Press, 2022), pp. 91–104

Mellor, Leo, and Glyn Salton-Cox (eds), 'The Long 1930s' [Special Issue], *Critical Quarterly* 57:3 (2015)

Miller, Gavin, 'Animals, Empathy, and Care in Naomi Mitchison's *Memoirs of a Spacewoman*', *Science Fiction Studies* 35:2 (July 2008), pp. 251–65

——, *Science Fiction and Psychology* (Liverpool: Liverpool University Press, 2020)

Mitchison, Naomi, *When the Bough Breaks and Other Stories* (London: Jonathan Cape, 1924)

——, *Nix-Nought-Nothing: Four Plays for Children* (London: Jonathan Cape, 1928)

——, *Comments on Birth Control* (London: Faber and Faber, 1930)

——, 'The Book and the Revolution', review of Gerald Heard, *The Ascent of Humanity*, in *Time and Tide* 11 (January 1930), p. 80

——, 'Some Comments on the Use of Contraceptives by Intelligent Persons', in Norman Haire (ed.), *Sexual Reform Congress, London 8–15: IX: 1929. World League for Sexual Reform. Proceedings of the Third Congress* (London: Kegan Paul, Trench, Trubner & Co., 1930), pp. 182–8

——, *Black Sparta: Greek Stories* (London: Jonathan Cape, 1931)

——, 'Good News', review of Gerald Heard, *Social Substance of Religion*, in *Time and Tide* 12 (June 1931), p. 894

——, *An Outline for Boys and Girls and Their Parents* (London: Victor Gollancz, 1932)

——, *The Delicate Fire* (London: Jonathan Cape, 1933)

——, *The Home and a Changing Civilisation* (London: John Lane, 1934)

——, 'Arkansas through British Eyes', *The Living Age* (May 1935)

——, 'White House and Marked Tree', *The New Statesman and Nation* (27 April 1935), p. 585

——, *The Blood of the Martyrs* (New York: Whittlesey House, 1939)

——, 'Socialist Britain', *Pakistan Horizon* 4:1 (1951), pp. 12–20

——, *Memoirs of a Spacewoman* (London: Victor Gollancz Ltd, 1962)

——, 'Open Letter to an African Chief', *Journal of Modern African Studies* 2:1 (March 1964), pp. 65–72

——, *Return to the Fairy Hill* (London: William Heinemann, 1966)

——, *African Heroes* (New York: Farrar, Straus, and Giroux, 1969)

——, *The Africans: A History* (London: Anthony Blond, 1970)

——, *The Moral Basis of Politics* (Port Washington, NY: Kennikat Press, 1973)

——, *Small Talk: Memoirs of an Edwardian Childhood* (London: Bodley Head, 1973)

——, *Sunrise Tomorrow: A Story of Botswana* (Glasgow: William Collins, 1973)

——, *All Change Here: Girlhood and Marriage* (London: Bodley Head, 1975)

——, *The Cleansing of the Knife and Other Poems* (Edinburgh: Canongate, 1978)

——, *You May Well Ask: A Memoir 1920–1940* (London: Gollancz, 1979/London: Fontana, 1986)

——, *Images of Africa* (Edinburgh: Canongate, 1980)

——, *The Corn King and the Spring Queen* (London: Virago, 1983/Edinburgh: Canongate, 1990)

——, *The Bull Calves* (Glasgow: Richard Drew, 1985)

——, *Travel Light* (London: Virago, 1985)

——, *Among You Taking Notes: The Wartime Diary of Naomi Mitchison, 1939–1945*, ed. Dorothy Sheridan (Oxford: Oxford University Press, 1986)

——, *Early in Orcadia* (Glasgow: Richard Drew, 1987)

——, 'Growing Up Saturated with Science', *The Scientist* (December 1987)

——, *As It Was: An Autobiography 1897–1918* [comprising *Small Talk* (1973) and *All Change Here* (1975)] (Glasgow: Richard Drew, 1988)

——, *Solution Three*, afterword by Susan M. Squier (New York: The Feminist Press at the City University of New York, 1995)

——, *Lobsters on the Agenda* (Isle of Colonsay: House of Lochar, 1997)

——, *Small Talk with All Change Here* (Isle of Colonsay: House of Lochar, 2000)

——, *Beyond This Limit: Selected Shorter Fiction*, ed. Isobel Murray (Glasgow: Kennedy & Boyd, 2008)

——, *The Conquered* (Glasgow: Kennedy & Boyd, 2009)

——, *When We Become Men* (Glasgow: Kennedy & Boyd, 2009)

——, *We Have Been Warned* (Kilkerran: Kennedy & Boyd, 2012)

——, *Other People's Worlds: Impressions of Ghana and Nigeria* and *Mucking Around: Five Continents over Fifty Years* (Edinburgh: Kennedy & Boyd, 2021)

Mitford, Nancy, *Love in a Cold Climate and Other Novels* (London: Penguin, 2000)

Montefiore, Janet, *Men and Women Writers of the 1930s: The Dangerous Flood of History* (London: Routledge, 1996)

Morris, A. J. A., 'Trevelyan, Sir Charles Philips, third baronet (1870–1958), politician', *Oxford Dictionary of National Biography*, https://doi.org/10.1093/ref:odnb/36553

Murray, Isobel, 'Novelists of the Renaissance', in Cairns Craig (ed.), *The History of Scottish Literature*, 4 vols (Aberdeen: Aberdeen University Press, 1987), vol. 4, pp. 103–17

——, introduction to Naomi Mitchison, *Memoirs of a Spacewoman* (Glasgow: Kennedy & Boyd, 2011)

Neander, Joachim, 'The Impact of "Jewish Soap" and "Lampshades" on Holocaust Remembrance', in Christina Guenther and Beth. A. Griech-Polelle (eds), *Trajectories of Memory: Intergenerational Representations of the Holocaust in History and the Arts* (Newcastle-upon-Tyne: Cambridge Scholars, 2008), pp. 51–78

O'Connor, Frank, *The Lonely Voice: A Study of the Short Story* (London: Melville House, 2004)

O'Hagan, Andrew, 'Poor Hitler', *London Review of Books* 29:22 (15 November 2007)

Orwell, George, 'Names Sent to Celia Kirwan, 2 May 1949', in Peter Davison (ed.), *The Lost Orwell* (London: Timewell Press, 2006), pp. 140–51

Osborne, Peter, *The Politics of Time: Modernity and the Avant-Garde* (London: Verso, 1995)

Periyan, Natasha, 'Naomi Mitchison, Eugenics and the Community: The Class and Gender Politics of Intelligence', in Nick Hubble, Luke Seaber and Elinor Taylor (eds), *The 1930s: A Decade of Modern British Fiction* (London: Bloomsbury, 2021), pp. 91–122

Pimlott, Ben, *Labour and the Left in the 1930s* (New York: Cambridge University Press, 1977)

Plain, Gill, *Women's Fiction of the Second World War: Gender, Power and Resistance* (Edinburgh: Edinburgh University Press, 1996)

Pollard, Lucy, *Margery Spring Rice: Pioneer of Women's Health in the Early Twentieth Century* (Cambridge, UK: Open Book Publishers, 2020) [ebook]

price, kitt, *Loving Faster than Light: Romance and Readers in Einstein's Universe* (Chicago: University of Chicago Press, 2012)

Quijano, Aníbal, 'Coloniality and Modernity/Rationality', *Cultural Studies* 21:2–3 (2007), pp. 168–78

Quirke, V. M., 'Haldane, John Burdon Sanderson (1892–1964), geneticist', *Oxford Dictionary of National Biography*, https://doi.org/10.1093/ref:odnb/33641

Rich, P. J., *Elixir of Empire: The English Public Schools, Ritualism, Freemasonry and Imperialism* (London: Regency, 1989)

Richardson, Angelique, *Love and Eugenics in the Late Nineteenth Century: Rational Reproduction and the New Woman* (Oxford: Oxford University Press, 2003)

Robb, George, 'Race Motherhood: Moral Eugenics vs Progressive Eugenics, 1880–1920', in Claudia Nelson and Ann Sumner Holmes (eds), *Maternal Instincts: Visions of Motherhood and Sexuality in Britain, 1875–1925* (Basingstoke: Macmillan, 1997), pp. 58–74

Russell, Dora, *Hypatia; or, Woman and Knowledge* (London: Keegan Paul & Co., 1925)

——, *The Right to be Happy* (London: G. Routledge & Sons, 1927)

Rusterholz, Caroline, 'Testing the Gräfenberg Ring in Interwar Britain: Norman Haire, Helena Wright and the Debate over Statistical Evidence, Side Effects, and Intrauterine Contraception', *Journal of the History of Medicine and Allied Sciences* 72:4 (2017), pp. 448–67

Ryder, Jacqueline, 'Speaking as Tribal (M)other: The African Writing of Naomi Mitchison', in Carla Sassi and Theo van Heijnsbergen (eds), *With and Without Empire: Scotland across the (Post)colonial Borderline* (Newcastle-upon-Tyne: Cambridge Scholars Publishing, 2013), pp. 200–13

Said, Edward, *Culture and Imperialism* (New York: Vintage, 1994)

Salton-Cox, Glyn, *Queer Communism and the Ministry of Love: Sexual Revolution in British Writing of the 1930s* (Edinburgh: Edinburgh University Press, 2018)

Sassi, Carla, 'The Cosmic (Cosmo)Polis in Naomi Mitchison's Science Fiction Novels', in Caroline McCracken-Flesher (ed.), *Scotland as Science Fiction* (Lanham, MD: Bucknell University Press with Rowman & Littlefield, 2012), pp. 85–100

Saunders, Max, *Self-Impression: Life-Writing, Autobiografiction, and the Forms of Modern Literature* (Oxford: Oxford University Press, 2010)

Scannell, Paddy, and David Cardiff, *A Social History of British Broadcasting: Volume 1 – 1922–1939: Serving the Nation* (Oxford: Blackwell, 1991)

Shaw, Valerie, *The Short Story: A Critical Introduction* (London: Longman, 1983)

Shepherd, Nan, *The Living Mountain* (Edinburgh: Canongate, 2011)

Sheridan, Dorothy, 'Woven Tapestries: Dialogues and Dilemmas in Editing a Diary', *The European Journal of Life Writing* 10 (2021), pp. 45–67

Spender, Stephen, *The Destructive Element: A Study of Modern Writers and Beliefs* (London: Jonathan Cape, 1935)

——, *The Thirties and After: Poetry, Politics and People* (New York: Random House, 1979)

Spufford, Francis, *Red Plenty* (London: Faber & Faber, 2010)

Squier, Susan, 'Sexual Biopolitics in *Man's World*: The Writings of Charlotte Haldane', in Angela Ingram and Daphne Patai (eds), *Rediscovering Forgotten Radicals: British Women Writers, 1889–1939* (Chapel Hill: University of North Carolina Press, 1993), pp. 137–55

Stapledon, Olaf, 'A Sketch-Map of Human Nature', *Philosophy* 17:67 (July 1942), pp. 210–30

Stead, Henry, '"Comrade Doris": Lessing's Correspondence with the Foreign Commission of the Board of Soviet Writers in the 1950s', *Critical Quarterly* 63:1 (April 2021), pp. 35–47

Stears, Marc, 'Cole, George Douglas Howard (1889–1959), university teacher and political theorist', *Oxford Dictionary of National Biography*, https://doi.org/10.1093/ref:odnb/32486

Stirling, Kirsten, 'The Roots of the Present: Naomi Mitchison, Agnes Mure Mackenzie and the Construction of History', in Edward J. Cowan and Douglas Gifford (eds), *The Polar Twins* (Edinburgh: John Donald, 1999), pp. 254–69

——, 'The Female Figure in the Scottish Renaissance', *Scottish Cultural Review of Language and Literature* 11 (2008), pp. 35–63

Stray, Christopher, *Classics Transformed: Schools, Universities, and Society in England, 1830–1960* (Oxford: Clarendon Press, 1998)

Swingler, Randall, 'Apropos of Translation', *Greece and Rome* 7:19 (October 1937), pp. 1–10

Szreter, Simon, and Kate Fisher, *Sex before the Sexual Revolution: Intimate Life in England 1918–1963* (Cambridge: Cambridge University Press, 2010)

Szudzik, Matthew, and Eric W. Weisstein, 'Parallel Postulate', *MathWorld—A Wolfram Web Resource*, https://mathworld.wolfram.com/ParallelPostulate.html

Taunton, Matthew, *Red Britain: The Russian Revolution in Mid-Century Culture* (Oxford: Oxford University Press, 2019)

Thieß, Frank, Walter von Molo, and Thomas Mann, *Ein Streitgespräch über die äußere und die innere Emigration* (Dortmund: Druckschriften Vertriebsdienst, 1945)

Thomson, Mathew, 'Bowlbyism and the Post-War Settlement', in *Lost Freedom: The Landscape of the Child and the British Post-War Settlement* (Oxford: Oxford University Press, 2013), pp. 79–113

Upward, Edward, *The Spiral Ascent: A Trilogy* (London: Heinemann, 1977)

Vaninskaya, Anna, 'Introduction: Scotland and Russia since 1900', *Studies in Scottish Literature* 44:1 (2019), pp. 3–10

Viswanathan, Gauri, *Masks of Conquest: Literary Study and British Rule in India* (New York: Columbia University Press, 1989)

Vlach, Robert, 'Robert Burns through Russian Eyes', *Studies in Scottish Literature* 2:3 (1964), pp. 152–62

Wallace, Diana, *The Woman's Historical Novel: British Women Writers 1900–2000* (Basingstoke: Palgrave Macmillan, 2005)

Warner, Marina, 'Introduction' to Naomi Mitchison, *The Fourth Pig* (London: Princeton University Press, 2014), pp. 1–21

Wilford, R. A., 'The Pen Club, 1930–50', *Journal of Contemporary History* 14 (1979), pp. 99–116

Wilkinson, Rupert, *The Prefects: British Leadership and the Public School Tradition* (Oxford: Oxford University Press, 1964)

Williams, Raymond, *Orwell* (London: Collins, 1971)

—— (ed.), *George Orwell: A Collection of Critical Essays* (Englewood Cliffs, NJ: Prentice Hall, 1974)

Woolf, Virginia, *A Room of One's Own/Three Guineas* (Harmondsworth: Penguin, 2000)

# Index